THE WOODSMAN

B.C. LIENESCH

CARPE
CREATIVE
LLC

For Meg

My sentry,
my savior,
my soulmate.

"Grief can destroy you — or focus you."

— DEAN KOONTZ, *ODD HOURS*

PART I

MISSING PERSONS

1

Jackson Clay was good at finding things. It had served him all his life and today was no exception. Ditching his pickup truck at a remote parking lot, he'd spotted the post that marked the local trailhead for the Appalachian Trail as soon as it came into view. On the trail, he made out the path for the David Lesser Shelter even though the sign for it had been taken out by a fallen tree. Every landmark he'd memorized he spotted long before he got to it. It all would've made for an easy hike. But Jackson wasn't here for recreation. He was on a mission. He was here to find someone.

To anyone else, he looked the part. Tall and muscular, his body showed no strain in shouldering the large rucksack on his back. His brown, close-cropped hair was tucked away underneath an olive green ballcap much the way his hazel eyes were masked by dark wrap-around sunglasses. Add in his brown beard and the coat and pants he was wearing, and very little of his sandy complexion was left uncovered.

The leaves crunched beneath his boots as he traversed a stretch of trail that traced the Virginia-West Virginia border. He listened as the mostly barren branches rustled in the early spring breeze. It had been an otherwise temperate day, but now, as the sun set, a storm system was forming in the valley to the west. The sky grew dark behind Jackson as he walked towards the fading light.

The lack of foliage made it easy to spot the man coming up the trail the opposite way. Seeing him, Jackson instinctively reached for his Sig Sauer P320, sliding his hand around the cold metal grip and over the trigger. He slowed his pace and watched.

The man was pale and wiry, drowning in a rain parka two sizes too big for him. The way he seemed to trip on a root every few feet told Jackson the stranger wasn't exactly in his element.

When the man looked up and noticed him, he smiled and gave a friendly wave. Jackson returned the man's wave and tucked the pistol out of view.

"Afternoon," greeted the man, "How's it going?"

"Fine," Jackson replied, "And you?"

"Oh, I'm good," replied the man, "Just wrapping up my second mile for the day. It's about quitting time for me. A good solid two in a day? You can't complain about that."

The man was better at talking than he was at walking. Jackson immediately wasn't a fan.

"Say, do you know how far it is to the next shelter," asked the man.

"It's about a mile or so back that way," Jackson replied, "Looks like a tree took out the sign for it. Look closely for the path or you'll walk right past it."

"Oh, no," said the man, "You don't say. Looks like a storm's blowing in. And my flashlight is dead. You don't happen to have any AA batteries you could spare, do you?"

Jackson paused a moment, deciding whether or not to fix the man up. Better to get him squared away and moving, he thought.

"No problem," Jackson said.

He slid the rucksack off his shoulders and let it drop onto the ground. As he opened one of the front pockets, he slid his sleeves up, revealing the tattoo on his forearm.

"Whoa, that's some tat," said the man, "You served?"

The tattoo was a snake wrapped around a sword behind a shield. The shield was green and blue with a white sun and star and a red lightning bolt in the middle. The Ranger insignia. Over top of it was a furled banner that read 75 RANGER RGT.

"Yup, 75th Ranger Regiment," Jackson replied.

"Where'd you serve," asked the man, "Iraq? Afghanistan?"

Jackson's first deployment had been Kosovo, but the man wasn't wrong, either.

"Here's four AA batteries," Jackson said, ignoring the man's questions, "Is that enough?"

"Plenty, thanks," replied the man.

"Sure thing," Jackson said.

Zipping up the front pocket he'd rummaged through, Jackson slid the rucksack back onto his shoulder and buckled it across his vest.

"Good luck," Jackson said as he started to continue on.

"Thanks again. I'm Rick, by the way," Rick replied.

Jackson turned around and looked at Rick. He gave him a terse smile.

"Stay dry, Rick," Jackson replied, "You're going to want to beat that weather to the shelter."

Before Rick the talker could say anything back, Jackson disappeared around the bend in the trail.

He stepped up his pace now. Rick had slowed him down. His mind told him to double-check his GPS to see how far it was, but that would only take more time.

Time Jackson didn't have. He was on a mission. He was here to find someone.

And Jackson Clay was good at finding things.

2

Sara Beth Parker slammed the door so hard a couple screws came loose as the hinges rattled in recoil. Her mother was still yelling something at her, but she wasn't listening. She didn't want to hear it. What she wanted was to punch the woman she actually truly loved square in the face.

She paced the room angrily, her rage converting into pent up energy she wasn't quite sure how to expel right then. Sitting down on the edge of her bed, she reached for her phone, probably more so out of habit than anything else, and scrolled furiously through her social media accounts as she contemplated her next move.

All she wanted to do was what everyone else was doing. Okay, not everyone. But her friends, at least. Elizabeth Schuster's father had invited them all to Cabo San Lucas, Mexico for spring break. A trip with her name on it that wouldn't cost her parents a dime? She thought for sure she was in. That was, until she came home from school this afternoon and her mother quashed the idea with a quick and unceremonious 'no'.

Sara scrolled past Stephanie Adams' most recent post as she continued to brood.

10 days until Cabo Wabo!!!

"Bitch," Sara growled.

She scrolled some more. Her screen became a slideshow of selfies, memes, and animal videos. She was watching a particularly obese cat struggle to clean itself before her phone buzzed and beeped with an incoming FaceTime. The name Emily Green flashed across the screen. Sara hit answer.

"Hey," Sara Beth said in little more than a sullen whisper.

"Hey, I can barely hear you," Emily replied, "I can barely see you, too."

"Sorry, hold on," Sara Beth replied.

She pulled her hoodie off and brushed her dark chocolate hair away from her face. A pretty girl, Sara had a peachy complexion, large green eyes and thin lips that naturally curved into a smile, though now they were frowning.

"Uh, oh," Emily replied, "Didn't go as you expected when you got home, huh?"

"She fucking said no," Sara Beth stammered, "Can you believe that?"

"I'm sorry, hon," Emily said, "Did she say why?"

"No! That's the worst part of it! No reason! No reason whatsoever! Just a 'no'. And 'because I said so'. It's bullshit. I swear, the things that woman makes me think of doing."

"I wouldn't, orange isn't your color."

The two of them laughed until a brief silence lingered.

"Well, as long as you're not going anywhere," Emily said, "You might as well come out with us tonight."

"Ha, yeah right," Sara Beth answered, "Adolf downstairs just nixed a parent-supervised trip. You think she's going to let me go downtown alone with you?"

"It won't be just me," Emily said, "Jessica and Katia are going, too."

"Oh, terrific. Yeah, that'll sell her."

Emily laughed.

"She doesn't have to know, dummy," Emily said, "You could sneak out. And, hey, if you get busted, it's like you said: you're not going anywhere for Spring Break, anyway."

Emily's logic always seemed to have a way of getting Sara Beth in trouble. It was a particularly hazardous quality in a best friend.

"I'll think about it," Sara Beth said, giving in.

"Don't think," Emily replied, "Just do it."

Don't think, Sara Beth thought. That could be the title of Emily's memoir.

"Maybe," Sara Beth said, allowing a small smile to replace her scowl.

"Alright, lady," Emily replied smiling, "I'm going to hold you to that."

"Good! Bye," Sara Beth said, chuckling.

The screen went blank as the call ended. Sara Beth sighed as she scooted back into the bed and crossed her long legs. She opened Instagram up on her phone and searched for photos of Cabo San Lucas. Her screen became a sliding kaleidoscope of sun-drenched beaches and emerald blue water. She tapped on a photo of three women playing in the surf. She pictured herself as one of them, running and laughing as the warm ocean water lapped at her feet.

But she wasn't a woman on the beaches of Cabo San Lucas. She was a 16-year-old girl lying in her own bedroom of her family's quiet house in Harrisonburg, Virginia. Suffocating in the claustrophobia of her small town, drowning in the sea of things she wanted to do but couldn't. What did she know about Cabo? It might as well be Mars to her.

She flopped back and stared at the ceiling, replaying the fight with her mother in her head, when her phone buzzed. She looked over. It was a text message from Emily.

TONIGHT! COME!

Looking back at the ceiling, Sara Beth sighed again. It was bad enough she was going to miss Mexico, but if she had to stare at this ceiling all night with its chipping plaster and faded paint, she was going to go stir crazy.

Emily had offered her an out. And she was thinking about taking it.

3

Jackson was studying the sky as the first clap of thunder boomed in the distance. The temperature had risen as the air above had become more unstable and was now heavy with humidity. The storm would be on him shortly. On *them*, if he could make it there on time.

He checked his handheld GPS one more time. He was less than a half mile from the waypoint he'd programmed in. Perfect, Jackson thought. At this pace he'd be there in five minutes.

The branches of the oak and hickory trees rattled hauntingly overhead as the blue sky was slowly covered with dark gray clouds. The warm and sunny spring day was shaping up to be a stormy night.

Jackson had seen only two hikers since Rick the talker. They were an older couple headed north. Jackson had smiled politely as they passed, but now there was no one. Even the birds had stopped chirping. Jackson was alone and in his element.

He moved swiftly down the trail, taking each step as though he'd made it time and time before. He hadn't – in fact he'd never been on this stretch of the trail before – but Jackson had spent his life in woods like these. A childhood of playing in them had served him well in Boy Scouts and running cross country. His friends from school used to joke it took him getting deployed to the Syrian desert in Iraq to keep him from the woods.

A second clap of thunder broke the eerie silence, this time in the opposite direction of where the first had come. Jackson didn't slow down to look. A rain storm wasn't anything he couldn't handle, but he wanted to be in position before it hit.

Coming around a bend in the trail, the path straightened before jutting awkwardly around a small gully. That was the final landmark.

Jackson jogged to the spot and pulled out his GPS. Right on target. He checked the trail each way and scanned the woods to either side of him. There was no one.

"Go time," he said under his breath.

Dropping the pack off his shoulders, he unzipped it and pulled out a Winchester Model 70 rifle that could be folded in half to stow away. He assembled it and laid it on the ground.

Another clap of thunder. Jackson kept moving.

He pulled out his FLIR infrared monocular, gun holster, and his P320 pistol. Jackson put the gun in its holster and attached it to his leg. He put the monocular in a coat pocket, grabbed the rifle, and slung his pack back across his shoulders.

In less than two minutes, Jackson had transformed from recreational hiker to someone resembling a paramilitary operative. He looked around again before stepping off the trail and down into the gully as he headed for the side of the mountain. This is where he and the Appalachian Trail parted ways. The rest of his trek wouldn't be on this trail or any other.

4

The decision about what to do tonight had consumed Sara Beth for the rest of the afternoon and into the early evening. She had hardly said anything at dinner, stirring the tomato and cucumber salad around on her plate as her parents debated how the Burrows down the street could afford that new Lexus parked in their driveway. They'd probably taken her silence as her continued protest of their decision, Sara Beth thought. She didn't care. The less they knew, the better.

After all, if she was going to go out tonight, there would be no running it by them first. That much she had decided. She wasn't going to give them a chance to say no to her twice.

If she couldn't go to Mexico, she wanted to go somewhere. Did she think she'd really go out and make it back unnoticed? She didn't know. But in that particular moment, she didn't know if she cared, either.

Now back in her room alone, Sara Beth heard her phone chime and saw it light up as it lay on her desk. She walked over and saw a snap from her friend Jessica. The three of them – Jessica, Katia, and Emily – were making duck faces to the camera as they held various shades of lipstick in their hands. The text bar across the picture cut off the bottom of their hands.

GETTING READY!! R U?!?!

Sara Beth let out a little huff, annoyed. Another shameless sales pitch, she thought. She walked over to her mirror, snapped a selfie as she held up her middle finger, and sent it back.

HOW DO I LOOK?

She sunk into her bed, lying on her stomach with her phone beside her and turned on the TV. Flipping through the channel guide, she put on an episode of Gilmore Girls when her phone buzzed again.

"Unfucking believable," Sara Beth stammered to herself.

But it wasn't one of her friends. Not one of her girlfriends, anyway. It was a text from Kevin Polk.

Hey, u comin out 2nite?

Sara Beth studied the text message with suspicion. The timing felt like one of three certain girls put him up to this.

She responded. *Why? Who's asking?*

A message shot back. *I'm asking…who else?*

Butterflies churned in her stomach as prying suspicion gave way to the uneasy feeling that came when you felt as though you'd just said something profoundly stupid. The quandary of how to respond consumed her until she heard her mother shout from downstairs.

"Sara Beth!"

"What," she yelled back, rolling her eyes.

"It's your night to take out the trash. Please do it before you go to bed," her mother answered.

Oh, I'll take the trash out, Sara Beth thought, then I'll fucking keep on going.

"Fine," she shouted back.

Her phone buzzed again with another message from Kevin.

Come out…it'll be fun!

"Fuck it," she said to herself. She was going.

She went downstairs, pulled out the kitchen trash bag, tied it up, and took it out back. As she did so, she surveyed the lower floor. Only her father was downstairs. He was laid back, watching a college basketball game on TV, already half asleep. Her mother must've gone up shortly after yelling up to her.

Sara Beth took out the trash, came back inside and returned to her room where she began working on an outfit for tonight. Another hour or two and both of her parents would be sound asleep.

As long as she was quiet, she thought, neither of them would hear her sneak out the backdoor.

5
—————

Jackson sat perched behind a shrub and large oak tree atop a hill that overlooked the cabin in front of him. Weather-beaten planks that had seen better days made up the cabins siding, framing the building's equally ramshackle windows and doors. A roof with visible holes did its best in its late age to keep out the rain that was now falling.

Somewhere in that mess, Jackson thought, the person he'd come for was waiting.

He'd taken the gully next to the trail to where it joined a larger ravine. That ravine took him down the side of the mountain. From there, it was only a short hike through the Shenandoah backcountry to the hill he had set up on.

There was no car in the carport next to the cabin. Jackson had expected that, but it also meant he couldn't make his move yet. The person he'd come for wouldn't be the only one here tonight. The other – the one that had taken her and brought her here – would be coming back. That's when Jackson would strike.

Jackson took a swig from his water bottle as he continued to watch the property. The sun had set and now only a cloud-covered twilight hung in the sky. The initial onslaught of rain had yielded to a moderate drizzle. Jackson sat motionless, a boulder in the rainstorm.

His gaze moved farther out and he surveyed the narrow valley beyond, first with the scope attached to his Winchester rifle, then with the FLIR monocular. His eyes moved slowly, watching everything from the pasture of overgrown grass to the dirt road to the trees that dotted the opposite mountainside. Nothing.

As nightfall crept ever closer, the house was dark. No exterior lights had come on and no interior lights shone from inside. In an hour or so, you wouldn't be able to see the house at all unless you were looking for it. It's probably what the man who wasn't here had counted on.

He took another swig of water and tucked the bottle away. A light in the distance appeared moving down the highway from the north. Cars had come and gone sporadically over the hour or so Jackson had been sitting there. This one didn't seem any different. He paid it almost no mind until, out of the corner of his eye, he saw it begin to slow down. The car came to almost a complete stop before it turned right onto the dirt road that led to the cabin. The headlights were now pointed directly at him.

He shifted from his sitting position, getting up into a crouch leaning against the tree. Opening the bolt of the rifle, Jackson double checked that there was a round in the chamber, then did the same with his P320.

The headlights of the car bounced and swayed with the meandering road. Another 30 seconds and they'd be shining on the car port as the car pulled in.

Here we go, Jackson thought.

6

At ten o'clock sharp, Sara Beth's phone buzzed. It was a vibrating alarm she had set in case she'd fallen asleep. Of course, Sara Beth never got close to dozing off. Waiting impatiently for ten to come around, her mind had been consumed with what she planned to do. Little details came to her, things to remember to avoid getting caught.

She slipped on an oversized cream sweater and looked into the standing mirror in the corner of her room. Eyeing herself top to bottom, she shrugged, suppressing enough hormonal self-doubt to admit she liked the way she looked.

Holding her boots in her hand, she peeked into the hallway looking down at her parent's bedroom. The harsh LED light of the television cast an eerie shadow over her mother's figure wrapped up in the covers. Parent one, check.

From the open door of her room she could hear the television downstairs, still on a college basketball game. Her father probably had drifted off and was still down there. That wouldn't help things as she tried to go out the back door.

Sara Beth stepped out cautiously and walked downstairs, her thick, fuzzy socks muffling her footsteps as she went. Just as she went to check that her father was, in fact, asleep, a loud snore startled her. She let out a small gasp and then had to cover her mouth to keep herself from laughing. Parent two, check.

Slipping into the kitchen, she grabbed her black and red checkered coat off the hook and took one last look into the living area. The shadows of her father and the recliner flashed with the light from the TV.

"Bye, guys," Sara Beth whispered.

Closing the back door slowly behind her, she sat on the porch staircase to slide her riding boots on. She paused a moment and listened. There was nothing.

She had made it.

Euphoric, she whipped her coat on and walked briskly down the driveway towards the street. When she got to the front yard, she took one more look at her house. It looked as asleep as her parents did inside it. Turning for the sidewalk, she looked down to hide the proud smile she couldn't suppress.

Sara Beth made her way to the corner of Wolfe Street. The air was brisk but she was too pumped up to notice. This was happening, it was really happening. Her mind flashed forward to the thought of now surprising her friends. Their faces. The big, cheerful hug they'd give her. What would they even do? It didn't matter.

At Wolfe Street, she headed east. Wolfe Street would take her closer to her friends, assuming they were downtown. When she was just a few blocks from the area, Sara Beth thought, she would call Emily and the girls and surprise them with the good news.

Walking by house after house, she peered at the shadowy figures in the windows of the few with lights still on. A man sat at a table in one, a couple watched what looked like a cable news program in another, a second couple appeared to be working at something on their kitchen counter. Dishes, most likely.

When Sara Beth got to the intersection of High Street, she couldn't help but to smile again. This was really happening. She was here, on the edge of downtown. Sara Beth. Out on the town. Alone. Not some schlubby teenager in need of a chaperone.

She was looking at her Instagram feed at the light when she saw Jessica had posted a picture. She and Emily had posed for a selfie, holding peace signs up to their eyes. The filter on the photo made their already pale complexions seem ghostlike. But what really caught Sara Beth's eye was the Taj of India sign lit up behind them. They were on Court Square. She looked at the timestamp of the post. Three minutes ago.

Sara Beth chuckled to herself as she crossed High Street. This was too good. Better than calling them, she would show up and surprise them.

She changed course. Getting to Court Square would be fast if she could cut across the couple of city blocks between it and her. At a parking lot for an appliance repair store she turned diagonally off the street, cutting the corner towards Court Square. As she rounded the backside of the building, she checked her phone to see if her friends had posted anything else. No new updates. They were probably still there.

Just then her phone buzzed and chimed with an incoming Face-Time. It was Emily. Her friends hadn't given up on her. Did she answer it or stick to her plan of surprising them? She slowed down, staring at her phone, thinking, when it happened.

Walking around the building, Sara Beth hadn't noticed the black panel van parked behind the appliance repair shop. As she walked by it, looking down at her phone, she was startled when the back doors of the van abruptly kicked open. Four large, strong arms lurched from the darkness, grabbing her, and pulled her into the van. Sara Beth tried to scream, but a gloved hand covered her mouth. She looked inwards at the interior of the van as a shadowy figure in the driver seat punched the van into gear.

The van backed out, and turned down the street, turning back in the direction she had come. It drove past a crowded brewery. Sara Beth watched helplessly out the back windows as its patrons paid no mind to her abduction.

She kicked and punched and twisted her body trying to pry herself free of her captors. Her phone, she thought. She had to get to her phone.

Pulling her right arm towards her body, she reached in the pocket of her coat. It wasn't there. She slid her hand around frantically on the cold metal floor of the van as the two people in the back continued to wrestle with her. Her phone wasn't there. It wasn't anywhere. And just as she reached out once more, she felt a prick in her arm.

As soon as the pain had registered, Sara Beth felt disoriented. Her mind slowed. The burn from the prick in her arm lingered and throbbed. She could feel the sting soaking deeper, flowing through the skin and saturating the muscle below. She wanted to continue to fight, but fatigue set in. Sounds began to blur together just before the dark van turned black.

The man driving hung a left and turned south on High Street, heading away from downtown. Buildings became sparse as the city street narrowed to a small two-lane county road. City lights gave way to forest and farmland as the road bobbed and weaved around the encroaching hills. And the black van carrying Sara Beth Parker disappeared into the blackness of the night.

Back in the parking lot of the appliance repair shop, her phone buzzed for a moment on the cold asphalt. The screen lit up with a notification.

Emily – Missed FaceTime call

7

J ackson watched as the man he believed to have taken Ashley Sudfeld pulled into the carport and climbed out. Even from atop the hill in this rainstorm, he could tell it was him. The doughy, hunched physique. The disheveled gray hair. He even had the hitch in his gait described in the police file his connection had slipped him.

Walter Scruggs wasn't the kind of criminal that elicited empathy from the average person. Not that most did, but Walter was a lifetime predator. He'd spent his years a pariah in the communities where he lived when he wasn't incarcerated. He hated the world for it, but he also never changed.

So, Scruggs left what life he had and fled. He remembered his mother talking about an old hunting cabin in Appalachian Virginia her family used to have. It was remote, and what people were around didn't ask questions. It was perfect for him.

His newfound freedom emboldened his behavior. Eventually he would sit in his van and watch as the nearby high school let out. It wasn't long after that that a girl with baby blonde hair and striking blue eyes caught his eye.

Scruggs became obsessed with her. He stopped watching the school and started to watch her neighborhood. He would follow her as she went for runs or hung out with friends on her front porch.

But his craving grew deeper, and watching from afar was no longer enough. He'd follow the family into the store when they were out shopping or sit on benches around the route she always ran and wait for her to pass by. She would offer him a polite smile. He took it as much, much more.

So, it was on a cold, snowy February afternoon that Scruggs sat on a sidewalk. This time, though, he had a knife. And his van. Ashley Sudfeld never made it back home that day, and she'd be reported missing by her family before sundown.

It was this series of events that brought Jackson Clay to the same secluded cabin in the Shenandoah Valley on this night.

Jackson trotted down the hillside and crouched behind a stack of wooden pallets as Scruggs came around the far side of the van. The rain was driving against Jackson's body, heavy drops hitting the rigid brim of his ballcap. He watched as Scruggs moved towards the back of the house, walking towards Jackson. The hairs on the back of his neck pricked up with surprise. Fearing he'd been spotted, Jackson reached for the gun on his thigh.

But Scruggs turned away from Jackson and towards the back door. He was carrying a small bag of groceries in one hand and a bundle of firewood in the other. If he had seen Jackson, he certainly wasn't letting on. Scruggs got to the stoop of the backdoor and dropped everything. He reached in his pocket for his keys, fumbling in the darkness for the right one.

Jackson rose slowly, spotting the opportunity. He could hear Scruggs cussing to himself as he struggled to find the key. Jackson slowly unclipped and drew his P320 as he stepped out around the pallets, taking one slow, careful step after another.

Scruggs found the right key. He slid it into the deadbolt, turned it, and opened the door.

Jackson struck.

Covering the remaining fifty feet in just a couple seconds, Jackson hit Scruggs from behind with the entire force of his body, sending the two barreling through the door.

Jackson pushed himself to his feet as Scruggs was reaching for a knife on his belt. Jackson stomped on the arm and drove it away as Scruggs hollered in pain. Jackson took the knife, secured it in one of his pockets before rolling a writhing Scruggs onto his belly, putting his arms behind him and binding them together with zip tie handcuffs.

"What the hell do you want man," Scruggs groaned.

Jackson ignored him.

He drew a flashlight, lifted up his P320 and looked into the rest of the cabin. He moved down the hallway, clearing each room with the surefooted precision of a Ranger in the heart of Fallujah. There was a small den, a bathroom, and lastly a bedroom all the way at end. Nobody. It was clear.

Jackson moved back to the kitchen and stood Scruggs up.

"Where is she," asked Jackson.

"Where is who," Scruggs asked back.

Jackson swung Scruggs around and slammed his torso down on the table. He grabbed Scruggs' right arm and yanked it upwards. Scruggs screamed again.

"Listen to me," said Jackson, "This is going to go badly for you either way, the only question is how badly. I'm only going to ask one more time. Where is she?"

"I don't know who you're tal---"

Jackson didn't wait for Scruggs to finish his lie. He grabbed the zip tie cuffs around Scruggs' wrists and used leverage to direct him towards a support beam dividing the entry way into the kitchen. He pulled out two more pairs of zip tie cuffs, using one to secure Scrugg's ankles then another to bind the two sets of handcuffs together around the support beam.

"I don't know what you want, man," offered Scruggs, "I haven't got mu—"

Jackson scanned the area again, looking for something he missed.

"Trust me, I know what you have," said Jackson.

Jackson stepped out of the kitchen. He knew something was wrong. There hadn't been any other doors in any of the other rooms or in the hallway. Could he have a basement with access only from the outside? Possible, but it seemed unlikely.

Jackson moved his flashlight over everything in the hall and the kitchen once more. The light passing over a sink, a refrigerator, an oven, and then a door. A door. He had seen it the first time he searched the kitchen but assumed it to be some sort of pantry. Now, however, he looked closer. There was a key hole in the door knob. Pantries didn't need to be locked.

Walking over to it, Jackson put the light on Scruggs' face to see his reaction when he showed him he had spotted the door. Scruggs looked back at him with a blank stare.

Placing his hands on the countertop, Jackson bucked his left foot backward and booted the door open. He turned around, his P320 drawn, and looked. There was a rickety staircase leading down and a faint glow of light emanated from below. It appeared to be an unfinished basement. Jackson moved down the stairs slowly, his gun drawn.

The basement was little more than a 10' x 20' room with slab concrete for a floor and unpainted cinder blocks for walls. In the middle of the room was a rusty iron support beam. The light came from a camping lantern sitting on the floor. Next to it, the figure of a teenage girl lay on a mattress that looked like it had come from a dog kennel.

He hurried over to the girl when she screamed, "Please, no!"

He stopped, putting his hands up to show it was okay and holstered his gun, moving slowly to show her he meant her no harm.

"It's okay," he said, "I'm not going to hurt you. The other man isn't going to hurt you anymore."

"Are you the police," she asked.

"No, but I'm going to get them," he replied," I want to see that you're okay, though. Is that okay?"

She stared at him for a moment before nodding.

He walked over to her, checking her up and down. She was breathing okay, her heart rate was okay, and she didn't have any serious injuries. She was decidedly healthy for someone who had been held captive for a month. He pulled away the stained bed sheet – it was the only thing Scruggs had left her to keep warm as she lay down here in a shirt and panties – to reveal a metal cuff around her ankle with a chain. He followed the chain with his flashlight to a metal loop bolted on the wall.

That monster, Jackson thought.

Starting to realize Jackson was truly there to help, Ashley grasped him with both arms and began to cry. Jackson knew it wasn't over yet, but paused a moment, allowing her to embrace him.

"I'm going to get help," Jackson said, "Is there anything you need right now?"

Her eyes filled with panic as she buried her head into his side and tightened her hold on him.

"No! You can't leave," she replied, crying now, "Please, please! Don't leave me here!"

"I have to. Just a little while longer," Jackson replied.

Jackson began to pull himself away. Ashley didn't let go of him until he softly pushed on her arms, asking her to let him go. He walked back to the stairs. Jackson could hear Scruggs making noise upstairs, most likely trying to squirm free.

"Wait," Ashley said from across the room, "I'm cold."

"I'll get something," he replied, "And something for that chain, too."

"His keys," She offered, "It's a key. I think on the keys he carries."

Jackson nodded as he climbed up the stairs.

Scruggs had twisted himself around in a half-circle around the post. Jackson pulled Scruggs towards him and patted down his pockets.

"Hey," stammered Scruggs, bucking back and forth, "What are you doing?"

Jackson ignored him and continued to search. Nothing. Then he remembered. He had hit Scruggs from behind as he opened the door. The keys had probably been in his hand. He went back to the open door, shining his flashlight on the floor. Sure enough, there they were.

He grabbed the keys, then reached for his pack just outside the door. He opened a side pocket and removed a fire blanket he had packed just in case. Normally, it would be used to snuff out someone or something on fire, but it wouldn't be half bad at warming up a traumatized teenager, either.

He took the keys and the blanket and went back downstairs.

Ashley shuddered and backed away again as Jackson reappeared. How many times had she feared that door opening, Jackson thought.

"Still just me," he said, putting his hands up once more, "I found the keys and got a blanket."

She dropped her guard, allowing Jackson to come over to her. He unlocked the shackle around her ankle and slid it away. He watched and waited until her shivering became less violent.

"Okay, now," he said, "I need you to do me a favor."

"What," she replied.

"I'm going to call for help, but I need you to stay here."

Her panic kicked up again.

"No, no you can't," she begged, "Please, please take me with you."

"Listen to me," he said, trying to reassure her, "The man who hurt you is still upstairs. I have to make sure he doesn't hurt anyone else. I'll have him, and you will be safe, but only if you stay down here."

Still shivering a little, she was silent as she stared at Jackson, deciding whether or not to trust him.

"Okay," she finally relented.

"You promise me you'll stay here," asked Jackson.

"Yes. I, I promise."

Jackson got up. It was time to end this.

"9-1-1, what's your emergency," the voice on the other end of the call asked.

"Ashley Sudfeld, the girl who was abducted from outside Hillsboro, Virginia. She is at 2618 Summit View Lane, at the end of State Route 714," Jackson said.

He spoke in short, declarative statements, giving the operator and anyone who listened to the recorded conversation very little to identify him with.

"You say you found Ashley Sudfeld, sir," the operator asked.

"She is at that address. 2618 Summit View. Responding officers will also find Walter Scruggs. He is the one responsible for her abduction."

"Okay, sir, and may I have your name?"

Jackson ignored the question.

"Scruggs will be handcuffed and unarmed in plain view for arriving officers. Ashley Sudfeld is in the basement of the building.

She's stable, but requires medical attention. Likely mild hypothermia as well as cuts and scrapes. You'll want to start Fire and Rescue now. I'll leave this line open in case you are able to triangulate its position."

He put the phone down away from his ear. The operator on the other end was still trying to get information out of him, but her efforts were futile. She would never know who Jackson was. He was just about to put the phone down on the table when one more thought came to him as he eyed a bottle of Evan Williams sitting on the table. He put the phone back up to his ear as the operator continued.

"Sir, I need a name and num--,"

"Tell the responding deputies to look for the vehicle fire," Jackson said.

With that, Jackson placed the phone on the counter and turned towards Scruggs. He had given up trying to wrestle free. Something in him knew it was over. Jackson pulled out a knife and cut the zip tie bound around the post. He pulled Scruggs up by the pair around his wrists, the pain forcing Scruggs to reluctantly cooperate.

"Ow, man, c'mon let go," Scruggs begged.

Jackson marched him to the front door, opened it, and shoved Scruggs out before going back inside. He slipped his pack on, grabbed the bottle of Evan Williams and a dish towel by the sink and went back out the front door.

Scruggs had rolled over onto his back and was trying to get up when Jackson grabbed him by the cuffs around his wrists and helped him do just that.

"Walk," ordered Jackson.

"Listen man, listen," Scruggs said, continuing to beg, "A thousand dollars. A thousand dollars cash I have in there. It's all yours. Just let me go."

Jackson ignored the offer. He marched him over near the minivan in the carport and shoved him onto the ground once more. Opening the front door of the van, Jackson shined his flash light inside, looking for the hood release. He found it and popped it.

Before exiting, Jackson turned the flashlight into the van's interior and looked. The windows had been spray-painted black from the inside then covered with wire caging.

He stepped out and looked at Scruggs. Lying defeated in the mud as rain battered his meager frame. All this evil, all this pain caused, Jackson thought, and for what? A familiar anger began to burn in him.

He walked around to the front of the van, propped up the hood, and began popping open valves and unscrewing lids for fluids. He stuck the dish towel in the top of the bottle of Evan Williams and stepped back to a safe distance.

Lighting the rag, he tossed the makeshift incendiary at the engine. A whoosh of fire burst forth on impact and spread over the engine block before another, larger explosion caused the ground to shake as the whole car became engulfed in flames.

Returning to Scruggs, he grabbed him by his feet and dragged him to the post of the carport. He could feel the heat of the fire biting at his back.

"C'mon man, please," Scruggs said, now crying, "Don't kill me."

"No one's killing you. But this is over," Jackson replied.

He pulled out another set of zip tie handcuffs and once more bound Scrugg's hands and feet around a lamppost. Standing over him, Jackson took one last look at the man.

In a minute, there would be flashing lights on the horizon. Seconds later, they'd hear the sirens. Help would arrive. Scruggs would be arrested. Eventually, he'd be sentenced. And if all went the way it should, he would never be free again. Anonymity was important to Jackson, but he wanted Scruggs to remember the man that did this. That set those events in motion.

Scruggs looked up at him, sniffling.

"I didn't want to hurt her," he said.

Jackson looked off in the distance, anticipating the flashing lights.

"Yes, you did."

With that Jackson walked back towards the woods behind the cabin. He went back to the same perch behind the bush and tree where he had waited for Scruggs. He watched and waited, making sure Scruggs stayed put. Making sure help did arrive. Making sure Ashley was found.

The first flashing lights turned onto the gravel road, driving directly towards Scruggs and the fire. A pair of deputies came over, weapons drawn, and examined Scruggs. One of them motioned off towards the house and two others went for the front door. Lights flickered on through the windows. Jackson could see inside as they discovered the door to the basement and descended down the stairs.

It was over. Ashley was safe.

Jackson turned around and disappeared into the night.

8

Anne Parker awoke to the nasally beep of her alarm clock, a whining, analog brute that predated the turn of the century. She rolled over, slapped it, and stared at the ceiling until she felt fully awake.

Sitting up, Anne put on her slippers and robe. She headed down the hall for the stairs, but stopped outside Sara Beth's room. Normally, she could hear the television left on much too loud as Sara Beth slept. This morning, however, it was completely quiet. Strange, she thought, maybe she had gotten up already.

"Scott," she called out as she descended the stairs, "Scott, are you down here?"

Scott bucked forward in the chair as his mind leapt out of whatever dream he'd been having and back into the reality of early morning.

"Mmhmm, yeah," he said, shaking off the lingering sleepiness, "Yeah, I'm here."

"Is Sara Beth down here," she asked.

"Mm, no. No, I don't think so," he replied.

Anne walked into the living room and watched as Scott rubbed at his eyes.

"You're half asleep," she said annoyed as she walked past him into the kitchen, "Sara? Sara are you down here?"

"She's probably upstairs still asleep," Scott offered.

"Her T.V. wasn't on. Or, well, I didn't hear it on."

Scott chuckled.

"Well, did you actually look," he asked.

"No, but –"

"I bet you she's upstairs right now fast asleep," he said walking past her into the kitchen, "You want some coffee?"

Anne shook her head as she went back upstairs. Outside Sara Beth's bedroom, she placed her ear against the door. It was still quiet. She knocked gently.

"Sara Beth, are you awake," she asked.

There was no reply. She knocked again.

"Sara Beth, are you in there?"

Again, there was nothing. She could have headphones on or something, she thought. She turned the doorknob slowly as she knocked again.

"Sara Beth, are you in here? I'm coming in," Anne announced.

Her eyes swung with the door as it opened. The room lay still. Anne felt a panic begin to build in her. Not only was there no sign of Sara Beth, but the bed, although a bit ruffled, was made. Even on her best days, Sara Beth never made her bed.

"Scott," she screamed, taking the stairs in small jumps, "Scott! She's not in there!"

Her feet nearly slipped out from underneath her as she swung around the bannister and ran into the kitchen.

"Did you hear me," she said breathing heavily, "She's not in there! She's not in her room!"

"Okay, okay, calm down," said Scott, "Let's call her cell phone."

Scott watched as Anne nearly ripped the cradle for the phone off the wall and frantically punched in Sara Beth's phone number. It rang twice before going to voicemail. Anne dropped the phone and began sobbing. Scott grasped her arms and rubbed them as he lowered his head to catch her eyes with his.

"Shh, it's okay," Scott said, trying to sound soothing, "Let's stay calm, okay? We don't even know what we don't know. She's probably somewhere fine."

Anne nodded through tears and sniffling.

"Text her," suggested Scott, "Keep trying her phone. Call her friends. Emily, right? That's her best friend?"

"Yeah," replied Anne, grabbing a tissue.

"Okay," Scott said, "see if maybe they know where she is. Or if their parents do. I'll check outside really quick."

Scott threw a coat on over his pajamas and turned back to Anne. She nodded, mustering a smile to match her husband's reassuring demeanor. He smiled back, much more convincingly, as he stepped out the door.

The brisk morning had left a coat of dew on everything. Scott held his arms against his side as he examined the backyard from the porch. Nothing looked out of place.

"Sara," he called out, "Sara Beth?"

He stood and listened. And waited. For what, he wasn't sure. If he were being honest with himself, he wasn't expecting Sara Beth to suddenly pop out from behind the garage. Still, he hoped.

"Sara Beth, are you out here, honey," he asked again, now stepping off the porch.

He walked to the middle of the backyard, turning slowly as he looked around. Back in the house, he could see Anne through the windows as she paced around their kitchen with the phone to her ear.

"Where are you," Scott asked under his breath.

Walking over to the driveway, he called out again. Again, nothing. When he got to the front yard he stopped and looked around just as he had in the back. Nothing seemed out of place.

As Scott walked down the driveway, he called out for Sara Beth a fourth time, and for a fourth time there was no reply. He stopped at the edge of the street, standing on the tiny grass strip between the sidewalk and the curb, and looked either way. The sleepy Harrisonburg neighborhood was just as quiet as his own yard. Scott sighed. He could count the number of times in his life when he'd been genuinely unsure of what to do next. This was quickly becoming one of those times.

He was still standing there, thinking, when footsteps came patting around the corner. Scott turned to see his neighbor Marty Hughes returning from what must've been a morning jog. Marty, seeing Scott standing there in a coat and pajama pants, pulled out his earbuds as he gave him a quizzical look.

"Hey, Scott," he said, "Everything okay?"

"Hey, Marty," replied Scott, "You haven't seen Sara Beth, have you?"

Marty paused, thinking.

"No," Marty answered, "I haven't seen her in a couple of days. But you know, I get home after the schools let out."

"Yeah, I know," Scott said, "But you were just jogging around, right? You didn't see her anywhere just now?"

"No," Marty replied, "Why, what's up?"

The question bounced around in Scott's mind like a mental pinball. What was happening? What *had* happened? He continued to think, never answering Marty.

The front door swung open and Anne stepped out. Both Scott and Marty turned to look at her. Anne looked out to them, fighting back more tears, shaking her head.

"Jesus, Marty," Scott said, "I think I need to call the police."

9

By mid-morning, a crowd of press and onlookers had gathered outside the West Loudoun Station of the Loudoun County Sheriff's Office in Round Hill, Virginia. News that Ashley Sudfeld had been found slowly leaked overnight.

A crime reporter for the Loudoun Times-Mirror had been at home monitoring his police scanner for any possible news when the Sudfeld's name had gone out across the air. He tweeted that Sudfeld, whose case had been in the news the past month or so ever since she disappeared, may have been found. Words spread over social media and by sunrise every major media outlet was sending people that way.

The small road outside the Sherriff's Office was now lined with satellite trucks that had raised their dishes and antennae as if placing their flag on unclaimed territory. Reporters hurriedly composed themselves as their crews set up equipment, each of them racing to get that live shot their news program demanded.

Walter Scruggs remained locked up in the Sheriff's Office Station for the time being. Despite being one of the largest counties in the state, this end of Loudoun County was mostly rural. As such, the Western Loudoun Station was a rather unassuming structure and felt more like a small-town police station than a regional precinct for one of the largest municipal police departments in Virginia.

No crowd, however, had gathered outside INOVA Loudoun Hospital where Ashley Sudfeld had been taken shortly after being looked at in a nearby Emergency Room. In order to keep it that way, only the nursing staff on the floor and her immediate team of doctors knew she was there. Even the two deputies assigned to watch the floor were in plain clothes so as not to draw attention.

The deputies at Western Loudoun, however, were very much in uniform and doing all they could to keep the siege of media and nosy neighbors at bay, trying to herd the onlookers in the road aside to allow vehicles in and out. One particularly green deputy was losing an argument to an elderly woman who wasn't taking no for an answer as a black unmarked Dodge Charger pulled in with two detectives, Patrick Malone and Ethan Reagan.

"Man, look at this circus," Malone said from behind the wheel.

"It couldn't have helped that Nancy Grace tweeted out the address of the station a couple hours ago," replied Reagan.

"Are you kidding me," Malone asked.

"Trust me, this thing is only spinning up. White girl abducted from one of the wealthiest counties in the country? I bet you it's a Lifetime movie by next year."

"I'll take that action."

Malone and Reagan climbed out of the car, perfect opposites of each other. Malone was tall, black, and trim with the sun shining off his perfectly shaven head. Reagan was shorter and pudgy, with a pale complexion and disheveled salt-and-pepper hair. Neither one of them looked like they were in their forties, though for vastly different reasons. As they walked into the station, they were immediately greeted by its commander, Captain William Amherst.

"Captain, it's a pleasure," said Malone extending a hand, "Patrick Malone. This is Ethan Reagan."

"Glad to have you," replied Captain Amherst, "How much do you guys already know?"

"We're about up to speed," answered Reagan, "Sudfeld was found off an anonymous 911 call. The likely suspect, Scruggs, was found bound with zip ties nearby."

Captain Amherst huffed out a chuckle.

"Yeah," said Captain Amherst, "Someone did a number on that guy. Almost had to transfer him to the hospital, too. The only question is who and is it our mysterious 911 caller."

"Well," replied Malone, "No better way to start than asking the man himself."

Scruggs had been moved to an interview room for them. It was small and windowless, with little more than a wooden table and two folding chairs to furnish it. Scruggs occupied one of said chairs, his hands and legs bound with shackles.

Malone and Reagan opened the door and stepped inside. Malone sat down in the open chair, placed a file on the table and pulled some papers out. Reagan leaned against a far wall and looked up at the closed-circuit camera in the corner of the room. Captain Amherst and a couple others were watching from a room nearby.

"Mr. Scruggs, how are we today," Malone began.

Scruggs didn't move, much less say anything.

"We have a couple of questions for you," Malone said, "Before we start, you can stop at any time and ask for a lawyer to be present. Do you understand?"

Scruggs gave a nod, still not looking up or making eye contact.

"Great. So, I'll cut right to the chase," Malone continued, "You're in a bit of a tough spot here, man. I spoke with one of the crime techs currently at your cabin and the early indications are it's a treasure trove of physical evidence. I mean, and like I said, I'm just laying my cards down on the table, man. I haven't spoken to Ashley Sudfeld, but, quite frankly, I may not even need her to tell me you did this."

Malone looked at Reagan. Scruggs continued to stare at the ground, quiet. Reagan shrugged.

"What I'm saying here, man, is you've got what's looking like a tough case stacked against you," Malone said, "I've got all this phys-ical evidence, I've got you, found just outside the cabin, Ashley Sudfeld, missing for a month, inside the cabin. I mean, really, my only question here is how did you end up tied to your own car port?"

Reagan grinned as Scruggs offered no reply.

"Who tied you up, Walter," Malone asked.

Scruggs continued to ignore them, but the two detectives just stared at him, allowing the question to linger.

"See, Walter," Reagan interjected, squatting down to get on Scruggs' level, "you're in quite a bit of trouble. But, if someone who had originally helped you do all this tied you up and left you there. Say, a friend or some—"

"Wasn't no fuckin' friend," Scruggs hissed.

"What was that," asked Malone.

"I said," Scruggs growled, looking up, "He wasn't no fuckin' friend of mine. Damn sure of that."

"Okay, Walter, so who was it?"

"I don't know. You're the fuckin' detective. Detect some shit."

"Walter—"

"What do you want me to say? The guy came out of fuckin' nowhere. Hit me like a god damn truck."

"Okay, he hit you hard. Did he set the car on fire?"

"You think I set my own fuckin' car on fire?

"Okay, he did that too. But who was this guy?"

"I told you, man. I don't know."

"So, a random guy comes to your house in the middle of nowhere, takes you down, and finds the girl you've got captive? That's what you want us to believe?"

Scruggs slumped lower into his chair, making eye contact with the floor again. Malone sighed in frustration.

"Could he be somebody Ashley knew," asked Reagan.

"Look man, all I know is what I know," Scruggs replied, frustrated, "I know I got hit from behind, the dude fuckin' tied me up inside, called you guys, and then tied me up outside. And blew up my fuckin' van."

"And then what," asked Malone.

"What do you mean and then what?"

"What happened to him?"

"The guy walked into the woods like it was nothin'. Probably the same place he came out of when he jumped me."

Malone sat back and sighed. He looked up at Reagan, who just shrugged his shoulders once more. He turned back to Scruggs, looking at him, weighing his story. Who was this man in the woods?

10

Anne was focusing on the ball of Kleenex in her hand as the officers talked to her. When Scott called to say they believed their daughter was missing, a BOLO alert – or Be On the Look Out – had gone out to all officers on patrol, two of which were dispatched to the Parker's home to take an initial statement. The two of them, identified by their nameplates as Kitt and Cho, were trying to get the information they needed from Anne, but Anne didn't feel like she was being asked helpful questions. She felt like she was being interrogated.

Every question they asked felt like a challenge to her capabilities as a mother. When did you last see your daughter? Last night. Does she have a habit of leaving without telling anyone? No, god no. Do you know who she would leave to meet up with? Maybe her friends. Anyone in particular? I don't know. Does she have a boyfriend? I don't think so. You don't think so? I don't know of one.

The coffee machine beeped from the kitchen.

"Would you officers like some coffee," asked Shannon Hughes.

"No thank you, ma'am," replied Officer Kitt.

As Scott had called the police, Marty Hughes hurried home to tell his wife, Shannon, what was going on. The two of them immediately threw on some regular clothes and came over in a show of support. Shannon was trying to be helpful by preparing some refreshments. Marty was calling people in the neighborhood they knew to see if they'd seen Sara Beth.

"Why don't we go over the course of events from yesterday one more time," suggested Cho, "You said Sara Beth came home and the two of you got into an argument?"

"Yes," replied Anne, "She wanted to go to Mexico with her friends for Spring Break. I said no."

"And that was the end of it," asked the Officer Kitt.

"Yes," Anne answered, "Basically."

"Basically?"

"Look, what do you want me to say? She's 16. Occasionally, she and I aren't going to see eye to eye."

"I understand, ma'am. We're just trying to make sure there's no detail that might help explain what has happened."

Anne felt a rage build in her. What has happened? What has happened is that her daughter has disappeared. What has happened is they called for help, but so far, the only two officers sent to help are spending all their time at the one place everyone knows she isn't. They even had the balls to search the house like she might be under the couch cushions.

"Look," interjected Scott, "Don't we need to put out an AMBER Alert or something? We can get you a photo of her."

"We're not quite there yet, sir," replied Kitt.

"What do you mean," Scott shot back, "Our little girl is missing. She's a minor."

"I understand. But there's a number of criteria that have to be met in order to issue an AMBER Alert. If your daughter's been abducted, right now we don't even know what to tell people to look for to help find her. That's why we're here. We're trying to get as much information as we can."

Just then, Officer Cho's phone rang. He stepped out the front door to answer it.

"So, let's continue," said Kitt, "You said you had an argument and she eventually went to her room."

"Yes," replied Anne, "She spent the rest of the afternoon in her room. She didn't leave until she came back down for dinner."

"Okay, and when she ate dinner, did she say anything," asked Kitt.

"She was sulking. She hardly said two words. She didn't even ask if she could leave, just scooped up her plate and tossed it in the sink."

"And she went back upstairs?"

"Yes."

"And that was the last time you saw her? At dinner?"

"Yes, I told her later to take out the trash, but I didn't actually see her when I did. But she responded. She was in her room."

"Okay, and did she leave to take out the trash?"

Anne looked at Scott.

"I heard her take out the trash," answered Scott, "I was in here, watching a game."

"And you definitely heard her come back in," asked Kitt.

"Yes," Scott replied, "She came in and she went back upstairs. I heard her shut her door."

Officer Cho, now off the phone, opened the front door and motioned his partner over. They spoke briefly before the two of them both came back into the room. Officer Kitt stepped forward and addressed the Parkers with a stern look on his face.

"Mr. and Mrs. Parker, would your daughter have any reason to go to Eddie's Appliance Repair?"

Scott and Anne looked at each other, completely confused.

"No," Scott answered, "I – I don't even know where that is."

"It's on Wolfe Street, towards downtown. Between High and Liberty," the officer continued, "There's no reason that she would go around there?"

"No, I can't think of one," Anne answered, "Why?"

Kitt looked at his partner before answering.

"We've located your daughter's phone."

11

By midday Detectives Malone and Reagan were back at their offices at the Loudoun County Sheriff's Office in Leesburg. Scruggs hadn't said much more in their interview, and the word from the hospital was that Ashley Sudfeld was under sedation after a long and traumatic night and still was not ready to be interviewed.

Malone unwrapped a Subway sandwich and began to take a working lunch at his desk. He could hear Reagan on the phone on the other side of the cubicle wall. With a handful of open cases, they were eager to clear the one case that had seemed to solve itself.

"Shit," Malone said to himself, cursing a dollop of mustard that landed on his shirt.

He got up and grabbed a napkin from the small kitchenette at the end of the office. Reagan, seeing Malone away from his desk, let the person on the other end of the line go and hung up. He popped out of his chair and intercepted his partner in front of the coffee machines.

"That was Paul Chen over at Fairfax County Criminal Investigations," answered Reagan, "Says our guy sounds like him."

"Sounds like who" asked Malone.

Reagan made an exclamation with his face and smiled jovially as he answered.

"Him."

It took Malone a second to realize what Reagan was talking about.

"Oh come, on, Ethan," said Malone, almost rolling his eyes, "Don't start with this again."

"Why is it so crazy," Reagan asked.

"Seriously," replied Malone, "A mysterious vigilante that's some sort of patron saint to abducted children? Come on, it sounds like a bad movie."

"Patrick, I'm telling you. Look at the history. 2006, Richmond. Tamara Brooks walks into a firehouse after being missing two weeks. Says a guy beat up her abductor, drove her to the firehouse and told her to tell them who she was. 2008, Hagerstown, Maryland. Anonymous tip says a van connected to the abduction of Amber Hyland is in this backyard garage and there's someone inside. Police find Hyland alive. The guy who took her is found knocked out in the living room, one hand cuffed to the radiator. 2011, Culp—"

"Yeah, I've heard it all before. I'm saying, you can't convince me some guy is going around rescuing abducted children in his free time."

"Look at the evidence. Isn't that like your job description?"

The two of them chuckled as their boss, Captain Brian Van Holt, ambled down the hall. He was flipping through a file as he looked up and saw them.

"Hey, guys, are you just back from Western Loudoun," asked Captain Van Holt.

"Yes, sir," replied Patrick.

"My office," said the Captain, gesturing, "Let's talk."

The three of them crossed the open floor dotted with desks and filed into the Captain's private office connected by a hallway. Captain Van Holt sat down in his chair. Detectives Malone and Reagan followed him in, shut the door behind them, and slid into the two seats opposite the Captain.

"So," began Captain Van Holt, "What did Scruggs have to say about last night?"

"He says he was returning to the cabin when a man essentially bull rushed him inside and overpowered him," answered Malone, "According to Scruggs, the guy took his time taking control of the situation, eventually called 911, dragged Scruggs outside, lit his car on fire, tied him up, and left him for us."

"And what happened to this guy," asked the Captain.

"Scruggs claims he just up and disappeared."

"Disappeared how?"

"Says he walked into the woods behind the house, never came back."

Malone shrugged before saying the last part. Captain Van Holt let out a snort of disbelief. He sat back in his chair as he reflected on the information.

"So, the guy disappears into the woods," said the Captain, "Nobody thought to look for him?"

"It took arriving officers some time to figure everything out," answered Reagan, "Apparently it was a half hour or so before anybody pieced together there may be a third party. And by then? In the rain? In the woods?"

Again, the Captain paused in reflection. Malone and Reagan looked at each other, unsure whether or not to continue.

"So, this," Captain Van Holt said, pausing as if to think of the word, "This woodsman. I guess I give up any hope of finding out who he is?"

"We can certainly do our best, sir," replied Detective Malone, "But quite frankly, there isn't a lot to go on. Scruggs didn't give much of a description. We could ask Sudfeld when she's ready, but it's anybody's guess how much she'll help. We could pull DNA from the property, but that's not looking likely. And even then, it wouldn't place whoever we found there *at* the time everything went down."

"What about this phone he left at the scene," asked the Captain, "Is there any way to trace it?"

"It's a pretty standard prepaid cell phone. Tracfone brand. Widely available. Can be purchased cash or credit at any one of a number of stores."

"What about the zip tie hand cuffs and this blanket he gave the girl?"

"The ties don't seem to be anything special. Black, nondescript. Plenty of places sell them, especially online. As for the fire blanket, again, nothing special. Can be bought at just about any major hardware or camping store. Some workplace suppliers, as well."

Captain Van Holt sighed, shifting his weight in his chair. Again, he paused, reflecting on all the information. After a moment or two, he bucked forward in his chair, as if coming back to consciousness, and sorted the file on his desk back together.

"That's okay," said the Captain, "I'm not going to breathe down your guys' necks to bring in a guy that'd probably get a medal before he got handcuffs, anyway. Make sure we nail down Scruggs and close it."

"You got it, Cap," replied Detective Malone.

The two detectives stood up and saw themselves out.

12

W ithin a couple of hours, the area around Eddie's Appliance Repair had swelled with activity. After the Parkers' cellular provider pinged Sara Beth's phone to find its location, Harrisonburg Police dispatched a nearby officer, who found the gold iPhone laying in the parking lot of the shop.

The officer called it in and closed off the entire property with crime scene tape. Eddie Romano, who arrived in the middle of his business being quarantined, fussed over his enterprise being shut down. It wasn't until he learned a missing girl's phone had been found nearby that he dropped his objections.

Other officers began interviewing people at nearby businesses, asking who had been working the night before, when they might have closed, and who else would have been there. There was the micro-brewery directly across the street, the bakery attached to it, and the three-store shopping plaza next door. A separate group of officers worked their way along nearby residences, also asking if anyone had heard or seen anything.

The rows of police vehicles on either side of the street began to draw onlookers. Cell phones dotted faces amongst the crowd as people took pictures and video of what was going on. Others seemed to ignore the activity entirely and just converse amongst themselves.

In the middle of all this, Detectives Sean Doherty and Angela Cole pulled up in an unmarked silver police car. Once the phone was found and there was a likelihood something serious had happened, the case was assigned to Criminal Investigations.

Getting out, they crossed underneath the police tape surrounding the repair shop's property and walked over to the police sergeant supervising the scene.

"Sarge, how's it going," asked Detective Cole, extending a hand.

"Not bad," replied the Sergeant, shaking her hand, "Pretty decent morning. Warm today."

"Yeah, Spring might finally be here," replied Detective Cole, "What've you got?"

"Phone was found exactly where it is, nobody's touched it. You see the boys are knocking on doors, but I haven't been told about anything noteworthy yet. We've walked over the property three times, haven't found anything out of the ordinary."

"What about the shop owner? What's his story?"

"Says he closed at 7 yesterday, and when he left, he was the only person here. No other car in the parking lot. Says he drove out of here probably around 7:30."

Detective Cole began scrolling through her phone.

"According to the initial missing persons report, parent's last contact with the girl was around 9," said Cole.

"Adds up with what he said about not seeing anything, I guess," replied the Sergeant.

Both detectives nodded.

"Alright, Sarge," said Detective Doherty, "If we have any more questions, we'll holler."

The Sergeant smiled and stepped over to talk with an officer who had been waiting for him. Detectives Doherty and Cole stood looking away from each other, both of them surveying the area. She was taller than him, with dark caramel skin and a head full of ash brown curly hair. He, on the other hand, was almost stereotypically Irish, strawberry blonde and a baby face heavy with freckles. Cole always felt he wore the oversized Oakley sunglasses that he did to mask as much of it as possible.

"Well, what do you think," asked Doherty.

"Empty lot, nothing overlooking it," replied Cole, describing the area, "Can't see it from the street, at least not back here, anyway. Good spot for trouble."

Detective Doherty looked up at the rooftop of the appliance shop.

"I suppose we wouldn't be lucky enough to have any cameras, would we," he asked.

Detective Cole looked up as well.

"I guess not," she replied, "Surrounding buildings, maybe?"

"I'll make sure they check around," said Doherty.

He stepped away and waved over the Sergeant. Detective Cole walked over to the phone lying on the asphalt. Crouching down, she studied it, her mirrored aviators reflecting the sight of the phone back onto itself. A long, clean crack ran diagonally across most of the screen. Cole wondered if it had been like that already or if it had cracked from being dropped here. She pushed back the sleeve of her grey blazer as she slipped on a latex glove and flipped the phone over. Stuck inside the outer case on the backside was a photo strip that looked to be from a photobooth. There were three shots altogether, each had the same three girls. Cole recognized Sara Beth from the photos she'd seen. The three of them looked happy. Cole smiled back at them.

"Okay," Doherty began, walking back, "The brewery across the street apparently has some, but they only face the parking lot and behind the bar. The bakery also has them only in the parking lot and inside. They're checking if there are any rear-facing ones for the stores over there and if any residents had Nest cameras or anything like that."

Detective Cole looked up at him, snapping off the glove, and sighed.

"Brewery was probably our best bet," she said, "Nothing else looks directly at the parking lot. Were they busy last night?"

"Apparently so," said Doherty, "They're still trying to work out if anyone saw anything. No one there now was working last night.

They're calling co-workers and whatnot. We can double back later tonight, maybe see if they have any regulars that were here last night."

Cole didn't say anything back. She stared at the phone on the ground, wondering where its owner was.

"Crime scene techs are en route," offered Doherty, watching his partner fixate on the evidence.

"Okay," replied Cole, standing up.

"How do you want to play it, Ange," asked Doherty.

Cole took one last look around the lot, as if Sara Beth Parker might be hiding and no one had noticed her yet. But she wasn't. Aside from scattered trash and overgrown weeds, the lot was vacant. Lifeless. Sara Beth Parker was somewhere, but she wasn't here. Cole turned back and looked at her partner.

"Let's go talk to the parents," she said.

13

Sara Beth slowly came to consciousness as her head banged against something hard. She remained fuzzy, struggling to completely shake off the sleep she had just departed. Or maybe she wasn't awake. Maybe she was dreaming, she thought. Right then, nothing felt clear.

She felt her body sway back and forth and realized it – she – was moving, adrift on a dark ocean, swaying and crashing into swells she couldn't see. Stranded somewhere she didn't know.

As she continued to feel her body undulate, Sara Beth became more alert and the fuzzy images of what had happened now came into focus. Sneaking out. Her phone. Her friends. The parking lot. And then, darkness. Those arms. The menacing figures. The prick in her shoulder.

Her eyes shot open in bloodshot terror as everything came back to her. Someone – no, some people – had taken her in that parking lot. She had fought them. Clearly, she had lost.

She looked around in panic. She was moving, but she wasn't in a car anymore. Her head was pressed up against metal bars crisscrossing one another. It was some sort of cage.

She could hear the rattle of wheels below her. Not big wheels, but little ones, whiny and unforgiving. Like a desk chair. Or a cart. But this wasn't those. The metal bars were all around her. And that's when it hit her. She looked down at her feet to see a door with two latches, both padlocked. Was this a fucking dog crate? Yes, it was. But it was covered. Some sort of dark cloth enveloped it and her, rustling in the passing air as the cart moved.

What the hell was going on, she thought. An instinct burned in her to scream for help, but maybe whoever was out there wouldn't like that. Fear of reprisal kept her silent. She needed to figure out what was happening.

She closed her eyes and listened, trying to hear something, anything that might tell her where she was. The wheels rattled beneath her, shaking the entire crate every time they hit a bump. Still, they seemed to roll with ease. She must be inside somewhere with a hard floor, she thought.

Lights overhead shown through the tattered cloth around her as the cart moved along. She thought she could hear the whining of electricity passing through them. The whole thing had an industrial feel to it. She definitely was inside, she thought, being moved somewhere.

Suddenly her body slammed forward as the cage crashed against something and pushed past it. She heard the squeak of hinges swinging. Something or someone had used her to push a door open.

She heard the hinges swing again followed by the thud of some kind of door. The wheels beneath her began to slow.

The cage crashed into something again, but this time stopped completely. Without the wheels rattling now, she could make out footsteps behind her. They were walking away from her. Once more the hinges swung open, then closed, followed by the same sound of a door shutting.

Then quiet. Though, not completely quiet. There was some sort of sound, a familiar sound. What was it? She listened closer, pressing her ear gently against the metal bars. Then, in one snotty breath, she heard it. Someone sniffling.

"Hell--, Hello," Sara Beth got up the nerve to say.

"Shut the fuck up," a whisper snapped back.

But it hadn't come from whomever or whatever was sniffling. It had come from the other side of her.

She shifted herself in the cage.

"Please, I just nee--,"

"Seriously, shut up," the hushed voice snapped again, "They're going to come back if they hear you or her. Shut her up over there, too."

With that, the sniffling on the other side of her broke out into uncontrolled sobbing. There were at least three of them there. The voice telling her to stop talking also sounded like a girl.

"Jesus Christ, I'm not kidding," said the snappy voice, "Shut up. Shut the fuck up."

Sara Beth had so many questions. Where was she? Why had she been taken here? And who else was there? Two people? Maybe more? She wanted to ask all these questions and more, but figured the voice next to her would only scold her to keep quiet again.

Slowly the sobbing on the other side of her died down and it became quiet. She could, in fact, hear the electricity whirring through the lights overhead, breaking up what otherwise would be a cold and dark silence.

Sara Beth waited, but no one came back as the snappy voice had warned. Perhaps, they – whoever *they* were – were alone now. Sara Beth worked up the courage to speak again.

"Please," she said.

She waited for some variation of "shut up" to be swiped back, but her talking went unchallenged.

"Please," Sara Beth repeated, "I just want to go home."

"Yeah, well you're not going home," said the voice that had told her to shut up, "I don't think any of us are going home."

With that, whoever had been crying next to her spoke for the first time.

"We're in their home now."

14

As night fell over Harrisonburg, Doherty and Cole were sitting in their unmarked police car half a block from the repair shop where Sara Beth's phone was found. Doherty was scrolling through an email on his phone as Cole watched the now vacant lot. A team of criminalists had swept through in the afternoon and hadn't found much of anything useful. Mostly just cigarette butts and broken beer bottles that could've belonged to anyone. A couple items were bagged to be tested back at the lab, but neither Cole nor Doherty were holding their breath.

Cole's eyes traced the sidewalk as it led down to the empty store and parking lot. Everything must've looked just like this last night when Sara Beth disappeared, she thought. She pictured the young girl walking in the black and red checkered coat her parents had noticed was missing. She imagined her taking a turn at the parking lot and entering it. And then, nothing. Sara Beth Parker was gone.

"She missed a FaceTime call from an Emily Green a bit after 10 last night," said Doherty, "That was the last activity to the phone until her mom tried to call it early this morning when she discovered her missing."

"One of her closer friends," replied Cole, "That's what her mother told me this afternoon. Let's make sure to talk to her tomorrow."

Doherty nodded, not breaking eye contact with his phone. The email was a list of activity on the phone the past 24 hours.

"She actually connected on a FaceTime call with Green yesterday evening, a few hours before the missed call," said Doherty, "Oh, here we go. Text messages with a Kevin Polk. Not long after the connected FaceTime call with Green. Looks like he was trying to get her to go out last night."

"Go out where," asked Cole.

"Mm, doesn't say," replied Doherty, "There's a short back and forth between them. No specifics, though."

"Guess we'll be talking to Mr. Polk tomorrow, as well," said Cole. She checked her watch. It was 10:30.

"When was that missed FaceTime call last night," asked Cole.

"Uh, looks like 10:23 p.m. last night," replied Doherty.

"If she didn't answer because she couldn't, she was already taken by this time last night," Cole said.

She sighed. 24 hours missing and no lead. They had watched the repair shop and its parking lot for nearly two hours now. No one had so much as walked by it. Cole looked across the street at the brewery, its lights and music emanating out onto an otherwise quiet part of town. It looked busy.

"This is a bust," said Cole, "Come on. Let's work the brewery. See if anyone was here last night."

Doherty nodded in agreement and the two got out of the car, crossed the street, and walked the half block to the brewery. The inside of Brella Beer Company felt very much like any college town bar, dimly lit and loud with the beat of pop rock staples. Cole could feel the bass thump as a song from Maroon 5 vied for attention amid the conversations and laughter. She was surprised how busy it was for a Tuesday night.

"Where do you want to start," asked Doherty.

Detective Cole nodded over towards the bar. Walking over, she leaned on its polished wood counter as they waited patiently until the bartender saw them and made his way down to their side.

"How are you guys doing," said the bartender, "What can I get you?"

"No drinks, thanks," replied Detective Cole, pulling out her identification, "We're with the Harrisonburg Police Department. Do you have a minute to answer a couple questions?"

Immediately the bartender looked uneasy.

"If this is about serving a minor or something, maybe I should get my manager," the bartender answered.

"No. No, it's nothing like that," replied Cole, "Did you work last night?"

"Yeah, 5pm to close," the bartender said.

"Can we ask you about it? Do you have a minute," Cole asked.

The bartender hesitated for a moment, still looking uneasy. Cole flashed him a reassuring smile.

"Sure," the bartender answered, "Just let me find someone to cover."

The bartender grabbed a fellow employee's attention, one who was waiting tables, and motioned to her that he was stepping out. As she nodded, he grabbed a vape pen from under the cash register and motioned the two detectives towards a back door.

Stepping back outside was like stepping into another world. As they shut the door behind them the lights and music were gone, replaced by the dark and the quiet of the alley.

"You guys don't mind if I take my smoke break while we talk, do you," asked the bartender.

"Not at all," replied Detective Cole, "My name is Angela Cole. This is Sean Doherty. We're detectives with Harrisonburg Police Major Crimes."

The uneasy look returned to the bartender's face.

"I – I'm not sure what I can help you with," said the bartender.

"Well, we were hoping you could help us answer a few questions," replied Detective Cole, "I don't think I caught your name."

"Oh, my bad. Jake. Jake Diaz," the bartender said, extending a hand as he took a long drag from the vape pen.

"Jake, Angela. Nice to meet you. So, listen, you said you closed this place down last night?"

"Yeah, I close it down most nights. 2 a.m. when JMU is mid-semester like it is now. Last call is 1:30. I leave probably 3 or so."

"Around 10, 10:30 last night, did you notice anything with the repair shop across the street? Or maybe with the parking lot?"

"Maybe? I don't know. I'm sorry, when you're back there behind the bar alone it can get pretty busy."

"No, I understand. So, you don't remember anything with the place across the street?"

Jake took another drag and thought about it as he hugged his scrawny frame to stay warm.

"No, sorry," said Jake.

"You don't remember anybody going into the lot back there, or a car or something maybe," asked Detective Cole.

"No, sorry," replied Jake.

"Okay, what about last night in general. Anything odd happen? Anything that stuck out?"

"Um, guy dumped his girl or something at a table. She caused a bit of a scene for a second. That's about it."

"Anyone else here working tonight that also worked last night?"

"Yeah, Syd and Leah worked last night."

"You think you could grab one or both of them on your way back in and ask them to talk to us?"

"Yeah, no problem."

"Thanks, we'll just wait out here."

"Kay."

Jake opened the door and went back inside. Detective Doherty breathed into his hands trying to keep them warm as Cole turned towards him.

"Well, what do you think," asked Cole.

"Better hope one of these two other people remember seeing something," he replied, "We have next to nothing to go on right now."

"Yeah," said Cole.

She looked down at her watch. It was almost 11. The 24-hour marker burned bright in her mind, both warning and taunting her. This was only the second missing persons case Cole had worked, but she knew the statistics. In 48 hours, witnesses' memories begin to fade.

At 72, the leads slow down dramatically. After a week, the numbers say you're most likely looking for a body.

She rubbed at her wrist just below the watch.

Time wasn't on their side.

15

The sun was just climbing over the houses on the next street over as Anne sat on the stairs leading up to her back porch. Wrens and swallows chirped as they flew overhead. In the distance, Anne could hear the muffled sounds of cars as the morning commute began. Her hands took refuge in the warmth from her coffee mug as steam danced off the surface into the crisp morning air.

Her eyes were bloodshot from a restless night of endless worry. At first, she'd gone to bed, hoping to wake up to the sounds of her daughter downstairs, safe at home. But sleep never came. She lay in bed, thinking how she'd slept so soundly the night before as her daughter was god knows where, taken by heaven knows who. Sometime after that, continuing to beat herself up over the situation, Anne Parker decided rest wasn't something she deserved.

She'd descended downstairs and taken the TV remote from Scott who'd dozed off in his recliner again. A late-night cable news program was talking about authorities finding Ashley Sudfeld up in the northern part of the state. Watching the coverage, she saw Sara Beth in Ashley's story. As the story noted that Ashley's captor was a registered sex offender with a history of sexual assault, Anne buried her head into her James Madison Alumni hoodie and released the tears she'd been fighting back all night. Her daughter was out there, somewhere, and she was helpless to do anything about it.

So now she sat, emotionally and physically exhausted from a night of panic and self-loathing, staring blankly at her backyard. She imagined a young Sara Beth playing there in the yard, kicking a soccer ball at the garage door or chasing fireflies with a mason jar. There wasn't a single thing she wouldn't give to go back to one of those days right now.

Anne was imagining one of those warm, happy nights when the door behind her opened, sucking in a waft of cold morning air and snapping her back to reality.

"There you are," Scott said, "I've been looking all over the house for you."

"Sorry," replied Anne, "I couldn't sleep. I didn't want to bother you."

Scott sat down beside her and rubbed his hands together. Anne offered him the cup of coffee but he shook his head at the gesture.

"Detective Doherty called the house," Scott said, "Did you hear it ring?"

Anne looked at him with alarm. Immediately she felt a wave of guilt. How could she not have been waiting by the phone for news of her daughter? She shook her head as she looked at him desperately for some kind of good news.

"They want to do a press conference or something today," Scott said, "Get her picture out there. Get it in the media that she's missing and we're looking for her. That sort of thing, I guess."

Anne nodded, deflated that it hadn't been news about Sara Beth.

Scott turned and looked at her, now seeing the finer details of stress. Her eyes red from crying, the dark bags underneath them from a sleepless night, the fidgety arms of a woman who had had too much caffeine and not enough food. He grabbed her with his right arm and pulled her into him.

"It's going to be okay, hon" Scott said.

"You don't know that," Anne whispered back to him.

Scott didn't say anything else. He wanted to console his wife, but he had always been a man of practicality and logic. It had always made him the one who kept a cool head in stressful times like this. But now it was also the thing telling him that his wife wasn't wrong.

16

Doherty and Cole pulled into Thomas Harrison High School as the first classes of the day were beginning. Cole had called the school's office before they left and confirmed Emily Green and Kevin Polk were in attendance that morning and asked that a room be set aside where they could talk.

Situated on a modest hill overlooking a grassy pasture, its red brick and cream façade with large pane glass windows was the kind of uninspired contemporary architecture that screamed municipal building. School buses lined the street, creating a wall between the school and everything beyond it. Walking around them, the two detectives went to the school's office where they were greeted by Corporal Alex Rhys, the school resource officer.

"Detectives, how are you," he asked as he walked them over to an empty conference room, "I'll let you guys get situated and go track down Emily and Kevin. Who do you want to talk to first?"

"Emily Green, I suppose," replied Detective Cole.

"You got it," said Corporal Rhys, "Be right back."

Cole sat down and looked over what little information the school had legally been allowed to provide her about the two students without obtaining some sort of judicial order. Like Sara Beth, they too were 16 years old and sophomores at the school. Detective Doherty ran a background check on both of them from the office. Neither had a juvenile record.

A minute later the door swung open and Corporal Rhys ushered in Emily Green. Already seeming defensive, she hesitantly stepped towards the two detectives. Detective Cole stood up and offered her hand.

"Miss Green, it's a pleasure to meet you," Cole said, "My name is Angela Cole, I'm a detective with the Harrisonburg Police."

"Hi," Emily replied shyly.

"Why don't you have a seat," said Detective Doherty.

"Emily, first off you should know you're not in any kind of trouble. In fact, can we get you anything," asked Detective Cole, "A water? A soda?"

Emily shook her head as she slipped into a rolling desk chair.

"Are you sure, hon," asked Cole, trying to ease the obvious worry in Emily.

"No, thank you," replied Emily.

"Okay, well if you want something, you just let me know," Cole said.

"I will."

"So, Emily, you know by now your friend Sara Beth is missing."

"Yeah. People were talking about it all yesterday. And then I saw it on T.V. last night."

"Anyone say anything that stuck out to you?"

"This guy, Tony, said she ran away. Another guy, Trevor, said she probably got kidnapped. I think they're full of, I mean—"

"You can say it, they're full of shit. What makes you say that?"

Emily smiled sheepishly.

"They don't really know her," replied Emily, "I mean, Trevor isn't even in our class. He's a Senior."

"Uh huh, and what are their names again, just so I know," asked Detective Doherty.

"Tony Tran and Trevor Marcum," Emily answered.

Cole looked over at Detective Doherty. Both of them jotted down the two names.

"What about people who you do think might know what happened," asked Cole.

"No," replied Emily, "I would've said something. She was my friend. Is my friend."

"You two seem close," said Detective Doherty, "Let me ask, was she supposed to go out with you last night?"

Emily's faced turned flush. She sunk deeper into her hoodie as she played with the zipper.

"Emily," said Detective Cole, "I'm not here to get you in trouble. But if something happened, we need to know."

"I," began Emily cautiously, "I told my parents I was staying over at Stephanie's house. To study. They don't know we left her house."

"So, you went out last night," said Detective Doherty, "Was Sara Beth supposed to meet you?"

"We were trying to get her to come, but she was resisting. Eventually she stopped answering me. We never saw her."

"When was the last time you heard from her?"

"I guess yesterday afternoon. I sent her a snap trying to get her to come out. She replied with a snap of her middle finger."

Detective Cole grinned, amused, as she noted the last contact with Emily Green.

"What about actually talking to her," asked Detective Doherty.

"Earlier that afternoon, I FaceTimed her," replied Emily.

"Right, yes. We see that on her phone," Doherty said, double-checking the paperwork, "At 3:42 p.m. that afternoon."

"I guess, yeah."

"What did you talk about?"

"She was mad her mom wasn't going to let her go on this trip to Mexico over Spring Break. I told her we were going out, and she should blow off some steam by coming out with us. Like I said, though, she never said she was going to."

"You're 100% sure she never said at any point that day she was coming?"

"I wanted her to come. If she said she was coming, I would remember."

Detectives Doherty and Cole looked at each other.

"Emily," Detective Doherty said, stepping in, "The reason we ask is we found Sara Beth's phone. Coming from her house, she would've been headed towards the downtown area. You say she wasn't going to meet up with you. Do you know of any reason she would go down there?"

Emily turned white as she processed what Detective Doherty said. She closed her eyes as a tear rolled down her cheek.

"No," she said, "Oh my god, do you think she was coming to meet us? Am I? Am I the reason she's missing now?"

"No. No, of course not," Cole said quickly, trying to stop Emily from getting too upset, "We don't know why she left. But I tell you what, we're going to do everything we can to get her back."

Emily nodded as she lost the battle to hold back more tears. Corporal Rhys, who had been leaning in the corner, stepped over and offered her a tissue box from the table.

"I think that's good for now," said Detective Cole, "We'll let you know if we need you."

Corporal Rhys opened the door. Emily stood up, nodding, and was ushered out by Rhys.

"I'll go get Kevin Polk," Corporal Rhys said quietly as he shut the door behind him.

Detective Doherty stood up and walked to the window. An early morning physical education class jogged down the hill in grey t-shirts and purple mesh shorts. The teacher was getting on the few stragglers who seemed to prefer to socialize instead of run.

"You were good with Green," said Detective Doherty.

"Thanks, I think I should take Kevin Polk, too," replied Detective Cole, "If we don't divide and conquer, we'll be here all day running down every name these kids drop."

Detective Doherty turned around and walked back over to his notepad for reference.

"No problem," said Doherty, "You want me to run down this Tony Tran and Trevor Marcum separately?"

"Do you mind," asked Cole.

"No, not at all," answered Doherty.

"There's probably nothing there, like Green said, but we better check it out anyway."

"Agreed. I'll get Rhys to find the two. See if I can't find another one of these empty conference rooms."

Detective Doherty grabbed his files and stepped towards the door just as Corporal Rhys was knocking on and opening it. He gave the detective a polite smile as the two passed each other in the doorway.

"Detective Cole," said Corporal Rhys turning to look at her, "Kevin Polk for you."

"Yes, thank you," replied Detective Cole, "Kevin, why don't you have a seat."

Kevin plopped down confidently into one of the desk chairs. He didn't seem nearly as timid as Emily had.

"Kevin, it's nice to meet you," said Detective Cole.

"Nice to meet you, too," answered Kevin.

"Kevin, first of all, I just wanted to start by saying you're not in any kind of trouble," said Cole.

Kevin nodded.

"I assume you know by now Sara Beth Parker is missing," said Detective Cole.

"Yeah, everyone at school is talking about it," replied Kevin.

"Has anyone said that they know what happened to her," asked Detective Cole.

"Everyone has their theories, sure. But it's all just bullshit."

"Like Tony Tran and Trevor Marcum?"

"Yeah, and others. People who didn't know her."

"What about you? How well do you know Sara Beth?"

"I don't know. She's in a few of my classes. We talk a bit."

"You texted her two nights ago, a few hours before she disappeared."

Kevin shifted uneasily in his seat. He looked less confident now, as he muttered a reply.

"I just said, you know, she should come out," said Kevin, "But I never saw her. I didn't even go out that night."

"You didn't," asked Cole.

"No," replied Kevin, "I mean I was going to. But then I didn't. You can ask my dad. He found out I failed an English quiz. He grounded me that night."

"You could've snuck out."

"No way, you clearly don't know my parents. In fact, you can ask them. My dad yelled at me to get off my PS4 later that night. At like eight. Ridiculously early."

There was an edge to Kevin's tone now, as if he felt Cole was accusing him of something and he didn't appreciate it. Cole believed him, leaving her unsure where to go next.

"Look, can I go," asked Kevin, "Like I said, ask my parents."

Detective Cole let out a sigh and looked over the papers in front of her.

"Alright," she said, "Thank you. If I need anything else, I'll ask."

"Okay," replied Kevin.

He stood up and walked out. Now it was Cole's turn to get up and look out the window. Detective Doherty and Corporal Rhys were standing out there. They were looking off in the distance as one of the kids in gym clothes walked over to them. Must be Tony Tran or Trevor Marcum, she thought.

She hoped they'd find more than she had.

17

Jackson was listening to a news report on Ashley Sudfeld as he entered the sleepy village of The Plains, Virginia and pulled into a parking spot at Hart's Diner. He waited for a moment, listening to the end of the news story. The suspect, Walter Scruggs, was expected to be arraigned in court tomorrow. He was identified as the man authorities arrested when they found Sudfeld. There was no mention of someone capturing him before authorities arrived.

Satisfied, Jackson killed the engine and climbed out of his truck. He lifted up his left pant leg and examined the, bluish-purple bruise extending down to his ankle. Finding and freeing Ashley Sudfeld had not come without a cost to his body. He lowered his pants leg and stretched, trying to ease the pain away. As he did so, Frankie Hart, owner and operator of Hart's Diner, saw him and waved.

Jackson waved back before walking in and grabbing his usual seat at the counter.

"Jax," greeted Frankie, "How's it going?"

"Frankie," said Jackson, tersely returning the salutation.

"You want your usual for lunch," asked Frankie.

Jackson nodded. Frankie chuckled, flashing his signature beaming smile. These days, Jackson was a mostly private man, but Hart's Diner was one of the few places he had allowed himself to become known. He appreciated the low-key restaurant where he could get a decent cup of coffee and a bite to eat. It didn't hurt that it was less than 20 minutes from his timber-frame cabin nestled in the Bull Run Mountains.

"Turkey and swiss on wheat, bowl of corn chowder coming up," said Frankie, "You looked sore out there."

"Yeah, not going to run any triathlons any time soon," replied Jackson, "That's for sure."

Frankie disappeared into the kitchen as Jackson pulled out the copy of The Washington Post he had brought with him. He flipped through the pages, looking for more news on the Sudfeld case. He stopped when the words "Missing Girl" caught his eye, but to his surprise it wasn't an article on Sudfeld. A girl had apparently gone missing in Harrisonburg some time Monday night. Jackson flipped the paper over, folding it, and began reading.

"Sad thing about that girl," said Frankie, peering at the newspaper from the kitchen window.

"Looks like it," replied Jackson, "You know anything about it?"

"Just that some girl disappeared the other night," said Frankie, "Same night they found that other girl. Now that was a weird one. You hear about it?"

"I think I saw something on the news."

"Some dude calls 911, says there's this missing girl over in god knows where. Cops show up, find the dude that took her tied up."

"The girl tied him up?"

"No. Apparently some dude did. Didn't stick around for the cops to show up."

"I didn't hear about that. Where'd you hear that?"

"Ah, on Twitter man. Police won't say it, but there was someone else there. That's the one who called the police."

"Weird. Well, you know you can't believe everything on the internet these days."

"Shoot, the cops not wanting to admit some guy did their job for them? I'll believe that every damn day of the week. I wish that dude would come out and say it, too. I'd buy that man a damn beer."

Jackson grinned as he continued to read the article.

The police hadn't released much information other than to confirm she was a missing person with her physical description, but the article noted there had been a large police presence around an appliance repair shop less than half a mile from the missing girl's home.

The lack of information struck Jackson as odd. That usually meant they were sitting on something they didn't want to share, he thought. The other option was there wasn't a lot to go on. If it was the latter, that was bad news in a missing persons case.

Frankie pushed open the double doors to the kitchen and came around with Jackson's soup and sandwich.

"You want something to drink with that," asked Frankie, placing the food in front of Jackson

"Iced tea, unsweetened, please," Jackson said

"Man, you never change," Frankie replied, shaking his head as he smiled.

The article ended with a note that a press conference was scheduled for later today. If it hadn't already happened, Jackson wanted to catch it. He pulled his phone out of his pocket and googled the latest news on the case. Nothing mentioned a time let alone the press conference itself.

Frankie came around with the iced tea and placed it in front of Jackson who nodded as he took a bite of his sandwich.

"You know the girl or something," asked Frankie.

"Nope," replied Jackson.

"Awfully interested for someone that doesn't know her," Frankie said.

"Just curious, I guess."

"Uh huh, I see," Frankie said, "So you think someone took her?"

"Don't know, I'm not a detective."

"But you're curious, like you said."

Jackson *was* curious. In his experience – experience neither Frankie nor almost anyone else knew about – people didn't just disappear. Someone almost always saw something. If not a person then a camera, especially these days. But that didn't seem to be the story here. The more he thought about it, the more it made that gear inside of him tick.

He thought again about that press conference. He checked his watch; it was a little after one in the afternoon. If he hadn't missed it already, it was going to happen in the next few hours.

"Tell you what Frankie," said Jackson, "Can I get something to wrap up this other half of the sandwich."

"What's wrong," asked Frankie, "You got a hot date all of the sudden?"

"No, just forgot I had some stuff to take care of," replied Jackson.

"You didn't even touch your chowder."

Jackson smiled and patted his stomach.

"Probably for the best," he said.

Frankie laughed and shook his head again as he handed Jackson a Styrofoam container. Jackson pulled a 20 dollar bill out of his front pocket, told Frankie to keep the rest, and headed out.

18

C ole watched from a window as the microphones and cameras were being set up for the press conference on a small set of stairs in front of the Harrisonburg Police Department headquarters. An impressive red brick building, its glass pane front overlooked a fore-court at the corner of the city block. Detective Cole had been standing at one of those panes of glass for the better part of ten minutes waiting for Detective Doherty to let her know when the family of Sara Beth Parker arrived.

She watched as municipal employees and members of the news media quickly erected an area that would frame well for all the cameras. A line of vans and satellite trucks created a barrier on the street between the police department and the U.S. courthouse across the way. It was all an impressive effort, she thought. None of this was here two hours ago, and it would all be gone two hours from now.

She turned to throw her cup of coffee away when Detective Doherty opened the doors to the offices of the Major Crimes Unit just enough to poke his head in.

"They're here," he said.

Detective Cole nodded and followed her partner down the stairs. Anne and Scott Parker were waiting in the lobby. Even from across the floor, Cole could see how the trauma and stress of the last 36 hours had affected the two very differently.

Anne had her arms crossed over her belly, almost holding herself, as she leaned on Scott. She kept her head down, her long hair masking her face as she stared at a poster board in her hands.

Scott, to the contrary, looked like he was okay, all things considered. He stood quietly, an arm around his wife, engaged in conversation with those around him. As Detective Doherty approached, Scott saw him and extended an open hand and a smile. Anne barely moved.

"You guys remember Detective Cole," Doherty said.

"Yes. Detective, how are you," said Scott.

"I'm alright," Cole answered, "How are you guys?"

"We're doing the best we can," Scott replied.

The two detectives looked at Anne, waiting for her to say something, but nothing came. Up close now, Detective Cole could better see the poster. It was a collage of photographs of Sara Beth. An 8 x 10 of her most recent school photo was centered around several smaller ones, ranging from all stages of her life. A mother's monument to her lost daughter. The detective side of Cole wasn't sure how old childhood photos were going to help. The personal side of her, though, cringed with sympathy.

"Well," said Detective Cole, breaking the silence, "Why don't we sit down really quick over here to go over what will happen."

The four of them sat down on a set of upholstered chairs situated in the lobby. Detective Doherty asked Scott and Anne if they wanted anything to drink. Scott looked to Anne who shook her head.

"Do you guys have any questions," Cole asked.

"Someone from the police department asked us to prepare a statement," said Scott.

"Yes," replied Cole, "A spokesperson for the department will lay out the general information and give Sara Beth's description, then you will be able to read a statement if you'd like."

Scott looked at his wife.

"We – I – prepared something," said Scott, "I guess I should be the one to read it."

"Anne," said Detective Cole, "If you don't feel up to this, you don't have to go out there. Scott can do this."

"Yeah, honey," seconded Scott, "I can do this for us."

Anne shook her head.

"No, I need to do this," said Anne, "She might be out there. She might be watching. She needs to see I'm there."

Cole grabbed Anne's wrist and squeezed it gently, giving her a sympathetic smile.

"It looks like they're ready for us," Doherty said.

Together, the four of them stood up and headed for the plaza. The spokeswoman as well as Lieutenant Mike Ingle, the Major Crimes Unit Division Commander, and Captain Walter Faulk, the Special Operations Bureau Commander, had been by the front doors waiting for them. Anne and Scott were quickly introduced to the three officers before the group went outside.

A few cameramen began snapping shots as soon as the glass doors opened. A couple of television reporters who had been making live broadcasts quickly wrapped up what they were saying and stepped aside. The police department spokeswoman stepped in front of the group and centered the microphones towards her as she stepped up to the podium.

"Good afternoon," the spokesperson said, and began her briefing, "We're here today to ask for the public's help in locating a missing teenager, Sara Beth Parker."

Detective Cole looked out at the crowd of reporters as the spokeswoman gave the introductory briefing. They all looked so eager to get the information. Those who didn't have microphones set up held out recorders or cell phones. Others scribbled away at notepads.

"Sara Beth is 5'7", and approximately 95 lbs. She is white with dark brown hair, and may be wearing a black and red checkered coat or an off-white sweater."

Cole thought about what Anne Parker had said. That, if Sara Beth was watching, she needed her to know she was there. Was Sara Beth watching? Was she even in a place where she *could* watch? Cole had played out countless scenarios in her mind of what happened to Sara Beth. None of them had the missing teen snuggled up watching TV.

"Now, the parents of Sara Beth, Anne and Scott Parker, have prepared a statement," said the spokeswoman before stepping aside.

Scott began to reach for the paper in his back pocket and took a step forward before Anne abruptly cut in front of him and placed herself at the center of the podium. Detective Doherty and Cole looked at each other with worry. Doherty was ready to step in and usher her aside, but Cole grabbed his wrist, calling him off. This wasn't what they had planned, but she didn't want the evening news to play video of police trying to subdue a grieving mother who spoke out of turn.

"Please," began Anne Parker, "We just want our daughter home. If you have her, just let her go. Or bring her back. No one has to get in trouble. We just want Sara Beth back. Sara Beth, if you're listening, we miss you and we love you, honey. Come home, please."

Detective Doherty ripped his arm free and stepped forward before Anne could say anymore, politely ushering her back.

"We would like to thank the Parkers for their cooperation in this matter," said Detective Doherty, "My name is Detective Sean Doherty. I am one of the detectives working on the case. If you have questions, we will now take a couple."

The journalist fired a barrage of standard queries. Was there a person of interest in the case? Were other agencies getting involved? Was there a reason Sara Beth went out that night? Then, as Detective Cole thought the press conference was coming to its natural conclusion, a pair of questions caught her off guard.

"Detective Doherty," said a reporter, "Why hasn't an AMBER alert been issued for Sara Beth if she is missing?"

"The AMBER alert system is a nationwide emergency system that has a set of criteria that has to be met in order for it to be utilized," said Detective Doherty, "Without a known abductor or vehicle, we could not put out an alert asking the public to look for something we did not know."

The same reporter followed up with the second question.

"Is there reason to believe Sara Beth might not have been abducted? That she left on her own?"

Of course, she was taken, Cole thought. Who was this idiot? But Cole watched in disbelief as her partner gave a different answer.

"Nothing has been ruled out at this time and we are looking into all possibilities," he said.

The spokeswoman stepped forward as Doherty returned to Cole's side.

"Okay, guys, that's it for now," she said, "Thank you."

The group of police personnel turned and formed a circle around Anne and Scott as the group walked back into the department headquarters. Cole stared at Doherty, walking ahead of her, wondering why he had answered the way that he had.

19

The five-minute drive home from the police headquarters felt like an eternity for Scott. Neither he nor Anne said anything. A part of him knew why she did what she did at the press conference, but he wasn't sure how helpful it was. To him, this was a process. They needed to get their daughter back and they needed to go about it the right way. He wasn't sure that's what had happened back in front of the police building.

The silence between him and his wife continued as he pulled in and the two of them walked inside. Scott checked the time and walked to the fridge. It had been stocked with pre-prepared meals friends and neighbors had brought over in an effort to help – a hodge-podge collection of Tupperware and ceramic casserole dishes stacked on top of one another.

"What do you want," asked Scott, "lasagna or enchiladas?"

"I don't care," replied Anne from the living room.

Scott let out a sigh of frustration and pulled out the lasagna nestled in a yellow dish adorned with blue flowers. He remembered when the Donaldsons down the street had brought it over for a cookout last summer and how Anne had marveled at the dish. She had been so incredibly happy that day. He wanted desperately for that Anne to return to him.

The lasagna was covered with press 'n' seal wrap with a post-it note attached.

Preheat oven 375F, Bake 45 mins. If you need more, just ask. Let us know if you need anything. Love, Kat & Kevin

Scott turned the oven on and removed the wrap over the dish. He looked over at Anne in the living room. She was sitting in the dark, staring at the black television screen, the collage of Sara Beth still nestled under her arm. Scott sighed again. He needed a drink.

Going over to their liquor cabinet, he pulled out a bottle of Macallan and a rocks glass and poured himself a couple fingers. Taking a long drag, he stared down into the glass as he let the scotch play on his tongue. He closed his eyes and swallowed, savoring it as the alcohol warmed his throat. His eyes were still closed when he heard a knock on the front door.

"I've got it," said Scott as he left the kitchen.

But Anne paid him no mind. She sprung up from the sofa with the hope it might be good news and ran to the front door. The two of them got there at the same time. Anne reached for the knob first and opened it.

A man gave them a kind smile as Scott and Anne opened the door.

"Hello," said the man, "My name is Jeff Isaacs. I hope this is okay. I heard about what happened on the news and wanted to bring this over."

He raised his hands and presented a cookie tin and a thermos.

"I don't know if you've ever had Black Hills Coffee, but I love it," said Jeff, "And nothing goes better with it than some biscotti."

Anne's shoulders drooped, disappointed that it wasn't news of her daughter. Scott stepped towards Jeff, not wanting to seem ungrateful, and took the tin and thermos.

"Thank you," said Scott, "That's very kind of you. Please, why don't you come in."

Isaacs nodded obligingly as Anne stepped aside. Scott took the man's coat and hung it on their coat tree. Isaacs was average height, but his svelte frame and long face gave the impression that he was taller. Scott was struck by how immaculately manicured he was, as if he'd come here straight from the barber with his salt-and-pepper hair parted just so.

"Why don't I put these biscotti on a plate for all of us and get some mugs for this coffee," said Scott.

"Oh, no, please," replied Jeff, "They are for you to enjoy."

Scott grabbed three mugs anyway from the shelf above where he had just grabbed himself a rocks glass earlier and divvied up the thermos of coffee. As he went to grab a plate for the biscotti, he could hear bits and pieces of polite conversation in the other room. Compliments about the house. What a nice cardigan Isaacs was wearing. The conversation trailed off as Scott walked in with the refreshments.

"That really is far too kind of you," Isaacs said to Scott.

Scott nodded and smiled.

"I heard what happened to Sara Beth, and my heart just breaks for you two," said Jeff.

"Thank you," replied Scott.

"I actually know what it feels like to have a daughter go missing," said Jeff, "Seven years ago my Olivia disappeared one day after school. She was last seen walking home. And then, nothing."

Anne's hands started to shake as she struggled to hold back tears, thinking about her own daughter. Scott placed a hand on hers, trying to comfort her.

"My goodness," he said.

"We did all we could," Isaacs continued, "Or, at least, I tell myself that. For months, after people really stopped looking, I would just drive the roads at night, hoping to find her."

"This was here," Scott asked.

"No. No, I live about halfway between Staunton and Lexington. Steeles Tavern, in Augusta County?"

"Oh, sure. I've heard of it."

"Anyway, like I said, for months I was just beside myself. It seemed so unfair. Olivia was my sunshine. And she was gone."

He reached into his back pocket and pulled out a wallet-sized photo and handed it to Anne and Scott. A teenage girl in a maroon track top and shorts emblazoned with CMHS, she had striking hazel eyes and long brunette hair tied up in a pony tail.

"She's beautiful," said Scott.

"She was," lamented Jeff.

"I'm so sorry," replied Scott, "I didn't mean—"

"No. No, it's okay. You're right, she is pretty. Some days I can picture her still coming down the stairs in the morning. I couldn't believe how much Sara Beth looked like her when I saw a picture of her on the news."

Scott looked at the photo again. Jeff was right. The resemblance was there. Olivia did not have the signature dimples that Anne had always remarked that she loved on Sara Beth, but the similarities were definitely there.

"Yeah," said Scott, "Pretty incredible."

"Anyway," continued Jeff, "Like I said, for months I was beside myself. Then, one day, I decided I was over feeling sorry for myself. I decided, as much as it broke me losing Olivia, I didn't want any other parent to have to endure the pain that I did. And that's when I created PACTV."

"I'm sorry," replied Scott, "PACTV?"

"Yes. Parents of Abducted Children of The Valley. I know. It's a mouthful. We get to calling ourselves just Pact V. Or Pact Five."

"There are more of you?"

"Of us? Sure. You don't think there's just a couple of us in the entire Shenandoah Valley, do you?"

"I guess I never really thought about it."

"Well of course not. It's not like you ever thought what it would be like for your little one to go missing. That's actually why I wanted to speak with you. Pact Five is a dual-purpose support group and activist organization. We have volunteers from Roanoke to Winchester. You'd be surprised what a helpful resource that can be in this kind of situation."

"And you want to help find Sara Beth?"

"Of course, we do. We'd love to help find every missing child if we could. But of course, we can only do so much. And we stick to where we are, here in the valley."

"I don't know what you need, but we don't have much we can give. Especially right now."

"No. No, you misunderstand me, Scott. We just want to help. We don't want your money."

"I – We. We appreciate that. It's just – the police have been really helpful so far. We don't want them to think we're ungrateful."

"And they are great. They are," Jeff said, "But what you have to realize is these police officers and detectives, they aren't superheroes. They're ordinary people. The police work is their job. And they probably want to do well at their job. But at the end of the day, it's still just a job. But this isn't a job for us. These are our lives. We can't punch a clock at 5 o'clock and stop missing the ones we've lost. That's why we – *I'm* – here."

Scott nodded in acknowledgement. What Jeff said resonated with him. In the past few days, they must have met a hundred people insisting they were there to help, but none of them could begin to imagine what he or his wife were feeling. Jeff Isaacs understood. And for the first time since this all began, Scott felt like they might not have to go through this alone.

"Thank you, really," Scott said, "We just—"

"We just want our little girl back," Anne said.

Jeff reached out and placed his hand on hers.

"We all do," said Jeff, "We all do."

20

C ole leaned against the neon electric sign for Kline's Dairy Bar, watching the last rays of twilight fade over the far end of the city. She hadn't said much to her partner since the press conference except to agree to check out the appliance shop and brewery across the street one more time that night. With some time to kill between now and then, though, Doherty had proposed a stop at his (and most of Harrisonburg's) favorite ice cream shop.

Doherty, being a local boy, knew all the best spots. Pizza. Drinks. Even ice cream like with Kline's. It was an encyclopedic-like level of knowledge that had come from spending his whole life there. Joining the department almost right out of high school, he had had little reason to go anywhere else.

Not Angela Cole, though. No, she was a transplant and the first to admit it. Growing up in Washington, D.C., about two hours from Harrisonburg, she'd ended up in the charming valley town by way of a failed engagement. She was a young Metro Transit Police officer in the nation's capital when Cole and her fiancée planned to move to Harrisonburg to be closer to his family. Six months later she was a probationary patrol officer in a relatively strange town when her fiancée called it off. Planning on moving back home to D.C., she was convinced by a supervisor to stay. Even on days as crappy as this, she was glad she had.

She watched as Doherty fumbled with both their treats as he stepped away from the server window. She smiled, amused as he balanced a gargantuan serving of soft serve in a sugar cone, obviously his. Cole couldn't figure out where he put it all on his 5'8", 150-pound frame.

"Here, take yours," he said, a dash of panic to his voice.

"Thank you," Cole replied.

"Next week is blueberry cheesecake," Doherty added.

"Oh, we'll have to come back for that," said Cole.

Doherty nodded as he licked at the edges of the sugary mountain before him. Cole, playing with the straw to her milkshake, replayed the afternoon in her head.

After the press conference, they had had a meeting with their boss, Lieutenant Ingle, to brief him on where they were with the case. The image wasn't a pretty one. Anyone who had purported to know anything had been just as Emily Green described: full of shit. The other two girls who had been out with Emily, Katia and Jessica, corroborated what she'd told them, and a quick call to Kevin Polk's dad confirmed that Kevin, in fact, had never gone out that night.

To make matters worse, no one near the appliance repair shop that night remembered seeing anything suspicious. They'd begun checking with nearby registered sex offenders, but so far everyone they'd questioned had witnesses or evidence placing them some-where else at the time of the abduction. It was as if Sara Beth Parker had dissolved more than she had disappeared. As if she had simply ceased to exist. There, at home, in the evening. Gone in the morning.

Still, Cole's gut told her something awful had happened to Sara Beth, and it bothered her that any other theory was even being entertained.

"So, what was up with the press conference today," Cole asked.

Doherty stared at her, pretending to be confused by the question, but they both knew what she was talking about.

"What do you mean," Doherty asked.

"When that reporter asked if we had reason to believe she hadn't been abducted," Cole replied.

"I answered the question honestly," Doherty said

"Come on. Even if you believe she might not have been taken, you know if we don't drive it into the media that this girl is in immediate danger, they'll bury the story and we need people tuned in. We need eyes out there."

"Assuming she wants to be found."

Cole turned toward her partner. There was a sharp tone to her voice now.

"Assuming what now," she asked.

Doherty wiped his mouth with a napkin, and paused, choosing his words carefully.

"Look, we've been dancing around this the whole time now, so if I've got to be the one to say it, I'll say it," Doherty said, "We don't know that this is an abduction."

"The hell we don't," replied Cole angrily, "You actually think this is a runaway?"

"She got in a fight with her mother," Doherty replied, "She was pissed off. Pissed off kids rebel. It's what they do. And if she snuck out, where was she going? The only reason she had to go out were her friends and she said nothing to them."

"And what about her phone," asked Cole, "I suppose she took it with her just to toss it in some random parking lot."

"Maybe she realized it could be tracked. Maybe the FaceTime call reminded her she still had it. The only thing the phone says is she was out, and we know she left her house by her own choice."

"This is why the Lieutenant called us in today, wasn't it? They want to kill this case."

"Angela, we're Major Crimes. There are nine of us for a city of over 50,000. Every one of us is working multiple cases as it is. You know that. They just want to make sure we aren't using resources on a girl that doesn't want to be found. If she's a runaway, we can kick it to patrol and let them look for her."

The two detectives fell into another tense silence. Cole was glad they were standing across the parking lot from everyone now and hadn't drawn attention to themselves. She looked on at the crowd. Easily half of them were children. Not children that ran away or were taken. And the parents were happy parents, not ones wrought with grief like Anne Parker. These were happy families. The way families should look.

She knew Doherty and anyone else who thought Sara Beth Parker had run away was wrong. Deep down, somewhere inside she couldn't describe, she just knew. But she also knew, in a way, it didn't much matter. The way things were going, they needed to catch a break if they were going to bring Sara Beth home.

21

J ackson watched as the group of people plummeted 300 feet, screaming as they disappeared out of view behind the Play 'n' Win arcade directly in front of him. Slowly, they reappeared as the ride aptly named Drop Zone lifted them back up into the sky to do it all over again. *People pay good money for torture,* Jackson thought.

"Thinking of doing that next," asked a voice behind him.

Nathalie was giving him her signature sly smile, teasing him over his dislike of thrill rides. *You must be the only ex Spec Ops guy on the planet who hates roller coasters,* she would say, playfully challenging his bravado.

"That? That over there is called cruel and unusual punishment," Jackson answered, "And it's supposed to be banned by the constitution."

Nathalie threw her head back laughing as she reached for him and pulled him to her. Jackson looked down at her. The sun was catching her auburn hair, giving the impression she was crowned in a halo of light. To Jackson, she might as well be.

"Daddy, daddy, look," said a voice at Jackson's feet, "Basketball!"

Evan, their son, watched as a couple of teenagers took shots at hoops placed unnecessarily far away.

"I don't know, bud," Jackson replied, "You think you've got the arm for that?"

"*Uh huh,*" *Evan answered.*

Jackson and Nathalie laughed, leaning into one another again. They were out enjoying a day at King's Dominion, a theme park near their home in Richmond, Virginia. The idyllic day had drawn out the masses – Jackson had never seen it so crowded – but they didn't mind. Nothing was getting in the way of their little family.

"*Ok, well, Mr. Cruel and Unusual Punishment,*" *Nathalie said,* "*Mama wants to ride the Ferris Wheel.*"

"*Good luck with that,*" *Jackson replied.*

"*Come on,*" *Nathalie begged,* "*It's not even a roller coaster, it's a kiddie ride.*"

"*Well if it's a kiddie ride, then I guess I'm too old.*"

"*Ugh, you suck.*"

"*Language, Nat!*"

Jackson nodded down towards Evan. Nathalie smiled and mouthed the word 'sorry'.

"*Well, what about you, kiddo,*" *Nathalie asked Evan,* "*You want to go on the ride with mama?*"

"*Uh uh, no way,*" *replied Evan, as he bear-hugged Jackson's leg.*

"*You guys are killing me with your brotherhood of solidarity,*" *Nathalie said.*

Jackson smiled at her, picking Evan up into his arms.

"*Here, give me the camera, we'll get a shot of you,*" *Jackson said.*

Nathalie handed him their digital camera and ran on to the Ferris Wheel just as the operator was closing the gate. Nathalie took off and up in a slow-moving arc. Jackson booted up the camera and looked for her through the viewfinder.

"*Daddy,*" *said Evan fidgeting in his arms,* "*I want to do basketball.*"

"*In a minute, bud,*" *Jackson replied,* "*We're watching mama right now.*"

Jackson put Evan down as he continued to squirm, shaking the camera. Jackson's view of Nathalie was blocked as her basket crossed over the top of the wheel. He kept looking in the viewfinder, following her basket around. As she came down the far side, Nathalie reappeared, making a goofy smile as she waved at the camera. Jackson clicked a few shots.

"*Perfect, bud,*" *Jackson said,* "*Look, I got mama.*"

Jackson went to show Evan at his feet, but he wasn't there.

"Evan," Jackson called out.

He looked around him. Evan wasn't there. He looked over towards the basketball hoops. Not there, either.

"Evan," Jackson called out again.

He looked the other way. Nothing.

"You guys didn't see a little boy just now did you," Jackson asked one of the employees, "Green shirt? Blue shorts?"

The ride operator shook his head. Nathalie came jogging over, worried by the look of panic on Jackson's face.

"What's wrong," Nathalie asked.

"Evan," replied Jackson, "He – I don't know. He was right by me and then he wasn't."

"Evan," Nathalie shouted, looking around.

People around them now began to look on as their perfect afternoon devolved into the worst day of their lives. Jackson stood up on the counter for the basketball game, trying to look over the crowd. An employee implored him to get down but he ignored him.

"Evan," Jackson screamed, "EVAN."

JACKSON'S BODY bucked in his bed as his mind shot awake from the nightmare he was having. It was the same nightmare he had had more nights than he could count, the nightmare he had not only dreamt but lived. His eyes struggled to focus in the relative darkness as he rolled over to check his watch. The muffled pitter patter of steady rain tapped on the roof overhead. He pressed a button that backlit the face of his Casio Mudmaster. It was just after six in the morning. It was also 65° in the room, the air pressure was 1001 mbar, the watch was currently sitting at 911 ft. above sea level, and, sitting in his hand, the watch was presently facing north. Of course, sitting there half naked in bed, very little of that information mattered.

He rolled over to the edge of the bed and slowly sat upright, his joints aching as they expanded and contracted. He placed his arms over his head, stretching them upwards, and finally stood up. He had beaten the sun up, leaving Jackson to navigate his cabin even in complete darkness.

Still in his boxer briefs, he went to the sink and grabbed the pour-over coffee maker, a fresh filter and the small canister of coffee out of the pantry, and went to work. A corporal during his first tour in Afghanistan turned him onto the brewing method and Jackson hadn't made coffee any other way since.

After shaking enough ground coffee into the filter, he grabbed the tea kettle, filled it with water, and threw it on the stove. He thought about him now, Corporal Ramirez, as he brushed his hand over the scar just above the left side of his pelvis where a jagged piece of metal had torn into him as he pulled a bleeding Ramirez out of the line of fire.

Jackson's body was a tapestry of scars, evidence of a life lived harder than most. The bottle cap-shaped scar on his knee from being shot outside Fallujah. The jagged V in his left deltoid after an IED tore a nearby Humvee to shreds in southern Kandahar. And the two long slash marks on his right forearm from a bar outside Mobile, Alabama. No purple heart was awarded for that one.

He stood there in his boxer briefs and listened to the kettle begin to hiss on the stove. Jackson lived on his own in almost every way possible. His cabin was heated by a wood-burning stove situated just off his back porch, his water was well-based, and he got television and internet off of satellite dishes mounted on a post next to his driveway. In fact, the only thing actually hardwired to his cabin was the electricity, and that was only because his forested land didn't make a great spot to throw up solar panels.

The hiss of the steaming water turned over to a whistle as it began to boil. Jackson pulled the kettle off the stove and began slowly pouring the hot water over the coffee grounds. The smell of brewing coffee – rich notes of chocolate and hazelnut – began to fill the open-concept timber frame cabin. An early twilight backlit the clouds nestled overhead, painting the earth around Jackson's cabin in a bluish-grey light.

As the coffee finished brewing, he took off the grounds and filter, poured himself a cup, and walked over to his laptop. The logo on the cover lit up as he opened it and he heard the machine whir to life.

He searched for any more news on Sara Beth Parker. The results were disappointing as the police hadn't given much more information yesterday during the press conference. Aside from Sara Beth herself, there was very little for the public to look for. No suspect, no person of interest, no vehicle. Jackson frowned, both frustrated and curious.

One article, however, had mentioned that police recovered what they believed to be her phone and wondered what the police had found on it. He wouldn't be able to see her texts or calls, obviously, but there was other information that could be found.

Jackson opened up a new browser window and searched for Sara Beth Parker on every social media platform he could think of. Facebook, Twitter, Instagram, Tumblr. The list went on. As he expected, she had profiles on a number of them and virtually none were made private. He scrolled through her Instagram posts. Many of the more recent ones now had comments of people praying for her and begging for her to come home. Her last post had been on Monday, the day she disappeared. It was a photo taken from somewhere near her torso aimed at her legs and feet laying on a bed. He read the quoted caption below.

"This house is a prison! On planet bullshit! In the galaxy of this sucks camel dick!"

A quick google search told him it was a line from the movie Step Brothers. Perhaps she had been grounded or something, Jackson thought. According to news articles, it was believed she left her house willingly. It wouldn't be the first time a grounded teenager snuck out in rebellion. Just this time it seems like it had gone disastrously wrong.

He shut his laptop and stared at the wall in the dark, thinking to himself. The lack of information handed out to the public continued to bother him. He knew first-hand in cases like these the public is your best resource. It was possible Sara Beth Parker ran away, that she left her house and just kept on going, but his gut told him otherwise. Teenagers were not experts in trade craft. More times than not, a runaway left some sort of trail. Being spotted on camera at a bus station, or using a family member's credit card or telling a friend where they were. There was no trail for Sara Beth. Or, if there was, the police weren't letting on. That told Jackson something was wrong.

He reached for his phone on the desk, dialed a number, and waited for the person on the other end to pick up.

"It's me," Jackson said, "What do you know about the Parker case out of Harrisonburg?"

22

The loud clanging of metal awoke Sara Beth from a restless sleep, the first that hadn't been chemically induced since she had been taken. How long ago had that been, anyway, she wondered. Confined to a covered dog crate, she had lost any semblance of time. Surely, it must have been at least a day. Had it been more? Many more?

Now she could hear wheels rolling on the ground. Wheels that sounded like the ones she heard beneath her when she'd first awoken in the cage. Did they bring someone else in? Was there now a fourth person here with them? She waited to hear the metal hinges of the door swing again – a sign that whoever was here had left – and then worked up the nerve to say something.

"Hello?"

There was no answer.

"Maybe no one's there," said Meghan.

"Maybe whoever's there is knocked out just like we were," said Keera.

In the time that had past, Sara Beth had risked a few small conversations with the other captives. Meghan Anderson, the girl Sara Beth first knew as the one crying, was from Glen Allen, Virginia, a suburb of Richmond. Keera Caldwell, the one who had first scolded Sara Beth to shut up, was from Lewisburg, West Virginia.

Both recounted what they remembered about their abductions. Meghan had talked the night away with a guy in a bar and he was walking her to her car when she felt a sharp prick in her arm. The last thing she remembered was the man helping get her inside a car that wasn't hers. Keera had been driving home from work when she heard two loud pops and pulled over. Some nails had punctured two of her tires. Soon, a car pulled over. She was explaining to the driver she was fine when a cloth with a heavy chemical smell was shoved in her face. She told Meghan and Sara Beth she'd tried desperately to fight free from the man before everything went dark.

Initially, Sara Beth had been relieved when she first learned she wasn't alone. After hearing their stories, though, she was more terrified than she had been before.

"Hello," Sara Beth said again.

Again, her greeting went unanswered.

"I'm telling you. They're out cold," said Keera.

The muffled taps of footsteps could be heard in the direction of the squeaky door.

"Quick, shut up," said Keera.

The door swung about and bounced into something with force as a clumsy melody of thumps and bangs came ambling through. A moment later, the cloth over one end of the crate Sara Beth was in lifted up just enough that she could see a pair of jeans and boots from the knee down. Her heart lunged into her throat as fear coursed through her body.

A beefy pair of hands fed the nozzle of a hose through one of the openings in the crate and turned it on. Cold water shot out and splashed into Sara Beth's face.

"Stop," Sara Beth screamed, "What are you doing?"

"Drink from it or don't," said a man's voice, "I don't really give a fuck."

Sara Beth lay shaken, holding the hose in one hand. She didn't trust this man, clearly one of her captors, but she couldn't help herself. Her mind became overcome with how thirsty she really was. She looked at the flowing water for a moment before throwing all caution aside and burying her face into it. She slurped and chugged, taking only short, sporadic pauses to breathe. The water had that same metallic taste she remembered from days of playing in the sprinklers in her backyard. In a strange way, the off taste was comforting.

She was still trying to drink as much as she could when the stream cut off. The man ripped the hose out of the crate.

"Alright, that's enough," growled the voice.

She listened as he walked around the room, more metal clanging and the whooping of the hose being whipped around. Both Meghan and Keera made incoherent noises in successive order. Sara Beth assumed he was doing the same thing to them. A small act to ensure they didn't die, she thought. Yet, anyway.

Sara Beth found it curious that the man didn't seem to approach the far side of the room, where they heard the latest whatever it was being rolled to. Maybe there wasn't someone there at all. Maybe it was something else entirely.

The man did something with the hose just in front of the crate she was in before tossing it aside. Sara Beth heard it land to her left as the boots thumped towards the door and the hinges whined as the door swung open and shut. Then, silence again.

"Are you guys okay," asked Sara Beth quietly.

"Aside from having just been water boarded, yeah," whispered Keera back.

"I'm freezing now," said Meghan.

Sara Beth was about to say something more when she heard the muffled thumping of boots approaching the door again. This time, though, there was more than one pair. The men were talking to each other. Trying to listen, she couldn't make anything out until the doors burst open with a bang.

"Take that one. You, that one," said a voice.

It was the voice of the man that had been in just earlier with the hose. He had a gravelly voice – probably aided by years of tobacco use – with a southern drawl.

She heard Meghan scream followed by a barrage of profanity from Keera. Sara Beth was about to say something when the crate she was in shook. It rolled forward. Someone was moving her. Then she understood. They were all being moved.

"Stop it," yelled Sara Beth almost instinctively, "What do you want? Just let us go!"

She didn't expect an answer, but an answer of sorts came from across the room. Except whoever was speaking wasn't talking to her.

"No, dumbass," said the same gravelly voice, "The other one. Not that one."

The crate she was in coasted to a stop. She listened as wheels on both sides of her squealed as they rolled away. Both Meghan and Keera were screaming things at the invisible people in the room. Panic came over Sara Beth. As scared as she had been just a moment ago, she was twice as terrified now. Meghan and Keera were being moved and it seemed she was staying put. Staying put with God knows what they just put in here moments ago.

The door banged open again and Sara Beth covered her mouth to keep from screaming. She was about to be alone. This is it, she thought, it cannot get any worse than this. But just as she thought that, one of the other men spoke.

"What's with that one?"

The gravelly voice with the southern drawl answered.

"Don't worry about her. She won't be here long."

PART II

JACKSON NO MIDDLE NAME CLAY

23

Cole sat at her desk reviewing dashcam footage from a Harrisonburg Police Officer's patrol car. Swirling the wooden stirrer in her coffee, she watched as the patrol car drove down High Street approaching the downtown area and stopped at the traffic light at Wolfe Street. The patrol car was half a block from the parking lot where Sara Beth Parker disappeared. The timestamp on the video read 10:11 PM. Ten minutes later, it might've been right there as the abduction itself took place. Cole scowled in frustration.

It had been two weeks since she first got the call about a missing teen named Sara Beth. Officially, the case was still very much open and the police were actively pursuing all leads. Unofficially, those leads had dried up and Cole had been given the nudge to move on several times by her superiors.

But Sara Beth remained missing, leaving Detective Cole grasping at straws, reaching into the haystack, hoping to feel the pin prick of a needle. She continued to work the case whenever she could. If that meant being to work an hour earlier and leaving an hour later, so be it. She'd continue to look for Sara Beth on her own time if she had to. Moving on wasn't possible for her. Not on this one, anyway. Lying in bed at night, she'd see Anne Parker again, her head down as she clung to that poster with Sara Beth's pictures. Then Cole would think about Sara Beth, walking that night when someone had done something awful to her. She imagined her screaming, realizing what was happening. Cole couldn't help but think, wherever Sara Beth was, she was holding out hope that someone would come for her. Those around Cole seemed to have relinquished that duty. She would not.

Cole leaned forward in her chair, squinting at each person crossing the street, hoping she might catch a glimpse of Sara Beth Parker minutes before she was taken. A total of four people crossed High Street during the red light. None of them Sara Beth Parker. When the light turned green, the squad car drove forward, passing Wolfe Street.

"Come on, come on, circle back," Cole said under her breath.

But the officer never did. A block later, a call went out for a person loitering in front of a First Virginia Bank after hours. The officer radioed back he was responding, took a right on Market Street, and headed away from the downtown area.

Detective Cole sat back in her chair and sighed. She closed her eyes, trying to think of another angle, when her cell phone rang. Looking at the screen, it wasn't a number she recognized but had a Northern Virginia prefix.

"Harrisonburg Police, Detective Cole," she said with her official and professional greeting.

"Angela, hi. It's Jen Bailey, over at State," greeted the voice on the other end.

"Oh, yes. Hi, how are you, Jen," answered Detective Cole.

Jen Bailey was a detective with the Virginia State Police. She worked out of the Division VII Field Office, in the suburbs of Washington, D.C. commonly referred to as Northern Virginia. Cole and Bailey had met a couple years ago when Bailey had been working a murder of a state congressman and the suspect was believed to have fled to the Harrisonburg area. Mutual professional admiration had turned into a friendship as they stayed in touch, though Bailey admittedly made more of an effort than Cole did.

"I'm good, how are you," asked Bailey.

"Also good," replied Cole, "It's been a minute."

"It certainly has," agreed Bailey, "Actually, that's why I wanted to talk to you. I actually have meetings at the Area 16 Field Office in Harrisonburg tomorrow and the bosses are giving me an overnight. I was hoping maybe you'd be free for dinner or something."

"Yeah, of course. I can meet up for dinner."

"Great. Um, I should be wrapped up with everything by seven or so. Does that work for you?"

"Sure, that works great. I know a great pizza place down here."

"Pizza it is. Just text me the info and I'll see you tomorrow evening."

"Sure thing. Looking forward to it."

"Me too. Bye now."

Detective Cole ended the call. She began to punch in the address for Bella Luna Wood-Fired Pizza into a text message when Detective Doherty came around the side of her cubicle.

"Hey, who was that," he asked.

"A colleague of mine over at State. She works NoVa but is going to be down here tomorrow night and wanted to meet up," replied Cole.

"Ah, cool," said Doherty, holding a moment to change subjects, "So, listen. I was talking to my buddy in patrol and he says he's pretty sure his old partner was assigned a sector near the appliance repair shop the night Sara Beth Parker went missing."

"Will Halifax."

Doherty made a face, surprised.

"Yeah," he said, "How did you know?"

Cole nodded towards her computer screen.

"Just got done going over his dashcam footage," she said, "Nothing there."

"Really," asked Doherty.

"Nope," replied Cole, "He was on High Street headed in the right direction just after 10 p.m., but drives past Wolfe Street and then responds to a call up Market away from downtown. Doesn't clear the call until after our time window for the abduction."

"Well, damn."

"Yeah, damn."

Detective Doherty watched his partner staring at the still image on the screen. He wasn't sure what she was hoping to find. Missing almost three weeks with no suspects, there weren't many times this sort of thing ended well for the family involved. For the life of him, Doherty couldn't understand why his partner was so eager to get to such a moment.

"You got anything you need me to run down for you," Doherty asked.

"I'm good, thanks," Cole replied, "Appreciate it, though."

"Well, if you think of anything, you let me know," Doherty said.

Cole nodded as Doherty walked away. She righted herself in her chair, took a deep breath, and went back to work on the haystack.

24

The next evening, Cole and Bailey met up after work just as they had planned. It being a mild evening, the barn-style front doors to the pizzeria were open, giving the center corridor of the restaurant the feel of an open-air café. Here, the two detectives sat, enjoying dinner as a warm breeze welcomed itself in.

For the better part of an hour, the two women worked their way through a Margherita pizza that they had split as well as a bottle of Virginia Cabernet Franc. The conversation had meandered from work – both were doing fine – to family – both didn't get to see their folks as much as they ought to – to dating – neither had much time for it. They laughed as they admitted almost simultaneously this was their first social get-together in at least a month.

"Is there any more wine," asked Bailey.

"Just a little bit," answered Cole, "You want to get another bottle? My treat."

"No, I shouldn't," replied Bailey, "Even if you're paying."

Cole smiled, chuckling.

"Fair enough," she said, "How'd you like the pizza?"

"It was fantastic," Bailey answered, "Is this your go-to for impressing out-of-towners?"

"I took my folks here when they came down shortly after I moved," Cole said, "My father ate one of those pies by himself. That's when I figured it was pretty good."

The two women laughed. Detective Cole sat back, taking a sip of wine. Bailey followed suit, steeling herself for what she knew would be an uncomfortable conversation.

"So, you caught that Parker case, right," asked Bailey, "The abduction?"

Detective Cole nearly choked on her wine, surprised Detective Bailey knew about it.

"Yeah, I did," answered Cole, "How did you know?"

"Oh, I caught you on the T.V. a couple weeks back," replied Bailey, "Looked like a presser."

"Oh, right. Yeah," said Cole.

"How's that all going?"

Detective Cole sighed as she looked down at the table.

"It's not, actually," answered Cole.

"Oh? How so," asked Bailey.

Cole took another sip of wine as she sat up and leaned in towards Bailey.

"Between you and me," Cole said, "We're running out of ways to find this girl. If you can even say 'we.' My bosses are telling me to move on to more active stuff, and my partner half believes the girl is a runaway."

"But you don't," asked Bailey.

"My gut tells me this girl is in real trouble," Cole replied.

Detective Bailey nodded as she swirled the wine in her glass, watching it. Cole could now see she was struggling to say something.

"Have you ever thought about bringing in outside help," asked Bailey.

"Like who? You can't possibly be telling me State wants to get involved with a local missing persons," Cole asked back.

"No," replied Bailey," Not us."

"What then? The feds? I can't prove this girl went anywhere in particular let alone that she's crossed state lines."

"I was thinking more outside."

"I'm not sure I know what you mean then."

Bailey put her glass of wine to her lips and drank the last bit she'd been aerating during the latter half of their conversation.

"Maybe we should get the check before we continue this," said Bailey.

Cole nodded skeptically.

She paid the check – the two fought pleasantly, but Cole insisted – and they headed out to Cole's car on the top deck of the two-story parking garage across the street. Parked in the angle spot at the edge of the deck, the two women got to Cole's Jeep Liberty, walked past it, and leaned up against the brick wall. Bailey pulled out a cigarette as the two of them watched people pass by below. She offered one to Cole who shook her head.

"So, this outside help," said Cole.

Detective Bailey nodded, taking a drag from the lit cigarette.

"There's a guy," said Bailey, "A – I don't know how you would describe him."

"A private eye," asked Cole.

"No," answered Bailey, "Not officially, anyway."

"Ok, so then what are we talking about here? A bounty hunter?"

"No, nothing like that."

"Then what?"

"He's a—"

Bailey swirled her hand with the cigarette, conjuring up the word she was looking for.

"A finder, of sorts," Bailey finally managed to say.

"A finder? That's pretty cryptic," replied Cole.

"I don't know what you'd call him, but he can help," said Bailey, "This guy. He takes these cases when it seems like the vic is gone for good and he finds them. He goes into whatever hell took them and brings them back."

Detective Cole stared at her, a bit stunned by the picture she had just painted. In the years she had known Jen Bailey, she'd known her to be a down-to-earth, pragmatic woman. Not the kind to peddle the services of some vigilante.

Bailey took another long drag from her cigarette, killing it. She dropped it onto the concrete parking deck and rubbed it out with her shoe.

"Did you hear about the Ashley Sudfeld case," asked Bailey.

"Yeah, I think," replied Cole, "Girl disappeared out of Loudoun County, right? She was found a couple weeks back."

"That was him," Bailey said.

Cole snorted in disbelief.

"C'mon, Jen," she said, "And how do you know this?"

Bailey pulled out another cigarette from her purse, lit it, and blew the smoke into the twilight sky. She turned and made direct eye contact with Cole, as if a confession was about to come forth.

"I handle him," said Bailey.

"You what," asked Cole.

"I'm his contact within the police or whatever," replied Bailey, "At least, I think I'm his only police contact. I don't know, the guy's not exactly an open book."

"Jesus, Jen. You're leaking information to a civilian?"

"I guess if you want to be technical about it."

"Why on earth would you be so reckless?"

"Look, I'm telling you. This guy takes abduction cases that are cold and he finds them. He finds them and more times than not he finds the people that did it with enough evidence to convict. I don't know what your guys' cold case clearance rate is but ours is shit like everyone else's. And I'm telling you, this guy can help."

Cole turned around and looked at the parking deck behind them. A couple walked to their car across the way. Cole tried to process what Bailey had just told her.

"What makes you sure he even wants to do this," she asked.

"He called me," replied Bailey.

Cole smirked, incredulous, and shook her head.

"That's what this whole thing was about, wasn't it," said Cole, "You found out you knew the detective on the case and you figured you'd make an approach."

"Yes," replied Bailey, "I mean it was nice to see you again, too. But, yeah, I'm not going to lie to you. I told him I'd contact you."

"You worked me over like a witness," said Cole, "Like a suspect."

"Ange, it's not like that. You see how unorthodox it sounds. It's not exactly something you shoot out in an email."

"C'mon, get in. I'll drive you back to your hotel."

"Angela."

"I'll think about it, okay?"

"Okay."

Cole hit the unlock button and Bailey opened the passenger door. Cole fired up the Jeep.

"You knew you were about to pull all that, and you let me pay," said Cole.

"I tried to pay," Bailey retorted.

"Yeah," replied Cole, "Well next time try harder."

25

A half hour after dropping Bailey off at her hotel, Detective Angela Cole found herself circling the neighborhood in which the Parker family lived. She knew she wasn't ready to go home yet. She needed to drive. She needed to think.

The homes in the area were pretty, she thought. Two-story split levels that were erected as the area boomed along with its titular generation. Half a century later they still looked out over manicured lawns and trimmed hedges, shrines to the suburban lifestyle. It hardly seemed like the setting for the kind of nightmare the Parkers were enduring.

Cole took a right on Wolfe Street and slowed as the Parkers' house came into view. She pulled over and killed the engine.

The Parkers house now stood out from those around it. A large canary yellow ribbon was tied into a bow around the oak tree that shaded the front yard. A sign like a realtor's sign had been staked into the yard near the sidewalk with Sara Beth's sweet, dimpled face smiling at people that passed by. A sign attached below in red bold letters read HAVE YOU SEEN ME?

Cole could see the electric blue glow of a television in the living room. A part of her wanted to walk over and see if Sara Beth's parents were up and check in on them, but she resisted. Every time they had met or talked on the phone in the last week and a half, she hadn't had answers for them. Tonight wouldn't be any different.

Her mind circled back to Detective Bailey and the man. This finder of sorts, as she had put it. She couldn't shake the voice in her head telling her it was a bad idea. Detectives had lost their badges for less. Much less. She'd seen it herself a number of times.

But thinking about the Parkers now, the weight of any possible consequences waned. This was not just about Sara Beth, but Anne and Scott as well. She had promised them she would do everything she possibly could to bring their daughter home.

"Everything possible," she whispered to herself.

How could she say no to Bailey's offer and tell herself she'd kept her promise? She'd spent every spare minute of the past few weeks hoping to catch a break. Perhaps this was it. What if this man could help her find Sara Beth? Did she not owe it to the Parkers to try?

"God dammit," Cole said under her breath.

She pulled out her phone and called Detective Bailey.

"Hey, Angela," greeted Bailey after a couple rings, "I'm glad you called. Listen—"

"Your man," said Cole, "Set it up."

"He'll want to meet in the usual spot, up by me," Bailey replied.

"Text me the address. I'll be there."

Detective Cole ended the call. She still didn't know if she was doing the right thing. But she was doing everything possible.

26

Three days later, Cole got up at 4 a.m. on that Sunday morning to make the drive to the address Detective Bailey had given her. It was the harbor on the Old Town Alexandria waterfront. Driving the 135 miles of open interstate highway, she could count on one hand the number of cars she passed. The nation's most traffic-clogged metropolitan area was a wide-open thoroughfare this early on a weekend.

Old Town along the Potomac River waterfront was a popular spot for both locals and tourists. Rows of colonial-style buildings lined the narrow streets as the top of the Masonic Temple loomed overhead to the west. What hadn't been renovated into chic townhouses that started at well over a million became boutique shops and trendy eateries.

Later when the city awoke, the area would slowly fill with weekend warriors looking for brunch or perhaps a bar seat to catch the Nationals game. But here, now, an hour before the sun would rise, Old Town was deserted.

Cole sat in her car; the lone vehicle parked on the block directly adjacent to the marina. She'd arrived early, found a nearby 7 Eleven to grab a cup of coffee and now waited for Bailey or this man to show up next.

A part of her still wondered what she was doing. She liked to think she'd gotten to where she had thanks in large part to knowing where the line was and how not to cross it. As she sat in her car now, prepared to hand over sensitive case information to a man she'd never met, she wasn't sure she knew where she or the line stood.

A pair of headlights turned onto the street and pulled up curbside behind Cole's Jeep. She peered in her rearview mirror, waiting to see if she could make out who it was. Instinctively, her right hand reached for the Glock 22 holstered on her hip. But as the driver side door of the vehicle opened, she recognized the slender, leggy frame and long hair of Detective Bailey. Cole climbed out of her car and turned back to greet her.

"Good morning," said Bailey as she slipped her phone into her navy blazer.

"Morning," Cole said back as she, "So where's your boy?"

"He's probably here already," Bailey replied, "Come on. Let's walk."

She led Cole to the end of the building they had parked in front of, turning its corner onto an alley blocked off to vehicles. In the distance, lampposts lit up the outline of a row of boats that bobbed lazily in the currents of the Potomac.

"So, what's this guy's deal," asked Cole as they walked.

"What do you mean," replied Bailey.

"How many cases have you brought him in on," asked Cole.

"It's not like that. He contacts me asking for info on a case and I help him out."

"Okay so how many times has that happened?"

"I don't know. Maybe a dozen or so."

"And I'm assuming you checked him out before helping him."

"Of course, I'm not stupid."

"Well? What's his deal?"

"There's not much to know. At least not on paper. Born Jackson no middle name Clay. Nothing noteworthy on his record. Not much known work history. Joined the Army shortly after high school. Became a Ranger."

"You got that on a background check?"

"A search of his name turned up some military base addresses. I called a buddy who asked around. Served from '98 to '05. Married a Nathalie Grace in '04. He started the application process to become a private investigator in '05 as well but never finished."

"Nothing after 2005?"

"There wasn't much official information, so I searched around and found a Richmond Times-Dispatch article. A boy was abducted from King's Dominion on Labor Day weekend that year. The article named the parents as Jackson and Nathalie Clay."

"Christ."

"Yeah. I couldn't find much more on the story besides that article. Records show he divorced Nathalie in '07. I just sort of assumed the worst. His story seems to drop off after that. Pays taxes on a gray Ram pickup and a property about 40 minutes west of here. Other than that, there's not much."

"So, what's he been doing the last thirteen years?"

Bailey looked at Cole as she replied.

"I can tell you what he's been doing recently."

The alleyway flowed into a plaza directly in front of the marina. Bailey had led the two of them to a bench in the middle of the plaza as they talked. Cole looked around. A flag overhead flapped in the wind, harmonizing with the small waves that splashed against the docks. Aside from the breeze, the two of them were completely alone.

"So," said Cole, "Where is he?"

Detective Bailey punched something into her phone and looked over to a building further towards the river. It was a restaurant, its blue-gray façade blending in with the darkened sky behind it. A set of brick stairs met a white walkway that crossed over to the front doors. She was looking there when a figure emerged from the shadows underneath the walkway.

"There," said Bailey.

As he walked by an overhead light, Cole got her first look at

Jackson no middle name Clay. He was a taller man, athletically built with defined muscles. A ball cap hid most of his face, but she could see a trimmed brown beard that wrapped around the bottom of his face.

"Detective Bailey," greeted the man as he walked up to them.

"Jackson, good to see you," said Bailey, returning the pleasantry, "This is Detective Cole. Harrisonburg Police Major Crimes. She's been on the Parker girl's case from the beginning."

The man pulled his right hand out of his pocket and extended it open to Detective Cole.

"Jackson Clay," said Jackson.

"Angela Cole," replied Cole.

She pulled out the manila envelope she had tucked under her left arm and handed it to Jackson.

"Here you go," said Cole.

"These are the relevant case files," asked Jackson.

"Everything I've got," replied Cole.

Jackson unclasped the envelope, slid the files out, and began to thumb through them.

"You think she was taken from this appliance repair shop parking lot," asked Jackson.

"Yes, her phone was found there in the parking lot," answered Cole.

"Could've been tossed by those who took her," asked Jackson.

"It could've, but it was found behind the building. Why pull in just to dump the phone?"

Jackson nodded as he continued to flip through the papers. He opened up the section with files on the persons relevant to the case. Scott and Anne Parker. Obviously the parents. Emily Green, Jessica Compton, Katia Thomas, and Kevin Polk. Must be friends or classmates given their birthdates. Then, as he got to the last page, he saw the file of a man who seemed not to fit. The man had a pleasant face with a sanguine smile.

"Who is this Jeff Isaacs," asked Jackson.

"He's the head of a local victim's organization," answered Cole, "He's been working mostly with the family. Checking in on them, taking them to group events. He seems to be familiar with abduction cases in the area. Could be a resource for you to get your lay of the land."

"Alright," said Jackson as he put the file away, "Anything else?"

"Nope," replied Bailey, "That's about it. Detective Cole's card is attached to the front of those files. It has her number if you need to reach her. As for me, you know how to get a hold of me."

"Great," Jackson said.

Jackson stepped around them and began walking in the opposite direction he had come from. The abruptness of it caught Cole off guard. All this, all she was risking, and that was it. That was the big meeting. A panic fell over her. She felt like she had a hundred more questions to ask. Her brain raced to form words as she watched him walk away.

"Mr. Clay," Cole managed to say.

Jackson stopped and turned back to look at her. The light from a nearby lamppost caught his face and Cole could see Jackson Clay the man for the first time. She looked into his eyes, brown eyes that were staring back at her. They had an intensity that made her feel uncomfortable.

"I didn't want to do this at first," Cole said to him, "A part of me still doesn't. But I trust Jen. And I want to find this girl."

Jackson continued to stare at her as if she had more to say. Detective Cole's mouth was slightly agape, unsure if she had more to say herself, but nothing more came

"I want to find her, too," said Jackson, "That's why I'm here."

Cole paused a moment longer, still searching for what she wanted to say.

"I'm risking a lot reaching out to you."

Jackson stood there, working out what she was trying to say.

"Did you have something to do with her disappearance," he asked.

"No, of course not," replied Cole.

Jackson nodded.

"Then you have nothing to worry about," he said.

He turned and continued walking towards the far side of the plaza.

Cole watched him until he disappeared around the corner of a building. Whatever this was, whatever she'd just started, there was no undoing it now.

27

J ackson slung his axe downward onto the wedge of wood. He hit it dead center, splitting the half log into two quarter pieces that fell opposite ways off his chopping stump, each landing in a pile of similarly cut pieces.

After he had walked back to his truck at the Old Town marina, Jackson had sat in the driver seat skimming over the files again. The entire drive home he thought about Sara Beth Parker and her abduction. He sympathized with Detective Cole, now seeing there wasn't much in the ways of leads. She had done a good job; better than most detectives he had come across. There just simply wasn't a lot there. If he was going to find Sara Beth, it would have to start with finding something the authorities hadn't.

He placed another half log on the stump, stepped back, and swung the axe downwards. This time he hit left of center, creating two perfectly fine albeit different-sized wedges. Jackson sighed, annoyed.

When he'd gotten back to his house, he went over the entire file again, reading over what he'd already read twice, looking for an angle he hadn't yet seen. He agreed with Cole's theory that she had been taken from the appliance repair shop parking lot, but it was the fact that apparently no one saw anything that he found interesting. Sara

Beth's phone was found behind the shop. You couldn't draw a straight line from it to the street. If Sara Beth had been taken at that spot, it was a perfect blind spot to anyone passing by. Whoever took her had to have been lying in wait, he thought. They had known exactly what they were doing.

Jackson walked over and grabbed his canvas firewood carrier. He brought it to the pile of split logs, filled up the sack, and began carrying his fresh-cut firewood over to the pile he'd created by his wood-burning furnace.

Ultimately, the question was whether Sara Beth Parker was targeted or a victim picked at random. Her parents didn't seem to be exceptionally wealthy and no one that had been interviewed could think of a reason someone would want to harm her. Plus, there was the fact that Sara Beth had apparently never done this before. Her parents had said this was the first time she'd ever left home at night without telling someone first. Someone looking to take Sara Beth couldn't plan around something she hadn't done before. Sara Beth must've been a victim of opportunity, Jackson concluded. A girl in the wrong place at the wrong time. Like prey struck down by a predator.

A predator, Jackson thought. An idea came to him.

He tossed the canvas sack aside and hurried up the front stairs of his house. He sat down at his laptop and booted it up. He brought up an online sex offender registry and searched around the Parkers' address.

The greater Harrisonburg area had nearly 150 registered offenders. Jackson wasn't particularly surprised, but he'd hoped it would be less.

Zooming in on the Parkers' street, there were two registered offenders on the Parkers' block alone. He clicked on the one that was towards the direction she had walked. It was a 64-year-old male registered for possession of child pornography. Disturbing, thought Jackson, but not someone likely to subdue and abduct a teenage girl. He zoomed out and clicked on the other pin dot on the Parkers' block. Russell Daniels was a 34-year-old white male convicted of third-degree sexual battery in '09.

Jackson grabbed his phone, looking for Detective Cole's business card, and punched in her number.

"Detective Cole, Harrisonburg Major Crimes," she answered.

"Cole, it's Jackson Clay," he said, "Did you look at a Russell Daniels? 34-year-old registered sex offender on the Parkers' street."

"We looked at all nearby registered sex offenders," Cole replied, "It should be in the information I gave you. Hold on."

Jackson was patient as he heard papers rustle on the other end of the line.

"His grandmother says he came home at eight that night and never left," Cole said.

"Are we taking what his grandmother said as gospel," asked Clay.

"We talked to him, Clay," Cole replied, "To be honest, he didn't seem like the type. He and his grandmother even consented to a search of their house. It was clean. I mean, *clean clean.*"

"Alright, I guess. Thanks."

"You want to check him out, have at it. But I'm telling you, we looked."

Jackson ended the call. He rapped his knuckles on the desk as he thought. He had no reason not to believe Detective Cole, but there was something about Daniels. Something bothered Clay as he studied the man's photo and the pin dot over his address. He lived no more than 8 or 9 houses from the Parkers. It was too much of a coincidence. Maybe Daniels was, in fact, innocent, but Jackson decided he wanted to see for himself.

He grabbed his things and headed out.

28

Two hours later Jackson was parked in a shopping center on the southeast side of Harrisonburg. On the way down, he'd called Detective Bailey and asked her to see if Russell Daniels had a vehicle registered in his name. He did, a 1999 electric blue Honda Civic. When Jackson drove by Daniels' home address and didn't see the car, he looked up the work address listed on the sex offender registration.

The address, belonging to a cell phone retailer, brought him to this shopping center across town. Mostly vacant, it hadn't been hard to spot the blue Civic parked in the corner of the lot. Jackson parked several rows away with a good line of sight on both the store and the car.

He didn't have Daniels' work schedule, but the store's hours online said it would be closing soon. Daniels would more than likely be leaving not long after that.

Watching the store, Jackson pulled out his phone and googled Russell Daniels to see what came up. As a registered sex offender, Daniels wasn't allowed to have a Facebook account and one didn't show up. In fact, there weren't any social media accounts at all. Jackson hit the news tab on Google, hoping to find an article or report on Daniels' conviction. No luck. He was curious about the assault. Daniels' booking information put him at 5'6" and 120 lbs. and his photo made 120 seem generous. He didn't strike Jackson as the type to overpower someone, though, Jackson wasn't a 16-year-old teenage girl crossing a dark parking lot.

He sat there for another 40 minutes thinking about this and until, not long after 6 p.m., a man switched the OPEN sign in the front window. Even from half way across the parking lot, Jackson could easily see it was Russell Daniels, his pimply face sitting under a disheveled bowl of black hair. A moment later, Daniels stepped out the front door and locked it behind him. Jackson waited until he was in his car before firing the ignition on his truck.

Keeping a couple cars between them, Jackson followed Daniels. When Daniels stopped at a Taco Bell, Jackson drove past and waited in the parking lot of a Walgreens until he saw the Civic get back on the road. He stayed on Daniels all the way back to his house.

When Daniels pulled into his driveway, Jackson drove past and circled back at the end of the block with his headlights off. He watched Daniels awkwardly balance the greasy paper bag of food and soda cup in one hand, struggling to unlock the door. There was a good chance Daniels was in for the night, but Jackson would sit on the house a couple hours just to make sure.

He slumped back down in his seat, getting comfortable again, and took in the street. Down the street he could see the yard sign with balloons out front, a makeshift memorial to Sara Beth Parker in her own front yard. Russell Daniels lived within shouting distance of her. The Parkers might even know him. Jackson wondered if they knew he'd been convicted as a violent sex offender.

He grabbed his phone and began searching for information on Daniels' conviction again when the man himself reappeared from behind the house. Side stepping a van parked in the carport, he crossed the front yard and headed down the street, not towards Jackson but in the direction of the Parkers' home. Jackson felt the hairs on his neck prick up. He waited for Daniels to put some distance between the two of them and then began following him again.

Nightfall had crept over Harrisonburg and Jackson was losing sight of Daniels as he stepped in and out of the street lights overhead. Jackson pulled his FLIR monocle out of his pack and aimed it down the street. Against the cool front yards and vacant cars, Daniels was a fiery human-shaped blob on a dark blue sea. He came to and walked past the Parkers house without so much as look at it. When he turned the corner and took a left on Wolfe Street, though, he disappeared completely. Jackson dropped the monocle and sped up.

When he got to Wolfe Street, he stopped and looked, spotting Daniels continuing to walk. Jackson turned and followed a couple hundred feet further before pulling over. He parked, got out, and continued tracking Daniels on foot.

Cross traffic at High Street forced Jackson to draw an even distance with Daniels. They were standing in front of the crosswalks now on opposite sides of the street. The bill of his hat pulled low, Jackson watched Daniels out of the corner of his eye. If the man had spotted him, he wasn't letting on.

When the lights switched, Jackson walked as slow as he could without it looking out of place. Soon enough, Daniels had regained some distance on him. Jackson continued to follow from across the street.

Maybe he was going to the microbrewery, Jackson thought, looking for a nightcap to wash down that greasy fast food. But fifty feet short of the brewery, Russell Daniels turned suddenly and crossed the street. Jackson stepped sideways, ducking quickly behind a small tree and trash can, worried Daniels would see him. But Daniels didn't look his way. He got to the curb and didn't slow down. The hairs on Jackson's neck pricked up again. Russell Daniels stepped into the parking lot of Eddie's Appliance Repair, heading for the back of the shop. Jackson reached for the P320 concealed in the small of his back and disengaged the safety.

Now walking as fast as he could without running, Jackson rapidly closed the distance between Daniels and him. When Daniels disappeared around the corner of the building, Jackson broke out into a full-on run. Posting up against the side of the building, he drew his gun.

He turned the corner quietly. Daniels was doing something with the back door to the repair shop. Distracted and with his back turned, Jackson made his move on Daniels. In a split second, he was on him, pinning his face against the door. Jackson pressed the cold steel of the gun against the back of Daniels' neck to make it abundantly clear he was armed.

"Put your hands out at your side," said Jackson.

"Please, I didn't do anything," begged Daniels.

"Hands. Out. Now," ordered Jackson again.

Daniels splayed his hands against the door, palms open.

"Please, officer. I didn't do anything," Daniels said.

"I'm not the police," Jackson replied.

"Well I don't have any money, man," said Daniels.

"Stop. What are you doing back here?"

"What do you mean, man? I work here."

"Bullshit, you work at a cell phone store across town."

Daniels' expression was a mixture of panic and confusion.

"How did you—wha—I work here, too," Daniels said.

"It's not listed on your sex offender registration." Clay replied.

Panic overtook the confusion.

"Please," Daniels said, "I don't know what you—"

"Sara Beth Parker," Jackson said.

"Who's that," Daniels asked.

"She's the girl that disappeared right here three weeks ago. And now here you are, a registered sex offender, after hours, lying about working here."

"I—I do, though."

"If you worked here, this address would be registered. Or you'd be in jail. Or do I need to call someone to clear that up?"

Daniels breathing became erratic. He looked like he was on the verge sobbing.

"I do work here. I swear to Christ, man," said Daniels, "Just not, like, for real. I come in after hours, clean up the store and stuff. The guy here, he leaves me some cash."

Jackson was starting to piece it together.

"The owner's paying you under the table," Jackson said.

"I asked him for a job," Daniels managed to say in between short, panty breaths, "He said he would never hire a pedophile like me. That's what he called me. To my face. Then later he called me and said if I took out the trash and stuff after hours, he'd give me some cash. It's almost nothing, but it's tax free and I need it. So I do it."

Jackson engaged the safety on the P320 and dropped it to his side.

"So that's why you're here now," said Jackson, "To clean the place up?"

"Yeah, Eddie told me to come after the store's closed," Daniels answered, "I guess so people don't ask about me."

Daniels motioned with the keys in his hands towards the door, as if to ask Jackson if it was okay if he open the door. Jackson nodded.

"Your sexual assault conviction. What was that," Jackson asked.

"Eleven years ago, I was at a bar," Daniels began, "I started talking with this girl, I thought we were hitting it off. I had been drinking a bit and at one point I grabbed her inappropriately. She got scared. I said I was sorry, but she ran out. Next day, I wake up to cops at my door telling me she was 17. She had gotten in with a Fake ID. I'd assumed her being in the bar meant she was at least 21. When she told her parents what happened, they called the cops. I've been paying for it ever since."

Daniels got the door open. A few trash cans sat at the back door with a message taped to them. Daniels pulled it off and read it. He shook his head.

"Asshole," Daniels muttered under his breath as he shoved the note in his pocket.

A small part of Jackson felt bad for Daniels. He'd made a mistake at an age where people make mistakes. That didn't excuse what he did, but there were far worse people who hadn't paid the way Daniels had. Now Jackson knew what Cole meant about not seeming like the type.

"That's why I didn't say anything to the police, in case you're wondering," Daniels said.

"What," asked Jackson.

"When I saw the cops were looking around here for her," Daniels replied, "I asked Eddie if I should say something but he told me to shut up and keep my head down. So, I did."

"I don't understand. Why would you have talked to the police?"

Daniels looked at him with a puzzled expression. He seemed surprised Jackson didn't know what he was talking about.

"Because," he said, "I was here that night."

29

Scott pushed the tower of chairs he had just stacked over to the corner of the room, looking back to double check he hadn't missed any.

"Is that all of them," asked Jeff Isaacs.

"I think so," replied Scott.

On Sunday evenings, Isaacs held a weekly support group for parents or loved ones of missing children. It was an open-ended invitation, not just limited to the organization he had founded, but Scott had a sneaking suspicion that Isaacs saw it as a way to subtly indoctrinate those who attended.

"Thanks for helping clean up," said Jeff.

Jeff placed his hand on Scott's shoulder and gave him his signature wholesome grin.

"Not a problem," replied Scott.

Isaacs was always quick to offer a hug or an arm around the shoulder. Scott personally could do without it, but he felt like Jeff meant well, so he went with it.

After all, Jeff had done more to help them than most. The news and the media had moved on. Neighbors still wished them well, but they had their own lives. Even their interaction with the authorities had grown sparse. But Isaacs had remained. And with his wife at home mostly walling herself off from everyone, Scott, at least, was grateful.

"You want me to hit the lights," asked Scott.

"No need," replied Jeff, "The pastor said to go ahead and leave them on. Come on, I'll walk you out."

The meetings were held in a banquet room attached to Dogwood Mennonite Church on the edge of the Eastern Mennonite University campus in Harrisonburg. Scott had never met anyone involved with the church personally, but Isaacs had told him how supportive they were, going as far as to even pass along funds the church had raised to help PACTV spread the word when a child had recently disappeared.

The two men were leaving the church, making small talk as they went, when a car parked curbside caught their attention. Detective Angela Cole was leaning against her unmarked police car. She gave them her professional smile as they waved at her.

"Detective, what a lovely surprise," said Jeff.

"It's good to see you again, too, Mr. Isaacs," replied Cole, "You too, Scott."

"Good evening, Detective," said Scott, "What brings you out here? You working tonight?"

"I'm always working, I'm just not always paid for it," replied Cole, smiling again.

Isaacs laughed much harder than the silly joke warranted. Making an effort to be friendly as always, Scott thought.

"No, actually I wanted to talk to you," said Cole, looking at Scott.

"Oh, okay, sure," replied Scott.

The conversation paused, neither wanting to make outright eye contact with Isaacs.

"Ah, right," said Isaacs after allowing the awkward moment to linger a little too long, "Well, I'll be off then. Have to hurry home to feed the cats, anyway."

"Have a good night, Jeff," said Scott, "And thanks again."

"Don't mention it," replied Isaacs, walking towards his car, "See you later."

Scott leaned up against the police car next to Detective Cole. The two of them watched as Isaacs climbed into his car and pulled out of the parking lot.

"Didn't figure him for a pet guy," said Cole.

"Yeah," replied Scott, "Can't blame the guy. Must get lonely after all these years."

Cole nodded at the church.

"How are these things going," she asked.

"They're alright," replied Scott, "They fill the time."

"Anne not going anymore," asked Cole.

"No, it's not really her thing. I got her to go to the first one. Now, she just says I'm wasting my time. I don't know. Maybe I am, but I can't just sit at home and wallow."

"How's she doing?"

"Your guess is as good as mine. It's like she goes deeper and deeper into her own little world every day. I just figure when she's ready to talk, we'll talk."

Detective Cole nodded without saying anything more. She'd never been married and certainly never had a child of her own disappear. She couldn't even begin to imagine the despair Anne Parker must be feeling.

"So, what's up," said Scott.

"Right," answered Cole, "Well, I just wanted to tell you we haven't given up on Sara Beth. I haven't given up."

"No, I know," replied Scott, "And listen, if I haven't expressed how grateful I am, how grateful we are, that's on me."

"No, no. You're fine. I just meant I wanted you to know that there are people still looking for her. People more than just myself."

"I know, we really do appreciate it."

Cole smiled at him and nodded again. She wanted to just come out and level with him. That for whatever reason, something inside her told her this case was different. She wanted to tell him how far outside the box she was on this one. How far she was going for them. And maybe also herself.

"Well, I better get going," Scott said, "Anne's probably waiting for me."

"Sure," replied Cole, "Tell her I said hi. And you know, what I said."

"I will," said Scott, "Have a good evening."

"You too," Cole said.

She watched from her car as Scott climbed in his and pulled out just as Isaacs had, waving as he went by. She waved back. Tonight, would mark 20 days since the man's daughter, Sara Beth, disappeared. A fellow detective told her she should be bracing herself to find a body. That anything short of that would be a miracle.

Cole closed her eyes, praying for that miracle.

30

Jackson stared at Daniels as he processed the man's admission.

"What did you say," asked Jackson.

"I said I was here. The night that girl was taken," Daniels answered.

"And you saw something," Jackson said.

"Yeah. A van."

"They didn't see you?"

"I guess not, I didn't open the door. I looked out through the viewing slot."

Jackson looked at the back door. It had a speakeasy style peephole covered by a metal grate. Jackson's face had been no more than a few feet from it outside and he hadn't noticed it. Someone in a car wouldn't have seen it, either.

"Okay, a van," said Jackson, "Anything else?"

"No," replied Daniels, "I heard the engine outside. I thought it might be Eddie coming to check on me or something, so I looked out the slot. When I saw it wasn't him, I thought it might be someone trying to jack the place. So, I hid."

"You hid where," asked Jackson.

"Inside the store. Behind the register up front. I figured if they came in, I could break a window or something. I don't know. I wasn't thinking, I was scared."

"But no one came in."

"No."

"So, what happened?"

"Nothing. Maybe like half an hour went by. I wanted to leave out the front, but what if it was nothing, you know? Somebody calls the cops on me or tells Eddie I was out front? I wasn't about to risk my job or jail, man."

"Okay, 30 minutes went by. And what?"

"I don't know, I heard a couple doors slam shut and they left. They didn't rob the place or do anything to the back of it. I figured what I didn't know couldn't get me in trouble, you know? Then, the next day I heard a girl was missing from right around here."

"You saw them leave."

"I saw them pull out of the lot. I was looking from the front of the store."

"Which way did they go?"

"Up that way."

Daniels pointed towards High Street, the direction he and Jackson had come from. This was something. Even without anything else, now there was a van and a direction of travel. It was a start.

"The van, what did it look like," asked Jackson.

"I don't know, I didn't see it that well," Daniels answered.

"Well was it white, black, blue, purple, what," Jackson asked.

"It was dark. Black. Or maybe like dark blue. I don't know."

"And it turned that way towards High Street?"

"Yeah."

"Did you see anything else?"

"Not really, no."

"Did the van have anything that might identify it? Writing on the side? Noticeable damage?"

"Um, Its lights, kind of. It had those crazy bright headlights. The ones that are like bluish white."

"Xenon?"

"I guess. They aren't like regular headlights."

"I got it. Anything else?"

"No. That was it."

Jackson stepped back, giving Daniels room. He saw the keys Daniels dropped on the ground, picked them up and handed them over.

"Is that it," asked Daniels.

"For now," Jackson replied, "I know where to find you if I need more."

Daniels rolled his eyes before turning for the back door. Jackson watched as he fumbled with the keys, searching for the right one.

"Russell," said Jackson, "Let's keep this little meeting between us."

"Fuck man, you think I want to tell someone," asked Daniels.

Jackson gave him a nod and began walking back the way he'd come. When he was out of the lot and back on the sidewalk, he pulled out his phone, punched in Cole's number, and put it to his ear.

"It's Clay," he said, "I'm going to need traffic camera video from the night Sara Beth was taken."

31

S ara Beth listened as the van slowed. They'd put her back in there, the same one that'd taken her from everything she knew and everyone she loved at some point long ago. She wasn't sure how long, though. The construct of time was a house of cards to her that had since collapsed.

After being separated from Meghan and Keera, she'd been moved to a windowless room where she was moved out of the dog crate. Inside what was little more than a glorified broom closet, her disorientation continued. Her mind would switch back and forth, telling her the room was her sanctuary then turning around and screaming at her that she needed to get out. Without warning, her heart rate would spike and she'd struggle to catch her breath. The men outside who'd bang on her door and tell her to knock it off made it only worse.

She'd started to refuse to eat. When the door opened and two men grabbed her, she'd assumed they were about to force feed her to keep her alive. Instead, though, they'd shoved her back in the van and left the place with the crates and tiny rooms behind.

Now the two men held her down in the back of the van as it turned. She couldn't see their faces, just the leather vests and jeans they were wearing. Neither of them said anything except the occasional 'stop it' when she tried to move around.

They had their collective weight on top of her when the van's brakes wailed in pain. They came to a stop. Sara Beth's heart rate ramped up again and her breathing became shallow just as it had in the windowless room.

"She's fucking freaking out again," said one of the men as the van doors opened.

Standing in the opening was a third man, large and hairy with a handlebar mustache and receding hairline. Darkness surrounded him. Wherever they were, it was night out.

"She'll get over it," he said.

Sara Beth recognized his gravelly voice and southern accent. The man squatted down to Sara Beth's level as she laid on the floor of the van. He waited until she calmed down enough and met his eyes with hers.

"Now, we're gonna move ya," he said, "You gonna cooperate and do this easy?"

Sara Beth didn't think before she bucked at him and tried to scream. As she did, a hand shoved a cloth that smelled as bad as it tasted in her mouth, muffling her. A second hand came around with duct tape, securing the cloth in place. The men then held her wrists behind her back and her legs together as they applied generous amounts of duct tape to both.

As soon as they were finished, they lifted her out of the van and began carrying her. Sara Beth tried to look around but it was dark. Dark even by night standards. She could smell the grass below her and the fertilizer in the dirt. She'd always loved that smell. She took a deep breath in, trying to savor it as she assumed she was headed for another dog crate or windowless room.

The two men carried her up a short flight of stairs, and then, as she felt herself being carried through some sort of entryway, the brisk night was replaced with a kind of homey warmth. In dim light, she could see polished hardwood just inches from her face.

"Where do you want her," asked the large man.

"Downstairs," said a new voice.

This new voice was different. It was calm, almost genteel. Something about it made Sara Beth shiver.

"You heard him," said the large man.

The two men turned Sara Beth and continued carrying her deeper into wherever they were. A door opened, and the warmth and hardwood disappeared. It was dark again, but now there was no smell of fresh grass. The air was stagnant and had a chemical smell. It smelled of paint, Sara Beth thought.

She could feel herself being carried down a set of stairs before being unceremoniously dropped onto something firm but with some give. A mattress. They'd dropped her onto a mattress.

"Cuffs are right here," said one of the men.

"Hook is in the wall up there," said the other.

They cut the tape off her wrists and replaced it with handcuffs that they attached to something above her head.

"Leave the tape on her feet," yelled the gravelly-voiced man from atop the stairs, "And he wants her blindfolded."

"Where the fuck am I supposed to find a blindfold," said one of the other men.

"There's a tie over there," said the second, "Use that."

Not that she could see much of anything before, but now Sara Beth was really shrouded in darkness as she felt the tie slipped over her eyes and tightened.

"Are we done," asked the gravelly voice.

"Done," replied one of the men.

Sara Beth felt the two men step away from her and listened as they clomped up the stairs. A door slammed shut, and then, silence. Once again, she was alone. She used whatever the handcuffs were attached to to pull herself into a sitting position, then moved her head close enough to her hands that she could undo the tie. She looked around. Tiny windows lined the far wall near the ceiling. Enough ambient light came through them that she could just barely get a feel for the room she was in.

It wasn't a broom closet by any means. The room was cavernous and mostly empty save for a few things Sara Beth couldn't make out along the wall. It must be a basement, she thought. Or some sort of storage. A place people stored things until they needed them. Now, she was one of those things.

She closed her eyes and tried to not think about what she was needed for.

32

J ackson sat in his truck, parked in the parking lot of a Dunkin on
the far south end of Harrisonburg. He was waiting to meet Detective Cole who had told him she could get him the relevant
footage after running by her office first.

Figuring he'd be in the area a few days, Jackson had gotten a room
at an Econo Lodge in town after his talk with Russell Daniels. He
wanted to go back and talk to Eddie Vaccaro, the owner of the appliance repair shop but figured he wouldn't know any more than Daniels
did, and grilling Vaccaro might lead him to retaliate on Daniels in
some fashion. It would almost certainly do more harm than good.

Instead, Jackson focused on what Daniels told him. On his way to
the Dunkin parking lot, he ran into a gas station and bought a street
map of the area. He found the appliance repair shop and traced the
route Daniels said the van had taken with a pen. Heading in that direction, the fastest ways out of town were either US 33 to the northwest or
State Route 42 to the southwest. US 33 wound its way through the
mountains, eventually crossing into West Virginia. State Route 42
ended at US 250 just outside Staunton. Neither was a more likely
option than the other.

He was studying the map when he spotted Cole's unmarked police car pull in. Jackson flashed his headlights to make sure she saw. She pulled into a spot next to his truck, got out, and climbed into his passenger seat.

"There are six cars in the parking lot," said Cole, "You think I can't make your giant Ram pickup?"

"Just trying to help," Jackson replied.

Detective Cole reached into the breast pocket of her blazer and pulled out a thumb drive, handing it over to Jackson.

"That has the dashcams of patrol units that were in the vicinity of the appliance repair shop during that 10 o'clock hour," Cole said, "There's a couple stationary traffic cameras, too, but they're few and far between and mostly further downtown. I've been over it all a dozen times. I'm not sure what you're expecting to find."

Jackson wasn't sure he wanted to tell her about Daniels and the van. At least not yet.

"I might have something," he said, "I need to check it out for myself."

Cole shot him a look.

"What," she asked, "A person? A vehicle? From the lot?"

"I'll check it and if it's something, I'll let you know," Jackson answered.

"It was enough to put in a call for this footage," Cole said, "Come on, level with me."

Jackson didn't respond. He couldn't blame Cole for being eager, but Jackson wasn't interested in being micromanaged. Working alone meant moving faster. And in his experience, being fast was everything.

"You brought me in on this. Now you have to trust me."

"Trust you when you don't trust me," Cole snapped.

Again, Jackson didn't say anything back right away. She had a point. He was going to need her help. She'd put together a thumb drive of the footage largely without questioning him. It wouldn't help him if she decided to become less cooperative.

"I asked you about Russell Daniels," Jackson said.

"Yeah," replied Cole, "I told you we cleared him."

"He didn't take her, but he was there that night when it happened," Jackson said.

"What? How do you know this?"

"I followed him. Last night he left his house and went to the shop."

"And what happened?"

"Questioned him. He gets paid under the table to do chores. He was in there when it went down. Says he saw a dark colored van pull in to the back. A half hour later it took off."

Detective Cole sat back in the passenger seat, stunned. They had looked into Daniels. He was clean. Even his Parole Officer had attested to how much Daniels had been doing to get his life back together. They'd crossed him off and moved on. Now Cole couldn't help but wonder if they'd been careless.

"Did he get a make and model," asked Cole, "What about a plate? At least partial?"

"Dark work van, that's all he saw," answered Jackson.

Detective Cole went quiet as she thought to herself again.

"Let me work it," Jackson said, "If I need something more, I'll let you know."

"Alright," said Cole, "You let me know if you get a hit, though. Okay?"

Jackson nodded as she opened the door and climbed out. Before she'd even unlocked her car, he put his pickup in gear and pulled out. The coming night would mark three weeks exactly since Sara Beth had been taken. Jackson had ground to make up.

And fast was everything.

33

By the time Cole got back to her office, most of the other detectives, including her supervisors, were already there, prompting some curious stares. Normally, she was one of the first ones in the building in the morning and one of the last ones to leave in the evening. They hadn't come early enough to see her there when she'd grabbed the thumb drive and ducked back out. Cole didn't notice them, though. She was thinking about what Clay had told her.

A part of her was incredulous. How many nights had she staked out the repair shop? Russell Daniels never came wandering by while she was watching. She kept playing things over again in her mind, asking herself if she'd been too quick to clear Daniels. If they'd known about the van a couple weeks ago, maybe Sara Beth would be home now. The thought made Cole sick.

She chose not to think about that but instead think about the van. It was something, but without a license plate number, it was still a long-shot to find. There had to be dozens of dark-colored work vans in the Harrisonburg area. Even a make or model would help narrow it down. She was thinking about going to Russell Daniels and pressing him for details when there was a knock on her cubicle.

"Hey, where were you this morning," asked Detective Doherty.

"I was here at 8, like always," answered Cole, "I just ran back out real quick to grab coffee with an old friend."

"Well, look at you. Two social outings in as many weeks," Doherty said, chuckling, "Aren't you the socialite?"

He looked over at her screen and saw the dashcam footage from a patrol car up. Even without context, he knew what it was.

"What is that, your tenth time going over that stuff," said Doherty, nodding at the monitor.

"Something like that," Cole replied.

"Any kidnapper magically appear that we missed the first nine times," Doherty asked rhetorically.

"Have to try something, you never know what you'll see with fresh eyes."

"So, try something else. You're going to run yourself ragged looking at the same stuff over and over. It's not good for your eyes, staring at a screen like that."

"I'll be okay, thanks."

Doherty shrugged his shoulders and disappeared. She swiveled around in her chair, turning back to the computer, and pressed play on the footage. She was watching Officer Brad Cook drive around Court Square and the old courthouse, but Cole wasn't really paying attention. Doherty's estimate was on the conservative side of how many times she'd watched the same footage. She knew it so well she could give you the play-by-play. The Prius going much too slow in front of Capital Ale House. The woman struggling to walk two dogs at the intersection with Market Street. It all played out the same way it had a dozen times before.

Cole sighed, frustrated, and checked her watch. It was an hour until noon. She'd committed to only drinking caffeine in the morning, an idea supplied by Doherty after she mentioned how little sleep she got. If she went now, she could work her way through one more red eye coffee. She stood up, stretched, and walked down the hall, leaving the dashcam footage playing on her screen.

The video showed Officer Cook as he came around the west side of Court Square and turned right, heading northwest on Market Street. He drove three blocks before a red light at High Street stopped him.

The camera remained still as cross traffic drove along High Street, a medley of cars crossing left to right and right to left in random order. As the traffic lightened, the light turned yellow, then red, but not before one last car zoomed through the screen.

A black van with bright bluish white headlights sped to make the yellow light.

It was headed in the direction of the repair shop.

34

Jackson felt his heart thump hard as if it were bouncing off his chest wall as he watched his laptop screen. He stopped the video, skipped back, and played it again. And again. Sure enough, a black van with xenon headlights headed in the direction where Sara Beth had been taken. He looked at the timestamp on the dashcam footage. It read 10:06 p.m. Russell Daniels had said that the van had been behind the appliance shop for about half an hour. 30 minutes from 10:06 was right near the window when the police believed Sara Beth Parker disappeared.

He had the van.

As the van passed through the middle of the frame again, Jackson paused the video. It was a standard black panel van, a more recent model. It had the boxy shape and straight lines of a domestic make, he thought, most likely a Ford or Chevy.

Jackson pulled out the street map he'd bought and looked it over again. The patrol car was facing northwest on Market Street, which was also US Route 33. If the van had followed High Street into town, it had come from State Route 42, one of the two ways Jackson suspected the van also left town.

That highway paralleled Interstate 81 heading south out of

Harrisonburg. Jackson wondered if perhaps whoever took Sara Beth had been traveling that way to avoid major highways and the state troopers that patrolled them. It would've been the smart play, he thought, and whoever had taken her did not strike Jackson as particularly dumb. But that in and of itself wasn't much of a lead. Interstate 81 ran all the way into Tennessee.

He looked at the route the interstate took, tracing its way as the major thoroughfare through the Shenandoah Valley. The valley south of Harrisonburg was as good a place as any to start checking for registered vehicles.

Jackson pulled out his phone and called Detective Bailey.

"It's me," he said after a couple rings, "I need a favor."

"What is it," asked Bailey.

"I need a vehicle registration search," asked Jackson,

"Jesus, you have a vehicle already?"

"I have a description. Can you help?"

"Sure. What've you got?"

"I'm looking for a black panel van registered somewhere in the Shenandoah Valley between Harrisonburg and Roanoke, the closer to I-81 or Virginia 42 the better. Ford or Chevy make. Say 2003 or newer."

"Okay, it'll take a few hours."

"Alright. Thanks."

Jackson killed the call. He stared at his laptop screen thinking what to do next. The image of the black van crossing Market Street along High Street was still paused, a dark cloud of a figure filling the driver's seat. Who was that driving the van? Where had he come from? At the very least they had come from High Street south of Market Street.

Jackson grabbed his keys.

He wanted to see for himself.

35

The drive out of Harrisonburg for Jackson was a slow devolution of urban development. Where the intersection near the appliance repair shop was comprised of four city blocks built to the sidewalk, ten minutes further down the road Jackson found himself driving through rolling hills interspersed with the occasional warehouse or fast food chain. Another ten minutes and two towns later, it was nothing but rural farmland. Pure white clouds formed on the horizon, floating effortlessly across the valley towards the Shenandoah mountains. It was pristine country. For a moment, Jackson nearly forgot the dark factors that had brought him out here.

He imagined the van driving the very same road on a Monday night three weeks ago. Any other cars would have been few and far between. Driving through sleepy farm communities, whoever had taken Sara Beth would've been all but invisible.

As Jackson passed an elementary school, the rolling farmland gave way to a small cluster of rural houses, on the far side of which was what looked to be a gas station. Seeing it, he realized it was the first gas station he'd seen for miles, and wondered if he might get lucky a second time.

Pulling in, the sign out front read Duke's Country Store with the word Groceries painted in big blue letters. The metal canopy over the two gas pumps was faded green and didn't have a brand of gasoline like most stations did. The white brick building had two garage bays attached to it. Out front of one sat a rusted brown early 90's F-150. An older man with a weather-beaten face and unkempt white hair was working under the hood of it. He turned and looked at Jackson, grabbing a cloth from his tattered coveralls. Jackson gave the man a polite nod as he headed inside, but only got a wary stare in return.

Opening the store's front door, Jackson was welcomed by the scent of warm spices. The store itself couldn't have been more than twenty feet each way, crowded with tiny aisles of food that wouldn't expire for a decade. On the far side sat a checkout counter next to a display case glowing red with hot food under heating lamps. A paper sign handwritten with a Sharpie sat on top and read 'The Best Damn Fried Chicken This Side Of The Valley!' Jackson was reading the sign when a woman's voice spoke.

"We ain't lying," she said, "God's honest truth it is."

The woman appeared from behind the register, greeting him with a big smile as warm as the display case. Short and stout, the woman was wearing a red flowery apron that matched her ruby dyed hair.

"Did you make this yourself," asked Jackson, mustering what charm he could.

"I sure did," answered the woman.

"I'll take a couple of pieces for the road," Jackson said.

"Three pieces and you get a can of coke with it."

"A bottle of water and you have yourself a deal."

The woman gave another warm smile. Jackson had to hand it to her: she was a salesman as well as a cook.

"Do you mind if I ask you something," Jackson said as she began putting the food in a box, "Do you remember that night a while back that girl disappeared up in Harrisonburg?"

"I saw that on the news," replied the woman, "That was a few weeks ago, wasn't it?"

"Three weeks tonight, actually," Jackson answered.

The woman poked her head up over the display case.

"You a cop or something," asked the woman, curious.

"No, nothing like that," Jackson replied "But so do you remember seeing anything?"

"Not at night, nope," the woman said, "We close at 7 p.m. sharp every day. Have what's left in here for dinner, and go on up and watch TV. Monday's American Idol."

"Ah, I see. So, no one would've been down here after 7?"

"Uh uh."

The woman boxed up his food, slid it into a bag to go, and brought it over to the register.

"You said you want a water, hon," asked the woman.

"Yes, please," Jackson answered.

He pulled out his wallet as the woman went over to the fridge and grabbed a bottle of Deer Park.

"You need anything else, hon," asked the woman.

"No, thank you," Jackson answered.

"Then that'll be $5.34," said the woman.

Jackson handed her six dollars and she went into the drawer for his change.

"I never caught your name, honey," the woman said.

"Jackson," he said with a smile.

"It was nice to meet you Jackson, my name's Gertrude. Friend's call me Gerry," said the woman.

"Nice to meet you, too, ma'am," replied Jackson.

Gerry flashed her big, warm smile again. He smiled, waving good-bye, and began walking out before a thought popped in his head.

"Let me ask you one more thing, Gerry," Jackson said.

Gerry's smile grew bigger as Jackson used her friends' name for her.

"Of course, hon," replied Gerry.

"You don't know anyone around here with a black van do you," asked Jackson, "Maybe someone that strikes you as a little odd or suspicious?"

"Hm, can't say that I do. Harold Avery has an old black van, but I can't see him doing nothing wrong. Hell, I don't know if he could if he wanted to, the old fart."

"No, this would be a newer black van, maybe no more than ten years old."

"Nope, can't say that I know anyone with that."

"Alright then, have a good day."

"You too, hon. When you find out how good the chicken is you come back."

Gerry laughed, her belly jumping up and down as she did. Walking back to his truck, his phone rang. He grabbed it out of his pocket and looked at the screen. It was Detective Bailey. Jackson slid the green icon right and answered the call.

"Hey," Jackson said.

"Hey, I've got what you asked for," said Bailey, "I sent the info to you in an email. My personal email account, of course."

"Appreciate it," replied Jackson.

"Yeah, it's people here and there until you get to Roanoke, where it seems just about everyone probably knows someone who owns a black van."

"Make sense. Pretty big city and all."

"Yeah, I guess. Hey, where are you, I hear cars."

"At some country store south of Harrisonburg. Don't exactly know the town, if it even is one."

"Oh, you headed out to see Isaacs?"

"Who?"

"Jeff Isaacs. His info is in the case files. Remember, I told you his group had been helping. You said you were south of town; just thought maybe you were on his way to see him. He lives out that way in Steeles Tavern."

"No, I was just checking something out. Waiting for your call."

"Oh, okay. Well, this is your call."

"Thanks again."

Jackson ended the call. He opened up his passenger side door, slid the food in and pulled out the case files. He thumbed through the papers until he found the information on Isaacs again. Jackson opened up Google Maps on his phone and put in the address. The man lived about 40 minutes away. It couldn't hurt, Jackson thought.

He put the files away, walked around and climbed into his truck. The same older man working on the truck was still leering at him. Jackson nodded again and once again his effort was in vain.

He put the truck in gear and headed out for Steeles Tavern.

36

Jackson took a right off a rural highway and pulled onto a driveway that ended at a double garage attached to an impressive Victorian ranch style house. Creamy gray with slate blue metal roofing, the house and surrounding property were immaculately maintained. A modest yard enveloped the house on all sides like a manicured grass moat that separated it from the dense forest the home was snuggly nestled into, the same woods that surrounded the highway Jackson had taken to get there.

As he climbed out of his truck, Jackson saw Jeff Isaacs standing on the front porch, surprised to see someone drive up. Isaacs walked down the stairs and came over. Wearing a plaid flannel vest, matching cap, and jeans, he looked like someone who'd never hunted thought a hunter might look like.

"Hello there," said Jeff, "How may I help you?"

"My name is Jackson Clay," Jackson replied, "I heard you were familiar with the Sara Beth Parker case."

Isaacs look at him skeptically.

"A little bit, sure," Isaacs said, "Are you another detective?"

"Another," asked Jackson.

"I've met and talked to Detective Cole and her partner," Isaacs said, "What's his name? Doherty."

"No, I'm not with them. Or the police."

"So, you know the Parkers?"

"No. I'm just looking into the case. From what I understand, you yourself help out where you can."

An excitement came over Isaacs at the mention of his work.

"I, well, my organization more so really focuses on helping the family cope," he said, "We spread the word, sure, and get the missing's name and face out there. But I'm afraid we aren't some band of savvy investigators."

"But you're familiar with the Parker case," Jackson asked.

"Sure," replied Isaacs.

"I was wondering if I could ask you about it. Fill in some blanks for me."

"Sure. Actually—"

Isaacs looked around, as if unsure where to host his new guest. He turned the other way, facing the garage.

"You know, I was just about to head out to one of our PACTV groups," Isaacs said, "Not the Harrisonburg one the Parkers have been to a few times, but our Lexington one. It's not far. It'd be a good way for you to get a sense of what it is we're about."

Jackson was hesitant. He wasn't sure what meeting with a group of other victims would do to help him bring Sara Beth home, but if it gave him an opportunity to find out what Isaacs knew, maybe it was worth it.

"Okay," replied Jackson, "I'll follow you."

"Oh, there's no sense in taking two cars," said Isaacs, "You can ride with me. Don't worry, I'll bring you back in one piece."

Again, Jackson was hesitant.

"Alright. Just let me get my stuff," said Jackson.

"Of course, no problem," replied Isaacs, "I have to lock up and everything anyway."

Isaacs walked hastily down his walkway and trotted up the stairs.

"We'll take the Buick over there," Isaacs shouted before ducking into his house, "Feel free to get in. It should be unlocked."

Jackson walked around to the driver's side door of his truck, opened it, fetched his P320, and tucked it into the concealed holster clipped to his belt. He looked around, curious. The Buick was parked at the far corner of the driveway, far from the garage and the house. It struck Jackson as odd.

Double checking that Isaacs wasn't on his way out of the house, Jackson walked over to the garage doors. He cupped his hands around his eyes and put his face to the one of the windows. Inside was an Infiniti sedan and a Volkswagen SUV. No black panel van, not that Jackson really expected one.

He heard the front door shut around the corner and quickly stepped away from the house back towards his truck. Isaacs walked into view and gestured over to his Buick.

"Ready," asked Isaacs.

"Sure," replied Jackson.

The two of them got in and Jeff put the car in gear. As they pulled to the edge of the driveway, Isaacs' phone beeped and chirped in his pocket. He seemed to ignore it.

"Do you need to get that," Jackson asked.

"No, it's just an alert," replied Isaacs, "Sensors over the front of the driveway. They alert me when they've been tripped."

Jackson hadn't noticed it before, but now saw wood posts on either side of the driveway, knee high with infrared sensors.

"Fancy stuff," said Jackson.

"Well, you can never be too careful," replied Isaacs, "Evil is out there. I know more so than most. I suppose you do, too, if you look into stuff like the Parker case."

"I do," Jackson said.

They headed back towards Interstate 81, retracing the route Jackson had taken in but took the interstate south away from Harrisonburg. Jackson took in the view as farm land and truck stops dotted the valley landscape bordered by mountains.

"So are you a private investigator or something," Isaacs asked.

"Something like that," answered Jackson.

"I see," Isaacs said, "And the Parkers didn't hire you?"

"No, no one hired me."

"You mean you're here on your own time and dime? That's mighty of you."

"Just want to help."

"Yeah, I know the feeling. I lost my Olivia seven years ago. Went through a dark place but ultimately decided I didn't want anyone to have to go through what I did. And decided to help."

"That's noble of you."

"I don't know about all that. I just want to help, like you said. Terrible thing that happened to the Parkers."

"Sure is."

"I told them when I first met them, I couldn't get over how much Sara Beth looks like Olivia."

Isaacs leaned forward and fished a photo out of his back pocket and handed it to Jackson. He was right, Jackson thought. There was definitely a strong resemblance.

"She was beautiful. I'm sorry you lost her," said Jackson.

"Yeah, me too," Isaacs replied, "She was my world. Still is, really."

"And that's what your group is about," asked Jackson.

"Exactly. Once I started trying to help, I was stunned by how many like me there were out there. I think none of us were ever aware such a community existed. It's not like you advertise to people that your child was stolen from you. I decided to try and bring as many as I could together. To create a community where we could help one another."

"And that's what PACTV is?"

"Sure. Well, at least I hope so."

"Sounds nice."

"Well, you'll see for yourself."

Jackson was caught up in memories as he and Jeff drove through the rolling hills of the southern Shenandoah Valley, on their way to meet the broken families. Parents that had the thing they loved most in this world stolen from them. They would never know how much Jackson Clay shared their pain.

37

It was after midnight by the time Jackson got back to the Econo Lodge in Harrisonburg. The support group meeting hadn't been quite what Jackson expected. Though, if he were being honest with himself, he wasn't sure what he had expected.

Only four other people came besides Isaacs and himself, two sets of parents. Each had had a daughter taken from them. Jackson sat quietly and listened to them speak, but none of them talked much about their loved ones. It was clear the four of them regularly met there with Isaacs, making it more of a social event than anything else. The conversation meandered from the weather to the local baseball team to that one road the city refused to fix. Jackson couldn't help but feel his time was being wasted. He needed information that would get him closer to finding Sara Beth, not the local news latest.

As Jackson pulled into the parking lot of his motel, he saw the silhouette of a person leaning on the railing in front of his door. The full head of curly hair and gun-sized bulge on her right hip told him it was Detective Cole. Pretending not to notice, he walked over to the stairs and climbed them to his second-floor door. Of course, Detective Cole had seen him and was facing his direction as he turned the corner.

"Detective Cole," Jackson said, "You're up late."

"As are you, Mr. Clay," replied Cole.

"I don't remember telling you I checked in here," said Jackson.

"I'm a detective, Mr. Clay, I'm good at what I do."

Jackson took a deep breath, frustrated.

"What can I do for you, detective," Jackson asked.

"You had Detective Bailey run down black vans south of town," answered Cole.

"I did," replied Jackson.

"Ignoring why you wouldn't ask me, I assume your next step was to cross reference them with the state sex offender registry."

"It is, but I've been out chasing other leads down."

"Well, I wasn't. I cross referenced the names and got a hit. Albert Perry. He's registered for a first-degree rape conviction in New York state. Mr. Perry offered to drive a girl home from her high school after cheerleading practice let out. Instead, she was forced to have sex with him while he held a knife to her throat. He did twenty years and got out in 2015. His home address is registered outside a small town called Swoope about 35 miles south of here. Mr. Perry also happens to have a 2009 black Chevy Express."

Detective Cole handed him a manila folder with the information. He flipped through it, verifying everything she had said.

"So why don't you run it down yourself," Jackson asked.

"Come on," replied Cole, "Because I have you. The finder. The thing that goes bump in the night."

"And it's out of your jurisdiction on a case you're not supposed to be on, right," asked Jackson.

Detective Cole didn't say anything back.

"I'll get on it first thing in the morning," Jackson said, "Goodnight, Detective."

Detective Cole took the hint and headed for the stairs. But before she disappeared around the corner, she turned back to Jackson.

"What was the lead you were running," she asked.

"It turned out to be nothing," Jackson said.

She looked at him, suspicious.

"It was a literal dead end, Cole," Jackson said, his voice rising, "I'm not hiding anything from you."

Detective Cole gave a terse smile and nodded before descending the stairs. Jackson watched as she reappeared in the parking lot below, climbed into a Jeep Liberty, and left. He sighed again, still frustrated. Jackson Clay didn't appreciate being micromanaged.

He opened his hotel room door, and hit the lights. He tossed his keys onto the accent table and lowered himself onto the bed. Detective Cole's lead was a good one, but he'd been at it for 20 hours straight already. He set the alarm on his phone for four hours and closed his eyes. Minutes later, he was somewhere else entirely.

38

J ackson stared at the can of ginger ale. He could hear the carbonated bubbles plinking off the inside of the can, coming to the surface as their soft gurgling echoed. Nat was next to him, the two of them sitting in chairs in Detective Greg Teasley's office. He seemed like a nice enough guy, his desk adorned with photos of his two boys in Little League and Pop Warner uniforms. The youngest looked to be Evan's age. Jackson wondered if Teasley thought about him as he searched for Evan.

Detective Teasley opened the door and came in, sliding his ample gut between Jackson and Nat with a stack of papers.

"Okay, we put together a media packet with the photos you gave us," Teasley said, "We should start to see stories of him run beginning with the evening local news tonight. If stations want to interview you two, it would go a long way if you're up to it."

"Of course, whatever we need to do," Jackson replied.

Jackson looked at Nathalie. She didn't move, staring forward, a scowl tattooed on her face. Her leg was shaking. She did that when she was frustrated.

Evan had been missing almost 24 hours. Detective Teasley and others had told them they were doing all they could to find him. Jackson had been grateful *for their help. Nat, the few times she said anything, had only taken swipes at them for not doing more.*

"So, what do we do now," Jackson asked.

"Now, you let us do our job," Detective Teasley answered, "We'll pursue leads as they come in. Getting the word out will help. With a little luck, we'll be busy here the next few days. The best thing for you two to do is go home."

"You want us to just sit on our hands and do nothing," Jackson asked

"Like I said, if the media calls, take their interview. Talk with friends and family. Maybe something will come back to you that you remember."

Nathalie snorted as she stood up and left the detective's office, the door rattling as it banged against the wall. Jackson stood and thanked the detective for his time before leaving and jogging after his wife. He caught up with her just outside the front doors of the police station.

"Hey, Nat," he said, "What the hell was that?"

"It's bullshit, Jackson," she seethed, "It's all just bullshit."

"What are you talking about," Jackson asked.

"The flyers, the photos, the god damn media packet. It's all just a game to them. They go through the motions and maybe they find the kid or maybe they don't. But they checked their boxes so they're good. Except it's Evan now. It's my kid. And I'll be damned if they treat this like just another day at the office."

"They're doing their jobs, Nat. What more are they supposed to do?"

"Care, Jackson! They're supposed to give a fuck. Did that guy in there seem like he cared about anything other than when 5 o'clock rolled around?"

"Nat, they're just calm. They've done this before and they know what they're doing. We just need to trust them."

Nathalie snorted again.

"We," she echoed as she rolled her eyes.

"Yes, we, Nat," Jackson said, "Us."

"Last I checked, it wasn't we that let him disappear. It was you," she screamed.

"Come on, Nat. That's not fair."

She turned and stomped up the stairs, getting so close Jackson could feel her breath, warm and angry, against his face.

"No, I'm glad you said something," she said, "Because something needs to be *said. It's one thing that the cops in there don't give a fuck. It's not their kid. But he is yours, Jackson. So, where are you? Huh? You're the big, bad ex-Army Ranger that wants to be a private eye. Do some detective stuff, then. Find our son!"*

Indignation began to build in Jackson as he watched Nathalie storm off towards their car. He knew she was upset – hell, he was upset, too – but never would he go as far as to blame her for something as impossible as the situation they found themselves in. He could count on his fingers the number of times they had had a major fight. But now, standing on the stairs of the police station, the parental sin of losing his son placed at his feet by his wife, it felt as though something had broken that could not be fixed.

JACKSON OPENED his eyes not to the sight of Nathalie but a ceiling fan whirring and whining as it begrudgingly blew the damp air of the hotel room down onto him. He rolled over, sat up, and checked his watch. It was just before five in the morning. Ten seconds later, his alarm buzzed on his phone.

He got up, walked over to the bathroom, and tore open a packet of coffee. It wasn't his usual pour-over Gold Coast blend, but for free coffee it would certainly do. Listening as the little coffeemaker gurgled to life, he rubbed the rest of the sleep from his eyes. As his vision cleared, he saw the file Cole had dropped off last night. He grabbed it and began to thumb through the information on the man she'd found.

Albert Perry was convicted in 1995 for the 1994 rape of Lily McCall in the Finger Lakes region of New York state. Lily had been 16 just as Sara Beth was now. Perry was 31 when he was convicted, which would make him 55 now. Not too old that he couldn't overpower a teenage girl again, Jackson thought.

The last page was a printout of Perry's sex offender registry. He'd apparently moved last year from Watkins Glen, New York. Both his home and work had Swoope, Virginia addresses. Jackson couldn't think why the area sounded familiar to him. The work address said it was a gas station. He opened up the map he had bought and double-checked it wasn't where he'd stopped and grabbed Gerry's fried chicken.

Confirmed. Gerry's chicken was innocent.

He scanned the map looking for Swoope. As he found it, a cold, tingling sensation came over him. He opened up his laptop and googled both addresses. Both the gas station listed as his place of employment and his home were less than a mile off of Virginia 42, the state highway that made its way to Harrisonburg where inside the town limits it was called High Street. The same High Street the police car dashcam had seen the black van drive down the night Sara Beth Parker went missing.

"Son of a bitch," Jackson muttered under his breath.

He quickly threw on a pair of jeans and a t-shirt, grabbed his boots, slid a magazine into his P320 and holstered it. He grabbed his gear bag and was out the door in a matter of minutes.

39

Twenty minutes later, Jackson was nearing where his nav system put Perry's home address. As he came around a bend, he saw the silhouette of a large building in the early dawn twilight with a sign illuminated near the road. His stomach turned in knots again as he read it.

John Lewis High School
Home of the Fighting Irish

Jackson's nav system said he was less than a mile from the house. It was much farther than the 500 feet required by law, but with little else around, the revelation left Jackson with a sick feeling in his stomach.

As he drew near, he could see the house, perched on a hill, overlooking the rural highway. The house looked to be surrounded by open fields on all sides for at least a couple hundred yards. Jackson grunted as he saw this. Making his way up to the house wouldn't be easy.

He stopped at the next intersection and made a U-turn, doubling back to the high school. There, the side of the road Albert Perry's house was on was covered with trees. Jackson needed a place to leave his car and proceed on foot, but there weren't many options and none of them were great. Parked in the school's parking lot, his truck wouldn't look out of place, but even at this hour faculty were probably already arriving, and all it took was one person seeing him park his truck and run into the woods before the police were called out for a suspicious person.

Instead, Jackson parked just off the highway past a wooded private driveway near the open field next to Perry's house. With any luck, people passing by would assume the truck was with the residence at the end of the drive, and those in the residence wouldn't think much of a truck down by the road.

Killing the lights and engine, Jackson looked around for headlights or signs of activity. Nothing. He opened his door, slung his pack on over his shoulders and began hiking up the hillside into the trees.

He loped to the tree line along the open field as he moved parallel to the house. Jackson followed it all the way to where another field shaved off the back side of the woods, cutting it into a square.

Perry's house was less than a hundred yards away, nestled in a low bank of early morning fog that glowed with the first rays of sunlight. Jackson noticed the two fields were separated not only by wire fencing but a small trail. It was probably used by trucks and ATV's to move things in and out of the fields. The road ran up to the back of Perry's property as it wound its way around a small copse of trees. It was the best cover he'd have getting across the fields.

Keeping his upper half low, Jackson ran along the fence line, crossing the field fast and quiet. When he got to the trees on the far side, he ducked behind the thickest trunk and watched the house for movement. Nothing. Jackson had gotten across clean.

He turned and scanned the property. The only vehicle out in the open was an older model Subaru caked in dirt, but behind the house on the other side of the trees was a detached garage and a large shed, either of which were big enough to house the van. Maybe the van was in one of them, or maybe Albert Perry was out driving in it somewhere. There was only one way to find out.

Using the trees for cover, he made his way between the two structures where both had windows facing one another. He looked in the garage first. No cars. It had been turned into some sort of workshop.

Jackson slid back down into a squat and walked over to the shed, popping up to peer in its window.

There was something large inside covered with some sort of tarp. Whether it was a van or not was hard to see in the relative darkness of the early morning. He'd have to get inside for a better look. The only problem was the shed's doors were in plain view of the house.

Jackson moved to the corner of the shed and looked at its doors They were locked together with a metal clasp and large padlock, but the wood around the clasp was weathered and deteriorating. Jackson bet he could simply pry the whole assembly off.

He looked out at the house and scanned the windows one more time for any movement. They were dark and still.

Stepping slowly out from the cover of the two buildings, Jackson moved towards the shed doors. He pulled out his knife, jamming it in between the wood and metal, and pulled the handle towards him. The metal clasp and lock tore off the door and fell with a clunk at Jackson's feet.

Brushing the splintered wood aside, he swung open the broken door. Now with more light on it, Jackson could easily see it was a van with an auto cover on it. He lifted up a flap far enough to reveal a portion of the grill and hood. A gold Chevrolet moniker shined in the sunlight just now coming over the horizon. He lifted the cover a little further to see the body was painted black. Now he just needed to see about the xenon headlights.

But just as Jackson began to wonder if the keys to the van were in the shed somewhere, he heard the distinctive *click-click* of a shotgun behind him.

"And just who the fuck are you," asked a voice.

40

Jackson stuck his hands out to either side showing there was nothing in them. It was an attempt to deescalate the situation. He'd lost count how many times between the service and his life now he'd had a gun pulled on him. To him, this was merely a matter of procedure.

"I said who the fuck are you," the voice asked again, angrier, "You picked the wrong fucker to rob."

"I'm not here to take anything," Jackson replied calmly.

"Bullshit. Keep your hands up," said the voice.

Jackson raised his arms a little. He didn't want the back of his shirt to come up enough to show the P320 in its holster.

"I'm going to turn around, do not shoot me," Jackson said.

He rotated in place slowly, turning around to come face to face with the man. He was a shorter man whose age showed, with liver-spotted ruddy skin and white hair that flowed into a bushy beard. It was Albert Perry. Somewhere between the field and here, in front of the shed, Perry must've made him and gotten the drop on him. Jackson clenched his fists, angry at himself as he thought about it.

"Well, you say you ain't going to rob me. Who are you then," asked Perry.

"I'm going to reach slowly for my ID, okay? Do not shoot me," Jackson replied.

He reached slowly behind him and pulled his wallet out from his back pocket and extended it towards Perry with one hand. Perry stepped towards Jackson to examine it, taking one hand off the shotgun. He'd done exactly what Jackson wanted him to do.

In an instant, Jackson grabbed the barrel of the shotgun and pulled it forward, shoving the muzzle past his body and out of danger of shooting him. Perry's loose grip on the gun came free. Jackson turned into Perry, throwing a right elbow into the man's temple. When Perry brought his hands to his face, Jackson swung the butt of the shotgun into Perry's sternum. Rocked by the two blows, Perry stumbled backwards. Jackson marched at him, swinging a leg behind Perry and throwing him to the ground by his chest. Before he could process that he'd made a mistake, Albert Perry found himself on his back with his own shotgun pointed at him.

"Albert Perry," said Jackson, "We need to have a chat."

"How do you know—Wait, what's going on here," asked Perry.

"Get up," replied Jackson, "Walk over to the shed."

"What are you going to do, shoot me?"

"Weren't you just about to shoot me?"

"Fuck you, you're on my property."

Jackson ignored him. He motioned with the end of the shotgun.

"Up," Jackson ordered, "Over by the shed."

Perry stared at him long enough for his protest to register, then slowly pushed himself to his feet and limped over to the shed.

"There. Now what," Perry demanded.

"That black van under there. One just like it was seen right where a 16-year-old girl was taken from Harrisonburg three weeks ago," Jackson replied, "You have a history with teenage girls."

"Wha—Hey, I had nothing to do with that," Perry said.

"Didn't you?"

"No, I sure as shit didn't."

"Of the hundreds of registered sex offenders out here, it turns out there's only one with a black van, and he's a convicted rapist of a girl the same age as the one that disappeared. That's some coincidence."

"You say I used this van? Look at it. Hard to get it to Harrisonburg without an engine."

"What?"

"The transmission crapped out on it years ago. I've been scrapping it for parts. Go on look, the thing is gutted."

Jackson motioned over to the driver's door.

"Pop the hood," he said.

Albert shuffled sideways towards the van, not turning away from Jackson and the shotgun. He opened the door, reached in with one hand and pulled the hood release.

"Alright, back up," Jackson ordered.

Jackson walked over, keeping the gun trained on Perry, and opened the hood with one hand. Perry wasn't lying; there was a gaping hole where an engine should be.

"So, what," said Jackson, "This all could've been done in the weeks since."

"Transmission went a year ago," Perry replied, "I started selling parts not long after."

"You have some way to prove it," Jackson asked.

"Fuck you. You ain't a cop or you wouldn't be here like this. You prove it."

"You're right, I'm not a cop. Which should concern you, considering I've got your own gun pointed at you."

"I don't know what to tell you. Shoot me then."

Jackson thought to himself. He needed another way to either confirm or clear Perry.

"Three weeks ago, last Monday," Jackson said, "You know what you were doing?"

"What time," Perry asked.

"Between 10 and 11 pm," Jackson answered.

"Monday nights I work. The EZ Stop up the road. You can check for yourself."

"Someone going to vouch for you?"

"The hell if I know."

That was the place listed as his work on the sex offender registry. Albert Perry could be lying, but Jackson was starting to get the feeling he was telling the truth. With the gun still trained on Perry, he pulled out his phone and googled EZ Stop Swoope, Virginia. When the information came up, he pressed the phone icon. His phone dialed the number as he put it to his ear.

"EZ Stop," said a gruff man's voice.

"How's it going," replied Jackson, "My wife and I were traveling through a while back and she thinks she might've left a ring in the bathroom there."

"Mm, haven't seen anything like that," the man said, "When'd you say you lost it?"

"Must've been maybe three weeks ago. It was a Monday night."

"Ah, a different man's been working Monday nights around here recently. He's supposed to work tonight, in fact. I can ask him when he comes in."

"And who's that?"

"Al. Al, um, Perry I think his last name is."

Jackson ended the call.

"When do you work next," Jackson asked.

"Tonight," Perry said, "Why?"

Jackson pumped the shotgun. One by one the shells fell out of it and rolled into the grass. He tossed the shotgun deep into the shed and approached Perry, getting up so close to him he could smell the chewing tobacco on the old man's breath.

"I'm going to find out what happened to that girl," Jackson said, "If I find out you had anything to do with it, I'll be coming back. And if I come back here, it won't be to ask more questions."

Perry didn't say anything back. Jackson began walking backwards.

"Let's make this the last time we meet, Albert Perry," Jackson said, "For your sake."

Perry watched him, almost snarling. Jackson didn't turn away from him until he crossed the field, then turned and ran into the woods.

Hiking back down the wooded hillside, Jackson made his way to where he had left his truck. He got in and drove down the road until he had a view of Perry's drive way. Now that he had his face-to-face with Perry, he wanted to see how the man reacted.

But Perry didn't leave the property. Jackson sat on the house well into the afternoon. No one came in or out.

Maybe Perry was lying, but the man on the phone had said Perry was working tonight and then Perry confirmed it without knowing what the man had said. There was good reason to buy Perry's story, but it wasn't bulletproof. Jackson decided he wanted to confirm Perry's alibi.

Five minutes later, he pulled into the parking lot of the EZ Stop. As he walked in, a husky gentleman looked up from behind the counter. His upper torso looked as though it was trying to break out of the sleeveless camouflage constricting it. Tattoos competed with dark hair for real estate on his arms, back, and chest. Jackson wondered why he was minding a gas station in the middle of the afternoon and not playing tackle for the Steelers.

"Afternoon," said Jackson, "I was wondering if you could help me out?"

"With what," replied the man.

"A little girl was taken from Harrisonburg about three weeks ago," Jackson said, "Maybe you heard about it?"

"I think I remember seeing it on the news."

"Yeah, she's still missing. You didn't happen to be working here on a Monday night a while back? Three weeks from yesterday?"

"No, can't say that I was."

"Ah. See I'm checking gas stations for a guy. I was going to ask if you remember seeing him."

Jackson looked up at the camera over the man's shoulder.

"How long do you guys keep the footage for those cameras," Jackson asked.

"I'm not sure," the man replied, "I think a month or so."

"You mind checking if you guys still have footage from that night," asked Jackson.

The man stared at Jackson as if trying to get a read on him.

"Who did you say you were with, again," the man asked.

"I didn't," Jackson answered.

The man paused a moment longer, still seemingly trying to size up Jackson.

"There isn't a reason you wouldn't want to help is there," Jackson asked.

"No, I suppose not," the man said, "Back here."

He waved Jackson over towards a door next to the register and opened it. Inside was a cramped office littered with papers. The man squeezed into the tiny office chair and opened something up on the computer.

"You said three weeks ago from last night," the man asked.

"Exactly," answered Jackson, "Right around 10:30."

The man punched something into the keyboard and a window with grainy camera footage popped up. Jackson recognized from its frame of reference it was the camera behind the register. The two of them stared at the screen as the footage played.

"You know, it's funny, you're the second person today to ask about this night," the man said.

"Oh yeah," asked Jackson.

"Yeah," answered the man, "Some guy called right as I got in saying his wife left a ring in here that night. When I told him I hadn't been working, the guy just up and hung up on me. Asshole."

"It takes all kinds," Jackson said.

Shortly after 10:30, a couple of guys who'd clearly had a few too many walked into view of the camera. As they seemed to have a conversation, one fell backwards, knocking over a rack of sodas.

"Either of those knuckleheads the guy you're looking for," asked the man.

"Unfortunately, no," Jackson replied.

As the two struggled to right one another a third man came into the frame yelling at them. It was Albert Perry. Jackson watched as he got the two men away from the mess and then pointed to the doors, clearly inviting them to leave. The timestamp on the video read 10:38 p.m. Albert Perry was forty miles away when Sara Beth was taken.

"Thank you for letting me look," Jackson said.

"That it," the man asked.

"That's it," replied Jackson, "Have a good day."

Jackson stepped out of the office and waved as he left the store.

41

Jackson returned to Harrisonburg frustrated. He'd cross referenced the list of owners of black vans with the sex registry again. There was nothing. For all intents and purposes, he was back at square one.

Back in his motel room, he sat at a table with Sara Beth's missing persons report in front of him, the round, café-style table was up against the window. From his second-floor room, Jackson could see traffic taking turns going through the intersection outside. A random medley of all sizes and colors. He imagined waiting long enough and his patience being rewarded with the sight of the black van and its xenon headlights rolling by.

One should be so lucky.

Looking down at the file, Jackson thought about the Parkers. Not Sara Beth so much as her parents, Anne and Scott. Some time ago, Jackson had been Scott Parker. The happy father and husband. He thought about that happiness being taken away without warning and the pain that followed. The dread. The despair in knowing but also not knowing. It was a pain that had almost broken him. He was determined to find Sara Beth before it broke the Parkers.

Jackson was thinking about this when his phone chirped with a message. He slid it open and looked at it. It was a text message from Detective Cole.

You look into Perry yet??

Yes, he thought. It's been a day. Obviously, I've looked into Perry. The question annoyed Jackson. So much so he was tempted not to reply. But Detective Cole didn't strike him as the type that took silence for a satisfying answer. He texted her back.

Dead end. He didn't take her.

Jackson closed out of the messaging app on his phone and tossed it onto the table where it landed on Jeff Isaacs' picture. He too must know that pain, Jackson thought. In fact, he could probably relate more to the Parkers than he could, with him also losing a teenage daughter.

Olivia Isaacs. A thought came to him. Two girls that looked eerily alike taken within maybe an hour's distance of one another? Seven years apart? The two could be connected. Almost all predators had a type. What if Olivia and Sara Beth were taken by the same person?

He tried to think. Did Jeff tell him her age? As similar as they looked, did it matter? Probably not if you were the kind of person capable of that kind of evil. Jackson grabbed his phone off the table and called Detective Bailey.

"It's me," he said, "Can you get me the case files on Olivia Isaacs?"

"What? Why," asked Detective Bailey, who had clearly been asleep.

"Just, can you get them," Jackson asked again.

"It's almost midnight, Clay. I'll see what I can do when I get to the office tomorrow morning."

"First thing?"

"Good night, Clay."

The call ended. Jackson put the phone down and looked over at the bed. His help was asleep. He might as well try to get some rest himself. Even if Detective Bailey ignored his request, Jeff Isaacs was probably the only case file he needed. It probably made sense to pay him another visit. He would do just that tomorrow morning.

42

S ara Beth sat shivering on the lumpy mattress in the basement. She could hear the man upstairs yelling at someone. There was no other voice, so she guessed he was on the phone. Either way, her captor now suddenly angry made her nervous.

Tonight marked the third night she'd been held down here, hand-cuffed to the wall. She'd started using the chains binding her to make indentations on the wall to keep track, fearing the number of days she spent here would grow.

When the sun rose the first morning, light filled the empty base-ment and she could see where the smell of paint came from. Someone had hastily painted the corner she was chained to bright pink. An old beat-up bookshelf and dresser sat next to her adorned with random items. Posters lined the wall above her with pictures of bands and famous actors. It was as if someone had tried in vain to make her prison cell feel like some kind of bedroom, except something was off.

Not the chains and handcuffs – that much was obviously wrong – but the posters and the trinkets on the shelf felt old. The posters were of Nelly, Avril Lavigne, and some young-looking actor she'd seen before but didn't who he was. She'd heard of stuff by Nelly and Avril Lavigne, sure, but she didn't actually *listen* to them. It was as if the so-called bedroom had been put together by someone who didn't really get what a teenage girl would be into. At least not these days.

That revelation somehow only further terrified Sara Beth.

Had it all been put together by the man upstairs? The one with the genteel voice? She hadn't actually seen him yet – always quickly putting the blindfold back on when the door opened – but he'd seemed strangely nice. At least in their first interactions.

The night Sara Beth arrived, the man came down shortly after the others had left and brought her a peanut butter and jelly sandwich and some potato chips. He'd softly grasped her arm and guided it to the plate, encouraging her to eat.

"You eat, now," he'd said in a warm tone, "We'll talk soon."

The next morning she'd awoken to find another plate of food – buttered toast and a hard-boiled egg – next to her mattress. She was surprised the man could come and go without waking her, as fretful as her sleeping had been since she'd been taken.

All of that had given Sara Beth hope that things might get better wherever she was now, but that hope was crushed when the man came down later that night. His steps down the stairs were loud and frantic, unlike the soft steps she'd heard before.

"Here, eat this," he'd said.

"I can't see," she'd replied.

He grabbed her arm like he had the first night, but now he was forceful and unfriendly. His hand was cold and clammy, not warm like it had been before.

"Here, it's right here," he'd said, sounding annoyed.

The food now was just a can of tuna. The man hadn't even bothered to open it. As Sara Beth fumbled for the tab on the lid, she heard the man stomp back up the stairs and slam the door behind him.

Her two encounters since then with the man had been just as cold. Each time another can of tuna practically thrown at her as he said little more than 'eat' before he disappeared again. Now he was upstairs yelling at someone on the phone. Sara Beth didn't know what it all meant, but something inside her told her it didn't add up to anything good.

She sat quietly, trying to make out what the man was saying. There was something about a different man. Something was wrong about him. The man upstairs told whoever he was talking to he needed to deal with it.

The ceiling creaked overhead as the man paced around. As he moved into another part of the upstairs, Sara Beth could more clearly make out what he was saying.

"I don't care, I'm done. I'm out," the man yelled.

A pause.

"Keep the money, I don't give a shit. But I'm out."

Another pause.

"I'm not going to say shit. But you need to handle this."

The next pause was longer. The footsteps stopped. Sara Beth thought the phone call might've ended, but a chill rushed over her as the man yelled into the phone one last time.

"You get her and do it yourself."

43

Jackson was wide awake and staring at the ceiling of his motel room when his alarm went off at 4:30 the following morning. Sleep had eluded him most of the night as he thought about Olivia Isaacs and why no one had considered a possible connection before. Maybe there was something about the Isaacs case he didn't know that ruled out a connection. Either way, he had to find out.

It was too early to expect Detective Bailey to have the case files ready for him just as it was probably too early to pay Jeff Isaacs another visit. He rolled out of his bed, started making coffee in the little coffeemaker in the bathroom and sat down at his laptop.

After double checking that Bailey had not sent him anything, he brought up Google and searched for Olivia Isaacs. A slew of articles came up. Jackson clicked through them one by one and read about her disappearance.

Olivia Isaacs disappeared some time during the afternoon of May 6, 2012 shortly after her high school had let out for the day. She was 15 years old at the time. According to an article in the Daily News-Record, a Harrisonburg-based newspaper, Olivia regularly walked the mile and a half home from school. On the afternoon of May 6, though, a thunderstorm had blown through, leading some to speculate that she'd accepted an offer of a ride. But it seemed that was pretty much anything anyone had. Suppositions and theories. Without tangible leads, the case must've gone cold.

A separate article in the Daily News-Record focused on Jeff Isaacs, the grieving father who was starting an organization for fellow grieving parents. The article mentioned how he hoped the organization would create more attention for missing kids, starting with Olivia. The article was framed in the light of new hope and optimism for Olivia's case and others. Reading it with the knowledge of how everything ends made it all the sadder, Jackson thought.

He spent the better part of the next hour reading articles with largely the same information. Even when he found the website for PACTV, which admittedly hadn't been kept up very well, the About Us section shared little he hadn't read somewhere else. It all painted the picture in broad strokes for Jackson. Now he wanted the finer points.

He checked his watch. It was almost six. Going to the window, he pulled back the curtains and watched the city outside. The sky was just starting to fill with the light of a coming day. He wondered how soon was too soon to visit Jeff Isaacs. Maybe if he took his time grabbing some breakfast, it would be long enough. He was thinking about it as his phone buzzed from across the motel room.

He expected it to be Bailey calling in with the information, but as he picked up the phone, the Caller ID didn't say Bailey. It was Detective Cole.

"Morning, Det—" Jackson began to say before Detective Cole cut him off.

"Clay," she said in angry exasperation, "Tell me you did not contact the family."

"What, no," replied Jackson suddenly on the defensive, "Why would I—"

"Clay, promise you didn't do something as stupid as make contact with them."

"Cole, would you listen to me? I haven't talked to anyone in the family."

"You promise?"

"Yes. Christ, Cole, what the hell is this about?"

He felt his body tingle with the sensation of a million tiny needle pricks as she answered him.

"Anne Parker is missing."

44

As Cole and Doherty pulled up to the Parkers' house, the street was already lined with squad cars. A couple of officers were out with next door neighbors, no doubt asking if they had seen anything or had talked to Anne Parker recently.

"Pull up right around that cruiser," Cole said.

Her door was open and she was climbing out before the car had come to a stop. Marching up the stairs, she nodded to the officers standing by the front door as she walked in.

Inside, Scott Parker was sitting on the living room couch, his head in his hands, as a half dozen officers surrounded him. Two other detectives from Cole's unit, Ben Pemberton and Sam Ross, were flanking Scott on opposite sides, scribbling on their steno pads as they asked him questions. Detective Cole slid in through the contingent of officers encircling Scott.

"Scott, are you okay," Cole asked.

Scott nodded, not making eye contact with her or anyone else.

"Angela, what are you doing here," Detective Pemberton asked.

"Their daughter's been missing over three weeks," answered Cole, "I'm sure you've gotten to that by now."

"Yes," replied Pemberton, "We're working it."

Detective Cole nodded over towards an empty corner of the room, gesturing for the two other detectives to step over for a word.

"Mr. Parker, just a minute," said Detective Ross.

The two of them stood up and followed Cole, forming a small huddle.

"This is obviously related to their daughter," Cole said, "Let Doherty and I work it."

"We've been on the ground here an hour already," Pemberton replied, "Getting you caught up is time wasted that we could be spending looking for her."

"Listen, I know them, okay," Cole said, "Getting *you* guys read in would take even more time. At least let us assist."

"Okay, fine. We asked him if he knew of any place she'd go to get away. He couldn't think of anywhere. Can you?"

"Get away? The call said missing persons. You're already sure she left on her own?"

Detectives Pemberton and Ross looked at each other.

"Scott Parker called 9-1-1 when he went to check on Anne in their bedroom," Pemberton said, "She was gone and there was a hand-written note on a piece of paper on her pillow saying she was sorry."

Cole felt her heart lurch into her throat. Anne Parker had been handling everything worse and worse each time she saw her. Now she had hit her breaking point. Cole went back over to Scott, pulled the coffee table closer to the couch, and sat on it facing him.

"Scott," Cole said, "What about Sara Beth? Is there a place *she* would go?"

"No, she never ran away," Scott answered, "I told you that the very first day."

"I know, I know," replied Cole, "What about together? Was there a particular place she enjoyed going? Something that meant a lot to all of you?"

"I don't know," Scott said as tears began to run down his cheeks, "I'm sorry, I just don't know."

Detective Cole patted his hand, comforting him. She stood up and walked back over to Detectives Ross and Pemberton.

"I assume you have a BOLO out for her," Cole asked the two detectives.

"BOLO out for HPD and State Police on her and her car," Detective Pemberton said.

"Her car," Cole echoed, confused.

"Yeah she took her car. Forgot to mention that. A 2010 Subaru Outback."

"Can we track it? What about her phone?"

"We're trying to figure that out as we speak."

As Pemberton talked, Cole's eyes looked past him at a uniformed officer suddenly raising his radio to his ear.

"Detectives," he said, pausing to listen to the radio a moment longer, "9-1-1 caller reports a woman on Pleasant Valley Road standing on the I-81 overpass. Possible jumper. Description matches Anne Parker."

Detective Cole looked at Scott who met her eyes with his, tears streaming from them.

"I can't lose her, too," he said.

45

Running down the front walk way, Cole shouted to her partner, Detective Doherty, who was talking to some officers by their car.

"Pleasant Valley Road at I-81. Let's go now," she said.

The two of them slid into their unmarked patrol car. Doherty took a sharp U-turn in front of the Parkers' house and punched it down the road, their lights and siren waking what parts of the neighborhood remained asleep.

Cole grabbed her radio from the center console.

"This is One-David-Twenty responding code three to the possible jumper on Pleasant Valley. Tell arriving units to stay back and not to make contact. We are five minutes out."

Cole held onto the overhead handle as if the car might leave her behind. Doherty wove in and out of the light traffic, crossing over to the opposite side of the road when necessary. They raced across town, two patrol cars following, a streaking convoy of red and blue lights.

Four minutes later – Doherty would brag later about how he shaved time off their ETA – the three police cars arrived at a tangled knot of emergency vehicles. A couple of officers had taped off the area to keep onlookers at bay and were now enforcing that line as a crowd gathered. Cole ducked under the tape and looked for the patrol supervisor. An officer saw her looking and motioned her towards the front of the vehicles.

"You must be Detective Cole," said an officer with the chevrons of a sergeant on his sleeve.

"I am," answered Cole, "Where are we at?"

"She's right there, sitting on the railing," said the sergeant, "Hasn't said anything to us, hasn't even looked our way. No one's attempted to interact with her per your order."

"I appreciate it. Where are we at logistically?"

"I've got the road shut down both ways, clearly. Rescue's drawing up a plan to intervene."

"Let's see if we can talk her down first. Have State Troopers shut down the interstate at the first exit each way."

"Copy that."

"I'm going to go talk to her. No one else approaches unless I say to."

"You got it."

Detective Cole felt her heart begin to beat harder. There was nothing but gray concrete between her and Anne. It couldn't have been more than a few dozen feet but it felt like it might be miles.

Anne Parker was sitting hunched on the railing of the overpass, her hair covering her face as she looked down. She was gripping the railing for balance on either side of her. Detective Cole took that as a promising sign.

She began to walk out to her, walking slowly as if Anne were an animal that might easily startle. When she got about halfway, she called out.

"Anne," Cole said, "Anne, it's me. Angela."

Anne's head turned. Detective Cole could see her looking back through a break in her long, brown hair.

"Anne, I just want to make sure you're okay," said Cole.

"Nothing is okay," Anne murmured back.

A helicopter thumped overhead. Detective Cole could barely hear her. She reached for her radio and called back to the patrol supervisor.

"Whose bird is that," she asked on the radio.

"Not sure. It's not one of ours," the sergeant radioed back.

"Well get it out of here," Cole responded.

She put the radio back on her hip as the Sergeant burst a quick transmission acknowledging her. Cole took a couple steps closer to Anne.

"Talk to me, Anne," she said, "Why are you out here?"

"I can't do it anymore," Anne replied.

"Anne, I know you're upset, but this isn't the way to handle it," Cole said, "Hurting yourself isn't going to fix this."

"It's what's right. It should be me who suffers. I lost her."

"No, Anne. You didn't lose her. She's out there somewhere. We're going to find her. And when we do, she's going to need her mother."

"Where? Where is she? She's gone. It should be me. I should be gone."

"No, Anne, you should be right here, waiting for your daughter. You don't want to do this. What if Sara Beth comes home tomorrow? Or the next day? Imagine all she'll have been through. She's going to need her mother. She's going to need you, Anne."

"What if I can't? What if I'm not strong enough?"

"You are, Anne. You've made it this far. I can't even begin to imagine what you've been through, and you've made it this far."

Cole was now within arm's reach of her. She put an arm out, placing her hand carefully on Anne's back.

"Anne, it's okay," Cole said, "You can't blame yourself. You have been so amazing. We want to help you. We want to bring Sara Beth home to you. But first, we want you to be safe. And okay."

"I'm not okay," Anne replied, "Look at me. Look at all this. This is not okay."

"This is okay, Anne. We're all here for you," Cole said, "We just want you to be safe."

"I can't. I can't go back."

"Why not, Anne?"

"The not knowing, the empty house, it's too much."

"If it's too much to be at home, Anne, you don't have to be at home. But this, this railing. This isn't the place for you. Let's come back over to this side."

"There's nothing for me back there."

"Anne, there's nothing for you down there. We're all right here. Me, Scott, your friends. We're here for you. We just want you to come off the railing."

"Tell them I can't, Tell them I'm sorry."

Anne's hands began to fidget, sliding up and down the railing. She looked further down, past her feet at the ground below. Her breathing turned shallow and rapid. Cole was losing her.

"Anne," she said, "I'm sorry."

In one motion, Cole swung her arms underneath Anne's, bear-hugging her from behind. She lunged backwards, tugging Anne off the ledge and directly onto her as the two of them fell to the ground.

Immediately, a handful of firefighters and police officers rushed to their aid. Onlookers in the distance began to clap, but all Cole could hear were the guttural cries bellowing from Anne.

"No, please, no," Anne cried, "I need this to end! Please, no!"

Detective Cole didn't let go of her as she kicked and twisted, trying to get free. Cole squeezed tighter.

"I'm sorry, hon," she said softly into Anne's ear, "I'm so sorry."

Firefighters and police officers surrounded them and helped control Anne. Cole held back tears as the first responders pleaded with Anne to calm down. Detective Doherty came running in, ordering other officers to get her off of Cole. The chaotic pile of arms and legs shifted sideways and Cole slid out from underneath, propping herself up on her elbows.

"You okay," asked Doherty, squatting down beside her.

"Yeah, I'm fine," Cole answered, catching her breath.

A handful of firefighters got Anne onto a stretcher where she laid back sobbing. She wasn't fighting them anymore, more tired than anything.

"That was some slick move," Doherty said, "You saved her."

Cole watched as they buckled her in, pinning down her arms and legs. Anne Parker didn't resemble the worried mother Detective Cole first met. She was something else. A creature of her own devastation. Wounded and disoriented.

"It sure doesn't feel like it," Cole replied.

She picked herself up off the concrete, shooing away a gesture of help from Doherty and walked back to the end of the bridge that was abuzz with activity. The patrol supervisor stopped barking orders into his mic just long enough to pat Cole on the back as she walked past. Cole didn't feel it. A numbness came over her. Police officers, paramedics, and firefighters crisscrossed every which way around her. She didn't notice any of it. They were blurs to her. Currents in a river. Someone leaned over and said something to her. She ignored it and kept walking.

It wasn't until she got to the other side of the mess that she felt like she could breathe. She leaned against an ambulance and put her hands on her knees as she tried to calm herself.

When she felt she'd calmed down a little, Cole looked up and took stock of the crowd of people that had gathered. Just beyond the yellow tape, a grey Dodge Ram caught her eye. Jackson Clay was leaning on the front of it, watching the scene. Watching her.

Detective Cole walked over to him, ducking underneath the yellow tape. An officer who had been keeping his eye on Jackson, wary of the man but nervous about confronting him, saw her approach and eased his stance.

"You look like shit," said Jackson.

"I'll be fine," replied Cole.

"For what it's worth, I'm telling you the truth," Jackson said, "I haven't had any contact with the family."

"I know. This was her. She'd been going downhill ever since it started. I didn't think it was this bad. I should've seen it coming."

"Bull. You're not her psychiatrist. You don't know what's in her head."

"No, I'm just the dick that didn't find her little girl."

Jackson didn't say anything back. The two of them stood for a moment in silence, taking in the scene.

"We're running out of time, Clay," Cole said.

"I get that feeling, too," Jackson said back.

"You sure Albert Perry is clean," Cole asked.

"I saw it with my own eyes. He was an hour away from here when it happened."

"Fuck."

"I have something else I'm going to check out. Was about to head out before you called me."

"Let me guess, you'll let me know if anything comes of it."

"Sounds good to me."

Jackson pushed himself off the truck and walked past Cole as he fished his keys out of his pocket. When he got to the door of his truck, he stopped and turned back to her.

"I know I don't have to tell you," Jackson said, "But all this, this isn't on you."

"Yeah, I know," said Cole.

Jackson nodded and opened the truck door.

"Clay," Cole said.

"Yeah," Jackson replied.

"Find her."

Jackson nodded again and climbed into his truck. The engine growled as it came to life. He backed up slowly and turned around. Cole watched as he pulled out to the street and turned left, heading south. A moment later, the ambulance carrying Anne Parker maneuvered through the crowd and turned the opposite way, rounding a blue Hospital sign on the side of the road as it went.

46

I t was late afternoon by the time Jackson headed out for Jeff Isaacs'
house. When he returned to his motel to grab his gear, he noticed
the information from Detective Bailey had come in. He grabbed a
sandwich from the Subway across the street as he went over it. There
wasn't much his research hadn't already told him save for a couple of
people that had been looked at. Jackson jotted their names down and
continued to get ready to go, figuring Isaacs would be more than able
to provide context to the information anyway.

As Jackson headed south towards Isaacs' house, Detective Cole
texted him to let him know Anne Parker was being kept at RMH
Medical Center on what was called a 5150, or a 72-hour involuntary
psychiatric admission to the hospital. Jackson could sympathize with
what she was going through, Helplessness had driven her to contem-
plate leaving that overpass. It had nearly pushed him to do equally
destructive things a lifetime ago. The hardest part of being pushed that
far was coming back from it, and not everyone did.

As he got to the exit for Steeles Tavern and took the off ramp, an
orange dot lit up on his dashboard. His fuel gauge was beginning to
touch the white 'E' at the bottom. The gas station at the traffic light was
the last one before Isaac's house.

He pulled in, hopped out, and walked into the store. A young girl with a mouse-like face was behind the register. Jackson grabbed a bottle of water and put it on the counter.

"Will that be all, sir," asked the cashier.

"That and 20 in gas, please," Jackson replied, "Pump, um—"

He turned, looking back out the window to read the number on the pump he'd parked in front of. Instead though, Jackson's eyes caught the back half of a black van stopped at the traffic light.

"Sir, the pump number," asked the cashier.

Jackson didn't hear her. He stepped towards the window, not taking his eyes off the van. Its front half was obscured by the 18-wheeler in front of it. Something inside him told him what he would see.

"There are other customers, sir," the cashier pleaded.

The light turned green. The 18-wheeler lurched forward. Jackson didn't blink. As the semi rolled forward the van came into full view.

Its xenon headlights burned like two bright blue balls of fire.

47

Jackson read the number off his pump and turned back to the cashier, jumping in front of another customer she had taken.

"20 on pump ten, please," He said, "You keep the rest. Thanks. Sorry."

He ran out to his truck looking for the black van, fearing he'd lose it before he could get enough gas in his tank to follow it. But the van didn't continue on down the road. Instead it turned into the gas station and parked in front of the storefront.

A man climbed out of the side door with what looked like a scratcher ticket in his hand and went inside. He was young with blonde hair and a boyish face. His hoodie, jeans, and boots were all caked in dirt.

Jackson grabbed the gas pump and began filling up his truck, watching the man inside the store. He'd climbed out of the back of the van, which led Jackson to believe there were at least two more men in it taking the front two seats. There was no way to see from where he was standing, though.

The man inside waited patiently in line before cashing the ticket and then using some of the money to buy a pack of cigarettes. As he walked out, Jackson looked at the meter on the gas pump.

The gallons and dollar amount climbed slowly as gas poured into his tank. 16 dollars. 17.

The man climbed back inside the truck. 18. 19.

The van backed out and pulled away, heading for the interstate. 20.

The pump cut off with an abrupt click. Jackson put the nozzle back and jumped into his pickup, firing it up. He put it in gear and pulled out of the gas station, cutting off an old Trans Am whose driver flipped him off. Jackson didn't see it. He didn't take his eyes off his target.

Weaving in and out of traffic, it took him less than a minute to catch back up with the van as it drove the speed limit in the right-hand lane. Jackson pulled into the lane a couple cars behind and began following.

He pulled his P320 out from behind him and set it on the passenger seat. His mind raced, playing out scenarios how to intercept the van. Given the man had come out of the back, he assumed Sara Beth probably wasn't inside, but he couldn't be sure and knew he had to be ready for anything.

The van drove south on the interstate a half hour longer before getting off and picking up the Blue Ridge Parkway, winding its way around the spine of the Appalachian Mountains. With almost no traffic, Jackson had to place more distance between him and the van to keep from being spotted. Keeping it in his sights was tough, mostly catching glimpses of its taillights before it swung around another bend. Jackson wasn't worried about losing them. Out here, roads were few and far between. Jackson would spot it if the van turned somewhere.

They continued on for almost an hour eventually making their way to the small town of Rocky Mount, where the van pulled into a dark parking lot. Jackson drove past, stopped at the next intersection and doubled back. Just as Jackson guessed, two men climbed out of the front. The guy that had run into the gas station climbed out of the back and joined them in front of a building that had clearly seen better days. A dimly lit sign labeled it as Crossroads Bar & Grill.

Jackson waited for the men to go inside before turning off the street and pulling into the parking lot himself. He climbed out, grabbed his P320 off the passenger seat, and slid it into its concealed holster on his belt.

He walked over to the van and looked quickly inside. The center console was littered with candy wrappers and cigarette packs. Two double gulp cups from 7-Eleven filled the cupholders. Jackson looked up behind the front seats. There was no barrier between the cabin and the rest of the van. He stepped back, looking around quickly for anyone watching, then pointed a flashlight inside the van. It was empty. He grabbed his phone and snapped a shot of the license plate then walked around to the driver's side and did the same thing with the VIN before heading into the bar.

Crossroads Bar and Grill took the term dive bar to the extreme. An impressive collection of neon signs for just about every cheap domestic beer imaginable struggled in their dual role as interior lighting. A couple of pool tables sat in the back, their kelly green felt fading to a disreputable shade of seafoam underneath stains and water rings from countless drinks. The shelf behind the bar featured a handful of bottom shelf liquors and a tap limited to beers that started with either 'Bud' or 'Miller.' A vinyl sign below the TV showed a schedule of NASCAR races from three years ago. Time had literally passed the place by.

The three men he'd seen get out of the van had taken up seats along the bar itself and were having an animated conversation about something. Jackson stepped in and took up a spot on the far corner of the bar, several seats down from the three men. A bartender, wary of Jackson's unfamiliar face walked over to him and placed a napkin on the bar.

"What can I get you," he asked.

"Whatever's good and cold," Jackson answered.

The bartender nodded, reaching underneath the bar. He came back up with a Rolling Rock, twisted off the cap and placed it down on the napkin in front of Jackson.

"$2.50," said the bartender.

Jackson reached into his back pocket and fetched his money clip, taking out a $10 bill.

"How about 10, and let's keep them coming," Jackson replied.

"Just as long as you save some for a tip," the bartender said.

Jackson stared at the beer, holding it in front of him with both hands, as he listened to the three men continue their lively conversation. The two men that had climbed out of the front of the van had long sandy hair and were clearly related. Their matching leather vests had some sort of insignia on the back. Jackson supposed it might be a bike club. They seemed to be giving the third guy, who was noticeably younger, grief over not getting some girl's phone number back at the gas station. The ribbing turned into playful fighting as one of the men put the younger guy in a headlock and the other took his phone. Jackson watched, amused, as the younger guy tried in vain to break free while simultaneously flailing his left arm around in an attempt to get his phone back

As the play fight died down, the guy who had had his friend in a headlock sat back in his chair, looking over at Jackson who had been watching them. Jackson looked away and took a long sip from his beer. The guy got the other vested man's attention and nodded over in Jackson's direction. Smiling a menacing smile, he leaned over the bar, staring at Jackson.

"Say, friend," the guy said, "You're new here."

"Passing through," Jackson replied, "Just stopped to take a break."

He took another sip from his beer.

"This isn't the kind of place your type stops at. What, was Starbucks closed," the guy asked, his friends laughing, "Couldn't get a frosted mocha-chino this late?"

"Wouldn't know," Jackson answered.

The three men looked at each other. The guy who'd been talking to Jackson whispered something. The trio laughed.

"I think what my buddy is trying to say is you might be lost, friend," said the other guy in a biker vest.

"I know right where I am. Friend," Jackson said back.

The two men in vests got up off their chairs, their joking nature gone. The younger guy in the dirty hoodie seemed worried by how fast things had escalated.

"Yeah, you looking for something," asked the first vested man.

"As a matter of fact, I am," Jackson said, turning towards them, "Young girl went missing a few weeks ago. She was taken away by a van looking a lot like yours. But you wouldn't know anything about that, would you?"

The two vested guys rounded the corner of the bar and stepped closer. Jackson took another swig from his beer, not breaking eye contact with them. The younger guy watched nervously from his bar stool.

"You some sort of cop," asked one of the vest-clad men.

"No, he's not a cop," said the other, "But whatever he is, he talks too much."

"I guess that means we're done talking then," Jackson said.

The first guy lunged at Jackson. Jackson slid to the side, dodging the man's grasp as he smashed his bottle of Rolling Rock into the man's face. The second guy threw a telegraphed right-handed punch that Jackson ducked before coming back up and planting a fist of his own into the man's sternum. The man doubled over, gasping for air. Jackson planted a boot on his chest and kicked outward, propelling him backwards into the far wall. Jackson then turned back to the first man, took him by the head and rammed him into the bar. Neither man got up from the ground. Jackson looked at the third, the younger one, who was now ghost white with panic. As Jackson stepped towards him, he turned to run but a swinging pool cue came down and cracked him in the chest. A man as thick as a bourbon barrel came around the far side of the bar, tossing aside the pool cue he'd just struck the guy with.

"And just where do you think you're going," asked the large man, "This fine gentleman asked y'all a question."

The three men collectively groaned in response. The younger one crawled like a crab backwards towards the far wall as Jackson and his newfound husky ally approached him from opposite sides, cornering him.

"Fucking kill them, Mack," one of the other men whined from the floor.

"Mack, huh," said the large man, "That's a cute name."

Jackson watched as Mack pulled a butterfly knife on the man, who in turn chuckled.

"Oh, Macky boy," the man said, "You ever hear the one about the guy who brought a knife to a gun fight?"

The man reached into the small of his back and pulled a Smith &

Wesson

Wesson .357 revolver from underneath his Mossy Oak camouflage coat.

"I don't know about him, but I sure as shit have," said a voice behind them.

Jackson and the large man turned to see the bartender place a shotgun down on the bar top.

"Perhaps you all best leave," the bartender said.

Mack took advantage of the momentary distraction to run past Jackson for the front door, doing his best to corral his two friends off the floor as he went. Together, the three of them stumbled out into the night. A minute later Jackson heard an engine come to life followed by the squeal of tires spinning.

"You all, too, now," said the bartender.

The large man put his arms up, obliging the bartender and headed for the door. Jackson pulled a $20 dollar bill out of his money clip and put it on the bar.

"Sorry about everything," Jackson said.

The man only gave a short, annoyed grunt in response. Jackson followed the large man outside.

As the door opened, a cool breeze blew into Jackson. He watched as the man who had helped him walked over to a fire truck red Chevy Suburban that had to be from the early 90's.

"Have a good night," Jackson said as he walked past.

"I'm Bear, by the way," said the man, "In case you were wonderin' who saved your hide back there."

The man spoke with a southern accent as thick as gravy. His name piqued Jackson's curiosity.

"Bear," Jackson said, "As in the animal?"

"Yep," Bear said, "I have a real name, too. Long as hell. But folks just got to calling me Bear. So, Bear it is"

"Alright, Bear," Jackson replied, "Thanks for your help back there."

Jackson turned to continue walking, but Bear wasn't done.

"Y'know, if you need help trackin' those clowns down, I can give ya a hand," Bear said.

"That's alright, I'll manage," Jackson replied.

"Sure, sure. Well, can't say I didn't offer," Bear said back.

The statement stopped Jackson again. This time he was the one that wasn't done.

"You've seen those guys around before," Jackson asked.

"Of course. Those dingleberries are always around causing trouble," Bear answered, "Them and their lot."

"Their lot," asked Jackson.

"Sure. There's a whole group of 'em. Live off in the woods maybe 30-40 minutes from here."

"There's more of them?"

"Oh, plenty more."

Jackson turned back now, walking towards Bear. The large, burly man who had whacked one of the guys he'd been following with a pool stick now had his undivided attention.

"Alright, Bear," Jackson said, "Is there a place we can talk?"

"There's plenty of places, but I don't meet with strangers," Bear said giving a big, boyish smile.

It took Jackson a moment to understand what Bear was getting at.

"Sorry about that," he said. "I'm Jackson. Jackson Clay."

"Jackson Clay, good to meet ya," said Bear extending a hand, "Name's Archibald Beauchamp."

"Archibald Beauchamp," repeated Jackson.

"Yeah. My folks are from New Orleans. Ma was a big Archie Manning fan. Don't ask."

"I didn't."

"Anyways, like I said, you can just call me Bear."

Jackson met his hand with his own and shook it.

"Alright, Bear," Jackson said, "So is there a place a we can talk?"

"Well," Bear replied, "I suppose you could buy me a beer. You know, on account of I didn't get to finish mine back there. Thanks to you."

Bear flashed another boyish grin.

"You got another place to get that beer," asked Jackson, "I'm guessing Moe Szyslak in there isn't going to welcome us back anytime soon."

"Moe, like The Simpsons," said Bear, letting out a hearty laugh, "Well, man. Shoot, I don't know. Actually, you know, there's an Applebee's on up the road and I could go for some riblets. I was going to get dinner here. But you know."

Bear's cravings were leveraging the situation. Jackson smiled and nodded.

"Sure, Bear. Food's on me," he said

"Alright then," Bear said with a giddy smile, "Meet ya there?"

Jackson gave him another polite smile.

"No problem. I'll follow you."

48

Ten minutes later, Jackson was seated opposite Bear Beauchamp in an Applebee's, as Bear had promised, just down the road in Rocky Mount. On the way over, he'd called Detective Bailey and asked her to run Bear's record. She'd already gone home, but put Jackson in touch with a detective still there who ran Beauchamp and sent Jackson the information.

Aside from a couple of speeding tickets and one "Willful Discharge of a Firearm in a Public Place," Bear Beauchamp was a 38-year-old Martinsville resident who had few run-ins with the law. Jackson couldn't help but wonder if the man had an angle beyond just a free meal in all this, but for now he was happy to have whatever Bear knew.

On top of the riblets, Bear had decided he needed to start off with some wings. He'd eaten one too many without anything to wash it down and was now panting as he looked around for the waitress.

"Okay, hon, we didn't have any Miller High Life, so I brought you a Miller Lite," said the waitress, "Is that okay?"

Bear nodded hastily, motioning with his hand for her to bring it over. He took it from her hand, nodded in thanks, and put half of it away before coming up for air. Jackson had never seen anyone with such a voracious appetite for fermented grain and meat.

"How is it," asked Jackson.

"It's no High Life, but it'll do right now," Bear answered.

"High Life's that good, huh," Jackson asked.

Bear put down the beer and looked at him with a serious stare.

"It's the champagne of beers, Jack," he answered before letting out a breathy howl.

Bear laughing the hardest at his own punchlines was becoming a thing.

"It's too bad they don't serve it no more in yuppie places like this," Bear said, "Everyone wants microbrews and IPAs and organic ciders these days. Can you imagine? Microbrews. Who wants a tiny little beer?"

Bear slammed his fist and laughed again.

"Applebee's is a yuppie place," Jackson asked.

"Any place with clean bathrooms is a yuppie place to a rural lifestyle enthusiast like myself," Bear said smiling.

"Rural lifestyle enthusiast?"

"Yeah, it's like redneck, but more polite. Us rednecks prefer the term."

Jackson had known many self-described rednecks in his life. He'd never heard the term before. The waitress returned, dropping off a stack of napkins at the table. If Bear had noticed the insinuation, he didn't seem particularly offended.

"Are you sure I can't get anything for you, hon," the waitress asked Jackson.

He watched as Bear actually let out an involuntary growl biting into a chicken wing.

"I'm good, thanks," answered Jackson, "I'll stick with my iced tea."

The waitress smiled and headed off to another table. Jackson watched as Bear made a slurping noise, pulling a bone lengthwise between his lips. He dropped it on the plate and grabbed a couple of the napkins, wiping buffalo sauce from his beard.

"So, those guys back there," Jackson said, "You say you knew them."

Bear nodded as he tore into another wing.

"Everyone around here knows their type," answered Bear, "No one's particularly fond of them, neither."

"What do you mean 'their type'," Jackson asked.

Bear waited a moment, chewing what was in his mouth and swallowing it before leaning in closer to Jackson and speaking in a hushed tone.

"The Lokos," Bear said.

"The who," Jackson asked.

"The, um. Hold on, I know their full name. The Living Order of the Kingdom of Solomon," Bear answered, "You ever heard of them?"

Jackson wasn't sure if this was a set up for another one of his jokes.

"No, can't say that I have," Jackson answered.

"They're a group. A, what do you call it, a cult, I guess," Bear said.

"You're saying these three are members of a cult," Jackson asked skeptically.

"Yeah. I mean, what else do you call a group of people that live off in the woods and keep to themselves?"

"That's what they do?"

"Yeah. A group of them have a place in the woods. They have some name for it. The New City or whatever. The people out there call themselves the Living Order of the Kingdom of Solomon. I just got to calling them Lokos for short. You know, on account that they're batshit crazy."

"Lokos?"

"Yeah. Like the Mexican word for crazy or whatever. Their name, it spells out—"

"I got it. So, what do they do out there?"

"Shit, whatever the hell they want. No one messes with those fuckers. If for no other reason than they're armed to the teeth."

"And they all stay at this place? The New City?"

"Lokoville. That's what I call it. Easier. Sure, they'll go out and do shit. It's not unlike them to be at a bar like they were. But they spend most of their time there. All of them live there."

The waitress came by again and dropped off Bear's riblets as well as a handful of wet-naps. Again, Bear didn't seem to mind the implication as he slid aside the devoured chicken limbs and began pulling off pieces of barbecued pork and popping them into his mouth.

"So, do you know where this place is," Jackson asked, "Do you know how to get there?"

"I can do you one better," answered Bear, "I can show you myself. Not now, though. Too dangerous at night. Tomorrow morning, we can go if you want."

"You'd do that," Jackson asked.

Bear nodded as he began dissecting his second riblet. Jackson realized in all that had happened he'd never visited Jeff Isaacs to ask what had happened to Olivia and whether or not it could have anything to do with Sara Beth. Obviously, the van was more important. And now there was all this. And Bear, who had seemed to wiggle his way into the middle of it for very little. Now Jackson was curious.

"Let me ask you something," Jackson said, "Why are you doing all this? First stepping in at the bar, and now with this group?"

Bear put down the riblet and stared at Jackson. He seemed almost offended by the question.

"You said this was about a little girl, didn't you," Bear asked. "Someone took her or something?"

"A sixteen-year-old girl from Harrisonburg, yes," answered Jackson.

"Well who wouldn't want to help find some poor girl," asked Bear. "And besides, those guys are assholes."

Jackson didn't say anything back. The simplicity of his reasoning was refreshing. Jackson had spent the last three days turning over rocks, looking in places people didn't want to think about, looking for a little girl. And here, in all this wrong, was Archibald 'Bear' Beauchamp, who wanted to help for no other reason than help was needed. A little smile stretched across Jackson's face.

"Say, Jack," Bear said, "You want to go halfsies on dessert?"

49

The next morning, Jackson met Bear on a quiet stretch of farmland road where one two-lane highway intersected with another. The area – exceptionally rural even for southern Virginia – was between Smith Mountain Lake and Martinsville, the small town known for its NASCAR events.

Jackson spotted Bear's old red Suburban as he came around the bend and pulled up behind it. Bear was unloading a 4-wheel drive UTV with side-by-side seats and a small storage bed in the back, all covered in a RealTree camouflage wrap. He backed it up off a trailer attached to his truck and parked it facing down a dirt road that pointed directly at a wooded mountainside to the west.

"That's quite the vehicle there," Jackson said, getting out of his truck.

"Yeah, us rural lifestyle enthusiasts love our toys," Bear replied.

"Are we just leaving our trucks here," Jackson asked.

"Yeah, we'll just lock 'em up. Nobody will bother 'em out here."

"Alright, if you say so."

Bear grabbed a jerry can of gasoline out of the tailgate of his truck and put it in the back of the UTV. He shut the tailgates on both vehicles and walked around to the passenger-side door of his Suburban.

"Are you strapped," Bear asked.

"I have a Sig Sauer P320 in my truck," answered Jackson.

"Probably best if you grab that," Bear replied.

Jackson remembered Bear saying the Lokos were armed, but was surprised when he saw Bear step out of his truck carrying a Ruger AR-556 Rifle with a holographic sight, foregrip, and flashlight. Jackson had carried less special equipment as an Army Ranger.

"Is that really necessary," asked Jackson, nodding towards the rifle.

"What, this? You know what they say in boy scouts: be prepared," Bear answered.

"I don't remember many boy scouts having assault rifles," Jackson said.

"Must not have been in our troop, then," Bear replied.

Jackson fetched his pistol out of his truck and slid it into the leg holster on his side.

"You ready," Bear asked.

"Yup," Jackson replied.

"C'mon then, hop in," Bear said.

The UTV growled to life as Bear keyed the ignition. He put it in gear and took off down the dirt road. The field of soy beans on Jackson's right gave way to a thicket of trees as they slipped in underneath the wooded canopy. The road transitioned into a gravel grade barely wide enough for two cars side by side. Climbing in elevation, it wound its way around the face of the mountain, with the earth ascending upwards towards the sky on Bear's side and sliding downwards into a steep ravine on Jackson's side. Without the luxury of some sort of guard rail, Jackson had a clear view all the way down as the UTV traced the edge of the road.

Bear took the twists and turns of the road at speed, anticipating each bend the way only someone very familiar with the area could. Jackson was leaning out of the UTV looking down the steep mountainside when a large limestone boulder flashed past him, brushing him backwards into the vehicle. Bear let out a boyish cackle and helped Jackson right himself.

"You okay, buddy," Bear asked, still laughing.

"Fine, thanks," Jackson retorted, less than amused.

He looked back at the boulder that had nearly taken his face off. It was one of a pair of monstrous rocks that dotted each side of the road like an entranceway.

"This road is the only road across these mountains here for miles," Bear yelled over the engine of the UTV, "It has some official county name, but folks here just get to callin' it the mountain road."

"And this goes right to where this group is," Jackson asked.

"Their place is off of this," Bear answered, "Trust me, you won't get there before running into dudes with guns."

"Is that the plan for today?"

"Hell no. Not if I can help it. I know a spot where you can see the place. Just have to keep an eye out. The area is always crawling with those lokos."

The road climbed to a peak where an even smaller dirt road intersected it. A wooden sign read Callands-Gretna Gap with an arrow pointing. Bear pulled the wheel hard to the right, the UTV skidding sideways as it made the turn. This smaller road, barely wide enough for the UTV, climbed even higher from where the other peaked. Bear took the UTV all the way up it before coming to a stop as the road leveled off.

"We'll walk it from here," Bear said, "Any closer and the lokos will hear the Ranger from the overlook."

Jackson assumed he was referring to the UTV.

"I'd make sure there's a round in that peashooter of yours," Bear said grabbing his rifle.

"Are these guys really that dangerous," Jackson asked.

"Up here, yeah," Bear answered, "Down in town, they'll mind their P's and Q's as much as they can, but this is their turf. They have a knack for, what's the phrase, shooting first and asking questions later?"

"Law enforcement doesn't get involved?"

"Law enforcement? Local sheriff figures what they do out here on their own is their business. Sure, if one of them has one too many in town they end up in the drunk tank, but out here? This isn't the town."

"And you just come out here to what? Mix it up with them?"

"I've been hunting these grounds ever since my daddy took me out here before I was even in school. The way I see it, they're stepping on *my* toes, not the other way around."

Up ahead in front of Bear, Jackson could see there was a break in the trees. As Bear got closer to it, he began to walk in a crouch before going all the way to the ground, army crawling. Jackson followed suit. As he scooped dead leaves past him, Jackson made his way just barely into the opening. The trees had parted on the edge of a steep mountain face that over looked a clearing in the forest below.

"There you go," Bear said, handing him a pair of binoculars, "Welcome to cult country."

Jackson looked down at the area. An array of buildings dotted the clearing with more nestled in the woods. Most of them were simple wooden structures except for a large, weathered, red brick building near the edge of the clearing. A rusting smoke stack came out of the back of it and towered over the forest surrounding it.

"What's that large brick building," Jackson asked.

"Part of an old abandoned lumber mill," Bear answered, "The rest of it burned down decades ago. Folks who ran it never repaired it and just left. The first lokos lived in there before branching out as they got bigger."

Jackson put the binoculars up to his eyes and took a closer look. People, mostly men, milled about like ants on an ant hill. Unlike ants, though, just about everyone was carrying a gun of some kind. Mostly hunting rifles slung around shoulders or pistols on the hip, but there were others walking around with assault-style rifles. It even looked to Jackson like a couple might be wearing body armor.

"These guys really believe in the second amendment, huh," Jackson said.

"Oh, they love their guns alright," Bear replied, "Can't say that makes them very different than the rest of us around here, though."

The doors to the red brick building swung open and out walked one of the men Jackson had gotten into it with at the bar. It was the guy whose face Jackson had smashed a beer bottle into. Someone had bandaged his face up with gauze wrapped around his head. It left his face partially concealed, but he was still wearing the same biker vest and faded jeans.

"It's one of the guys from the bar," Jackson said.

"The Kerley brothers, yeah" replied Bear, "I wasn't lying when I said they were part of all this."

Jackson watched the man as he walked around one of the wooden buildings and headed into the tree cover. A moment later a black van emerged, following a dirt-covered path between the buildings until it disappeared into the woods on the far side of the clearing.

He wondered if the Kerley brothers were the men who took Sara Beth that night. Had they brought her here? The van was here. An uneasy feeling came over Jackson as he thought about Sara Beth down there, a hostage to a community of armed, as Bear put it, lokos. Was she okay? Was she even still alive?

Jackson thought finding who took Sara Beth Parker would bring answers. For now, all it had brought was more questions.

PART III

STORM

50

The next day, Jackson was sitting in a motel in the tiny town of Gretna, unpacking his things. The Pitts Inn, a drab, one-level enterprise, had rooms arranged in a horseshoe that opened into a courtyard with a pool that hadn't seen any kind of care for weeks. When Jackson asked if he could pay cash, the clerk asked if he was paying by the hour.

The Pitts Inn was aptly named, Jackson thought.

Overnight, he'd packed up and headed out of Harrisonburg and moved closer to the wooded valley the lokos called home. He'd returned quickly to his home outside The Plains to grab some extra equipment. If Sara Beth Parker was being held by the people in that complex, getting her out was going to be far different than what he normally dealt with. He picked up three more guns – two rifles and a shotgun – and all the camping and outdoor equipment his truck bed would fit.

Jackson had laid out each firearm on the bed in front of him, meticulously stripping down each, inspecting it, then cleaning it. He was halfway through working on the shotgun when his phone buzzed. It was Detective Bailey returning his call.

"Are you alone," Jackson asked.

"Hello to you too," replied Bailey, "No, I'm not. I'm in the office."

"Get some place alone and call me back," Jackson said.

Jackson put the phone down. He finished up the shotgun and put it aside, then went over to a large case and pulled out his digital SLR camera with a large telephoto zoom lens attached to it. He looked through the viewfinder and snapped a test shot when his phone buzzed again.

"Alright," Detective Bailey said, "What's up?"

"I need some information," Jackson replied.

"What else is new," Bailey replied.

"I need some info I think you're going to want to deliver in person. No emails."

"That's cryptic. Are you still in Harrisonburg?"

"No. Gretna."

"Where?"

"Gretna. It's a town southeast of Smith Mountain Lake."

"Jesus, what are you doing out there?"

Jackson paused.

"What do you know about the Living Order of the Kingdom of Solomon," Jackson asked.

"The Living Or—you mean the gun nuts out there," Bailey asked back.

"Yeah," Jackson replied, "Are you familiar with them?"

"A little. Not enough to – wait, you think they had something to do with the Parker girl?"

"We can talk when we meet. Can you pull everything you guys have on them and meet me tomorrow?"

"All the way down there?"

"I'll meet you halfway. Charlottesville. That park we used on the Dormer case."

"Okay."

Jackson ended the second call. He checked his watch. It was an hour before noon. He'd promised to meet Bear at his place for lunch and "talk about what to do next". Jackson got the idea that this was all some sort of adventure for Bear, that he didn't fully appreciate what was at stake. Still, Jackson knew he would be nowhere near as close to finding Sara Beth without the man's help. He was thankful for that.

Getting all the extra equipment situated could wait. Jackson grabbed his things and headed out.

51

Bear lived in a quaint Craftsman bungalow north of Martinsville, its white siding in need of a good wash. Adjacent to the house was a camper trailer and a large, warehouse-style shed. It was from this large shed that Bear emerged in a seafoam green Ford F-350 Super Duty with a utility body as Jackson pulled up. Bear gave him a hearty wave before backing the truck into a tree. The paint marks on the trunk seemed to imply it wasn't the first time.

"Son of a bitch," Bear growled, hopping out to assess the damage.

"You alright," asked Jackson, walking up.

"Yeah, I need to just cut that goddamn tree down," Bear answered.

"That's quite the color on it. The truck, I mean."

"Yeah. Forest Service paint job. I bought her at auction a couple years ago. Just pulling her out to make room for the tractor."

"You need any help?"

"Nah, c'mon. Where's my hospitality? Let's get some grub."

Bear walked him up the front porch adorned with two couches clearly not intended for outdoor use and led him through the house. A living area just inside the front door had little more than a recliner, lamp and unnecessarily large TV. The room opposite had more furniture, all of which was centered around a mantle that held what looked to be collectible McDonald's glasses.

"Did I lose ya in here," shouted Bear from further in the house, "Come on out back."

The house had a back deck that overlooked an impressive piece of property. A rolling grass hill slid down into an algae-covered pond tucked up against the woods beyond. Jackson figured it had to be no less than a couple acres.

"This is quite the place you've got here," Jackson said.

"Thankya. I put a lot of work into it," Bear replied, "You want a beer?"

"No, thanks," said Jackson, "Little early for me."

Bear shrugged and opened the can he had offered to Jackson. He walked over to the grill at the end of the deck and ignited the propane burners.

"Some burgers good with you," Bear asked.

"Sounds great," Jackson replied

The grill hissed with gas before igniting to life as Bear stepped inside for a moment and returned with a tray of patties, placing them on the table next to the grill.

"So, what does one do for a living to get themselves a place like this, if you don't mind me asking," asked Jackson.

"Oh, this and that. Mom and Dad left me a good bit of money, to tell ya the truth. Used to raise ostriches for meat and eggs," Bear replied.

Jackson looked up at him, skeptical.

"I shit you not," Bear said raising his hands, "I bought a hunting shop right in town over there. Another fella and I own it together. Nice guy."

"Is that how you came to know these lokos," asked Jackson, "Through the shop?"

"Oh, you can't live within 10 or 15 miles of Lokoville without knowing who lives out there," said Bear, "Maybe if you live under a rock or something, I suppose. Shit, some people out here do."

"What do they do out there in Lokoville besides keep to themselves? They into anything? Drugs or anything like that?"

"Don't really know, to tell you the truth. They don't exactly let people in and have a look around."

"Do you think they're the type to take a little girl?"

"Let's just say I don't think they're out there just for the peace and quiet, you know what I mean? There ain't much they could be mixed up in that would surprise me."

Bear threw the first patties on the grill, the meat sizzling as it hit the hot metal. He took out a salt shaker, sprinkled a handful into his beefy paw, and cocked his elbow and wrist in opposite directions, making a swan-like pose with his arm.

"Ha, you get it," Bear said, "Like that salt bae guy on YouTube."

Jackson gave him a gratuitous smile and nod. He didn't have any earthly idea who Bear was talking about.

"Do you think that's why they pack so much firepower," Jackson asked.

Bear shrugged without looking up from the grill.

"More people have guns out here than don't," Bear said, "Them being armed might be the least crazy thing about them."

"What makes them crazy, then," Jackson asked, "You say they're a cult. They have some sort of mission?"

"Not really that I know of," Bear answered, "Mostly to do what they want and be left alone. Like I said, they're not a friendly bunch. Even the ones that work the marina. You'd think they'd put on a smile for the customers. Uh uh."

"The marina?"

"Yeah. They run a bait and tackle shop on Smith Mountain Lake with a small dock attached. Guys there call it the marina. I assume it's how they pay for all that they have in the woods there. Must be pretty good business during tourist season."

"I'm going to want to check that place out, too, then. Do they carry guns around there the way they do in Lokoville?"

"No, no. Like I said, out with the rest of us, they lay low as much as they can."

Bear flipped the burgers on the grill and sprinkled them with salt again, this time without any theatrics. He polished off his beer, crushed it in his fist, and disappeared inside once more.

"I saw what they carried out in the woods, though. I ran back home and got some heavier stuff myself," Jackson said, talking louder so Bear could hear him.

Bear reappeared at the door with a devilish grin on his face.

"Oh, brother, you didn't have to do that," he said with a menacing chuckle, "You want firepower, I've got your firepower right here. Follow me."

Bear motioned him inside and led him down a hallway. The last room at the end of the hallway held little more than a large desk and a chair, but on the far wall was a built-in bookshelf filled to capacity. Bear walked over to the center of it, grabbed a hold of something, and pulled forward.

The center of the bookshelf swung outward like French doors to reveal an armament that rivaled a small barracks. Jackson clenched his jaw, feeling like it might drop if he didn't keep it in check.

"Impressive, ain't it," Bear asked with a beaming smile.

"That'd be one way to describe it," Jackson replied.

He looked the display over. There had to be over a dozen guns in all. Closer to two dozen, probably. There was everything from 9mm pistols to stuff he hadn't seen since his Ranger days.

"Is that an M2 .50 Cal machine gun," Jackson asked, doubting what he was seeing.

"Yeah," Bear answered, "She's a beaut, ain't she?"

"Sure," Jackson replied, "This all can't be legal, though. I mean, there's no way—"

"Eh, legal-ish."

"Legal-ish?"

"You know. Quasilegal. What I like to say is, what big brother don't know about, big brother don't need to worry about."

Jackson didn't dare ask him how he went about acquiring such things and kind of feared this hunting shop Bear co-owned might be a front for something more nefarious. It was clear Bear could bring a gun fight if need be, but Jackson didn't want it to come to that. Shootouts put holes in people. He didn't want Sara Beth Parker anywhere near one.

Bear closed the bookcase and led Jackson back out to the back deck.

Grease had pooled on the bottom of the grill and now a small inferno engulfed the ground beef on the grill.

"God, dammit," Bear stammered as he rushed over to the grill.

Quickly, he scooped the burgers out of the flames and onto a plate, but the damage had already been done. All he'd salvaged was a pile of hockey pucks that loosely resembled burger patties.

"Well, I don't think we're having burgers today, I'm sorry to say," Bear said, staring at the charred remains.

"That's alright, I'm not super hungry, anyways," Jackson replied.

Bear shut the lid of the grill to snuff out the fire. He opened up the trash can with his foot and shoveled the burnt beef into the garbage.

"Well, can I get ya a beer now," Bear asked.

"Still good. Thanks, though," Jackson replied.

Bear reached into the cooler and fetched himself another one, popping it open and taking a noisy slurp before wiping the excess foam off his beard.

"So, what's the next step," asked Bear.

"Well," Jackson began, "We have to find out if the lokos really have Sara Beth. They must, but I have to be sure. And I have to know where."

"You mean we have to know," Bear asked, "Do you know why they'd want her?"

"God knows. You tell me."

"All I know is those people are in it for themselves. If they've got her, and she ain't one of them, she's in trouble."

Jackson sighed. Bear was only saying what Jackson had thought. That Sara Beth was in danger was a given from the start. But these people, these lokos, were a different beast.

He turned away from Bear and looked out at the backyard as he leaned against the railing. Jackson watched as a heron stalked something in the pond. It watched the dark void below, finding its target and moving stealthily around it. Then, in a blink, it struck downwards, hitting its prey with lethal precision.

"With you owning that shop and all," Jackson asked, "you like to hunt?"

"Of course, yeah," Bear answered.

"That's good. That's real good, Bear," Jackson said, "Because we're going hunting."

52

The next morning, Jackson met Bailey at McIntire Park in Charlottesville, a sprawling recreational campus north of downtown just a few miles from the infamous 2017 protests led by white supremacists. With baseball fields, a skate park, hiking trails, and even a small golf course, it was a monument to suburbanite weekends. But here, on a weekday morning, the park was practically deserted save for Clay, Bailey, and a few park employees who kept a curious eye on the two cars parked side by side.

Bailey got out of her car and climbed into Jackson's truck.

"Morning," said Jackson, "Got you a cup of coffee."

"That was nice of you," Bailey replied.

"Least I could do," Jackson said.

Bailey took the coffee as well as the two sweetener packets Jackson had left on top of it, and mixed them together, stirring with her finger.

"So, what have you got," Jackson asked.

"Here," she answered.

She reached into her bag and pulled out a folder overflowing with documents. She shuffled through them quickly, double checking everything was there, and then handed it over to Jackson.

"The Living Order of the Kingdom of Solomon," Detective Bailey began, "Or LOKS, as we call them—"

"Lokos," Jackson interjected.

"What," Bailey asked.

"Nothing. A local I talked to calls them Lokos. Like crazy."

"Ah. Well, most agencies' shorthand for them is LOKS. Anyway, they don't fit neatly into any one category. They're part religious cult, part private militia, part co-op community. They basically check every box to ensure the authorities don't lean on them too hard."

"What do you mean?"

"It's guns and religion. You push too hard and miss, you're looking at a lawsuit. Hell, most of these groups are right wing but you'll have the ACLU coming to their defense. No one wants that kind of a headache. Plus, unlike most religious groups, LOKS isn't very big on recruiting. They mostly keep their numbers a close-knit group."

"Making it hard to get someone inside."

"Right. That's usually what's needed to break these types of cases. Both FBI and ATF have tried a couple of times over the years. Neither got close."

"Are they truly religious or is it just for show?"

"The honest answer is we don't know. The guy that seems to be in charge is named Solomon Ash. He was born Benjamin Asher, but changed his name a few years back, well, we're guessing for the Kingdom of Solomon bit. He has a brother, too. Silas Asher. He seems to be in some sort of leadership role, as well. It's all in those files there."

"I see."

"In terms of legitimacy, they tried and failed to file as a 501(c) charity. That's how most religious establishments avoid taxes and prying eyes from the government."

"So they aren't officially a religious group?"

"Not necessarily. The IRS has the strictest standards for proof. Anyone trying to prosecute them in court would have a much harder time. Judges aren't quick to mess with the first amendment, even if it involves a pair of career criminals."

Jackson thumbed through the files until he came to the information on the Ashers. Both had been born to a Lilith Asher, Benjamin – or Solomon – in 1984, and Silas in 1990. Lilith Asher was born in 1969, making her just 15 when she had Solomon. Her official record began when she was an adult, at 18. A series of soliciting and possession charges for the better part of two decades until her death in 2006 at age 37.

"Tough family life," Jackson said.

"Yeah," Bailey replied, "Solomon and Silas were wards of the state for the vast majority of their childhood. It's not in there because the files are sealed, but their mother's legal trouble began the year after Solomon was born. Her parents took care of Solomon for a few years, hoping their daughter would get clean. But sometime after she developed a record as an adult, they gave the kids up."

Jackson continued to read Solomon's and Silas' files. Neither one finished high school. Solomon attempted to enlist in the Army but washed out. The next year he became Silas' official guardian. From there, their records told most of their story. Silas appeared to be simple and violent. A slew of aggravated assaults that were never pursued, an aggravated robbery, and a resisting arrest with assault on a peace officer. Solomon's record, on the other hand, read like a sociopath's origin story. Animal cruelty, grand theft, destruction of property. Jackson put a finger on the page when he got to one line in particular.

"What's this attempted kidnapping with Solomon," Jackson asked.

"Well, Benjamin at the time," Bailey answered, "Apparently he bought a car from this guy only to find out the car was missing several parts. The guy thought he could sell some chump the car and then hold onto some parts to sell to someone else. Asher shows up to this guy's house with a snub nose revolver and holds the whole family inside the house until the guy gives him his money back."

"What a guy," Jackson exclaimed.

"Which one?"

"Exactly. Do you think he could escalate to actual abduction?"

"Who knows. Probably. I think the question to ask is to what extent? He doesn't strike me as a sex predator, so what would be his need for taking a girl like Sara Beth?"

"I guess that's for me to find out."

"I guess so."

Detective Bailey zipped up her bag as Jackson continued to flip through a few pages. She looked down at the page he was studying. It was the business information on the bait and tackle shop on Smith Mountain Lake that the Lokos ran.

"What do you know about this business of theirs," Jackson asked.

"Not much," Bailey answered, "They opened it shortly after their 501(c) application failed. Probably got some good advice to make their finances look legitimate. They claim the profits off of that place pay for everything at their compound. It's hard to prove otherwise, given their secrecy."

"Maybe it's time someone took a closer look," Jackson said.

He closed up the file packet and put it on the rear seats. As Detective Bailey watched him reach back, she noticed the Pelican case sitting on the rear seat. She spent enough time in law enforcement to know it was for a gun.

"Jackson," Bailey said, "I know I don't have to tell you this, but if you're going to go looking around at these guys, be careful."

"I always am," Jackson replied.

"I'm serious," Bailey said, "From what my colleague in the ATF told me, these guys don't fuck around. The local law enforcement looks the other way on most everything. If you go snooping around out there, these aren't the kind of people who call the police to report a trespasser. These are the kind that shoot you and dig a hole in the woods."

"I've got it."

Bailey gave a nervous smile and nodded before climbing out of the truck.

"If you need anything else," she said, "Just call."

Jackson watched as she walked over to her Jetta and pulled out. He took out his phone and punched in a number.

"Bear," he said, "It's Jackson. Meet me at the Lokos' marina this afternoon. It's time to get to work."

53

P enhook Bait & Tackle sat like a hangnail on one of the countless fingers of land that clawed at Smith Mountain Lake. A large asphalt parking lot sun washed by years of existence sloped down into and dwarfed the quaint sky-blue shop that sat at the edge of the water and the small array of docks that lay beyond. Next to it, a strip of large garages, no doubt intended to house boats, lined the bottom of the parking lot with a tattered trailer home bookending it on the other side.

Jackson and Bear rolled up on the parking lot slowly, scoping the place out. Unlike the New City of David, which had been busy with people scurrying about in every direction, the bait shop looked deserted from the outside. Only one truck with a boat trailer was parked in the parking lot.

"Doesn't look like much," Bear said, "Maybe they're closed."

"No, there's someone in there," Jackson replied, "Just isn't busy."

Jackson drove across the lot and parked in front of the bait shop. He climbed out and looked around. The area was serene. Houses and docks dotted the sprawling coastline, interspersed with sassafras, oak, and maple trees. He imagined in mid-summer the area filled with the sounds of vacationers and day trippers relaxing on the lake, kids playing as boats roared by. Now, though, it was just quiet.

Behind him, a creaky door kicked open and a man in a dirty shop apron stuck his wiry frame out from the bait shop.

"Can I help y'all," the man asked, almost suspicious of them being there.

"Yes, you can, actually," Jackson said, "Sorry, I was taking in the view. It's beautiful here."

"Yeah, I suppose," replied the man, "What do you need?"

"Actually, my friend here and I were looking to keep our boat around here somewhere and we figured we'd check out your shop."

"Alright, well come in here. I'll get you our information on dockage."

Bear and Jackson followed the man into the shop. Inside, the store was filled with cramped aisles lined with fishing and boating equipment. A counter on the far side had pricier items like poles and reels behind it.

"You break anything, you're paying for it," the man said, minding Jackson's wandering eyes, "I've got your information over here."

He stepped behind the counter and began looking below. Jackson watched him from the far end of the counter. The man was an older man, with a short, unkempt beard and receding hairline, both of which were venturing to gray. His denim shop apron was smeared with a confused mixture of grease and oil and got in his way as he shuffled things around on the ground. Jackson heard the man rattle off a few four-letter words before popping up with a large binder. He opened it and swung it around to face away from him.

"These are the rates by length of time," the man said, "If you sign up before the end of the month, you get a 5% early discount."

"Alright, perfect. Thanks," Jackson replied, walking over.

He pretended to look over the rates as a prospective customer would. When he felt he'd studied them long enough, he looked back up at the man.

"Seems pretty reasonable," Jackson said, "You mind if we walk out there and take a look for ourselves?"

"Fine," the man said, "Just don't go wandering off. And like I said, you break anything, you're paying for it. I don't care if it's for sale or not."

"Not a problem," Jackson replied.

He walked out the side door with Bear in tow and followed the steps down to the water. The center dock was built on posts driven into to the lake bed. Smaller floating docks affixed with stairs branched off on either side forming the boat slips. The whole thing struck Jackson as a barebones operation.

"I don't very well think she's down there, buddy," Bear said from behind.

Jackson turned to look at him.

"No, but there's those garages and a trailer over there," he said, "We need to have a look in there."

"And how do you plan on doing that with Oscar the Grouch in there," Bear asked.

"You're going to chat him up," Jackson answered.

"I'm going to what? About what?"

"Talk to him about fishing or something."

Jackson walked past him and began heading back towards the store.

"Fishing," Bear said with a look of disgust, "I use a gun, Jack. No pussy stick and string."

"Then ask him about shooting fish," Jackson retorted.

Bear muttered something under his breath but Jackson couldn't make it out. He took the stairs to the store two at a time. When he got to the back corner of the building he turned and looked at Bear walking at a more leisurely pace, protesting his role in the plan. Jackson waited until Bear was looking back at him then made a gesture with his face for him to go into the store. Bear, continuing passive rebellion, ambled towards the store and opened the door.

"Say, uh, what kind of motors do most folks run around here," he asked as he disappeared inside.

The door shut and a muffled conversation continued.

Jackson waited a minute and then slowly crossed the back of the store. From there, at the point of the little finger of land, Jackson was concealed from everything except the water.

He checked the gap between the store and the garages. There was no one. Ducking down, he hurried across the opening and continued making his way along the back of the garages.

At the far end was a door with a window. Sliding his way down to it, Jackson put his face to the glass and looked inside. Each bay of the garage housed a boat in a varied stage of disrepair. All four were raised up, making it easy to see the rest of the garage area by the light that filtered through the large door windows on the other side. There was no one inside.

The last thing he needed to check before doubling back to Bear was the trailer. But situated in the open several hundred feet from the garages, there was no way to get there while remaining hidden. Jackson had no choice. Checking that no one was watching him, he stood up and casually walked over to the trailer.

The trailer itself was 30 feet long, sitting on four tires and a trailer post. The mud caked on the outside complimented the brown and beige paint scheme.

All four windows on the face of the trailer, including the ones on each door, had the blinds drawn. Jackson walked up to the first door and knocked on it, listening carefully. No one answered, nor did he hear any movement inside. Carefully, he checked the door handle. It was unlocked. Jackson looked around, double checking again that no one was watching, and opened the trailer door.

"Hello," Jackson said to the empty space inside.

Nothing returned his greeting.

He stepped up on the metal step hanging from the bottom of the trailer and leaned inside the door. From there, he could see the interior from end to end. It was empty. With a sigh, Jackson stepped down and shut the trailer.

Walking briskly, he headed back to the shop not worried about being spotted. Even before he got to the door, he could hear the clerk yelling something inaudible inside. Jackson steeled himself for a confrontation.

"Is everything okay in here," asked Jackson.

Bear turned and looked at him with an incredulous look on his face.

"Jack, this man has never seen *Cannonball Run*," Bear said, flustered.

Jackson exhaled, both relieved and unamused.

"I'm sorry for my friend. Low blood sugar and all," Jackson said to the store clerk as he grabbed Bear to usher him out, "I had a look around. Nice place you've got here. We'll be back for sure."

Jackson waved and stepped out, shoving Bear in front of him, before the man could reply. Bear was chuckling as the two of them walked back to Jackson's truck.

"Smooth," Jackson said.

"What," Bear asked with a devilish grin, "He was so annoyed with me, he didn't bother to wonder where you were."

Jackson didn't say anything back. Bear was smarter than he let on.

"So, did you find anything," Bear asked.

"No, no signs of her here," Jackson replied.

"So, what's next," asked Bear.

"I want to get a closer look at the compound. Lokoville. Is there a way to get closer?"

"There's always a way to get closer, it's just a matter of whether or not we're noticed."

"We need to find her. If she's not there, someone there knows where she is. First thing tomorrow morning, we go back in there."

"You got it."

The two of them climbed into Jackson's truck.

Across the long, sloping parking lot, hidden underneath a thicket of low-hanging oak trees, the Kerley brothers, each nursing wounds a few days old, watched from their black van as the two men that had pummeled them in a bar fight pulled out of the bait shop parking lot.

"It's them, alright," said the one in the driver's seat, "Call him."

"Fuck that," said the other, "*You* call him."

The driver stared at his brother, but the staring didn't coerce his sibling to make the call. Muttering something under his breath, the one behind the wheel pulled out his phone, punched something in, and put it to his ear.

"Sir, it's them," he said, "The two guys I told you about. They're snooping around the marina."

A gravelly voice with a southern drawl answered back on the other end of the line.

"Follow them."

54

As Jackson headed back to his motel in Gretna, he thought about the Lokos' compound in the middle of the woods. The couple hours he and Bear had watched the place it had been a hive of activity with little or no chance for someone to sneak in undetected. Going in at night probably wouldn't be any easier. The Lokos seemed to value privacy above all else.

Jackson headed East on State Route 40, the sun reaching out behind him with its last few forlorn rays of light as he drove into the indigo sky ahead. The road cut an east-west trail just south of Smith Mountain Lake through the woodlands of southern Virginia, pockmarked with the occasional small farm. A brisk wind rippled through his open windows as the warmth of the day disappeared with the sun.

Coming around a bend in the road, he slowed as he saw brake lights ahead. A construction crew was working on a bridge up ahead and had closed the road down to just one lane. His side was stopped as cars headed the other way passed through one by one.

It took only a minute or so for the cars to drive past, then the red taillights in line ahead of Jackson began to move into the other lane. Jackson lumbered forward in his pickup with the traffic. When his turn came to drive around, he waved at the flagger waving him through.

The flagger waved back before putting his hand up in a "stop" gesture to the next car in line. Jackson was the last one allowed through.

But as he drove around the construction, he heard commotion behind him. One car honked, followed by a second car. Men from the construction crew yelled as a car in line behind him decided it too was coming through and cut off the cars ahead of it as it pushed its way across the bridge.

What a jackass, Jackson thought.

But as he drove on, he noticed the car that had been in such a rush to push through was now hanging back, almost intentionally. Traffic was moving slow enough that those who had been waved through together were still almost bumper-to-bumper. The car behind Jackson, though, kept its distance. Something was wrong about it.

As he approached Gretna, Jackson took a sharp left away from his motel. The headlights behind him followed. When he got north of town, he took the first exit, a right turn, for Blue Ridge Drive. The headlights behind him took the same turn. Blue Ridge Drive looped back in a meandering arc south towards Gretna. Jackson took it the whole way, driving 5 mph under the speed limit. The headlights behind him followed, always keeping their distance. They'd followed Jackson almost in a complete circle around the small town.

He was certain now. Someone was following him.

Jackson reached for his phone and called Bear, whose quick answer surprised him.

"Jackie boy, I was just about to call you," Bear said, "Those Lokos from the bar. They were in that black van with the bright headlights. I think they're following me."

"Yeah, I've got a tail, too," Jackson replied, "Someone must've not liked us snooping around the marina."

"That's what I was thinking," Bear said, "What do you want to do?"

"Don't go home. Don't even go near your house."

"Yeah, no shit."

Jackson's thoughts ricocheted around in his mind, formulating a plan. Either he or Bear or both of them were going to need help shaking the people following them.

"Head for Rocky Mount," Jackson said, "Try to lose them on the way. I'll call you back."

Jackson ended the call. He got back on State Route 40 and headed back out of town the way he'd came. By now, whoever was following him must've realized they'd been made, but it wasn't fazing them. They kept following. Jackson switched the screen on his center console over to the truck's navigation map so he could see the roads nearby and where they went.

He drove past the exit for the marina and headed for Rocky Mount, all the while looking for an opportunity. A couple miles later, he saw one in the form of an 18-wheeler.

Pulling up behind it, Jackson slowed down to the truck's speed and followed it closely, waiting. He looked in his rearview mirror. The car following him had slowed down as well, keeping its distance. Jackson watched the oncoming traffic, waiting for the right moment.

Around a lazy turn, the road straightened out. Headlights appeared on the horizon up ahead. This was the chance he'd been looking for.

He waited until the car coming at them was closer, then swerved into the other lane and floored it. His Dodge Ram bucked upwards and charged forward as the engine revved past 6,000 rpm. Jackson drove right at the oncoming car, which was now frantically flashing its head-lights. The car following him tried to do the same, but it was too late. Jackson had gotten the jump he was looking for. He got past the semi and dove back into the right lane. The car he'd just played chicken with honked at him, the driver yelling out his window as he drove past. Angry as he might be, the driver had served his purpose, cutting off the car trying to follow Jackson, who had to duck back behind the truck and wait to pass.

Jackson sped ahead, creating distance between him and whoever was tailing him. When he finally lost sight of the headlights in his rearview mirror, he took the next turn off the highway and then the first turn off that road. He continued to do this for the next several minutes, taking the first turn off of every road that wasn't a dead end.

Convinced he'd lost them, Jackson pulled off the road and killed the lights. He looked at the navigation screen on his truck to see where he had ended up. It showed that he was north of a town called Glade

Hill. Route 40 was the most obvious way to Rocky Mount, but whoever had been tailing him would likely be on there, hoping to find him again. Jackson looked for a different, less obvious way to get to Rocky Mount and put it in the nav system.

As he continued on, he reached for his phone and called Bear back.

"What's going on, buddy," Bear said.

"I lost whoever was following me," Jackson replied, "What about you?"

"Nope, haven't been able to shake these assholes," Bear answered, "They're not being subtle, either. They've run two red lights to keep up with me."

Jackson had hoped Bear lost his tail, too, but it didn't matter. He'd shaken his and now he had a plan.

"Is there a department store or something over there," Jackson asked, "Something with a big parking lot that'll still be busy?"

"Yeah, there's a Walmart," Bear answered, "People are there all hours of the day."

"Great, drive over in the area of the Walmart," Jackson said, "Still try to shake them, though."

Jackson ended the call before Bear could respond. His navigation system said he was 14 minutes away, but as he raced down the backroads of southern Virginia, he shaved 4 minutes off that time to make it an even ten. When he saw the sign for the Walmart, he called Bear back.

"Are you near the Walmart," Jackson asked.

"Yes, sir," Bear replied.

"Okay, pull in to the parking lot and park around a lot of cars, but where you can still see what the van does," Jackson said.

"Gotcha."

"Tell me what they do."

Jackson turned left across the road and pulled into the parking lot himself and scanned it, looking for Bear. Sure enough, there was Bear in his red Suburban pulling in from the other entrance. He watched as Bear took a right down a row of parking spots and pulled into one. A second later, the van rolled in.

"They're looking at me, they just drove by the row I parked on," Bear said.

"I see them," Jackson replied, "Sit tight."

"I'm missing The Bachelorette right now, just so you know," Bear said.

Jackson ignored him. He watched the van amble through the walking shoppers as he circled it from the edges of the parking lot. The van turned off the main drag in front of the store and went down a row of spots two rows over from Bear. A car backed out of a spot and the van pulled through and parked with a perfect view of Bear's suburban. Jackson moved closer in his truck.

He saw the car directly in front of Bear back out and leave.

"Bear, pull forward so you don't have to back out when I tell you to go," Jackson said.

Bear didn't reply, but his red suburban rolled into the next parking spot. The set up was almost perfect. Jackson just needed the last piece to fall into place. He drove down one lane over from the van, buying more time. Just then, an old lady in a PT Cruiser pulled into the spot behind the van. They were boxed in on three sides. Jackson had his opportunity.

"Some old bag just pulled in behind the van," Bear said.

"I saw," Jackson replied, "I'm coming around now. When I tell you to, get lost."

Jackson turned onto the row with the van. When the lane cleared itself of shoppers, he hit the gas.

"Get ready," said Jackson.

He slammed on his breaks, all four tires screaming in pain as his truck slid to a stop in front of the van. The three Lokos from the bar – Mack and the Kerley brothers – were inside it, their eyes large and white.

"Now," ordered Jackson.

He opened his door, and headed for the driver side of the van. The three men inside slid away from the door, frantically hitting the lock button. Jackson pulled a knife out from his belt and punched the front tire. He stood back up, and looked at them, the trio watching him from the passenger seat with fear.

"You boys have a good night," Jackson shouted through the window.

He climbed back into his truck, taking the first exit out of the parking lot, and disappeared down the road.

Heading south, Jackson avoided the area he'd been around all day. As he drove, he noticed his phone was still connected to Bear. He picked it up off the passenger seat.

"Did you make it out clean," Jackson asked.

"Yes, sir, buddy boy," Bear answered, "Got nothing but darkness ahead and behind me."

"Good," Jackson replied, "Hurry on home. And get some extra sheets out for your couch. I'm sleeping over."

55

Jackson opened the door to his and Nathalie's townhouse in the Oregon Hill district of Richmond. Nathalie was sitting on the couch in the living room, nursing a glass of water, staring at the television. It wasn't on.

The coffee table in front of her, the very first piece of furniture they had bought together at an urban flea market, was overflowing with envelopes, most of them unopened. The mail since Evan disappeared had become a chore in and of itself. On top of the usual bills and junk mail now came hundreds of letters from strangers. Most of them were well-wishers offering their condolences. A small minority were nasty attacks directed at either them or Evan. Those were the ones Nathalie couldn't forget.

Jackson walked into the living room and sat down opposite Nathalie, his elbows on his knees and his hands clasping a stack of papers. He'd been reinvigorated with a sense of purpose.

"Nat, I found him," Jackson said.

Nathalie looked up from the blank television. She didn't look hopeful.

"You found Evan," Nathalie said, the doubt sharp in her tone.

"I think I found who took him," Jackson replied, "This guy, he was a seasonal worker at the park. He was in jail for—"

Nathalie stood up and walked to the kitchen, slamming her glass on the counter as she stared into the empty sink.

"What is it, Nathalie," Jackson asked.

"So, what? You're a detective now," Nathalie asked, "You're, what? Sherlock Holmes all of the sudden?"

"Come on, now," Jackson replied, "That's not fair. You told me to find him, I'm trying to find him."

"No, what's not fair is that my son is missing, no one seems to give a shit about it, and now I have to hear my husband's cockamamie theories as to who took him."

"Yeah, well, at least we're doing something about it, Nat. I'd rather be out there and try and fail 100 times than sit around here and mope and do nothing like some people."

"What am I supposed to do, Jackson? Hop in the mystery machine with you and the rest of the gang and pretend this is some big adventure?"

"No one here is enjoying this, Nat, least of all me. But you were right. We have to find him. We have to try. We can't just do nothing. Or, at least, I can't."

A silence fell over the kitchen, bringing an intermission to the argument. Nathalie turned on the faucet, waiting a moment for the water to get cold, and refilled her glass. She took a long, slow slip, before putting it down, still staring at the sink. Jackson rounded the kitchen island and approached her carefully, placing the papers on the counter. When he spoke again, his voice was calm.

"Would you at least look at what I found, Nat," Jackson asked, "Please? I really think there's something here."

"And what, Jackson," Nathalie asked back, "What if he did it? What are you going to do, arrest him?"

"I'm going to get our son back," Jackson answered.

"And what if he isn't there, Jackson?"

"Then I'll keep looking."

"That's not what I mean."

"Then what do you mean, Nat?"

Nathalie began to laugh. Or, at least, Jackson thought she was laughing. She looked like she could be crying just as well.

"I mean, Jackson," Nathalie said, her voice rising again, "What if he's gone? Not from that guy or whoever you find next, but gone for good."

"Nat, you can't think like that," Jackson answered.

"No, you see, Jackson, I do," Nathalie said, "Because you and your friends and your little cop pals are all running around here like it's only a matter of time before one of you saves the day. And none of you will say it. That he's been gone for over a month. That if he were going to be found, someone would've found him."

"What are you saying, Nat?"

"I'm saying he's gone, Jackson!"

"You don't know that."

"I do, Jackson. Deep, down inside, I know."

Jackson felt a rage build inside him. He knew he wasn't just angry at Nathalie. He was angry at everything. At the situation. At life for being so cruel. But right now, all he had in front of him was her.

"If he really is gone," Jackson seethed, "Then he went without his own mother doing a damn thing about it."

Nathalie turned and stared at him in disbelief, her face stricken with utter shock. Shock and betrayal. Her mind seemed to be searching for the words to say, but nothing came. She marched past Jackson, brushing him sideways with her shoulder as she passed, and continued out into the hallway.

"Where are you going," Jackson shouted.

"You want me to do something," Nathalie screamed back, "I'm doing something."

Jackson didn't leave the kitchen as the front door swung open before being slammed shut.

JACKSON FLINCHED from the sound of the door slamming as if it happened in Bear's living room and not just his head. His body jerked sideways, flipping off the couch. Jackson stuck his hands out, breaking his fall.

Bear leaned through the entryway from the kitchen, stirring something in a mug.

"You look just like a fish that landed on a boat of mine once," Bear said.

"I thought you didn't fish," Jackson replied, peeling himself off the floor.

"I didn't say I caught him," Bear said, "Damn thing jumped right onto my boat."

Jackson gave Bear a gratuitous smile, acknowledging the humor, as he sat back and plopped himself upright on the couch.

"You want some coffee," Bear asked.

"Sure," Jackson replied, wiping the sleep from his eyes.

He listened as Bear disappeared into the kitchen, cuing a melody of cabinets banging, mugs clanking, and a profanity-laced rant. There was also the sound of something sizzling on the stove, a fire had been started in the fireplace, and the coffee table now held an array of guns and spare magazines. Bear had clearly been awake for some time.

"I checked the wildlife cams I set up on the road and driveway last night," Bear said as he came in with two mugs and handed one to Jackson, "No one came snooping around after we got in here."

"We got lucky last night," Jackson said, "They underestimated us. They won't do that again."

"What do you want to do," Bear asked.

"I need to get back to the motel in Gretna, make sure they didn't make the place."

"Why would they? You didn't go there, did you?"

"No, but I circled around Gretna. They could guess I'd set up nearby and get lucky. Plus, we don't know who around here talks to them."

"Might make sense for you to pack up and just work out of here. It's private. And you know at least I'm not one of them Lokos."

"No, I don't think they have a t-shirt in your size."

Bear let out a laugh that sounded more like a growl. Whoever nicknamed him Bear had done so appropriately. He stood up and walked into the kitchen.

"You want some eggs and bacon," he shouted.

"Sure, thanks," Jackson shouted back.

That explained the sizzling on the stove. As Jackson finished his coffee, Bear walked in with two plates of food, placing them on the table between Jackson and him.

"So, we'll go round up your stuff first," Bear said.

"Yeah," Jackson replied, "And make sure they aren't sitting on the place. Which reminds me. You've got other cars around here, right?"

"Buddy," Bear answered, "What rural lifestyle do you know that don't own a bunch of old trucks?""

"You're the only one I know, but, good. You better ditch that Suburban now that they can make it. In fact, we should put it in that shed or tarp it over or something."

"Done and done. So, we get you out of there, and then what?"

"They're keeping Sara Beth somewhere. We need to find out where."

56

It took Jackson and Bear the better part of the morning to do everything necessary to carefully retrieve what Jackson had left in the motel in Gretna. Knowing the Lokos knew to look for Jackson's Ram and Bear's Suburban, they hid the two under tarps behind a pile of scrap. Bear loaned Jackson the keys to the old forest service F-350 while he pulled out a black 1985 Dodge D100 he'd restored.

"That's some pickup," Jackson had said as Bear came around the shed in it.

"Built her back myself," he said, smiling proudly and patting the dashboard, "My baby."

When they got near Gretna, they circled the small town twice, checking for a tail, then surveyed the motel parking lot from across the street, looking for someone sitting on the room. As it turned out, no one from the Lokos had made the motel.

That hadn't stopped Jackson from acting out of an abundance of caution, though. He entered his motel room through a small window in the bathroom that couldn't be seen from the street, packed up his gear, throwing it out the same window, and left the motel key along with a note for the housekeeping staff that he wouldn't be back.

Considering he'd paid for another week, he doubted they would mind his Irish goodbye.

Leaving Gretna, Jackson and Bear took separate routes back to Bear's house, both retracing several stretches of road at least once to look for someone tailing them. Neither of them spotted anyone following.

Bear was now busy transforming his dining room table into something of a black-market bazaar, laying out only his most spectacular and illegal firearms in an array of potential carnage.

"Is that all really necessary," Jackson asked.

"Hey, those Lokos come knocking around here," Bear replied, "We're going to knock back, Jack."

Bear chuckled as he fed bullets into the .357 he'd had on him back at the bar.

"So how do you plan on finding out where the Parker girl is," he asked.

"Not sure," Jackson answered, "The obvious way would be to go in and find out for ourselves."

"Ha," Bear snorted, "Easier said than done with that group."

"Yeah, my thoughts exactly. You haven't checked out the place at night, have you?"

"No, but I'm sure they've got folks watching out."

"That'd be my guess as well. They were on us just for snooping around the marina."

"You think they think this is still about the girl, after you asked back at the bar in Rocky Mount?"

Jackson didn't say anything. He'd forgotten he'd brought it up to the three Lokos there. Now he regretted that he had. What if he'd put her in more danger letting them know he was looking for her? The thought left Jackson feeling queasy.

"How do you think they made us at the marina," Jackson asked, "We never asked the store clerk about Sara Beth."

Bear shrugged his shoulders.

"Not sure," he answered, "He's a Loko, the guys at the bar were Lokos. Maybe they were on us just thinking us being there was suspicious. The guys on me were the ones from the bar. They could've ID'd either of us if they were sitting on the marina."

"Maybe," Jackson replied, "Either way, we bothered them enough that they wanted to know what we were up to. I wouldn't be surprised if they're out right now still looking for us after we lost them last night."

He thought about how aggressively the Lokos had pursued them after just a couple of encounters. Whatever was going on, they didn't want prying eyes around. It made him wonder what they had to hide. Then a thought struck Jackson.

"How many Lokos are there in all," Jackson asked.

"I don't know," Bear answered, "100? 150?"

"Over 100 and the same three knuckleheads ended up tailing us," Jackson said, "Do they have guys specifically tasked with doing security stuff?"

"Not sure. Why do you ask?"

"Maybe we don't need to get all 100-150 out of our way to have a look around. If there's a handful tasked to security, maybe we can thin them out."

"And how do you suppose we do that?"

"They're looking to go after us. Let's give them something to go after."

Jackson sat forward and booted up his laptop. He brought up Google Maps and searched the area where the Lokos had their compound in the woods. Only about half of the buildings Jackson remembered seeing could be seen on the satellite imagery. The rest were obscured by the trees overhead.

"How many times have you gone out there looking at their place," Jackson asked.

"Maybe a half dozen or so," Bear answered.

"Could you draw me a layout of their set up," Jackson asked.

Bear nodded and disappeared down the hall, returning with a piece of paper.

"There's one entrance in and out near as I can tell," Bear explained, "It intersects with the mountain road. You know, what we drove in on.

I know that because I've seen guys sit out front with their guns like they're guarding the place."

Bear scribbled on the paper, illustrating the foliage that blocked views of the place from the mountain road. Behind it, he began to draw a series of squares and rectangles.

"From what I've seen above," Bear continued, "there's a bunch of smaller buildings up front, near the entrance. Then you have the old abandoned mill in the middle of that opening here. And there are more small buildings that go around it sort of in the shape of a horseshoe."

Jackson noticed the buildings Bear diagrammed didn't go all the way around to the other side of the mill, opposite the entrance to the place.

"What about back here," Jackson asked, pointing to the empty spot on the diagram, "What's back here?"

"Not a whole lot," Bear answered, "I think they use it for target practice mostly. Shooting off into the woods. There's not much more than some random stuff stored back there."

"So that's where I'll set up. It's the least likely place people will be to begin with, and we'll see how much emptier you can make it when you give them something to go after."

Bear looked at him quizzically.

"And how exactly am I going to do that," he asked.

Jackson stood up from the couch and looked out the window at where they had covered up Bear's red Suburban, the silver bowtie emblem catching the sun as the end of one of the tarps flapped in the breeze. He turned to Bear.

"We didn't want them to make your Suburban," Jackson said, "Well, now, let's make sure they do."

57

Six hours later Jackson was lying prone on the forest floor northeast of the Lokos compound. He was a few yards from the tree line that broke into the clearing where the mill was located with a good view of the back half of the place. More importantly, though, nobody could see him.

Bear had insisted Jackson use a ghillie suit — camouflage clothing that would have its wearer resemble a walking piece of vegetation — he had, but Jackson convinced him it wouldn't be helpful if he had to have a look inside the buildings. It would be too bulky and cumbersome in close quarters. Bear wouldn't compromise on Jackson wearing a bullet resistant vest, though, and Jackson slipped one on over his RealTree hunting jacket.

Now Jackson lay on his belly, the earth scooped around him for better concealment, and watched one of the Lokos leaning against the backside of the mill, smoking a cigarette.

"You still hear me good, buddy," Bear's garbled voice blasted into Jackson's earpiece.

Bear didn't know how good cellular service was near Lokoville – he'd seen guys use cell phones around the compound but wasn't sure about the surrounding woods – and had suggested they use a couple of radios he had for hunting. Jackson attached an earpiece to his radio to limit the noise.

"Yeah, I've still got you," Jackson answered.

"I'm looking at a big, black sky behind you," Bear said, "Looks like a storm might be rolling in. Don't know if that changes how you want to do this."

"Rain or no rain, I need to get in there," Jackson replied.

He began crawling on his stomach, approaching the tree line. The guy leaning against the back of the mill had finished off his cigarette and lit another one. Jackson started to slowly raise himself into a crouch when the door on the backside of the mill flew open as if someone had kicked it. The sound startled the man leaning against the wall, who straightened up as two other men trotted down the stairs from the backdoor.

Jackson put his binoculars to his eyes to get a better look.

"Son of a bitch," Jackson muttered to himself.

The two men were Solomon and Silas Ash. Jackson recognized them from the photos in the packet Detective Bailey had given him. The two brothers were in a heated argument with one another, though Jackson couldn't make out what it was about.

"Bear, I've got Silas and Solomon Ash on the back side of the mill here," Jackson said quietly into his radio.

"Ash," Bear replied, "That's their last name?"

"These days it is," Jackson answered.

"So, these guys aren't Lokos so much as they are Ash-holes."

A staticky laugh prodded at Jackson's ear drum.

"Bear, focus," Jackson said, "They're back here arguing about something."

"Okay, so what do you want me to do," Bear asked.

"I think it's time you greet the neighbors," Jackson replied.

Three quarters of a mile away on the other side of The New City of David, Bear sat in his Suburban on the mountain road. He held his radio up to his ear as Jackson's message transmitted. A boyish grin stretched across his face. He put the SUV in gear and rolled forward.

58

B ear moved slowly down the road in his Suburban, the downward slope propelling him forward more than the V8 engine itself. He rounded a bend, navigating the towering oak trees on either side of him and came into the clearing in front of the Lokos' compound. Just as he'd seen the half dozen times he'd driven past before, two men watched the road leading in.

They were just in front of the thick brush that sheltered Lokoville like a wall. One of the men sat on an ATV, the other leaning against a stubby black willow tree. Bear hit the brakes hard to grab their attention. The suburban skidded on the gravel, its front fender kissing the grade road as the SUV's generous suspension gave under the weight of the large vehicle and the man driving it. The Loko on the ATV hopped off and stared out at Bear, gripping his hunting rifle with both hands. The one leaning against the tree flicked out a cigarette and followed suit.

"Alright, looks like they see me," Bear said into the radio.

"What are they doing," Jackson asked.

"Looking at me," Bear answered, "I think they're talking to each other."

The two men turned to one another, their conversation becoming more and more animated until the one that had been on the ATV pulled out a radio twice the size of the ones Bear and Jackson were using.

"One of them is talking to someone on a radio now," Bear said.

"Yeah, the goon next to Solomon and Silas over here just approached them holding a radio," Jackson said. "They seem to be talking about whatever was said."

Bear stared at the two men, anticipating some sort of move towards him. The two Lokos stared back, waiting for an order to do just that.

"Hold on, Silas just took the radio from the guy over here," Jackson said, "He's talking to someone."

Just as Jackson said that, the man out front put his radio to his ear. He said something back into it before hopping on the ATV and firing it up.

"They're coming," Bear said.

"Let's go," Jackson replied.

"Roger," Bear said.

The ATV veered off the drive and took a direct line at Bear in his suburban, tearing through tall grass as it went. The other Loko began walking towards him. Bear hit the gas, all 200 horses of the Suburban's modified V8 engine coming to life at once. Just as the fender had dipped when he stopped, it now bucked in the air as the truck kicked forward. The man on the road put his gun to his shoulder and aimed down the sight. Bear leaned right and ducked behind the dashboard as a round came flying through the windshield.

"Jesus H Christ," Bear yelled over the sound of shattering glass.

He popped back up just in time to see the man who'd shot at him dive out of the way of his Suburban. The ATV flew out of the tall grass, picking up the grade road behind Bear's Suburban, pursuing the red SUV. As Bear headed into the woods on the other side of the clearing, he looked back just in time to see another car roar out of the compound and take up position behind the ATV.

"I've got two on me," Bear radioed to Jackson, "An ATV and what looks like a Jeep SUV."

"Copy that. You've stirred the hornet's nest in here," Jackson replied, "You know what to do. Head for Harrisonburg, if you don't shake them by the time you're close, make the call we talked about."

"Got it," Bear said, "Good luck, brother."

Bear bobbed and weaved the truck around blind turns as the road wound its way up the mountain on the northside of the valley. Fishtailing around the switchbacks on the road, the Suburban kicked up clouds of dust so thick the Loko on the ATV had to put his head down to power through it. Seeing that, Bear had an idea.

As the road turned through a switchback and broke out onto a level plane, Bear powered the SUV around the turn. Keeping his foot on the gas, the Suburban kicked up a wall of dirt and dust until it regained traction down the straight stretch. That's when Bear hit the brakes and skidded to a stop, kicking up even more dirt. He waited. A second later the ATV came flying out of the cloud. The Loko driving it didn't see the Suburban until it was too late.

The ATV slammed into the back of Bear's truck, throwing the Loko riding it into his tailgate as he bounced off and hit the ground. Bear laughed menacingly as the Jeep swerved to avoid the mess. He hit the gas again, gaining distance between him and the last of his pursuers. The Jeep righted itself on the road and took off after him, leaving the downed ATV rider to fend for himself.

As the dirt road emptied onto a rural highway, Bear hung a right, using the paved road as opportunity to open up what his truck's engine could do. He hopped from highway to highway, zigzagging his way past Smith Mountain Lake as he headed north. Outside the small town of Buchanan, Bear picked up Interstate 81. From there, it was a straight shot to Harrisonburg.

For the better part of 90 minutes, the Jeep stuck with Bear and his Suburban. Bear wasn't particularly worried about losing them. If they were following him, they weren't on Jackson. Plus, he had a plan.

The sun had disappeared into the crevasse between the western mountains and the approaching storm. As the skies opened up, rain tattered Bear's broken windshield, dripping through the bullet hole just below the rearview mirror. As his wipers swooshed the water away, his headlights lit up a sign next to the highway.

HARRISONBURG NEXT 3 EXITS

Bear made a phone call.

"How're ya doing," Bear said, "I think Jackson Clay told you I might be calling. Him and I need that favor."

The voice on the other end said something back.

"First exit for Route 11, you've got it," Bear said, "See you then."

As he hung up, Bear saw the exit for Route 11 approaching. He swerved across two lanes of traffic to catch the exit ramp. The Jeep behind him followed, nearly hitting a Ford Focus in the middle lane.

Bear merged on to Route 11 and stayed in the right lane. Up ahead, a silver car sat in the parking lot of a State Farm Insurance office facing the road. Bear flashed his headlights twice and sped up. By the time he passed the car, he was doing 10 mph over the speed limit and the Jeep behind him had followed suit. As it streaked past the silver car, the car pulled out into traffic and sped up to get right on the Jeep's back fender. Bear watched in his rearview mirror as the silver sedan came to life in a disco of red and blue lights, signaling for the Jeep to pull over.

Bear convulsed with laughter.

"See you Ash-holes later," he yelled to no one in particular.

The police cruiser came to a stop behind the Jeep and focused its searchlight on the back window. The door opened and a figure got out, slowly approaching the Jeep. The man driving the Jeep rolled down the window. He waited as the figure, a woman in a navy pantsuit with a full head of curly hair, came to his door and lifted up the badge dangling around her neck.

"Good evening," said the officer, "Detective Angela Cole with the Harrisonburg Police Department. How are we doing this evening?"

59

Jackson watched as news of Bear stirred Lokos inside the compound into a frenzy. He could see Solomon Ash yell something at his brother, Silas, who in turn began yelling at a handful of armed men and women around him. Jackson couldn't tell if Silas was admonishing them or giving them orders, but when he was done, the group fanned out, most of them heading away from Jackson.

"I've got two on me," Bear shouted into his radio, "An ATV and what looks like a Jeep SUV."

Jackson could barely hear him over the background noise. Bear must be in the thick of it now, he thought.

"Copy that. You've stirred the hornet's nest in here," Jackson replied, "You know what to do. Head for Harrisonburg, if you don't shake them by the time you're close, make the call we talked about."

"Got it," Bear said back in a garbled transmission, "Good luck, brother."

The distraction had certainly gotten people's attention inside Lokoville, but Jackson wasn't sure it had had the desired effect. The same lone man stood by the back door to the mill, and instead of lazily filling his lungs with poison, he was now alert and looking around.

Jackson knew he couldn't make it across the open field to the man before he'd alert others, and shooting him would draw attention as well. Instead, he rotated himself along the tree line in an arc until he was to the lookout's side. Now, a small stack of oil drums and a parked tractor broke up the open ground into shorter stretches and Jackson could see around the side of the old lumber mill towards the front of the compound. No one else was coming. It was time to make his move.

Staying low, he stepped out of the clearing and jogged hunched over to the oil barrels. The man at the back of the mill didn't notice. Jackson looked to his right towards the clearing. A woman climbed onto an ATV and took off towards the front of the compound, disappearing from view. He was still good.

From the barrels Jackson crawled on his belly using the large back wheels of the tractor to shield himself from the man. As he got to the tractor wheel, he slowly peeled himself up off the earth. Rising, he peeked over the top of the tractor. The man standing guard looked less alert than he had a minute ago. Boredom was already returning.

Jackson shifted around to the front of the tractor and crouched down behind the tractor's bucket. It was a thirty-foot gap of open ground to the side of the mill. He had no choice but to go for it. When the man looked the other way, Jackson made his move. Breaking out into a run, Jackson crossed the gap in just a few seconds. The lookout was distracted by something the other way. He didn't stand a chance.

At full speed, Jackson hit him like a linebacker, driving a shoulder into the middle of his back as he grabbed the man's legs from underneath him and planted him into the dirt. Shooting up onto one knee, he grabbed the man's two wrists and put them behind his back. The man didn't resist. He was too busy trying to catch the breath that Jackson had knocked out of him.

Jackson reached into one of his cargo pockets and grabbed a pair of zip tie cuffs and restrained the man. Jackson looked down at him. The man was trying to look back at him out of the corner of his eye as he panted for oxygen.

"Listen to me very carefully," Jackson said in a low voice, "That door to the mill, is it locked?"

The man shook his head, still sucking wind.

"What about inside," Jackson asked, "Is there anyone on the other side of the door?"

Again, the man shook his head.

"I don't think I need to tell you lying would be very bad for you here," Jackson said.

"No. No one," the man managed to say.

"Good boy," Jackson said.

He tore off a piece of duct tape and put it around the man's mouth.

"Don't go anywhere," he said.

Jackson climbed off the man and took the stairs up to the door two at a time. He drew his P320 as he stayed crouched and checked the door. It was, in fact, unlocked. Slowly, Jackson opened it, moving with the door and scanning the room, his gun drawn. The room was a small office. There was an old metal desk with an accompanying desk chair. On top of it, papers were strewn about. In the corner stood an empty coat tree and a shelving unit filled with tools. Aside from the dated furniture, though, the room was empty. The lookout had told the truth.

Jackson hopped back down the stairs, grabbing the bound man, and dragged him up into the office, shutting the door behind them. He began to search the room for evidence of Sara Beth. The papers scattered on the desk seemed to be a mixture of receipts and manuals for hardware equipment, most likely the stuff on the shelves. Jackson was looking at these when he heard a loud bang come from somewhere deeper inside the building. He looked in the direction it had come. There was a second door to the office.

Jackson put his ear to this door, then turned the knob slowly and began to open it, his P320 at the ready. Peeking outside the door, he saw a long hallway. A large, cavernous opening in the center of the building was divided from the walkway by a railing. Opposite the open middle were an array of doors with frosted windows carved into a cinderblock wall. The place was a maze.

He turned and looked back at the man he had subdued, who was watching him nervously. Jackson crouched down, his gun in hand and in view of the man.

"You're not going to fight me, right," Jackson asked.

The man gave a jittery nod.

"If I take this tape off your mouth," Jackson continued, "You're not going to scream, right?"

Another nod.

Jackson reached out and slowly removed the tape, giving himself the option to quickly put it back if the man decided not to cooperate. But the only sound the man gave was a little groan as the adhesive peeled away at his skin.

"The girl," Jackson said, "Where is she?"

The man gave him a confused look.

"I don't understand," he said.

"What's your name," Jackson asked.

"Cliff," the man replied.

"Cliff, I thought you said you were going to cooperate."

"I did. I – I am."

"Then where is the girl?"

"Which one?"

"The girl you and your friends out there took."

"Who are you talking about?"

Jackson brought his gun closer to Cliff's face.

"Cliff," Jackson said, "I'm going to ask you one more ti—"

"I'm not doing nothing," Cliff replied, his voice stricken with fear, "You said where's the girl. You got to tell me which one of them you're talking about."

Jackson's heart began to thump hard in his chest. He feared he already knew the answer to his next question.

"Them," he said, "You mean there's more than one?"

Cliff nodded.

"There was never just one."

60

Jackson stared at Cliff, not wanting to believe what he'd said. A clap of thunder exploded somewhere nearby, causing Cliff to flinch. Jackson didn't move. He was a world away in his own head. How many girls did these people have? How many Sara Beth Parkers were here? A rage began to burn in him.

Reaching into one of his pockets, Jackson fetched a photo of Sara Beth and put it up to Cliff's face.

"This one," Jackson said, "Her name is Sara Beth Parker. Where is she?"

"I – I haven't seen her. I haven't seen most of them. I'm not supposed to," Cliff said, "I just know they're here."

"They're here where," Jackson asked.

"Down inside further. They keep them in an old storage area that's been secured until they're gone."

"What do you mean until they're gone?"

"Until they go."

"Where? Where do they go?"

"To whoever they go to."

Jackson's anger burned inside him as what Cliff told him only got worse. He'd finally gotten here, to the people who had taken Sara Beth, and she might not even be here. He couldn't think about it. Sara Beth had to be here. He had to find her.

"You're going to take me to where they keep the girls," Jackson said.

"I can't," Cliff replied.

"My gun to your back will say otherwise," Jackson countered.

"I can't just go to them. There are people in here. They'll see me. See us. I'm not supposed to be in here unless I'm told to."

"We'll worry about that when we get there."

Jackson began pulling Cliff to his feet when the door behind him swung open.

"The fuck is this," said a gravelly voice behind him.

In one swift motion, Jackson dropped to the floor, turning sideways, and drawing his P320 in the direction of the doorway. He landed on top of Cliff and pointed his pistol up at a large, barrel-chested man with small tree trunks for arms. The man smiled down at him over a thick handlebar mustache.

"Well ain't you cute," said the man with a southern drawl.

Jackson noticed the holster on the man's hip, a large grip of what had to be a high-caliber pistol jutting out. The man's hand was sliding slowly towards it. From his position, Jackson had only one play. Squeezing the trigger, he planted two 9mm rounds squarely into the man's chest.

Outside another clap of thunder boomed, echoing the thunder that had just rang out inside. The man stumbled backwards, raking at the gunshot wounds, before falling against the far wall. He was dead before he hit the ground.

Jackson tugged a crying Cliff off the floor.

"Come on," Jackson said, "We've got to move. Now."

He shoved him through the door and began to march him down the hallway when he looked up. Standing at the far end, watching, was Silas Ash. A six-shot revolver dangled limply in his hand.

"Shit, you killed Big Jed," Silas said.

"He didn't give me much of a choice," Jackson replied.

Turning his torso sideways to make himself a smaller target, he grabbed Cliff by the back of his shirt and put him squarely between

Silas and himself. Cliff made a noise Jackson hadn't ever heard a man make before.

"All I want is Sara Beth Parker," Jackson said, "Just give her to me and we'll go."

Silas began to laugh.

"Oh, you dumb fuck," Silas said, "You don't even know what you don't know."

Jackson doubled down.

"The girl," he said, "Give her to me."

Silas began to walk forward. Jackson lifted Cliff upright by his shirt and pointed his P320 at Silas over Cliff's left shoulder. Silas laughed again.

"You think I give two shits about ole Cliff," he asked.

Before Jackson could answer, Silas' arm snapped up and fired a round, hitting Cliff in his abdomen. Jackson lowered his gun, trying to catch the suddenly limp body in his hands. Silas fired again, hitting Cliff in the collarbone. He hadn't lied about caring for Cliff's wellbeing. Jackson realized he had only seconds before his only cover would be bleeding out on the floor.

"I'm sorry about this," he muttered into Cliff's ear.

Grabbing him even tighter, Jackson pushed him forward, rushing Silas and using Cliff as a shield. The charge caught Silas off guard, who fired his next four shots frantically, each one of them catching Cliff. When Jackson counted the sixth shot, he let go of Cliff who fell lifeless to the floor.

Jackson charged Silas directly now, who turned and reached for something. It was too late, Jackson hit him with the broadside of his arm, clotheslining him, and knocking both of them to the ground.

As Silas fell backwards the contents of the pocket he'd been reaching into scattered onto the floor. He moved for a knife that rattled across the concrete floor, but Jackson saw it. He grabbed Silas' wrist and twisted his arm behind him, then pulled up until he heard a pop. Silas shrieked in pain. Jackson had dislocated his shoulder.

Whipping an arm around Silas' neck, he placed him in a chokehold and pulled his head close to his.

"Sara Beth Parker," Jackson growled, "The girl from Harrisonburg. Where is she?"

Silas didn't answer as he groaned in pain.

Jackson began to squeeze harder when he heard a door kick open around the corner.

"Silas," a voice called out.

Laying against the wall with Silas in a chokehold, Jackson poked his head around the corner. Three men with assault rifles were moving cautiously down the hallway towards him. When they saw him, they fired.

Jackson ducked back as chips of paint and concrete splintered into the air. With his free hand, he drew his P320, reached around the corner, and returned fire. Emptying the entire magazine, he looked down at Silas who was out cold now. Jackson let him go, grabbed another magazine and reloaded.

More gunfire came from around the corner. As pieces of debris peppered the floor, a black rectangle caught Jackson's eye. It was a phone. Silas must have dropped it during the fight. A bullet crashed into the wall next to it, sending it sliding. Jackson wanted that phone, and he wanted it undamaged.

Pulling himself up onto one knee, he turned and faced the corner of the wall. When there was a break in the gunfire, he leaned out with his P320 drawn. A man ducked behind cover as Jackson squeezed off two rounds. The other two men, seeing the third get hit, ducked inside a door and closed it. Jackson emptied the rest of his magazine in their direction. He reached for the phone and ducked back behind the wall. A second later, gunfire came booming from around the corner once more.

Jackson clicked on the phone. It needed a finger print to unlock. He looked over at the unconscious Silas. He grabbed the man's hand and placed his limp thumb onto the phone's screen. It unlocked. Jackson quickly changed the security setting on the phone so it wouldn't need a finger print to unlock again and put it away.

Loading his final magazine, he knew he didn't have what he needed to sustain the gunfight. By now, more men were surely on the way. It was time to take the phone, hoping it was enough, and go.

Standing up, he slowly backed down the hallway towards the office he had entered in from. As he neared the office doors, two shadows appeared around the bend in the hallway. Jackson fired two shots. The shadows disappeared. This was the best it was going to get. He ducked into the office, ran out the door and sprinted across the clearing behind the mill into the night.

As he ran across the open field, his lungs filled with the smell of the imminent storm. Thunder clapped as he ran towards the lightning.

"There he is, shoot him," he heard a voice yell behind him.

Gunfire rang out as Jackson made it to the tree line, but he didn't slow down. He kept running. Hot lead collided with tree trunks and splintered their wood. Leaves whipped and snapped as large caliber rounds pruned them from their branches. He flinched as a round hit a large hickory tree and peppered his face with splintered wood. It didn't stop him. It couldn't stop him. His lifespan in that moment was measured by the distance he could put between him and his pursuers.

Two men ran into the woods after him but Jackson ran faster and climbed harder. Now he was in his element. He could weave in and out of the trees like a running back reading a defense. As the skies opened up above, he continued on, scaling the steep and muddied terrain on all fours.

When he made it to the first ridgeline, he stopped to get his bearings. This was the first landmark, his way of mapping in his head what to look for without a GPS or compass. He could hear voices below him but didn't see anyone. The rain and night hadn't deterred them from continuing their pursuit. He pulled out his P320 and checked the magazine. Counting the one in the chamber, he had three rounds. He put the gun away and followed the ridgeline east, running hard on the even terrain.

The storm began to pick up in intensity. Drops of rain turned into sheets blown sideways by the violent winds. Trees whipped back and forth, fighting the weather's attempts to snap them in two if not uproot them completely. Loose branches fell from above, striking the ground like crooked javelins.

Jackson kept running. He had the advantage now and he was

determined to leverage it. He'd spent his entire life in woods just like these. He was comfortable here. He was dangerous here.

The wind and rain drowned out the voices behind him. Jackson looked back. The storm had cut visibility down to virtually zero. If the men pursuing him didn't know where he was headed, pretty soon he'd become impossible to track.

He continued along the ridge until he found Bear's UTV. The two of them had parked it on a state forest trail. Jackson grabbed the keys out of his pocket, climbed in, and fired it up. Turning the wheel, he punched the gas and the UTV whipped around in a semi-circle. He shifted it into high gear, and continued climbing the mountain, now with 120 horses to aid him.

By the time the two men found the trail, Jackson was almost two miles away.

61

Jackson took the trail all the way north until it ended alongside a rural highway. There, he and Bear had stashed his truck out of view, covering it with camouflage netting. The plan had been to rendezvous there when Jackson had Sara Beth Parker with him, but that hadn't happened.

Instead, all Jackson had was the phone of a goon cult leader. As he climbed into his truck to escape the mid-Atlantic monsoon overhead, he fished the phone out of his pocket and tried to turn it on. It was dead. Jackson looked at the bottom of it and saw it used the same Micro USB charger as his. He plugged it in and turned on the truck to let it charge. The phone came to life with a picture of an empty battery and a brand logo Jackson didn't recognize.

Watching the scroll wheel circle as the battery percentage climbed from zero to 1%, he grabbed his own phone and called Bear. The roar of wind whipping by answered the call.

"What's the good news buddy," Bear said, yelling over the storm, "You get that little girl?"

"No such luck," Jackson replied, "I'm not sure she was there anyway."

"Wait, what do you mean," Bear said, "Where would she be then?"

"I don't know. It's bad, Bear."

"What's going on?"

"They've taken multiple girls. The guy I worked over said they take them and keep them at that place until they're gone. I never got out of him what that means."

"Christ. It sounds like some sort of, what do you call it? Trafficking ring or something."

"Yeah, that's what I'm afraid of."

"What if they don't have her no more?"

"I can't begin to think like that."

Jackson could hear Bear's windshield wipers thump back and forth as he struggled to find the right thing to say.

"What's the play," Bear finally asked.

"I don't know," Jackson replied, "I got Silas Ash's phone off of him in a fight. Hopefully it has something on there. I guess meet me here at the trailhead like we planned."

"You got it," Bear said, "And Jackie boy?"

"Yeah?"

"We'll find her, brother."

Jackson ended the call. He wasn't so sure. It was nearing a month since these people had taken her, *if* they had taken her. He was no human trafficker, but he couldn't imagine holding onto a living, breathing payday for that long. Even if she hadn't been sold to someone, there was always the chance they – Jackson couldn't even bring himself to imagine it.

Closing his eyes, he tried to refocus. Think about what you can control, he thought. You don't know that she's gone. And if there's a chance, you're still in the game.

He was listening to the rain plink against the fiberglass body of the truck when the chirping of a phone interrupted. He looked down, thinking at first Bear had called him back, but it was the other phone. Silas' phone. It had received a text message.

Jackson punched the message open. It was just a spam message alerting how much data had been used on the phone, but it gave Jackson an idea. He opened up the text messaging app on the phone. There were suspiciously few conversations, especially for someone who is supposedly ordering around cult militia members all day.

He opened the apps menu on the phone and browsed. As he swiped alphabetically, he got to 'T', and saw Telegram. He knew Telegram was a go-to messaging app for people who preferred their privacy, particularly criminals. A couple years back, the Russian government had even toyed with the idea of blocking the app altogether given its prevalent use amongst terrorists.

Jackson opened up the app. This was where Silas had been communicating. There were dozens of chats open including a number of Secret Chats. Secret Chats was a feature where messages could only be accessed by the device sending the message and the device receiving it, making hacking or eavesdropping virtually impossible.

He scanned the messages on the Secret Chats, none of which looked good. The most recent had come a few hours ago from a username 3vang3l1st.

Subject 2. $50,000.

Before it, Silas, or someone using this phone, had sent the user photos of three women inside cages. The boldness of it all shocked Jackson. They hadn't even bothered to set self-destruction timers on their messages, another feature of the app. He supposed Silas needed the record of messages to keep up with the business of selling humans. The thought reinvigorated the rage inside Jackson.

He continued to scroll through the Secret Chats, reading each briefly, hoping he'd get a clue or perhaps a photo of Sara Beth. A chat with a user called Amhaaretz last had a message sent three days ago. It was a message from the user to Silas.

We need to talk about the girl.

Jackson slid the window up and read the older messages. There were exchanges working out various details and setting up times to meet. The user mentioned "my place", leading Jackson to wonder if they were local. He continued to scroll. As far as Jackson could tell, Silas had not sent this user any pictures. He wondered if perhaps the conversation had begun with pictures sent, a sick sort of shop laying out its merchandise to a predator customer.

He scrolled all the way to the top and began reading. The conversa-

tion between the two started off simple enough. They exchanged pleas-
antries, then Amhaaretz indicated to Silas who they were, without
exchanging names.

*Think you should remember me. Our mutual acquaintance introduced us
at the lake yesterday.*

Jackson wondered if he was referring to Smith Mountain Lake at
the marina. According to the timestamps, the conversation went quiet
for a few days before Amhaaretz sent another message. Reading it,
Jackson felt himself go cold.

The girl from Harrisonburg on the news. My friend says that was you.

Silas replied acknowledging they had taken her. Jackson's fingers
went numb as he held the phone. He held it tighter as he continued
reading. There was a back and forth, discussing what had happened
before the user Amhaaretz sent a message as simple as it was sinister.

Her. I want her.

Scrolling faster, Jackson began speed-reading the conversation as
fast as he could. Looking for any sort of clue.

"Come on. Reveal yourself. Who are you," he muttered to himself.

The messages were intentionally vague. An exchange had clearly
been set up and Sara Beth Parker had been given to this person.
Shortly after a conversation working out the details of handing her
over, messages stopped until a little more than a week ago when
Amhaaretz started sounding nervous. Unsolicited, the person had sent
Silas a message.

This case of hers isn't going away.

A sporadic back-and-forth continued. The user sounding worried.
Silas reassured them it would go away. Then, as Jackson scrolled
further down, he nearly dropped the phone.

Amhaaretz had sent a picture file of Jackson. It looked like a still
taken from a security camera. Jackson was walking across what looked
to be a road or parking lot. He scrolled down to the next messages. The
words stabbed into Jackson like tiny daggers as he read.

*This man came to my house looking into the girl. I had to take him with
me to Lexington so he wouldn't find her.*

Jeff Isaacs had taken Sara Beth Parker.

62

Jackson tore down the highway, his truck cutting through the torrents of rain like a torpedo. Even on their max setting, his wipers couldn't keep up with the barrage of water hitting his windshield. But he couldn't slow down. He had to get to Jeff Isaacs. He had to get to Sara Beth. He had to be there now.

Seconds felt like minutes. Miles seemed to stretch on forever. He reached for his phone and called Bear. It went to voicemail.

"God dammit," Jackson said, "Come on, Bear, pick up."

"Hey, it's Archi – er – Bear. Uh, you know that to do," said a pre-recorded message.

"Bear, it's me," Jackson yelled over the wind and the rain, "Listen to me. Jeff Isaacs. He has Sara Beth. He lives off of Route 606 in Steeles Tavern. Take exit 205 from I-81 and go East about a mile. Wait for me there."

Jackson tried to think of the cars he saw at Isaacs' house.

"If you see a light blue Buick SUV, a white Volkswagen Atlas, or a black Infiniti sedan in the area, follow it and call me immediately," Jackson added.

He ended the call and looked at the time. It was almost 10. He estimated he was about an hour and 45 minutes away from Jeff Isaacs' house. With a little luck, he could shave that down to 90 minutes.

Jackson's mind raced as fast as his truck. Could the Lokos connect him to Isaacs? Could they warn him before he got there? Would they warn him, or would they rather start dropping bodies? Maybe whoever had followed Bear to Harrisonburg was headed there now. There were too many variables. Too many unknowns. Jackson had to get there.

He was rounding the city of Roanoke, catching Interstate 81 north, when his phone rang. It was Bear.

"Bear," Jackson said, "Talk to me."

"I think I'm outside the house," Bear said, "You didn't give me an exact address so I called that detective lady."

"You didn't tell her Isaacs has Sara Beth, did you," Jackson asked.

"C'mon man, give me some credit. No, I told her I was supposed to grab some information on the way back and needed the address."

"Alright, stay on the highway. He has motion sensors on his driveway. God knows what else there is if he's keeping abducted kids there."

"Gotcha, I'll wait for you."

"I'm an hour out. Sit on the driveway. If anyone leaves, follow them and call me. Otherwise, stay put."

"10-4, brother."

Jackson ended the call and drove harder into the storm. For a week now, he had crossed half the state looking for a teenage girl whose only crime was showing a little rebellion for the first time in her life. Jeff Isaacs hadn't just preyed upon her, he'd preyed upon her family, giving them false hope and comfort. Jeff Isaacs owed them more than just their little girl, he owed all three of them their lives back.

Jackson Clay was coming to collect.

63

Half an hour before midnight, Jackson pulled up behind Bear's Suburban on a lonely stretch of road near Jeff Isaacs' home. He saw the door of the SUV open as he killed his headlights. Bear's brawny silhouette stepped out into the stormy darkness and met Jackson at the back of his truck.

"Any movement," Jackson asked in a hushed voice.

"No. It's completely dark, actually," Bear replied, "I noticed two other houses pitch black on the way in. I think the power might be out around here."

"Let's assume it isn't," Jackson said, "Even if it's out, he might have a backup generator."

Bear opened the back doors to his Suburban. Inside was a large assortment of the firearms and tactical equipment from his house. Jackson estimated he must've brought half of his personal armory with him.

"I grabbed a few things when we were heading out; always better to be prepared," Bear said as he slipped on a generously-portioned bullet resistant vest, "You still good with your pistol there?"

Jackson looked at the display of firepower. He didn't peg Jeff Isaacs for the gun-toting type, but he hadn't suspected him to be involved with Sara Beth's abduction, either. Besides that, he'd already been caught outgunned in one shootout tonight. He wasn't about to let that happen again. He reached in and grabbed a Sig Sauer assault rifle equipped with a foregrip, scope, and laser sight.

"Actually, you mind if I borrow this," Jackson asked.

Bear suppressed a grin, pleased an ex-Ranger approved of his curated collection of carnage.

"By all means," Bear replied, "In fact, I've got extra mags for that."

Jackson took the extra magazines from Bear and slid them into the pouches on the front of his vest. He scanned the weapons depot in the back of the truck once more, reaching in again and grabbing a throat microphone for his radio and a pair of night vision binoculars.

"Better take these, too," Jackson added, "Just in case."

Bear could no longer suppress his smile.

"Good thinking," he replied.

"Let's go," Jackson said.

The two crept slowly into the woods, disappearing into the dark foliage. Jackson couldn't see more than a few feet in front of him, only catching glimpses of the house in the distance as lightning flashed across the sky. He pulled out the night vision binoculars and put them up to his face. Bear was right, the house was completely dark. If he hadn't known better, he'd think the place was abandoned.

Jackson tapped Bear on the shoulder and signaled for him to move to the far side of the house where the garage was while he went the opposite way. Bear nodded and split off.

Jackson stalked forward slowly, his gun raised. In front of him was the tree line where the woods he was using for cover gave way to Isaacs' manicured lawn. Posting up against a large oak tree, he got down on one knee at the edge of the yard and looked the property over through the green hue of the night vision goggles. He could see Bear on the far side, crossing the large driveway and heading for the garage.

"Bear, can you hear me," Jackson said, the microphone around his neck picking up the vibrations of his vocal cords.

"Loud and clear, bud," Bear replied.

Jackson switched on the infrared pointer on the laser sight which shot out a beam of light only visible with the right equipment on. He waved the barrel of his gun, flailing the laser in the air to show Bear where he was. Bear did the same thing back.

"Check the garage," Jackson said to Bear, "Are all three cars I mentioned there?"

"There's a Volkswagen and an Infiniti inside the garage," Bear replied, "And there's a Buick on the far end of the driveway."

"He's got to be here," Jackson said, "Front porch stairs. Let's move."

Their rifles up and pointed at the house, the two converged on the front porch stairs from opposite directions. There, Jackson signaled for Bear to follow him. He ascended the stairs quietly and scanned the windows for movement. As he stepped to the door, Bear came around to the opposite side. He looked at Bear and nodded. Bear nodded back.

"On you, brother," he said.

With one swift strike, Jackson swung his steel toed boot into the door, knocking it off its hinges. The storm blew through the splintered door frame, the wind whipping rain into the entryway.

Jackson's rain-soaked silhouette stepped through the opening into the house. It was pitch black. He moved through the house in a counterclockwise direction, sweeping from room to room. As he scanned down a hall on the other side of the living area, the lenses of his night vision binoculars flared up from light coming through a doorway on the far end. Bear looked at him. Jackson motioned for him to follow.

Moving down the hallway and getting closer, Jackson could see the glow was coming from the kitchen. Flipping off the night vision, he stepped off the wall into the hallway and scanned what he could see of the room. A light source was flickering, casting cabinets and small appliances in an eerie, dim radiance. As he got to the doorway, he leaned back against the wall and listened. Something metal clinked. Jackson moved.

Stepping in, he covered the room in a sweeping arc, his rifle out in front of him. Jeff Isaacs was sitting at a table, a pair of candles illuminating his sullen face. He was looking down at a bottle of Johnnie Walker and a snub nose Ruger revolver in front of him.

"You move for that gun, it'll be the last move you make," Jackson said.

"I was wondering when you would put it all together," Isaacs replied.

"Did you hear me," Jackson asked, "Move and I'll shoot you."

"Detective Cole mentioned your friend here found the Living Order. I figured it was only a matter of time."

"I'm serious, Isaacs."

Isaacs looked up at Jackson, baring his soul in his eyes. They were red from crying. But it was more than that. They were heartbroken. Afflicted with overarching guilt.

"I'm not going to shoot you," said Isaacs, "I know how this ends."

"Stand up, move over there," Jackson replied, motioning towards the kitchen counter.

Letting out a sigh, Isaacs slid the chair back and did what he was told. Jackson kept the gun pointed at him as he moved across the kitchen. He put his hands on the edge of the sink and looked out the window at the storm causing mayhem outside.

"What now," Isaacs asked.

"Sara Beth," Jackson replied, "Where is she?"

Jackson watched as Isaacs' upper body began to shake, a faint, breathy cackle coming out of him. Bear looked at Jackson. Neither of them could tell if he was laughing or crying. Or both.

"Oh god," Isaacs said, "You don't know."

Hearing those five words, Jackson felt his knees become weak as his body tingled with a million pin pricks. The rifle grew heavy in his hands.

"What did you do," Jackson said, fear peppering his voice.

Isaacs' breathy cackle became more pronounced. A laugh of disbelief.

"What did I do," Isaacs echoed, "What did I do?"

Jackson dropped the rifle. It swung around his body on its sling as he charged at Isaacs. He grabbed the back of Isaacs' head and shoved it down into the sink.

"Where is she," he yelled, "Tell me, now!"

Isaacs' laughter devolved into hysterical crying. Jackson shoved his head down farther, so much so that it was pressed against the cold white porcelain of the sink itself. He grabbed the stopper off the counter, plugged the drain, and turned on the faucet. Cold well water splashed onto Isaacs' face as it pooled around his mouth.

"Where is she," Jackson yelled again, "What did you do with her?"

"I -- I," Isaacs muttered, trying to speak.

Jackson pulled him upright, spun him around, and slammed him against the counter. Grabbing him by the collar of his pastel green polo, Jackson pulled his face so close to his own he could smell the scotch on Isaacs' breath. He looked at the man, who now refused to make eye contact with him. His hair was wet and unkempt, his pupils dilated. Jackson thought he looked as though he had been caught out in the storm.

"What did you do," Jackson growled.

Isaacs wouldn't look up as he answered.

"I gave her back."

64

It took every bit of self-control Jackson had not to take his hands off Jeff Isaacs' shirt collar and place them around his neck.

"What do you mean you gave her back," Jackson snarled.

"I – I made a mistake," Isaacs replied, sobbing, "I just wanted my Olivia back. And that girl—"

"*Sara. Beth.* Sara. Beth. Parker," Jackson said, shaking him once, "She had a name. And it wasn't Olivia. She wasn't yours to have."

"I – I know that now. I thought that maybe I could just take her, and we could be a family. Like the one I had. But I was wrong. And then you came around, and I knew it was a matter of time."

"So, what? You gave her back to Solomon and Silas? Like some fucked up return policy?"

"It was the only wa—I didn't know what to do. I was scared. They wouldn't take her back at first, telling me she was my problem now. But I said I'd let her go to the cops."

"And so they took her."

"Solomon came himself. Said he had to figure out what to do with her. He sent some men, then, to scare me into not talking. Not long after that, they came back and tossed the place. Said right after they left here was the first time they ran into you and asked who you were."

Jackson thought back to the evening he'd first spotted the van. He'd been on his way to Jeff Isaacs' house when he stopped for gas. That's when he'd seen them. As he thought back now, the van had come from the direction of Isaacs' house.

Son of a bitch, Jackson thought to himself.

"What are you going to do," Isaacs asked.

Jackson thought, looking for the best solution. Looking for the play. He'd expected Sara Beth to be here. For her to be freed and Isaacs to be arrested. But her not being here made things complicated. Turning him over was still a possibility, but he didn't have Sara Beth. He needed cards to play if he was going to get her back. Jeff Isaacs was a card to play.

"You're coming with us," Jackson answered.

"Like hell this pedo-fucker is," Bear stammered, drawing his Desert Eagle from its holster.

Jackson turned and shot him a look. Bear stepped back and holstered his gun.

"You're coming with us and that is it," Jackson said assertively.

Isaacs' shoulders sagged, his upper body drooping and placing all its weight onto the clenched fists of Jackson.

"If you're going to kill me, just get on with it," Isaacs lamented.

"I'm not going to kill you," Jackson said, "But you don't get to walk for this."

Isaacs started to nod in defeat, but then the nodding became convulsive. He was going to be sick. Jackson spun him towards the sink just as Isaacs' guilt purged itself in the form of his stomach's contents.

"Oh for fuck's sake," Bear said.

"I'm sorry," Isaacs replied, "I truly am."

He reached for a dish towel on the counter and wiped his mouth.

"You good now," Jackson asked.

"Yes, sorry," Isaacs answered, "I'll go. Please, just let me clean myself up in the bathroom."

Jackson grabbed him by the shoulder and the hip and moved him towards Bear.

"Take him to the bathroom," Jackson said, "Leave the door open and watch him."

Bear nodded and led Isaacs around the table and into the hallway where the two disappeared. Jackson leaned against the cabinet, listening to the rain rap on the metal roof overhead. A muffled clap of thunder roared through the sky. He thought about what to do next.

Yes, Jeff Isaacs was a card to play, but the plays were limited. His fate ultimately played out two ways: being turned over to the authorities or being turned over to the Lokos. Neither option was great. Not while Sara Beth was still out there.

Jackson looked at the morbid place setting Isaacs had prepared for himself. The candles in cryptic black iron holders. The half-drunk bottle of Johnnie. The revolver that wasn't there.

Jackson shook his head, as if doubting his vision. Everything was there but the gun. He went to the table and looked. It wasn't there. He checked the kitchen counter. Nothing. Where was the gun?

And in one horrifying moment, Jackson realized what had happened.

"Bear," Jackson screamed.

But as he jumped into the hallway a loud bang echoed off the hollow wooden walls and vibrated through the floorboards below. Bear flinched, caught off guard, and fell to the ground.

Jackson ran to him, patting him as he looked for a gunshot wound.

"Are you hit," he said, panicked.

"No, no," Bear answered, "It wasn't me."

Crouching on the ground, Jackson turned and looked inside the bathroom. Jeff Isaacs' lifeless body laid on the black and white tile floor, a red hole the size of an orange replacing the upper part of his face. His hand was still clasped around the snub nose Ruger, a single trail of smoke dancing upwards from the muzzle. Blood splatter covered the mirror and the bathroom's art deco interior.

Jackson turned and looked back at Bear.

"I'm sorry, Jack," Bear said disappointed in himself, "I didn't see the gun."

Jackson looked back at the bathroom.

"This isn't on you," Jackson replied, "All of this. All of this is on him."

PART IV

THE MOUNTAIN ROAD

65

By dawn, Isaacs' property was saturated with law enforcement officials. Jackson couldn't be sure someone hadn't heard the gun shot and figured it was better to call it in himself. That way, at least, he could control the narrative.

Before he called 9-1-1, he'd told Bear to gather everything that they'd brought, take it back to his Suburban and leave. Then, he reported to the dispatcher he'd arrived at Isaacs' house wanting to ask him some follow-up questions when he'd heard a gunshot. He was worried, so he broke open the door and eventually found the body.

Within half an hour, the first sheriff's deputies were on scene. In two hours, a pair of detectives arrived. None of them particularly believed Jackson was telling the whole truth, but they didn't have the evidence to prove otherwise. When Detective Bailey heard that State Police were assisting with a dead body identified as Jeff Isaacs and that a Jackson Clay was being questioned, she called a colleague at Division III Headquarters to keep an eye on him as a favor to her.

"I don't know what's going on down there, but I know this guy and he didn't do anything like that," Bailey had said over the phone, "Don't let those inbred mouth breathers down there fuck it up."

That was when Jackson met a beefy State Police Detective by the name of Donald Butler. Detective Butler had blonde hair cut into a flat top with a mustache that stopped being stylish several decades ago. Whenever he wasn't poking holes in the Sheriff's Office Detectives' theories as they questioned Jackson, he'd stand no less than 4 feet away from him, working his way through a meaty paw filled with sunflower seeds, spitting the shells onto Isaacs' pristine lawn.

"Don't think he'll mind now," Butler had quipped when he caught Jackson looking at him funny for doing so.

Jackson was sitting on Isaacs' front porch stairs waiting for the deputies to give him the okay to leave when a silver unmarked police car pulled up. The driver's side door opened and out stepped Detective Angela Cole who immediately locked eyes with Jackson.

"Great," Jackson said at the sight of her.

"You know her," asked Detective Butler.

"Yeah, she's not going to be happy," Jackson answered, "Better spare yourself on this one."

When Detective Cole approached him, Butler didn't move to step in this time. Cole took one step up, then placed a foot on the second. Standing over Jackson, her figure eclipsed the early morning sun.

"Good morning," Jackson said.

"What the hell happened, Clay," Cole asked, clearly unhappy.

Her raised voice caught the attention of a nearby deputy who went to step in before Detective Cole showed him a badge and a look that told him to get lost.

"Well," Cole said, "I'm waiting."

"I don't know, go ask Isaacs," Jackson replied.

"You really want to get smart with me now," Cole asked.

"What do you want me to say? I came down to ask the guy some questions, and heard a gunshot. The guy shot himself."

"Why would he do that?"

"I don't know, Cole. He wasn't real talkative when I got to him."

Detective Cole pulled off her mirrored aviator sunglasses and leaned into Jackson's face.

"You're the only one in the house with a dead body," Cole said, "Look around. These guys want you for this. You need a friend right now, so I'd start talking."

"Do you think the tough cop bit is going to work on me, Cole," Jackson asked.

She stood up straight, tucking her glasses into the neckline of her blouse as she looked around.

"What were you going to ask him about," Cole asked.

"Olivia," Jackson answered.

"What about her," Cole asked.

Jackson nodded up over towards the sheriff's deputies.

"You really want to do this here," he asked.

Detective Cole looked up and noticed one of the Sheriff's Office detectives listening keenly to their conversation. She stepped back off the steps and motioned with her head for Jackson to follow her over to a quiet corner of the yard. The Sheriff's Office detective began to follow when Detective Butler stepped in front of him and asked him if he'd done a number of things he very well knew the detective had.

"Her case," Jackson said once the two of them were far enough away, "She was close in age and looks like Sara Beth. Probably also abducted by a stranger. I wanted to know more about her case, to see if there were parallels."

"And this came to you in the middle of the night," Cole asked.

"I'm looking for a missing girl," Jackson replied, "I'm not exactly keeping office hours."

"If you're going around asking about girls that have been gone for years, I'm guessing you're not much closer to finding Sara Beth."

"I wouldn't say that."

"So, you have a lead."

"Possibly."

"Oh, cut the shit, Clay. Are you on to something or not?"

"I told you, when I know something solid, you'll know. I can tell you this, being tied up here answering questions for a bunch of Barney Fifes isn't helping."

"Look where you are, Clay. Dead bodies don't just show up every day around here. They're going to hit this case hard."

"Doesn't change the fact that every minute I'm here, I'm not out there looking for her."

Jackson began to walk away when Detective Cole grabbed his arm.

"I'll see what I can do about speeding things up," Cole said, her voice calmer.

Jackson looked at her a moment and then nodded in thanks.

"If you need information on Olivia Cole's case, I can call Bailey and see what State has in its files," Cole said.

"Forget it," Jackson said, as he continued walking, "I got what I needed. If you want to help, get me kicked loose."

Detective Cole stood there, watching Jackson walk back to the house, wondering what he'd meant by he'd got what he needed.

66

A little before noon, the Augusta County Sheriff's Deputies finally let Jackson go, at which point he headed directly to Bear's house. As he drove south, he couldn't help but take unexpected turns and run the occasional light, double checking that no one got the idea to follow him from the scene, whether they be Lokos, police, or anyone else.

As he drove, he thought about the position he found himself in. Not only were the Lokos undoubtedly after him now, but at least one police department suspected he had something to do with a man's death, and a detective from another probably felt he wasn't being completely honest about what he knew about an abducted minor. A clear way out of the mess didn't immediately come to him. But he wasn't worried about himself, he was worried about Sara Beth.

Jackson pulled into Bear's driveway. Bear had his truck backed all the way up to his front porch and was unloading the arsenal he'd brought with him to Isaacs' house.

"Well you're here and not in handcuffs," Bear said as Jackson walked over, "I'll take that as a good sign."

"They're not buying what I told them," Jackson replied, "But they can't prove anything. Not yet, anyways."

"Well that's less than good," Bear asserted.

"Least of our worries, at this point. You got my SIG Sauer?"

"Over on the seat there," Bear said.

Jackson fetched the gun off the seat as well as his leg holster. He strapped the holster to himself, then checked that the magazine was still full before sliding it back in and cocking the gun to put one round in the chamber.

"We expecting company," Bear asked, watching him load up.

"Right now, I don't know who's coming around that corner," Jackson answered.

Bear paused for a minute, then placed one of the rifles he was unloading by his side.

"Is Silas' phone with my stuff," Jackson asked.

"Should be," Bear replied.

Jackson went back to the Suburban and found the phone and its battery tucked in the middle seat. He'd turned off the phone and taken out the battery in case the Lokos tried to locate it somehow. He put the battery back in and turned the phone on.

Once it booted, Jackson went back into the Telegram app. He opened up the Secret Chats and scanned them again, looking for another mention of Sara Beth Parker perhaps by someone else. The user 3vang3l1st, the first message he'd seen last night, had either become impatient or paranoid and had told Silas to forget any arrangements. That's one life potentially saved, Jackson thought.

None of the other private chats seemed to mention Sara Beth, but they all seemed to be clients, not fellow Lokos. Perhaps Silas communicated with other members another way, he thought, and went back into the phone's contacts. He was scanning the contacts for Solomon or any other name he recognized, when a call flashed across the screen. It was an unknown number.

Bear heard the phone ring, and came around the truck looking at Jackson. Jackson looked up at him, then swiped the green phone icon and put the phone up to his ear.

"Mr. Clay," said a voice on the other end, "It would appear you have something of mine."

67

The voice on the other end wasn't like Silas or the other Lokos Jackson had talked to. It was smooth and even-toned. Eerily calm.

Jackson put the phone out in front of him and put it on speakerphone so that Bear could also hear.

"You mean this phone," Jackson supposed.

"That would be it, yes," replied the voice.

Jackson stared at Bear, contemplating something in his head.

"Don't you mean I have something of your brother's," Jackson said before pausing, "It is Solomon, isn't it?"

An amused chuckle came back on the other end of the line.

"Quite the detective, we have here. You are sharp, I'll give you that," Solomon Ash said.

"Ain't a pussy, neither," Bear barked at the phone.

"Ah," Solomon said, "This must be the human sasquatch my men have been chasing around the woods."

Bear inhaled, about to give Solomon Ash a piece of his mind, but Jackson held up a hand, telling him to stop.

"I wanted to thank you, by the way, for taking care of Mr. Isaacs," Solomon continued, "He was a loose end I had been meaning to tie up.

Imagine my surprise when I found out the guy giving me all these headaches had done it for me."

Jackson's grip tightened on the phone, wishing it was Solomon's neck. Jeff Isaacs by no means was a saint, but he'd been preyed upon by the Ash brothers, promised false dreams of the family he'd lost. If Isaacs' grief had propelled him down such a dark road, it was Solomon that had given him the initial push.

"I'm not the good Samaritan type," Jackson said, "What's in it for me if I give you back the phone?"

"What would you like," Solomon asked.

"You know exactly what I want," Jackson replied, "Where is she?"

"Ah, yes. The girl you've been asking around about. That's a lot to ask for just one phone."

"I could always turn it over to the authorities. I'm sure they'd be interested to learn what you all have going on out there in the woods."

There was silence on the other end. Solomon Ash didn't say anything.

"Cut the crap, Ash," Jackson said, "We make a deal for the girl or I'm in the car driving this phone over to the Richmond FBI Field Office."

The silence lingered a moment longer before Solomon Ash spoke.

"Alright," Solomon said finally, "What do you propose?"

"We meet," Jackson answered, "Today."

"Yes, well, unfortunately it's going to take me a bit of time to gather what you want," Solomon replied.

"Tomorrow then. Sun up. That gives you plenty of time."

"Alright. First thing tomorrow. And where is this exchange supposed to happen?"

Jackson thought quickly. He needed a place someone like Ash would be comfortable with but a place where he had the edge.

"The mountain road," Jackson said looking at Bear, "At the two limestone boulders south of your compound."

"Fine, that'll work," Solomon replied.

"You bring anything more than one truck, we don't have a deal," Jackson said, "You bring Sara Beth Parker alive and unharmed. Then you'll have your phone."

Jackson ended the call before Solomon could agree. It was non-negotiable. Jackson put the phone down and slid it into his pocket.

"There you have it," Jackson said, "We have a meet."

He stepped around Bear and continued to unload weapons from the back of the Suburban. Bear came around the side of the truck, watching him work.

"Buddy, I hate to state the obvious," Bear began, "But there ain't a snowball's chance in hell they'll give her up. She's seen too much. She knows too much."

"He needs the phone, he'll bring her," Jackson replied, "Then it's up to us to get her out of there."

Bear didn't say anything. Instead he just looked at Jackson, seemingly uncertain. Jackson felt his wary stare.

"Listen" Jackson said, "This is what it's come down to. This is the play. You've seen how this has all gone. We're running out of time. It's this or she doesn't come home. This has to work."

Bear nodded and patted him on the shoulder.

"Alright," Bear replied, "You say this is how we do it, this is how it'll get done."

Jackson nodded and smiled.

"So," Bear said, unloading the last two guns, "What's next?"

"It's going to be a tough one tomorrow," Jackson said, "We better rest while we can. We're on the move tonight."

68

Cole sat at her desk at the Harrisonburg Police Department headquarters, staring at an empty cup of coffee. She was thinking about that morning and her conversation with Jackson Clay when her partner, Detective Sean Doherty, walked up and knocked on her cubicle wall.

"What's up, Sean," Cole asked.

"Thought you'd like to know two fed looking types just walked in and sat down with the boss," Doherty answered.

Detective Cole stood up and peered over her cubicle wall. Indeed, two men, one in a navy suit and one in a gray one, were seated with her superior, Lieutenant Mike Ingle. As they spoke, Lieutenant Ingle pointed in her direction and the two men looked over. Detective Cole shrank down into her office chair.

"You think this has anything to do with your field trip to Steeles Tavern this morning," Doherty asked.

"I don't know," Cole said, "But I'm going to find out."

As she left her desk and walked down the aisle that split the Major Crimes Unit in two, the men were stepping into the conference room just off of the Lieutenant's office. Ingle was flipping through some papers when he looked up and saw Detective Cole approaching.

"Ah, good," Ingle said, "Angela, you're just who I was looking for. You mind stepping into the conference room for a minute?"

"For what," asked Cole, suspicious.

Ingle held open the glass door for her without answering her question.

"It'll just take a few minutes," he said.

Reluctantly, Detective Cole stepped in and took a seat opposite the two strange faces at the table, who paid her no mind until Ingle made a formal introduction.

"Gentlemen, this is Detective Angela Cole," Ingle said, "Angela, these are Special Agents Frank Rivera and James Blair with the ATF."

"The ATF," Cole echoed, surprised.

"That's right Detective," said Agent Rivera, "Angela, is it?"

"Detective Cole will be fine, thank you," replied Cole.

"Angela," Lt. Ingle said, displeased with her tone.

Agent Rivera held up his hands in a gesture of surrender. Detective Cole got the feeling she was being worked over as if this was an interrogation.

"Okay," Rivera said, "Detective Cole, do you know a Jeff Isaacs?"

"You obviously know I do," Cole replied, "So why don't you cut the bullshit and get on with it."

"Cole," Ingle admonished again.

She shot the Lieutenant a look.

"No, it's okay, Lieutenant," said Agent Rivera, "Detective Cole, we've been investigating a group that calls itself the Living Order of the Kingdom of Solomon. LOKS for short. You may have heard of them."

"I've heard of them, yes," Cole replied.

"We've suspected for some time that they were into a number of nefarious things," Agent Rivera continued, "Mostly from our end, we were looking at them for possession and distribution of illegal firearms and explosives. A criminal informant of ours said there might be something more going on, though, mainly human trafficking."

"Human trafficking?"

"That's what he said. He was a low-level guy we were able to flip on a methamphetamine charge. His name is Cliff Bridges."

Agent Blair slid the man's mugshot across the table.

"Do you know him," Agent Rivera asked.

"No, I don't," Cole replied, looking up from the photo.

"He was supposed to check in with us this morning," Agent Rivera said, "But he's been radio silent. He's never missed a check-in. Now, he's six hours overdue and counting."

"I'm sorry your man hasn't checked in with you, but what's this all got to do with me?"

"Isaacs. How do you know him?"

"I'm working – I worked a case of a teenage girl. Abduction off the street. He ran a non-profit that helped families of taken children. He'd been helping the family of the girl that was abducted."

Agent Blair slid another photo across the table. The photo, clearly a surveillance photo, showed Jeff Isaacs meeting with two men, both of whom looked familiar.

"He also seemed to know some interesting people," Agent Rivera continued, "This is Isaacs at a marina owned by the LOKS on Smith Mountain Lake. The marina is how they explain the legitimacy of their revenue stream. The man on the right there is Solomon Ash, the leader of the LOKS. The other man is Jerry—"

"Jerry Johns," Cole said.

"That's right," said Agent Rivera, "The televangelist."

"Sure, I've seen him on TV Sunday mornings."

"He's the president of Christ Sovereign College over in Virginia Beach, as well. But near as we can tell – and believe me, we did our homework – these three have no official connection whatsoever, making this photo of them at a dock at Smith Mountain Lake quite interesting."

Detective Cole picked up the photo and studied it. What the hell had Jeff Isaacs been into, she thought.

"A minute ago, you said Jeff Isaacs *ran* a non-profit," Agent Blair said, "I'm assuming by your phrasing you know he's dead."

Lieutenant Ingle looked up at Agent Blair and then over at Detective Cole with alarm. Clearly, Isaacs' death was news to him. Detective Cole was searching for the words to formulate an answer when Agent

Blair slid another photo across the table. This one, another surveillance photo, was of her at the crime scene at Isaacs' house.

"Are you kidding me? You're surveilling crime scenes now," Cole asked rhetorically.

"You have to look at it from our point of view, detective," Agent Rivera said, "Here, we know this guy, now dead, is mixed up in something with some notable people, and then here comes this detective who knows him throwing her weight around at a crime scene that's not hers."

"I wasn't throwing my weight around," Cole said, annoyed, "I was—"

Agent Blair slid yet another photo across the table. It was of her standing on Isaacs' lawn talking to Jackson Clay.

"Finish that sentence," Agent Blair said, "You were, what? Having a private conversation with the suspect?"

"Oh, for fuck's sake," Cole snapped, "He's not a suspect. There *is* no suspect. Isaacs put a gun to his head and pulled the trigger. If you had your intel right, you'd know that."

"We do know the COD appears to be a self-inflicted gunshot wound," Agent Blair replied, "The question is why does it interest you?"

"Because there's still a little girl out there somewhere and maybe this guy had something to do with it. Look, if you want some sort of witch hunt, find another witch. I'm not your girl."

"We just want to understand what's going on here. Right now, we have a lot of interesting puzzle pieces, and we need to understand how they fit together."

"Yeah. You and I both."

She turned to her Lieutenant.

"Am I done here, sir," asked Cole.

Ingle didn't give her a reason to stay.

"Terrific," Cole said, "You gentleman have a nice day."

She walked angrily out of the conference room and marched down the center aisle of the office.

Sliding back into her desk, she put her head in her hands and forced herself to calm down. Whatever was going on, she was behind the curve. It was a feeling she didn't much care for and one she was going to fix.

She flipped through her notes to find the information of the man that had called her asking to verify Isaacs' address as a favor to Jackson.

Turning to her computer, she put in the name and searched Archibald Beauchamp.

69

Solomon Ash sat in the passenger seat, quietly judging the cretins on their drives home. The boors that slaved their way to and from work every day, spending a third or more of their life at jobs they hated to put food on the table for people they quietly resented. That wasn't Solomon. That was never him. To him, the American dream was a hoax. A piece of propaganda to get schlubs to pay their taxes and participate in the PTA. He had no time for that. He never did.

He watched as his Land Rover – other people drove him in it, sure, but make no mistake, the car was his and his alone – flew by the traffic jam, driving in the other direction. The thought made him grin. He'd never been one to go with the flow. To clock in at 9 and clock out at 5, that was for the imbeciles. Not him.

He looked in the backseat at the two large men taking up a bench seat for three. Baron and Lester were Solomon's personal muscle. If he were being completely honest, he trusted Baron and Lester more than he trusted his own brother. They were no less violent then Silas, but they were disciplined and dependable. His brother, bless his heart, was too emotional for his own good.

"Safeties off, boys," Solomon said to Baron and Lester, "Tell the boys in the other car, too."

Silas and three more men were following in another Land Rover. Baron and Lester unholstered their handguns, cocked them, and flipped off the safety before returning them to their holsters. Baron pulled out his phone and made a call.

"We're almost there," he said, "Boss says lock 'n' load."

The driver turned off of US Route 58 a few miles west of Clarksville, following a rural road north. The road climbed gradually, traversing a small field, before diving down through land thick with the woodlands of southern Virginia. Meandering back and forth, it emptied into a private driveway that ran its way to an impressive Colonial style house on the mouth of the Dan River.

Pulling in, the two Land Rovers diverged like bent fork prongs, blocking the three cars – two Cadillacs and a Lexus – in the stone-paved driveway. The men from both cars disembarked and fanned out, each knowing their job. Two jogged around the house towards the back door while two more posted up on the entrance of the driveway. The remaining two, Baron and Lester, followed Silas and Solomon to the front door.

As Solomon casually jogged up the steps to the porch, the front door swung open and out stepped an older man visibly angry.

"What in god's name are you doing here, Sol," said the man, "My family's here, you fuck."

"First of all, Senator, it's Solomon," said Solomon, "And second, we know the family's here. We were hoping they might join us."

Harlon Graves was the Virginia state senator for the 15th district, a confused polygon that spread out through south central portions of the state. Calling himself a pure nationalist, his coziness to a number of white supremacist groups had made him far too radioactive for any political party. But he had managed to stoke the flames of bigotry and intolerance in the area enough to steal a senate seat as an independent in a district that was 66% white. He'd run under the pretense that he was a working man and political outsider simply looking out for his fellow blue-collar friends and family. In truth, though, his family came from old money in the tobacco industry of pre-civil war Virginia, making the hardest thing he had to do on a day-to-day basis cashing out investments to fund his family's lifestyle.

"What the fuck are you talking about you little twerp," stammered Graves.

"Why don't we go inside and talk about it," replied Solomon.

"Why don't you get the fuck off my property before I call the sheriff," Graves growled.

A door kicked open behind the Senator inside the house and the two men who had circled around back now stepped through, one of them holding Graves' wife by the hair, a ball gag muffling her shrieking.

"Unfortunately, that's not going to happen, Senator," said Solomon, "Why don't we step inside?"

Solomon looked past Senator Graves to the man who wasn't holding the senator's wife.

"Get the daughter, she must be upstairs," Solomon said.

Senator Graves went to yell for his daughter, but as he breathed in, the barrel of a .45-caliber Colt 1911 pistol pressed into his neck.

"Why don't we use our indoor voice from here on, Senator," Solomon said.

Baron pushed the senator inside and together the statesman and his wife were marched to their large antique walnut dining room table. The group heard a scream come from upstairs, which caused Graves' wife to start crying. A moment later, the man who went upstairs returned with a teenage girl, cuffed and gagged.

Solomon's men sat the mother and daughter side by side in the middle of the table and forced the senator down into a seat at the far end. Solomon scooted out a chair and took a seat next to the senator.

"So, the reason we're here, you must be wondering," Solomon said.

The senator stared at Solomon, his eyes filled with rancor, but didn't say anything.

"Well, senator, due to situations beyond my control, we are regretfully going to have to take possession of that item you took delivery of the other day," Solomon continued.

"Go fuck yourself, I don't know what you're talking about," Graves replied.

Solomon looked at him confused.

"Are you sure," he asked, "I mean it can't be every day one takes ownership of a young lady."

Solomon looked around at everyone, amused

"I mean, hell, I'm *in the business* of it," he said, "and even for me it never gets to be, you know, routine."

Solomon turned to the wife and daughter.

"You have to understand, it's about the money for me," Solomon said, "Though I suppose for people like Harlon here, it's about something a little different. Isn't it, Harlon?"

"I'm warning you," Graves seethed, "Do not do this here, now."

"Is it about the missus?" Solomon pretended to ask quietly, leaning forward, "Things just not what they once were in the bedroom? You need something younger? Not unlike your pretty daughter over there."

"You leave her out of this, you understand me, asshole."

"Wait, wait. Did you take a girl *because* she's like your daughter, Senator? I mean that is some kind of reverse Electra complex mindfuck if I've ever seen one."

Solomon let out a forced chuckle. Senator Graves tried to lunge at Solomon before Baron and Lester grabbed him by the shoulders and planted him firmly back in his seat.

"Calm down, senator, we're just having some fun" Solomon said, "Now, like I said, we are going to have to take the girl back. So, where is she?"

"Fuck you," Graves replied.

"Senator, you're not making this any easier on yourself," Solomon said, "Normally, I would be happy to carry on like this. You use a four-letter word, I make a witty comeback, and we go 12 rounds like that. But for me, today, time is of the essence. That's why I brought these men with me. We can do this transaction clean and easy, or, well, we can go the messy route."

Silas walked up behind Senator Graves' wife, brandishing a bowie knife, and pressed the blade gently into the side of her neck.

"Stop it," Graves yelled, "Leave her alone!"

"Tell us where the girl is," Solomon said, his amusement gone like he flipped a switch.

"I don't know what the fuck you're talking about," Graves replied, still yelling.

The man that had grabbed Senator Graves' daughter from upstairs came back into the dining room.

"There's a separate building out back, looks like an office," he said. "Down a walkway across the garden. Near the river."

Solomon looked at Senator Graves with piqued interest.

"Oh, Senator," he said, "You wouldn't be playing Slick Willie down by the river, would you?"

Senator Graves didn't say anything. Solomon turned back to the man.

"Check it out," he said before turning to Silas, "Go with them."

Silas and the goons disappeared through the kitchen and out the back of the house. Solomon turned back to Senator Graves, who now sat quietly, his head slumped down, his elbows on the table.

"She's there, isn't she," Solomon asked quietly.

Senator Graves didn't answer him.

"I asked you for your cooperation," Solomon continued, "I told you we would find her."

Solomon shook his head, feigning disappointment.

"Such a foolish man," he said.

"Please," Graves said, his voice starting to crack, "Please, just let them go. They don't even know what's going on."

Solomon patted Senator Graves on his hand.

"Oh, Senator," Solomon said, "You and I both know we're past that."

Graves slumped down further in his chair and began sobbing. Seeing this and reading what it must mean, his wife let out a muffled shriek through her gag and began to whine violently. Their daughter, confused, darted her eyes frantically between the two.

"If it gives you any comfort, Senator," Solomon said, "You should know, to me, this is strictly business. But, like I said, you put yourself in this position."

Senator Graves' sobbing turned into something guttural, almost an animalistic howl, as he heard the backdoor kick open and bang against the wall with force. A young voice screamed as kitchenware knocked and clanged around. Silas appeared in the doorway, grabbing a teenage girl who was flailing in his arms.

"Found her," he said, giving a menacing smile, "Playboy here had a secret room below his home office. Regular sex dungeon. Kinky fuck."

"Ah, Miss Parker, I believe it is," said Solomon.

Standing up, he approached Sara Beth Parker who stopped flailing, suddenly paralyzed with fear. Solomon cupped her chin, softly stroking her bottom lip with his thumb. Sara Beth dry heaved as if she was going to be sick.

"You know, I am not normally in the practice of learning my commodities' names," Solomon said, "But you, you have caused me a great deal of trouble. Truth be told, if I could do it all over again, I never would have had Silas and his goons snatch you from that parking lot in Harrisonburg. We would've taken someone, anyone else had we known what a handful you were going to be."

Sara Beth did nothing but stare at him, terrified even to blink. Solomon shook his head, as if he had been somewhere else in his head for a moment.

"Anyway," he said, his voice distant before gathering himself, "Take her to the car, would you?"

Solomon turned and placed his hands on Senator Graves' shoulders.

"Well, Senator, it's been fun, but I must be going," he said.

Lester, standing behind the senator's wife and daughter, drew a semiautomatic pistol and attached a silencer to the end of the barrel. Senator Graves' daughter began to cry just as hard as her mother.

"Please, god," Senator Graves murmured.

Solomon leaned in to the senator so close that the 69-year-old man could feel Solomon's breath on his ear as he whispered the last words he'd ever hear.

"You're a child fucker, Harlon. You don't get god. You get me."

Senator Graves closed his eyes as Lester fired two rounds into the back of his wife and daughter's heads. He put his head down and sobbed as Lester matter-of-factly walked around the table, put the gun to the back of the senator's head, and squeezed the trigger two more times.

At that, the room became silent. Solomon took one of the cloth napkins and wiped at some blood splatter on the cuff of his shirt before stuffing it in his pocket. He turned to Silas.

"Crack the safe to make it look like a home invasion then burn it all," Solomon said, "Don't be home late."

Silas nodded and smiled. As Solomon walked out the front door, Baron dropped off two jerry cans filled with diesel fuel on the porch then followed him out to the car where Lester was closing the tailgate to the Land Rover.

"Are we good," Solomon asked.

"She's sedated, now," Lester answered, "She'll be out for the duration."

"Good," Solomon replied, "Let's go."

70

Jackson sat in his car across the train tracks staring at the small white cottage. Nat had moved out and most of their friends chose to keep their distance. Unable to concentrate on anything else, his pursuit of a Private Investigator's license had fallen by the wayside. All he had was this. Tracking down the man that took his boy from him.

Now, he had found him. Or at least he had convinced himself of that. This small white cottage, at the end of a block of houses, snuggled up against the train tracks just west of the Port of Richmond, was where Dale Jeffers lived. Convinced Jeffers had taken Evan, he'd followed him for weeks, learning where he went. He knew now, on a Friday night like this one, Jeffers came home after stopping at 7Eleven for a pack of Busch and wouldn't reemerge until sometime Saturday afternoon.

Jackson put his car in gear and slowly pulled off the road, coasting into a field of tall grass, hiding it from passersby. He killed the engine and climbed out. Winter had come early in the form of a late November ice storm. Shards of frozen water pelted his face, as if admonishing him, begging him to turn back and go home. He stood on the train tracks and stared at the house. The electric blue light of the television illuminated the windows, flickering as the scenes changed.

Reaching into his coat, Jackson pulled out an M9 Beretta. Fond of the model when he'd used it in the Army, he'd bought himself this one with custom work done to the barrel and the grip as a retirement present when he left the armed forces. The model, M9, had made him smile when Evan was born on March 9. He'd imagined the day Evan would turn 18 and he would give him the gun. He looked down at the it, thinking about that day that wouldn't come now. It wouldn't come because it had been taken from him, and Dale Jeffers was the man that had taken it. He clenched the gun in his hand and began walking toward the house.

Of course, the gun was registered to him. He didn't know everything about criminal forensics but he knew enough to figure there was a decent chance he'd be tied to whatever he did to Jeffers tonight. He didn't care. He had lost everything. No. Rather, he had had everything taken from him. Now it was time to take whatever Dale Jeffers held dear.

Walking up to the house, he quietly checked the door. To his surprise, it was unlocked. Jackson turned the knob slowly and pushed open the door.

The front entrance opened into a quaint living area that felt even smaller with the piles of junk strewn about it. Bookshelves were lined with empty beer cans broken up by the occasional photo or knickknack. Old mail and paper-work littered a desk in the corner. In the center of the room, Jackson saw the top of a man's head in a dirty plaid recliner facing a television that had to have been from before the turn of the century. Some old movie was on, strobing the room in varying flashes of gray and white.

Slowly, Jackson approached the recliner. He stuck out the M9 Beretta and placed the muzzle against the back of Jeffers' balding head. The sudden sensation of cold steel against his scalp caused Jeffers to jump in his seat. Jackson noticed the recliner swiveled. He grabbed the edge and spun it, bringing Jeffers around to face him.

"I ain't got much money," Jeffers said rather calmly, "What – whatever I have is yours, though."

"Dale Jeffers," Jackson said.

"What," Jeffers replied.

"You are Dale Jeffers, no?"

"Wha – I – What's this about?"

"This is about something you took from me."

"Now hold on, I didn't take nothing from no one."

Jackson reached into his coat and pulled out a photo, a picture he had taken *with Nat and Evan last Christmas. The three of them had big, goofy smiles on their face. Evan smiled through a Santa stocking that was too big for his head. He tossed it to Jeffers.*

"His name was Evan Randolph Clay," Jackson said, "He didn't do a damn thing to anyone. And you took him from me."

Jeffers searched for the words to form some sort of denial but Jackson saw the acknowledgement in his eyes. To him it was as good as a confession. He stepped towards Jeffers, cocking the Beretta, as the old man continued to babble indecipherably in his chair.

Jackson debated whether he wanted to say anything more before squeezing the trigger and being done with it when something banged against a door over his shoulder. Jackson stepped back, unsure of now where to point his gun. It hadn't been an intentional knock, one done with someone's knuckles, but a clumsy one, as if someone had bumped into the door.

"Who else is here," Jackson asked.

"No one," replied Jeffers, "There's no one else here. Only me."

Dale Jeffers looked as though he was more nervous now than when he had faced imminent death. Jackson moved towards the door and turned the knob. It was locked.

"You don't lock your front door, but you keep this locked," Jackson asked rhetorically.

"It's nothing. Really," Jeffers replied, "It's just storage. Something must've fallen down."

Jackson wasn't buying it. He turned back to Jeffers, about to demand the man open the door, when he noticed a key around the man's neck for the first time. It sat, flat on his chest, nestled amongst the man's patchy chest hair. He aimed the gun at Jeffers, then leaned forward and ripped the key from around his neck. He slid it into the lock on the knob at turned it. The door opened to reveal what was indeed a small closet, but there was nothing stored here. Nothing except for a little boy.

Jackson stepped back, almost breathless. The boy had olive skin and short black hair. He looked up at Jackson expressionless. Not crying, not fighting to get off the soiled mattress he sat on, just innocently inquisitive of this man that had opened the door.

The more Jackson looked at him, the more he realized the boy looked familiar. He'd seen him somewhere. And then it hit him.

A few days earlier there had been a report on the news of a young boy missing. He'd last been seen with his family at Byrd Park in the Fan District of Richmond. Jackson remembered watching the mother and father sobbing on camera. He could relate exactly to what they were going through.

Jackson turned back to Jeffers who now sat silent with his head down. His rage for the man intensified, something he'd previously thought wasn't possible. How many more boys just like his Evan had there been? How many families torn apart by grief?

A slew of violent reprisals flashed into Jackson's head like a rotating carousel of possible acts of vengeance. But as he stood in the middle of the living room, the little boy simply staring at him, expressionless, he realized he didn't have the nerve to do it. Not in front of the boy. This poor boy who'd been taken from the only things he'd known in this world. As much as he wanted Dale Jeffers to hurt and to pay for what he'd done, this boy had been through enough. He couldn't harm Jeffers. Not in front of the boy.

Jackson scanned the room, looking for something to help him. Over in the corner a roll of duct tape lay around the handle of a hammer sitting upside down. Jackson grabbed it and ordered Dale Jeffers up. Jeffers began to say something, but Jackson rolled the duct tape around his head, covering his mouth and quieting him. He ripped it off and did the same thing around Jeffers' wrist and ankles.

Finished, he tossed it on to the plaid recliner and grabbed Jeffers underneath his arm.

"Hop," Jackson ordered.

Jeffers jumped up and down awkwardly, making his way to and then out the front door of his house, where Jackson sat him down on the porch. He then went back inside and retrieved the young boy, picking him up and cradling him in his arms. The boy giggled as Jackson slid a forearm under his bottom and placed him against his chest. He walked out the door and led the boy over to the hood of a white Ford pickup parked in the driveway.

"You do anything other than sit right there and I'll kill you, you understand," Jackson barked from the driveway.

Jeffers didn't say anything back.

Jackson reached into his pocket, fetched his phone, and dialed 9-1-1.

"Yes, hello," Jackson said, "That boy on the news. The one that disappeared from Byrd Park. I found him. A man named Dale Jeffers had him. We

are all at his house now. 5601 Earnhardt Avenue. Can you send the police, please?"

Jackson continued to converse with the operator, cooing the little boy during pauses in the questioning. The little boy would giggle and smile up at Jackson, who smiled back. It wasn't Evan smiling at him, but it was someone else's Evan. And in that moment, exhausted from his own hate and anger, that was good enough for Jackson. He knew there'd be tough questions to answer. But in that moment, with that little boy looking at him, the promise of a fulfilling life returned to a young, innocent soul, Jackson didn't care.

He continued to play with the boy, cooing him. The rest of the world faded from focus. Around him, the darkness slowly became awash in blue and red flashing lights. There were sirens, but Jackson didn't hear them. All he heard were the giggles of the little boy in front of him. The boy he'd saved.

JACKSON CLAY OPENED his eyes not to the image of a little boy but Bear Beauchamp's front yard cast peacefully in the midnight moonlight. Rubbing his eyes, he looked at the empty Miller High Life bottle sitting on the table next to him. Bear had offered it to him as a four-in-the-afternoon nightcap, and, too exhausted to spurn his offer, Jackson had obliged him.

Not long after that he must've dozed off in the Adirondack chair on Bear's front porch because that's where he found himself. Without any porch lights on or light coming through the windows from inside, the area was bathed in a peaceful twilight just bright enough to make out the features around him. Jackson paused a moment longer, taking in the night, before getting up and going inside. The sun would be up in a few hours and there was work to be done.

On the coffee table in the living room, Jackson found the yellow mailer he'd asked Bear for before dozing off. He took it over to his bags and fetched one of his prepaid burner phones, then got Silas' phone.

Jackson knew the first thing Solomon would check is that the SIM card and storage card were still in the phone, so he'd have to leave them there. He wasn't sure he could copy the information on the cards and he was even less sure he could copy them without it being discovered. Instead, he opted to do things the low-tech way.

First, opening up the back of the phone, he snapped photos of any and all identification numbers he could find, including on the battery. Then going into the phone's settings, he pulled up all the identification information he could find. The phone's serial number, the SIM card's serial number, the service provider account information, and snapped photos of all of that as well.

After that, Jackson spent the next two hours methodically going through the phone, snapping photos of every damning conversation, email, and photo he could find. When he found photos of what appeared to be abducted people with their faces to the camera, he searched missing persons cases across the state of Virginia and tried to identify anyone he saw in the photos. He was successful on a number of them. The first one he found was Meghan Anderson, a college student who disappeared after last being seen at a bar in the Richmond suburbs. He used the missing persons site he found her on to identify numerous others. Pamela Capp, Lynn O'Hara, Bea Gould, Katie Carter, Danielle Hardy. Jackson documented each of them.

In all, Jackson snapped almost a thousand pictures and typed in thousands of words of notes in the phone's memo app. It had nearly eaten up all of the cheap little phone's memory. When he was done, he powered the phone off and removed the battery so the phone wouldn't inadvertently turn itself on. Then he grabbed a piece of paper and wrapped it around the phone. With a marker, he wrote on the front of it.

CHECK PHOTOS AND MEMO FILES
DO NOT LET THEM GET AWAY WITH THIS

He put the phone wrapped in the note inside the mailer along with the battery, and sealed it with the adhesive strip. He flipped the mailer onto its front and addressed it.

DELIVER TO DETECTIVE JENNIFER BAILEY
VIRGINIA STATE POLICE DIVISION SEVEN HEADQUARTERS

Below he wrote down the address, then placed more than enough stamps for postage in the upper right-hand corner. All that was left was to write down the return address. He never had any intention of putting his own name and address down in case it never got to Detective Bailey, but now an idea came to him. He uncapped the marker and wrote.

SARA BETH PARKER

Underneath, he wrote down the address of the repair shop parking lot where she had disappeared.

Jackson sat back, looked over his work, and sighed. He didn't know what was about to happen, but should he not make it out or get Sara Beth back, he figured this was the ace up his sleeve. His measure taken to ensure justice was done should he not be able to do it himself.

He stood gingerly, stretching his legs, when a flicker of light through the back window caught his eye. Curious, he walked into the kitchen to see. Bear was in the backyard, seated at his fire pit, a bottle of beer cupped in between his hands.

Jackson walked out to join him.

"Couldn't sleep," he asked as he walked up to Bear.

"Nah, I slept fine for a bit," Bear answered, "I got my solid seven. No need to overdo it."

"Sure," Jackson replied.

The fire popped and crackled, shooting the occasional ember wayward as Jackson took a seat on a log opposite Bear. The two of them didn't say anything as they stared at the fire. Bear tilted his head back and polished off a beer before reaching behind himself and grabbing another. He extended it to Jackson in invitation, who smiled politely and shook his head. Bear shrugged, opened the beer with his lighter, and slid it into his koozie.

"So, this thing today," Jackson said, breaking the silence, "I don't know what it's going to be like, but chances are it's going to be rough."

"Knowing those peckerwoods, I'd bet on it," Bear replied.

"You know, I couldn't have gotten this far without your help," Jackson continued.

"Uh oh."

"What?"

"Starting off with how nice it's been and all that. I know how this goes."

"What do you mean?"

"You're breaking up with me."

Bear's whole body shook in jolly pleasure as he laughed, quite literally slapping his knee with his non-beer hand. Jackson couldn't help but grin and chuckle himself.

"No, all I'm saying is," Jackson said, "I signed up for this. I took this on."

"I took this on, too, brother," Bear replied.

"No, I know you offered your help and all that," Jackson said, "I guess what I'm saying is, I don't know how this is going to go down today, but whatever happens, I'm good with it. I decided that a long time ago. But that's my choice. You've got to know you don't have to go out there today because of choices I've made."

Bear didn't say anything. He took a long sip of his beer, holding it for a moment in his mouth, before swallowing. He leaned forward, his elbows on his knees, and stared into the fire. Jackson watched him, waiting for him to say something, but Bear didn't say anything.

"Bear," Jackson said.

Bear looked up at him.

"I heard ya," Bear said, "I ain't goin' nowhere."

Jackson smiled and nodded. He'd been doing this sort of thing a while and had gotten used to going it alone. He'd always figured it was a path for him and him only. That first boy he'd found had stopped him from killing a man while he sat watching TV. Regardless of what that man had done or what he did or didn't deserve, that boy had stopped Jackson from crossing a line he knew he hadn't been ready to cross. That boy had been his salvation, showing him a way to move on. Moving on had always meant going it alone. But, now, as he sat across from Archibald 'Bear' Beauchamp, he was thankful to have him.

"When do we go," Bear asked.

"Soon," Jackson replied, "We need to be in position before the Lokos get there and we've got work to do before then. I don't know what they plan to do, but one thing's for sure: they aren't going to get the drop on us."

"Amen to that," Bear said, "I can bring the Suburban or the D100 around and start loading it."

"No, we'll load up my truck," Jackson said, "But we'll bring your Suburban and the Ranger and drop them nearby. Give ourselves some options."

"What do you want me to bring out in terms of firepower?"

"All of it. Last night I brought one pistol to a full-on firefight. That's not a mistake I plan on making twice."

Bear gave a boyish, menacing smile.

"When you say *all* of it," Bear began.

"I mean that stuff you showed me behind the bookcase," Jackson said, ".50 Cal and all."

"Buddy," Bear said, "Don't toy with my emotions."

"I've seen what these monsters are doing, what they are capable of," Jackson replied standing up, "I'm not fucking around anymore."

71

Cole was the only driver on the highway just after midnight. She'd tried to get some rest, but the thought that something was about to happen plagued her. Slumber never came, and she grew tired of waiting for it.

She'd hopped in her car and decided to head to Bear Beauchamp's last known address. Maybe Jackson Clay was there, maybe he wasn't. But she figured the man she had helped out a couple of days ago would know where to find him.

Her GPS had taken her on a series of remote rural highways off of US Route 220, snaking a path towards the north end of the town of Martinsville. The moon, nearly full, flickered in between the passing trees, casting a low light on the sleeping world. It was in this light she saw a trailer being backed down a driveway half a mile ahead. She looked at her GPS. It was the driveway her route ended on.

As she neared the driveway, she slowed down and killed her headlights. Creeping towards the clearing in the trees, she leaned forward, peaking down the asphalt path. A man was driving some sort of all-terrain vehicle onto the trailer she'd seen as another man waved him forward. The man shifted, the headlights of the vehicle briefly flashing across his face. It was Jackson Clay.

Detective Cole turned down the drive way and pulled forward, putting her unmarked police car nose to nose with a red Chevy Suburban the trailer was hitched to. Her arrival startled Jackson, who drew a gun from the small of his back. The other man, who she now saw to be Bear Beauchamp from his DMV photo, came around the front of the truck with an impressive-looking shotgun in hand. As she climbed out of the car, and stood looking at the two of them, Jackson dropped his guard. She heard him tell Bear it was okay.

"Lady, you got some death wish rolling up on a private citizen out here like that," Bear scolded as he went back to what he'd been working on.

Jackson approached her with the walk of a man not amused to see her there. He grabbed her forearm and pulled her towards the back of her car.

"What the hell are you doing here," Jackson said, clearly angry.

Cole jerked her arm free.

"I told you before. I'm a detective, Clay," she replied, "I'm good at what I do."

"You shouldn't be here," he said.

"Shouldn't I," she asked, "Seems a lot's going on for someone that doesn't know anything for certain yet."

Cole turned and waved an open hand at the sight of their two trucks, the all-terrain vehicle, and the guns Bear was working on on the front porch.

"Are you guys going hunting?" she asked rhetorically. "Because this seems a bit overkill for quail if you ask me."

Jackson looked at her. The determination in her eyes. Trying to keep her in the dark wasn't going to work anymore.

"Look, what do you want from me," he asked.

"I want to know what's going on," Cole said.

"I'm working on bringing Sara Beth home," Jackson replied, "That's the truth."

"How? By storming the gates of the LOKS place?"

"What?"

"I know about them, Jackson. The Kingdom of Solomon guys. They're just north of here, right? I had two ATF agents grill me like I might be a part of the whole thing, when actually I knew nothing about it."

"Why are the ATF asking you about them?"

"Because they're watching them, Clay. They have photos of Jeff Isaacs meeting with their leader at some marina on Smith Mountain Lake."

"Do they have eyes on Lokoville?"

"Lokoville?"

"Their compound in the woods. Are they watching there?"

"I don't know. They didn't show me any photos like that. Just of the marina and the crime scene at Isaacs' house. They wanted to know who you were and why I was talking to you."

"What did you tell them?"

"I didn't tell them anything, but that's not going to satisfy them. You've got to tell me what's going on here, Clay. I mean, what is that?"

Cole pointed past Jackson at Bear who was sizing up a piece of camouflage netting.

"What is going on here, Clay," she asked.

"I told you. I'm working on getting Sara Beth back," Jackson replied.

Cole crossed her arms in frustration.

"That's the truth, Cole," Jackson said, "I have a play for Sara Beth and I'm making it."

"It looks like you're going to war," Cole replied.

"I'm bringing her home," Jackson said, "I'm not playing games with you. You need to trust me on this."

"You knew about all this yesterday, right? When you told me you were still working things? How am I supposed to trust you?"

"Not all of this, no."

Bear shut the tailgate to Jackson's truck and walked over to Jackson and Cole.

"We're ready to go, Jack," Bear said, "What's the word?"

Jackson looked at the detective.

"I don't know," he replied, "You going to let us go, Cole?"

Detective Cole looked at the two men. Asking her to trust either of them seemed impossible. But her instinct told her she'd be putting

Sara Beth further in harm's way if she stopped them. She stepped towards Jackson, and looked directly into his eyes.

"Bring her home," she said.

Getting back into her car, Cole backed down the drive way and pulled out onto the rural road. Jackson and Bear drove past in the two trucks. She watched as they headed down the road until their taillights disappeared from view. Cole had let them go reluctantly. Whatever they were about to do worried her. She couldn't sit by and do nothing.

An idea came to her, but it made her uneasy. It required her to trust someone else she wasn't sure that she did, and for them to trust her. Cole opened up her glove box and looked for the business card she'd been given. With it in hand, she pulled out her phone, punched in the number on the card, and put the phone to her ear.

"Agent Rivera, it's Detective Cole, Harrisonburg Police," she said, "I think you need to get down to southern Virginia."

72

Jackson sat in his truck, the engine humming, and stared at the stretch of mountain road ahead of him. Fifty feet ahead lay the two large limestone boulders that sat like a gateway to this stretch of road. From where Jackson sat, the road disappeared around a bend into nothing, leaving only the mountainous horizon and the sun just now peeking out from behind it.

He'd sat there, just like that, for hours, watching as the sky slowly illuminated with the dawning of a new day. The scene had been idyllic. Jackson knew it wouldn't last.

"You still hear me okay, buddy," Bear said into his ear.

Jackson put a finger on the earpiece in his ear. The two of them were once again communicating by radio. They had gotten out on the mountain road and set up in the early morning hours. As Jackson sat in his Ram, Bear was hundreds of feet back and to Jackson's left, lying prone on a ledge near where the mountain road peaked. He had his M2 heavy machine gun on a tripod as well as a Windrunner M96, a large-caliber sniper rifle with an effective range of over a mile. Together, the three of them lay under camouflage netting. Looking up from where Jackson sat, Bear was impossible to spot.

"Yeah, I've got you," Jackson replied, keying his throat mic, "Any movement on the road yet?"

"Nothing yet," Bear answered.

Bear had scanned the mountainside with a pair of binoculars all morning, making sure the Lokos didn't do precisely what the two of them had: place a hidden shooter with a view of the meeting area.

Jackson looked at his watch. It was 15 minutes before seven. He looked around, studying the area around him. The Lokos hadn't tried anything yet, which made him nervous.

"So, assuming they show up and bring the girl with them," Bear said into the radio, "We expect them to just give her up?"

"The phone can fuck them just as easily, which is why they'll play ball," Jackson replied, "Solomon doesn't strike me as stupid. He'll try for both, but that's why you're up there. To make sure that doesn't happen."

"To make sure you two get out," Bear doubled down.

Or, at the very least, Jackson thought, to make sure *she* gets out.

"Hold on, there's dust kicked up on the bend in the road after yours," Bear said, "Might be a vehicle coming towards you."

Jackson looked down at the Sig Sauer assault rifle, the same one he'd used the other night, and checked that the safety was off and there was a round in the chamber. He then drew his P320 from his hip and did the same thing. He put them back and looked down the road. Bear didn't continue his report.

"Anything," Jackson asked.

"Hold on, I'm watching," Bear answered.

Jackson sat still and focused, trying to keep his heart rate low. Down on the road, he couldn't see what was coming. It had made him uneasy all morning. That feeling was only heightened now.

"Yup, brother, I think it's them," Bear said, "Looks like that black van coming towards you."

Jackson couldn't help but note the irony. The black van, the vehicle that had started all this, the first break he'd gotten – the vehicle he'd chased halfway across the state, the one that had led him to Bear, that led him to the Living Order – *that* was the van bringing Sara Beth Parker to him finally.

"Are you ready up there," Jackson asked.

"Ready," Bear replied.

"Good," said Jackson, "Let's finish this."

73

J ackson rapped two fingers against the cold steel of the P320 strapped to his thigh. He stared forward, motionless, waiting for the van to come around the bend in the road.

"Let me know what they're doing," Jackson said, keying his mic.

"They're still moving towards you," Bear radioed back, "Taking their sweet time, but they're coming."

Bear watched the van amble down the road, bobbing awkwardly with every hole it hit. He winced as the whole body bucked forward with the front bumper smacking the ground. The van had come to a stop.

"Hold on, they're stopping," Bear said, "I think this road might've ripped the van a new one."

But just as he radioed Jackson, the van began moving again. As it continued forward, Bear spotted two men on the road. They must've come off the back of the van. With rifles slung around their back and draped in camouflage, they began climbing up the slope of the mountain, following the road. As they climbed into thicker brush, only their movement made it possible to spot them.

"They're moving again, but we've got a problem," Bear radioed,

"Two shooters in camouflage came off the back of the van. They're on your high side."

"Watch them," Jackson replied, "I've got the van."

Jackson waited for the van to come into his line of sight before climbing out of the truck. Knowing that men were sneaking up on his side actually put him at ease. He knew the Lokos would try something, now he knew their move and could anticipate it.

As the van moved slowly towards him, he stepped out, sliding the assault rifle he had over into the driver's seat. He reached into the cubby on the driver-side door and pulled out a second handgun – his M9 Beretta with a custom grip and barrel – and slipped it into his waistband.

The van came to a stop several feet short of the limestone boulders, mirroring Jackson's truck. Silas Ash climbed out of the driver's seat, a shotgun already in hand. Jackson heard the backdoors of the van open and the three men Jackson had originally met at the bar in Rocky Mount came around to the front. The Kerley brothers were carrying assault rifles; the one Jackson knew as Mack toted a pump-action shotgun.

Solomon Ash studied Jackson from the passenger seat a minute more before opening the door of the van and standing up, looking down at Jackson with his elbows rested on the door and the hood.

"It is a lovely day in the Virginia wilderness, isn't it," Solomon said.

Jackson was quiet. When he didn't say anything, Solomon shrugged his shoulders and climbed down, snaking his way through the trio of goons to stand in front of them.

"That's a lot of firepower for one cell phone," Jackson said.

Solomon smiled.

"Hey, you said bring one car, you didn't say how many it could hold," he replied.

He made a show of looking over the area, both high and low, before turning back to Jackson.

"And I presume your redneck friend is around here somewhere," Solomon said.

"I'm right here, asshole," Bear chimed into Jackson's ear.

"Sara Beth. Where is she," Jackson asked Solomon.

"Where's the phone," Solomon asked in reply.

Jackson reached into his pocket and pulled out Silas' cell phone in a clear Ziploc bag, holding it up for the band of Lokos to see.

"Sara Beth," Jackson repeated, "Now."

Solomon turned and said something to one of the Kerley brothers. The man disappeared briefly behind the van before coming back around marching a girl in front of him.

There she was. Even with her wrists bound, her mouth gagged, and her body worked over with bruises and cuts, Jackson recognized Sara Beth from the countless times he'd looked at her photo. That dark brown hair. Those big green eyes. Sara Beth Parker, finally in the flesh.

"The phone now, Mr. Clay," Solomon said.

"Let her come to me," Jackson replied, "Then I'll give you the phone."

"That's not how this is going to go down, Mr. Clay," Solomon said.

"That's exactly how this is going to go down. That is, if you want the phone back."

"Look around, Mr. Clay. You're in no position to negotiate anything."

"Exactly, look around. It's five men on one. I'm not going anywhere. Let her walk to me, and I'll toss you the phone."

Solomon thought to himself for a minute, then turned to the man holding Sara Beth's wrists and nodded.

Bear watched through the scope of the sniper rifle as one of the Lokos he recognized from the bar marched Sara Beth forward, then stopped as he tried to cut off the zip ties around her wrists. Bear shifted the scope up and looked at the two men in the woods. They were no more than a couple feet apart, moving past the boulders and coming around to Jackson's side.

"The two shooters in the woods are moving to flank you," Bear radioed to Jackson.

Jackson tried to look out of the corner of his eye to see if he could see the men. He couldn't. Then a snapping sound brought his attention forward again.

Sara Beth grabbed her wrists and rubbed them as if it had been a while since they'd been free. Solomon walked over to her and pulled the cloth gag off her mouth, letting it drape around her neck. He smiled at her, then turned and faced Jackson with his hand on her back as if ready to usher her forward.

"One more thing, Mr. Clay," Solomon said, "The gun on your leg. Kindly lose it, please."

Jackson stared at him. He didn't mind dropping the gun with a second one tucked into his pants, but he wanted to sell Solomon on his reluctancy to keep him from suspecting he had a backup.

"Now, Mr. Clay," Solomon demanded.

With two fingers, Jackson slowly unclipped the holster and withdrew the gun, presenting it in front of him before moving to place it on the ground. When his mouth was hidden from view, Jackson keyed his radio mic.

"When I make my move, drop the guys in the woods," Jackson said.

"Got it," Bear radioed back.

Jackson stood up, his arms outstretched and his hands open. He looked at Solomon with a begrudging scowl.

"The girl now," Jackson said.

Solomon smiled at him.

"Very well," he replied, "Off you go, my dear."

Solomon gave her a gentle nudge with the hand on her back. She hesitated, looking at Jackson with fear and uncertainty. Jackson swung one of his outstretched arms towards her and motioned with his hand.

"It's okay, Sara Beth," he said, "I'm here to take you home."

"The guys in the woods are at your three o'clock," Bear radioed, "Whatever you're going to do, you need to do it now."

Jackson took a step towards her.

"Sara Beth," he pleaded, "It's okay."

"That's far enough, Mr. Clay," Solomon said.

"Let me take her," Jackson replied, "I have the phone."

He took the phone in the Ziploc bag and held it out for everyone to see again. Cautiously, he began walking towards them, towards Sara Beth, all the while maintaining eye contact with her.

"Sara Beth, you have to trust me," Jackson said, "I'm not like the other men he's given you to. I'm here to bring you home."

Nervous, she took a jittery step towards him.

"That's it, good," Jackson said.

He continued to walk towards her slowly until he was standing in between the two limestone boulders. He stood there as she came to him, seeming to trust what she was doing more and more. Her steps became more sure-footed. Her body stopped shaking. Maybe something told her to trust Jackson, or maybe the hope of going home had overtaken her fear. By the time she got to Jackson's arms, she was practically jogging. Jackson didn't stop looking at her, reassuring her with a smile. She started to smile back, those signatures dimples starting to form, when Jackson saw Solomon pull out a gun and point it at them.

Jackson grabbed Sara Beth with both arms, holding her as he threw both of them to his left behind one of the limestone boulders. They hit the ground as two shots rang out almost simultaneously. Jackson heard one ricochet off the rock. He looked over his shoulder to see a man on the mountainside above him be thrown backwards against a tree before falling and tumbling down, his body coming to a stop at the top of the other boulder.

As the man fell, Jackson saw the second one stand up where the first had been shot. The man leveled a gun directed at the two of them laying on the road. Jackson pulled the M9 out from behind his back and fired two shots, winging the man and throwing him off balance. Another shot rang out from above and behind Jackson. He was looking at the camouflaged gunman when the .50 caliber round effectively crushed the man's skull, tossing his body like a rag doll.

"Got them," Bear radioed.

"Get that M2 and light them up," Jackson replied.

Jackson looked towards the gap in between the boulders, placing himself between Sara Beth and the others. One of the Kerley brothers, the one that had taken Sara Beth out of the van, came around the rock, his rifle pointed in their direction. Jackson squeezed off another two rounds, hitting the man square in his chest, then pointed it at the man's head and fired a third round. The man's head kicked backwards, guiding his lifeless body to the ground.

The valley became filled with the *rat-tat-tat* of the powerful machine gun overhead. Jackson could hear as lead rounds punched holes into the van with a melody of metal being pierced and glass shattering.

Jackson looked over at Sara Beth who had balled herself up in the fetal position and was covering her head with her hands. He shook her gently as he shouted over the gunfire.

"Sara Beth, we have to go," he said.

She didn't move.

"Sara Beth, you have to trust me," he tried again, "We have to move or we will die."

She turned her head and peeked out at him through the bend in her arm. Jackson held out a hand. She took it and stood up with him. Jackson keyed his radio.

"Cover us, I'm getting the girl out of here," he said.

He turned to Sara Beth.

"Stand behind me," he said.

She nodded. Jackson squared his body in the direction of the Lokos, his gun pointed the same way. Taking one step at a time, he moved back towards his truck. He watched as Bear rained rounds down on them, crashing violently into whatever they hit like metal meteors.

He was halfway to his truck when he saw Solomon peek his head out from behind the van. He stuck his hand out with a gun and fired at Jackson.

Jackson returned his fire when the other Kerley brother came around the opposite side of the van with a shotgun. Before Jackson could react, the man pulled the trigger. Jackson was almost knocked off his feet as the slug slammed into the right side of his abdomen. Bear continued to fire in the man's direction, but the Loko was protected by the van. He pumped the shotgun, kicking a smoking shell airborne, then leveled the shotgun at Jackson again.

This time Jackson turned, grabbed Sara Beth and pushed her towards the truck. The Kerley brother followed their movement, firing off another round that obliterated the window of the Ram's open driver-side door.

Jackson picked Sara Beth up and shoved her into the truck's cabin before climbing in himself. Keeping low, he moved to put his feet on the pedals.

"Keep it up, I'm getting her out of here," he yelled to Bear through the radio.

He tried reaching to put the truck in gear but as he extended his right arm the pain became excruciating from his abdomen. Jackson looked down, pulling up his shirt. The slug had caught the vest, but right now it didn't feel like it. He looked over at Sara Beth who was huddled in the foot space of the passenger seat.

"The truck," he said, wincing, "I need you to put it in reverse."

Sara Beth reached out with a shaking arm, grabbed the selector lever and yanked it down.

"There you go," Jackson said.

He tried to give her a smile but there was no sugarcoating the situation. Bullet after bullet plinked into metal and glass, showering them with debris. Jackson kicked the gas pedal and the truck roared backwards. He heard indecipherable yells from the men firing at them. Grabbing the wheel with his left hand, he kept the truck straight in its retreat until a violent thump nearly threw him into Sara Beth.

The right front tire didn't pop so much as explode as a rifle round went through it. The truck careened right before whipping left, the back tires falling off the edge of the road. The Ram had jackknifed across the small road, placing Jackson between the Lokos and Sara Beth.

He looked at Sara Beth, who was desperately holding back tears. They needed to move. No, she needed to move, and she could move faster than him.

Outside, the metallic roar of Bear's M2 stopped and a quiet fell over the mountainside.

"I'm out of ammo on the MG," Bear radioed.

"The girl, I'm sending her to you. Get her out of here," Jackson replied.

"Both of you get your asses up here," Bear said, "I'll cover you with the rifle."

"I'm sending her, Bear. I'll cover her, too," Jackson said, "No matter what, she makes it out. You understand?"

There was a pause before Bear answered him over the radio.

"You're a good man, Jack," he said.

Jackson grabbed the assault rifle off the floor of the truck and looked up at Sara Beth.

"Listen to me," he said, "My friend is up that hill a ways. He's going to make sure you get home. But you have to go to him, okay?"

Sara Beth nodded as she wiped her nose with the back of her hand.

"Now when I say to," Jackson continued, "I want you to push that door open and run like you've never run before. Stay close to the side where the mountain goes up and keep your head low, okay?"

She nodded again, this time with some determination in her eyes. Jackson took a deep breath in.

"Now," he said.

Jackson threw himself upright, pushing past the pain, and came gun up facing down the road. Solomon, Silas, and the two Lokos still alive had begun walking down the road towards him. Jackson opened fire, pulling the trigger as fast as he could, laying down a barrage of gunfire. The four of them ducked down as they returned fire. In between the two sides' gunfire a loud crack rang out behind Jackson. Silas Ash jerked upright as Bear's rifle shot threw his body backwards. Solomon knelt down by his brother as the other two fired in Bear's direction. Jackson began to fire at them when a round ripped through his left shoulder, splattering the side of his face with blood. He leaned against the steering wheel, trying to take cover as he caught a glimpse of Solomon. He'd taken Silas' rifle and was now staring down the scope directly at Jackson. He fired another shot, clipping Jackson's ear as the round punched a hole into the passenger head rest.

Jackson yanked his rifle with one arm in Solomon's direction and squeezed the trigger. But instead of the loud clap of gunpowder igniting as it sent a 45mm piece of metal down the barrel and towards its target, all Jackson heard was a metal click. The magazine was empty.

Jackson dove backwards deeper into the truck's cabin as Solomon fired at him. He reached for a second magazine in the glove compartment as the other two Lokos resumed firing in his direction.

"I've lost them behind trees," Bear radioed, "I can't see them."

"The girl," Jackson growled through the pain, "Get her."

Pulling himself towards the open passenger door, Jackson tumbled down and out of the far side of the truck. Coughing as he hit the ground, he loaded the new magazine into the rifle and slid a round into the chamber. His left shoulder essentially useless, Jackson nestled the butt of the rifle under his right arm pit and waited for the three to approach.

Almost in unison, they appeared from the other side of the truck, Solomon in the middle near the cab, the other two flanked out to the sides. Jackson fired at Solomon, missing as a second shotgun slug hammered into Jackson's chest. He gasped for air, his own breath becoming deafening in his ears. He hardly heard Solomon tell the others to stop, that Jackson was his.

Solomon climbed up and into the truck's bed and jumped down the other side, landing at Jackson's feet. Jackson searched for the strength to lift his gun at him, but no strength came. Solomon stepped on the gun and kicked it away. He was saying something to Jackson, but Jackson couldn't hear him. He had little interest in the man's taunts. Maybe he wouldn't see it, but Sara Beth would get home. She was gone, away from these monsters. She would go on. Survive. It didn't matter that he wouldn't. A dozen things in his life should've killed him. Fighting in war. Losing his son. Setting out to avenge his son. Truth be told, he might've done it himself long ago had it not been for that first child. The little boy. The first one he'd saved, who in turn saved him. Whatever all this had been between then and now, it had given his life purpose. He was good with that. Jackson closed his eyes and waited for the end to come.

But the end didn't come. As Jackson lay there, he heard a muffled thumping in between breaths, shaking the ground beneath him. A shadow crossed over his face. He opened his eyes to see a helicopter whip around the mountain overhead, a man in the open door leveling a large machine gun at the four of them. He looked up at Solomon, but Solomon wasn't looking at the helicopter or him. He was looking past him. All three of them were. Jackson arched his neck to look behind him. He watched almost in disbelief as a line of men in drab green tactical gear and body armor descended the mountainside, their weapons drawn. A large armored vehicle drove down the mountain road. Jackson read the yellow lettering on the side of it.

ATF SPECIAL RESPONSE TEAM

He looked back up at Solomon, who had dropped his rifle and raised his hands in the air. The other two men were already on the ground with Jackson, their arms and legs splayed out. In less than a minute, the tactical team was on top of them. Jackson watched as two of the men took Solomon into custody; five more had their guns trained on him. Jackson tried to get their attention. He pointed down the road and tried to speak. He couldn't hear if he was actually saying anything.

"Sara Beth Parker," he mouthed, "Sara. Beth. Parker."

One of the men in green knelt over him. He looked at the hook-and-loop patch on the man's body armor.

ATF POLICE MEDIC

He began looking Jackson over. Jackson continued to try and speak, but the man wasn't paying attention. As Jackson tried to point, the medic would grab his arm and pull it in. A second ATF officer came and knelt down beside Jackson. Jackson looked at him and tried to tell him. The man was saying something to him, but he couldn't hear. Again, Jackson tried. That's when he noticed the man was nodding. He placed a hand on Jackson's chest. Jackson stopped trying to speak and watched the man's lips. He read them.

"We've got her," the man said, "We've got her."

74

J ackson awoke in a room so brilliantly white it felt as if the air itself was sterilized. He squinted, fighting the brightness of an unforgiving florescent light overhead. Lifting a hand to shield himself, he looked down at his body. Draped in a gown with wires running every which way, he recognized he was in some sort of hospital.

The last thing he remembered after being tended to by medics, was being carried by stretcher to the armored vehicle, which drove him out of the mountains and to an ambulance waiting nearby. Shortly there-after, exhausted both physically and emotionally, he had closed his eyes and drifted off.

Now, Jackson took in his new surroundings. A monitor above read out real time updates on his vitals. His left shoulder was bandaged in a sling, his arm draped across his belly. He looked at the white bracelet on his wrist.

CLAY, JACKSON
ATTD PAUL ROTHWELL MD
"Expecting to see handcuffs," asked a voice across the room.
Detective Cole sat in a chair pointed at his bed, a cup of coffee in

her hand. Weak and tired, Jackson strained to find the words to talk to her.

"Where am I," he asked.

"Carilion Roanoke Memorial Hospital," Cole replied as she got up, "In Roanoke, obviously. You were taken to Franklin in Rocky Mount originally, but they had you airlifted here."

"Sara Beth," Jackson said.

"She's okay. They took her to RMH in Harrisonburg so she could be close to family and friends."

"Good."

Jackson used his good arm to lift a hand and rub at his eyes. He blinked, trying to shake off the sleepiness. Detective Cole tipped her cup towards him, offering, but he shook his head. Leaning on one elbow, he pulled himself up to a sitting position in the bed.

"Should I ask how an ATF Special Response Team raided the area," Jackson asked.

"Would you believe an anonymous caller reported shots fired nearby," Cole asked back.

Jackson smiled, acknowledging the bad cover story. He reached to his bed side table and poured water from a plastic pitcher.

"Is that the story everyone's going with," Jackson asked rhetorically.

"It probably sounds better than one man brought down an entire armed cult, all under the watchful eye of federal surveillance," Cole replied.

"I'm guessing they're going to have one or two questions for me," Jackson said.

"Probably, but don't expect more than a slap on the wrist. Something about you handing them a RICO Case on a silver platter has them looking the other way for a number of your transgressions."

The RICO Act allowed authorities to more effectively prosecute organized crime, specifically leaders of organized crime. It was made for a man like Solomon Ash.

"There is one thing they'll probably want explained, though," Cole continued, "The crime scene seems to be littered with large caliber rounds like a marine platoon tore through it. They found a bunch of shell casings on a bluff just off the road several hundred yards away, but no guns and no shooter. They interviewed a hunter in the area, an Archibald Beauchamp, who confirmed hearing the shots, but didn't see anyone."

Jackson smiled.

"Imagine that," he said.

"Yeah, imagine that," Cole echoed, returning the smile, "You wouldn't know anything about that, would you?"

"I'll tell you what, Detective," Jackson replied, "When I know something for sure, I'll let you know."

For the first time since they'd met, Cole laughed. She turned, tossing her cup in the trash, and walked towards the door.

"Now where have I heard that before," she said.

The two of them held a smile for each other as the silence between them lingered. Detective Cole opened the door but turned back and looked at Jackson once before leaving. Her smile slipped from one of amusement to one of appreciation. Her voice was softer this time when she spoke.

"You did good, Clay," she said, "Thank you."

"Don't mention it," he replied.

Detective Cole nodded and stepped out the door, shutting it behind her. Jackson slid back down in his bed and closed his eyes. She had put to rest what worries he still had. Somehow, in all this chaos, everything had worked out. He took a deep breath in then out and waited for sleep to come. When it did, there were only good dreams this time of his boy, Evan.

75

Three days later, Jackson was struggling to pull on a t-shirt as a nurse waited impatiently for him to finish signing his discharge paperwork. Jackson figured she was probably his age, with the same long, aging lines and slight frown of a life lived equally hard, though certainly in a different way. She tapped a pen on the clipboard in front of her as Jackson gingerly slid his recovering arm and shoulder into a sleeve.

"You sure I can't just cut the shirt," Jackson asked, "You guys did it to mine."

"What are you going to do when you get home," the nurse asked in reply, "Cut all your shirts open?"

"Don't think I won't," Jackson warned.

The gear Jackson had worn the day everything went down had been cut off him in the back of the ambulance. With the ATF still coming around, he hadn't wanted Bear to come by and bring more stuff just in case. Detective Jen Bailey had a state trooper she knew in the area drop off some gym clothes from the local division. The trooper must've been a fan, because in addition to the clothes he gave Jackson one of his signed Police Benevolent Association cards, a do-not-speak-about-this get-out-of-a-jam-free card to be presented the next time there were flashing lights in his rearview mirror.

With a deep groan, Jackson muscled the arm through. Before he had recovered, the nurse was shoving the clipboard in his face. Begrudgingly, Jackson signed the document and the nurse disappeared.

"So, I can leave now," Jackson shouted as she walked away.

"Wait for someone to wheel you out," the nurse shouted back, annoyed.

Some bedside manner, Jackson thought. He reached over to the table next to his hospital bed and grabbed the remote for the television and turned on the news.

They were covering Sara Beth's case as they played a clip of Anne and Scott Parker in front of an array of cameras and microphones. Jackson couldn't believe how much better Anne looked. The color had returned to her face and she was smiling as she answered questions. She looked nothing like the pale, distraught woman he had watched police pull off of the highway overpass.

"Good for you," Jackson said.

The news program cut back to the anchor quickly before playing footage of Solomon Ash being brought into court. Two police officers held his arms as he was taken out of a van and marched in shackles through a door, his orange prison jumpsuit covered with a bullet resistant vest. The authorities were showing more regard for his life than Solomon had for his victims.

The next footage played showed a different man being led away in handcuffs somewhere else. Jackson recognized the face but couldn't place him until a headline popped up on the screen.

TELEVANGELIST JERRY JOHNS ARRESTED

He was being led out of an impressive looking mansion. A man in a suit quickly ran up and draped a coat over Johns' head, trying in vain to conceal him. It was too late, though; the cameramen had gotten their shot.

"Evangelist," Jackson said, putting together the user he had seen on Silas' phone.

He had been just one of a handful of people in contact with Silas trying to buy young women like property. Jackson wondered how many more arrests would follow.

There was a knock at the door and Jackson looked up. A different, much friendlier-looking nurse stood in the doorway with a wheelchair.

"Are you ready to go, hon," she asked.

"I am, but I can walk out, thank you," he replied.

"Oh, that tough guy routine doesn't work with me, mister. You sit that rump right here in this wheelchair," she said.

Jackson shifted over into the wheelchair. The nurse took him to the elevator, down to the main floor, and pushed him towards the lobby.

"So, if I've got to call a cab, do I sit in the wheelchair and wait," Jackson asked.

Confused, the nurse looked down at a piece of paper.

"It says here you have someone picking you up," the nurse replied.

Now Jackson was confused, as well. Had Detective Cole come back down? Or perhaps Detective Bailey had arranged for someone else she knew to take him where he needed to go. Jackson was running through the possibilities in his head when he saw an old red Suburban parked out front. Jackson snorted. He should have known.

"Jackie boy, we sprung ya," Bear said with a goofy, childish smile.

"Pretty sure this nurse behind me did all the hard work," Jackson replied.

"Hard work? Just wait until we get back to my place and I have to give you a sponge bath," Bear said.

"You do that, and you'll be the one in here with gunshot wounds."

"I've seen your shooting, I'll take my chances."

Bear opened up the passenger door and gave Jackson a hand in. Hopping into the driver's seat, he waved at the nurse as he started the engine.

"She's cute," he said, "What's her deal?"

"Probably tired of backwoods hillbillies hitting on her," Jackson replied.

Bear let out a breathy chuckle as he put the truck into gear and pulled away from the hospital.

For most of the drive back to Bear's place outside Martinsville, Bear was a play-by-play man recapping his personal highlights of what went down on the mountain road. Not up for talking much, Jackson listened and let him do the leg work. He stared out the window at the endless miles of rural highway. There was a peacefulness to the passing wilderness. As the sun started to hang low in the sky, Jackson closed his eyes and basked in its warmth. Bear saw him with his eyes closed and let his stories trail off.

"Don't stop on my accord," Jackson said.

As they pulled in and drove down Bear's driveway, Jackson saw Bear's Dodge D100. Freshly washed and waxed, the black paint showed a beautiful depth and the metal trim shined with a luster as if it were brand new. It probably looked just like this the day it drove off a lot in 1985.

"You detailed the D100," Jackson said.

"Course I did," Bear replied, "I had to get it ready for ya."

Jackson looked at him skeptically as the two of them hopped out of the Suburban. Walking around to the front, Bear tossed him a set of keys.

"I figured you could use it while you work stuff out over your truck with the insurance company," he said, "Don't know what your policy says about bullet holes."

Jackson looked down at the keys.

"Thank you, Bear, I really appreciate it," Jackson said.

"No problem," Bear replied, "Come out hunting with me when you bring it back and we'll call it even."

"Don't you think we've done enough hunting recently," Jackson asked.

"Something else then. Plenty of stuff to do out here in the woods."

"How about fishing?"

Bear gave him a scowl and it was Jackson this time who chuckled. He extended a hand outwards and open towards Bear.

"Thank you for everything," Jackson said, "I really mean it."

Bear stepped forward, spurning the hand, and grabbed Jackson with both arms, picking him up off the ground.

"Ah, no problem, Jackie boy," Bear said jovially.

It suddenly dawned on Jackson how Bear had gotten his nickname.

Gently, Bear returned him to the earth. Jackson flashed him another smile as he climbed into the Dodge pickup and fired it up.

"She sounds good, doesn't she," Bear said.

"She sounds great," Jackson replied, "Thank you, again."

Bear nodded. Jackson checked the mirror, looked the controls over once, and put the truck in gear.

"You headed back home," Bear asked.

"Not just yet," Jackson replied.

Bear looked at Jackson quizzically, who patted him on the shoulder as he answered.

"I have to see someone first."

76

Jackson sat parked on Rockingham Drive a couple doors down from the Parker's home. On a night just like this one a couple weeks ago, Jackson had found himself on the very same street, sitting in a truck, looking at the Parker's house. Then, Sara Beth Parker had been missing for several weeks and the trail had gone cold. Tonight, he watched as three silhouettes sat around a table in their home.

Out front, the makeshift memorial had disappeared and the large wooden post that had held the 'Have You Seen Me?' sign was gone. In its place was a small patch of dirt covered by a layer of straw in an attempt to grow the grass back. In the end, that was all that was left for the Parkers to do. Cover up the scars of the past and do the best they could to move on with their lives.

In a different way, Jackson had done the same thing. In the wake of the same sort of pain, Jackson had found a way to move on. It had nearly led him down the wrong road, and it had nearly killed him, but it was ultimately through that journey that he found himself here, on this street, looking at a family reunited.

He watched as the silhouettes stood up from the table and disappeared from the window. Dinner must've ended. Jackson couldn't imagine the nights Sara Beth's parents must've sat at that table, probably eating in silence, wanting nothing more than their daughter to be home. And likewise, how many nights Sara Beth spent God knows where, wanting nothing more than to *be* home. It was the little things you don't think about, Jackson thought. Sure, there are the hugs and kisses and tears when you are first reunited and the joy of finally being able to bring that missing loved one home. But eventually, all that fades and life resumes. Work and traffic and taxes. Vacations and holidays with the family. Laughs over bad jokes and fights about who used all the hot water. Eventually, there's a return to normalcy. That's what it meant to truly survive, Jackson thought.

A figure emerged from the side of the Parker's house in their driveway. As she walked past the lamppost in the front yard, Jackson could see it was Sara Beth, pushing a wheeled trash can towards the street. Normalcy, Jackson thought again.

She pushed it to the curb, placing it just so, but paused before she turned back. She looked down the street at the black Dodge D100 parked there. Had they been actually able to see one another, Jackson and Sara Beth would be making eye contact. Instead, they looked at the shadows surrounding one another.

Sara Beth turned and walked up the driveway a ways before something compelled her to turn and look back once again. Now, standing by the lamppost, Jackson could see her face. It was not the face tattered with bruises and cuts under a mat of disheveled hair that he had seen on the mountain road. No, on this night, standing in her yard, Sara Beth Parker looked just as she had in countless school and family photos. There was no trace of the girl that had just endured unspeakable horrors. It was a testament to her resiliency.

Jackson feared perhaps he was making her nervous. That the out-of-place black truck sitting just down the road brought her back to the black van that had taken her and started all this. But Sara Beth didn't look fearful or even nervous. He had seen that Sara Beth a hundred miles away under a hail of gunfire. No, this Sara Beth seemed almost calm. Content. Perhaps somehow, she knew it was him. The man, a finder of sorts, that had found her and brought her back from the edge of a darkness that would've swallowed her whole. Perhaps she knew now that man was watching over her once more. And should she ever need him, he would be there again.

She walked up her front walkway and back into the house.

Jackson fired up the truck and drove home.

ACKNOWLEDGMENTS

This novel could not have been written without a small army at my back, all of whom have my most sincere gratitude. First and foremost, thank you to my wife, Meg, who continues to leave me in awe of her compassion, patience, and support. You are my dreamcatcher. Second, thank you to my close friends, Elizabeth Ellis and Madeline McMahon, who helped convince me to take that step off the ledge and begin this journey. Everyone should be so lucky as to have people like you in their corner. Third, thank you to my parents, Debbie Bleviss and Bill Lienesch, who were tremendously supportive as I took on this endeavor. I also want to thank everyone who lent their time and effort towards actually creating The Woodsman. This book was done on a shoestring budget and would not have been possible without these people volunteering themselves. There are dozens of friends and colleagues who I owe in this regard, and I wish I could mention them all here, but especially I want to thank my beta readers: Courtney Bumgardner, Leo Huynh, Rachel Lienesch, Emily Trautwein, and Austin Shirey, who gave their time and effort to this project, helping me craft this story and build this book. And last but certainly not least, thank you to Ursula Ellis, my copy editor, who took the chicken scratch I wrote and polished it into something resembling a novel.

ABOUT THE AUTHOR

B. C. Lienesch is a former freelance writer and featured columnist and editor for GuysNation.com but has done everything from owning a bakery to selling fireworks out of a pair of shipping containers. Born in Washington, D.C. and raised in Northern Virginia, he now lives in the same area with his wife, Meg, their two dogs, Kaia and Aria, and two cats, Luna and Hitchcock. THE WOODSMAN is his first novel.

Visit www.bclnovels.com or @bclienesch on social media for more.